Hidden City

for Ashley –
It's so lovely to meet you and your daughter today! I hope these earn a great place on your post-TBR shelf!
Best,
Je—

Hidden City

J.S. FURLONG

masterful
PERSON
COMPANY

Masterful Person Company Publishing
70 Willowmere Pond Road
Stafford, VA 22556

masterfulpersonco@gmail.com

ISBN: 978-1-7369891-3-5

Library of Congress Control Number: 2021907414

This book is a work of fiction. Any references to historical events, real people or real locales are used fictitiously. Other names, characters, places and incidents are the product of the author's imagination and any resemblance to actual events, places or persons living or dead is purely coincidental.

Some of the terms included in this book may be trademarks or registered trademarks. Use of such terms does not imply any association or endorsement by such trademark owners and no association or endorsement is intended or should be inferred. This book is not authorized by, and neither the Author or Publisher are affiliated with, the owners of the trademarks referred to in this book.

This book is also available in e-book, audiobook & paperback formats.

J.S. FURLONG

For Lizzi first.

Now for Roane & Emma, too.

Go get 'em, girls.

CONTENTS

1.

Sunday, June 17, 2001. New York City, NY.

I bit down hard on the chunky hand pushing on my mouth.

"Ow!" cried the fat kid, jerking his hand back.

I was too short to see over him and find out if anyone in the bustling hotel hallway had heard. I took a big breath to scream. Joseph Thornton shoved me back through the ladies room door. Up until that moment I hadn't been scared. Angry, yes. Surprised, yes, but afraid of these idiots? No. As I lost my breath hitting the door, that changed. A jolt of fear ran through me.

The kid I bit stayed outside, but the other crony followed. Luck was on their side. The bathroom was empty.

"Throw the match," Thornton growled, pushing me hard against the bathroom wall. "I need this win for college. And you," he paused, "*Miss* Goldman, are going to Throw. The. Match. Do you understand?"

My fights happened on chess boards, not in bathrooms. If you had told me an hour ago that this foul sack of teenager would have me pinned to the bathroom wall like a knight pinned to the edge of the board, I would have straightened my Amnesty International tee shirt and told you to be quiet. It was the new millennium for crying out loud. Beyond, in fact. It was two thousand *and one*. An hour ago, I would have thought civilized New Yorkers, even overly mature, hairy jocks with neck beards starting, were culturally beyond boys threatening girls in bathrooms.

An hour ago, I had eleven seconds left to win.

I watched closely as my opponent decided. Pretty brown eyes flicked over the board then lingered on my bishop. His forehead squashed together like he was attempting differential equations without a calculator. One mahogany curl bumped each cheek as his head tipped to scrutinize the board. Uh-oh. Did he see it? I'd spent my last five moves setting up this trap for his queen. I took a breath and waited, anticipating he was too logical a player to see my hidden mate.

I noticed his yarmulke, blue with an embroidered pattern that looked like pawns. Cute. The tiny velvet cap, no bigger than my hand, was bobby pinned to his hair right at the top of his head. Air-conditioning blasted from the vent above us as if the hotel thought people were actually dancing in this ballroom.

I imagined I heard the boy's brain ticking. Then his hand flashed up from his lap like a pilot light, snatched his queen and captured my bishop. Elation thrilled through my veins, an adrenaline rush that thumped my heart against narrow ribs. Two moves later, six seconds out of my eleven, I had him. Mate.

My opponent waved his hand for the proctor while I wrote down the final moves in my notebook. Once the proctor agreed that our board had a legitimate checkmate, we got up and nodded to each other. I would have stuck my hand out to shake, but orthodox boys aren't allowed to touch girls, even in a sportsmanship show of acknowledgement. I think it's a purity thing.

"Good game," I said following him out of the cone of silence. Ballroom door shutting behind us, I said "You used your tactics really well. That fork of my rook and knight in the middle game was exciting . . ." He shot me a glare and walked away. Well, that's the last time I think you have pretty eyes, I said to myself.

A tornado crashed into my side, hugging me with scrawny black clad arms. Meredith.

"Did you win, did you win? Of course you won! Look at your face! My god, woman, you're a machine! You need some water!" She grabbed my hand and dragged me down the hall toward the skittles room where we all kept our stuff during the tournament. My grandmother sat at one of the tables, feet propped on a chair with a fluffy, wool-looking project in her lap. She looked up when I came in and set aside her work. She stood, thick red socks blending into the hotel carpet and opened her arms wide for a hug. I embraced her and she squeezed me tight. "Four out of five?" she asked.

"Yup." $680 raised for my cause and one win away from my first actual title. National Master. It's not like I would be the only fourteen year old girl from New York City to hold a national master title, but it wasn't common either. I could count us on my fingers. She pulled back and took my face in her hands.

"Shayna," she said using her Yiddish nickname for me, "You are the smartest person in our family." She searched my face to make sure I knew she meant it. "And you can tell your father I said that. In fact you should tell him. He could use a little knocking off his fancy partner pedestal." She smiled at me, pride in my father and me gleaming from her eyes like her one gold tooth glinted from the corner of her top row of teeth.

"Thanks, Bubbe," I said. "But you'll have to tell him yourself. If I do it -- "

"He'll say you're bragging. Which," she said, brushing some escaped hair out of my face and back toward my braids, "you are absolutely entitled to do when you win today! One more game, right? What is it, thirteen more hours of this interminable waiting-death-by-boredom?"

"They say we'll be out by 8:00," I said.

"They say that every year. Will you stop bouncing like that?" Bubbe said to Meredith.

"I gotta use the bathroom," Meredith replied, "I was waiting til the end of the match so I wouldn't miss anything. And Stacy needs this." She waggled a bottle of water. I reached for it. "Come with me." My grandmother gave my best friend a raised eyebrow. Meredith aimed a pointed look at my frizzing hair and Bubbe let me go.

Meredith pushed open the ladies room door and ran to a stall. I had to pee, too, but not as badly as she did!

"How was the kid you played?" Meredith asked.

"Cute. In a Jane Austin sort of way. I think I played him a couple years ago. Might have beaten me. I forget."

"Liar. You remember every single game you play."

"I do not."

"You so do." She flushed and I heard the sink start. I adjusted my skirt and unlocked my stall. She appraised me in the mirror.

"You'd be a ton scarier behind the board if you would dress like a human being."

"I am a human being and I am dressed, therefore -- "

"You know what I mean. If you dressed like a *girl*. Please tell me at least you're wearing a bra?"

"My god, Mer! Of course I'm wearing a bra!"

"Last week you -- "

"Learned my lesson. Double A or not, bras it is."

She nodded her approval then sighed in disappointment. "You look like a fourth grader in that denim knee skirt."

"I look like a fourth grader no matter what I wear."

I learned just last month that there is a name for how I look to other people. Neanimorphic. It means looking younger than one's years. There's nothing wrong with me, I'm just small and don't look my age.

"Come on, Stace," Meredith said. "I gave you all those clothes!"

"They're all black."

"Black is sophisticated."

"Black is Goth."

Meredith pulled a hair brush, *my* hairbrush, out of a small canvas messenger bag she wore across her body and stood behind me.

"You have my hairbrush?" I said.

"I took it from your bag. It's gross if you use mine." She let out my braids as I guzzled the water she'd handed me. She popped the brush over my shoulder. "Use it."

When Meredith had a mind to change the way I looked there was no stopping her. Her own hair was dark brown, too but she had dyed it black. She wore thick eyeliner and purple lipstick with sparkles. Fine boned and delicate like a hummingbird, Meredith was made of love and colors and speed. She had been my other half since the first day of kindergarten when we promised each other to be friends forever.

"Did you grab my —" Before I even finished the sentence my wristwatch appeared in her hand.

"How many of these stupid things have I been to?" she said. Too many to count. I buckled the little blue strap and reached for my hair ties.

"Oh no," she said, swiping them out from under me and stuffing them in her pocket. "Wear it down."

"It's distracting that way. I need coffee."

"My god woman, you are pedestrian." Meredith opened her hand for my brush and swooped over my head. Four minutes later my long, straight hair wrapped around itself in a french twist behind my head. Her finishing touch was a strong tug on the collar of my tee to stretch it out. "I wanna see the necklace. It's so pretty." She tapped my gold Star of David pendant with her finger. It had teeny diamond chips at the corners and was probably the most expensive thing I owned. It was my bat mitzvah gift from Bubbe, saved for special occasions. Meredith had insisted today qualified.

"Beauty," Mer said with a flourish. "Now when you win your title and I take the picture, you won't look as much like a dweeb. Do you want lipstick?"

I wanted coffee and a sandwich. I rolled my eyes and exited past her out the door. I had one concern more pressing than food. My stomach rumbled, but I had to see if they posted the next rounds yet.

If he'd won his last game, I'd be playing Joseph Thornton, a square, jock looking kid who had needed a hair cut and a shave since he was twelve. He came from somewhere not

New York and we played each other every Nationals. If Joseph had lost, I'd be up against Jon Yu, a string bean Asian super nerd from the Bronx. I liked Jon. He was an aggressive player, very predictable, but also a very nice guy. I could not say the same of Joseph. Our matches ended in a seething draw every time. Not today, I thought. Not today. Today too much was at stake. I was ready. Today I refused to settle for a draw.

Rabbi Berman, my chess coach, careened around the corner.

"Stacy! Stacy! Asa won his match! Thanks to him winning and you winning, we might actually take this thing!" Rabbi's voice was quiet, but thrilled. His suit rumpled around him like a bathrobe forgotten in the dryer. He had trimmed his beard for the occasion and it matched his grey pin stripe suit in it's salt and pepper-ness.

"Have you lost weight since the last time you wore that suit?" I asked. His eyes opened in surprise.

"Matter of fact I have. Hello Meredith," he said as if seeing my friend for the first time.

"Are you okay?" I asked, concerned. "You're not sick or anything?"

"No, I started running a few months ago."

"Running? At your age?"

Meredith elbowed me hard in the side.

"Ow!"

"I'm not dead yet, Stacy. The Torah tells us everyday is a new opportunity to live a better life." He smiled. Did the

Torah say that? I couldn't remember, but I didn't think it did. "Your hair looks very nice." Rabbi turned to Mer. "When will you join our team, eh? We could use another brilliant player to cement these wins."

"Sorry, Rabbi," she said with a smile. "Chess isn't my thing. I'm just here to save her the trouble of telling me all about it later."

"What a thoughtful friend," he said shrugging his shoulders. "My wife has been my wife for forty-five years and she's never once in her life come to a tournament."

"I bet she would if you played," Meredith said.

"She would come if it was my funeral, but don't let that give you any ideas. Listen, Stacy, they just posted the final matches."

"Jon?" I said, hoping.

The corners of his eyes crinkled in concern.

My belly rumbled again, but this time I didn't feel just hungry.

"It's gonna be okay," he said. "You can do this. Joseph's coach is furious. Our team is tied with his thanks to Asa." Rabbi put his hands on my shoulders and leaned down. "And to you. Joseph's going to play an aggressive game. He'll try to psych you out. You must. Not. Let him."

I nodded.

"Whatever you do, protect your rooks."

Joseph loved to hide his rooks, capture yours and then use his to sweep up in a checkmate we liked to call 'The Lawnmower.'

"I got it."

"I know you do," Rabbi said. "Just do like always: Make a plan. Stick to the plan. Be ready to change the plan. Keep your mind on the mate."

I pushed my feet into the floor. Joseph, not Jon. Rats. It's really more fun to play with people you like.

This tournament was not for fun, though. This tournament was for a National win for my school team which had won exactly zero Nationals, for a National Master Title for me and for a little contribution to the NYPAG. Joseph was heading into his senior year, so for him, this would be about scholarships.

"I need to eat something."

Rabbi walked us back to the skittles room.

"How many sponsors did you all end up getting?" He asked me as we walked. "Fifty-four!" I replied. Thirty-four of them were mine. This tournament was also my first fundraiser since becoming president of the Youth Philanthropy Group at Beth Israel, the temple where my Grandfather used to be rabbi. We picked two charities a year to do a volunteer project with or help them raise money. I had chosen one of this year's charities, the New York Prisoner Advocacy Group. They fight to get prisoners who have been wrongfully imprisoned released and to get mental health benefits and treatment offered to prisoners who need it. I have a thing about wrongful imprisonment. I also have a thing about mental health care.

There are people that belong in jail, and there are people who don't. I knew one who did. I also knew that what that person did may not have entirely been their fault. It might have been something they couldn't help because they were sick. You don't get mad at a dog for biting someone if it has rabies. The dog can't help it. It's still bad someone got bit, but it wasn't really the dog's fault.

A month ago, I had the idea to turn this tournament into a fundraiser for my charity. For every game I won, my sponsors would donate money. I had won four games already and my average donor committed to five dollars a game. Three other teammates including Asa, had also gotten sponsors. Together we had fifty-four. I smiled in pride when I thought about it.

Arriving in the skittles room, my grandmother had laid out three sandwiches, soup, salad, knishes, iced teas and one giant cookie each from Jerry's. I think the real reason she agreed to be my chaperone at Nationals every year had to do with her enjoying buying us a much bigger meal than we could possibly eat and a bored Meredith always happy to get out and do the run to the deli.

Meredith slid her hand into mine as we sat down to eat. She squeezed, said nothing and let go, but I knew what she meant. She meant that she knew I was worried, she knew Rabbi was worried and that she had faith in me. She thought I would win. If you have to have only one friend in the whole world, pick someone who believes in you. Someone who thinks you're awesome and that you can do anything, is a valuable someone. I bit into my pastrami.

While Meredith and my grandmother cleaned up, I trotted back to the bathroom for a final break before the game. The final round started in less than ten minutes. When I came out, Joseph and two of his teammates stood across the hall.

"Hey Lesbo," he said. "Can we talk?" They started toward me.

"I don't talk to morons," I said.

"I don't talk to deviants but I'll make an exception for you." His cronies snickered.

I opened my mouth to blast him with a loud and furious lecture about the difference between homosexuality and deviance. I wanted to pound his ignorant, hairy face into the carpet. The bigger part of me knew to save it for the board.

"Sorry, Joseph. Go talk to someone who a) is a lesbian and b) gives a crap. I do not qualify." Very restrained, I told myself, feeling anger rushing to my face.

"Oh, I thought your girlfriend was here with you again. But maybe I saw you going into the bathroom to make out with someone else."

Something about him fired up a rare desire for me, the desire to go ballistic on someone. This is your plan? I thought, resenting him for disrupting my calm, winner mood. This is how you try to psych me out? You're going to have to think of something better.

I said nothing, turned away and started to walk down the hall. One of his cronies stepped in front of me. A black-haired kid with glasses. Not intimidating, despite being tall.

"Get out of my way."

The hall grew more crowded as players and coaches thronged back toward the ballroom.

"I'll scream if you don't move," I said.

The kid's eyes flicked to Thornton's bulk.

"I just want to talk," Joseph said, stepping closer.

"No."

They closed in on me, pushing me back toward the wall. I realized no one could see me. I opened my mouth to scream and Joseph's fat crony pushed his blubbery hand over my mouth.

2.

June 17, continued.

I sucked in a gasping breath. My body trembled under the force of Joseph's thick hands on my shoulders. He used his hip to pin mine so I couldn't kick up and hit him in the nuts.

"Look. I don't care anything about you or your hot girlfriend or what you do in private, but today I need this win and you will give it to me."

"I will not." My voice came out hoarse and scared.

"If you don't, I'll say I saw your coach giving you hand signals from the sidelines. That'll get you disqualified."

"I'll tell them you attacked me!"

"Your word against mine," he said. "No witnesses. All my teammates will back me."

I said nothing, but the heady mix of fury, indignation and the absolute commitment to not let him get away with this must've read on my face.

He paused. "Leak one word and I'll trip your grandmother down the stairs."

"You will not."

"Try me," he said. I gulped in a huge breath to scream. Joseph shook my shoulders. My head snapped against the wall so hard bright lights flashed in front of my eyes. "I am not kidding," Joseph said. "You resign before the 40th move, or give me the mate. I hope we're clear." A knock on the bathroom door.

"Joe, it's one minute to get in."

He grabbed my hand and gripped it tight, big fingers squeezing like a boa constrictor around my wrist. I was dizzy as he dragged me out of the bathroom. "Let's go. Friend."

Tears of anger and pain had sprung to my eyes when I hit my head. I staggered as he pulled me with him. He smiled at a group of three more team mates waiting outside the bathroom to escort us. He put his arm around my shoulders in a friendly way, walking me into the ballroom. I looked around desperately for Rabbi Berman. His back was to me as he exchanged some final words with Asa.

Joseph's coach waved us over to the middle table. He smiled a thin, wet smile and wished me a good game. My head hurt from hitting the wall, and I said nothing. Disgusting lizard.

Joseph was to play black. The varsity football jacket his coach draped over his shoulders reeked of deodorant and onions. Still clutching my hand, Joseph pulled my chair out. Finally letting go, he tucked me in, like we were dining at a fancy restaurant. My side faced Rabbi. The second Joesph sat down, I stood so fast my chair toppled. I bolted across the ballroom.

Grabbing Rabbi's jacket, I whispered "You have to get out of the ballroom!" He started to open his mouth in protest. "You can't watch us play!" I grabbed his sleeve and started tugging. "Please Rabbi! I can't explain, there's no time! Just go, now! And tell Meredith not to leave my grandmother under any circumstances! Not any! Please!" He nodded. I left my bewildered rabbi and turned to run back to my board.

"What did you tell him?" Joseph hissed once I sat. I stared at him with all the hatred I felt at that moment. I said nothing.

"What did you tell him?" Rage rose behind his eyes.

"That you raped me in the bathroom."

"What?" he shrieked.

"No talking!" called a proctor. "Shake hands." All dozen of us final rounders stood up. I noticed I was the only girl. And my watch was still on my wrist. I took it off and stuffed it in my pocket. Joseph's hands were twice the size of mine. We both squeezed too hard. It hurt. For a second I thought he might break my fingers. When we let go, my gaze shot to the door. Rabbi stood in the entryway, his shoulders tight with worry and confusion. I made a hard, pointed look at the door. He put his hands together to bless my game. And, thank god, turned and walked out of the ballroom.

I won't bore you with the entire game, but I will say that Joseph was not his usual self. He had gotten better since last I played him, sharper moves, better timing. He'd been memorizing patterns. He used tactics more aggressively. If he hadn't just physically hurt me and threatened me and my grandmother in the bathroom, it would have been a fun game. I wrote down every move and used the opening to calm my shaking nerves. I closed my eyes for a second before and after each move like Jill, my actress-turned-therapist step-mother, had taught me to do to keep myself calm and focused. I reminded myself of my goal: checkmate. Paralyze the king. I saw only the king . . . I did not look at the monster across the table. Forcing away the emotions pulsing under the surface of my mind, and the ache from my head hitting the bathroom wall, I saw only the board.

Chess for me is like dancing for Meredith. She loses herself in the music and volume and movement. Playing chess, I get lost. My body becomes irrelevant, my mind sorts through information like nothing outside of strategy and prediction exist. It is private and sweet and filled with surprises and adrenaline. It gives me space to be nothing, to become the game, to be just me.

An arm's length across the table, Joseph started getting creative. He moved a rook, setting a trap for my queen. A smile tickled the corner of my mouth. I shoved it away.

I did not capture his queen set out to lure my bishop into disaster. I moved fast so he would think he'd fooled me. Sacrificing my remaining b rank pawn, I pressed my knight to defend a pawn twice that had only one piece attacking it. It looked like a wasted move, but one move later it would open a diagonal file for my queen to wreak havoc on the center of the board.

Sociopathic Joseph hadn't expected that. He faltered, likely wondering how I could have made such an egregious positional error.

We danced in an out, trading advantage in position, for advantage in material. I captured one of his rooks and got the upper hand. If I lost it, I would not recover and he would win. Move 39. I had no intention of throwing this game.

The cavernous ballroom cocooned us in quiet. The silence amplified itself with every click of a clock in contrast.

Don't get cocky, Goldman, I told myself. Check everything. Studying the board fast, I observed: material: equal, meaning our captured pieces were worth the same number of points, position: his remaining rook floundered, pinned by my two pawns, his knight stayed stuck trapped on the edge of the board and his king crept toward the center, forced by my remaining bishop. The absence of the bishop he'd captured improved my position by opening a key file for my rook and for my open pawn to cross the board for promotion if I failed to win this exchange.

He hit his clock. I moved my knight into position at g4, a royal fork!

"Check."

His queen, pinned to his king, guaranteed a valuable capture for me while forcing him to move his king to one of two available squares. Both squares were better for me than for Joseph. And then I made a mistake. I looked up.

Joseph's blue eyes bored into me from a face shiny and pink. Sweat dripped onto the table from his forehead, his hair soaked. His fingers gripped the table. I'm used to seeing boys stress out when they play me, but I've never seen one look ready to throw the table over and leap across to rip out my throat. Meredith would tell me to curb the dramatics, but his expression stuck my breath in my chest.

I remembered his heavy paws on my shoulders, the feeling of his breath on my face as he slammed my head against the wall. He was not just a mean kid, something about him was different. His eyes gave me chills. An unfamiliar fury filled me, like what I had felt when he first approached me, only more intense. My face got hot. My skin felt itchy, like if I didn't reach over the board and hit him right now, I might start screaming and be unable to stop.

Goldman! I scolded myself. Who *are* you right now? Where is your mind? Come back and play this game! I looked back at the board, lost, and not in an in-the-flow way. I had no idea what had been happening. Had he moved? Had I? My clock ticked so he must've moved. Where had he gone? Valuable seconds later, I saw it. He had moved his king. Right, I'd been playing that fork. I captured his queen and hit my clock, still pushing the intense emotions away. He had one chance to redeem his game and play for a draw, but he threw one of his knights away by mistake and voila! I had him. Three more moves and BAM! I took his remaining rook with mine, simultaneously trapping his king. Checkmate.

I did not look at him again, choosing instead to only look at my notebook as I wrote down his last moves, and mine. Across from me, his breathing came thick and furious. I raised my hand for the proctor. Mate approved, I looked past my seething opponent, searching. Rabbi was nowhere in sight. Good Rabbi! I stood. Joseph stood too, and walked away without shaking my hand. I came back fully to my sane, logical self.

I guess I had after game cooties today.

"So you're asking to register an official complaint against the team?"

"Yes," I said. "Against Joseph Thornton first, and the team second. He asked me to throw our game."

"That's a serious offense."

"I'm aware."

"Are you sure he wasn't just teasing you?"

My brows scrunched together. Teasing me? Was he joking?

"I'm sure."

The proctor had sweat through his button down shirt and pushed his glasses up on his nose.

"Okay," he said, sighing in annoyance.

"You should be grateful I'm reporting this." I said as Sweaty Proctor Man shuffled through a large file box. "Who knows how many other kids he's threatened? What if all his wins today were faked?" Ignoring my comments, SPM pulled out a pink xeroxed form. "Write your complaint on the third line and sign here."

"How will I know this actually gets filed with the Federation?" I asked as I wrote.

"If you write it, it'll get filed."

"Can I track it? Is there a case number or complaint number or something you can give me?"

"What are you, a lawyer?"

I eyeballed the sweaty, nerdy man. Pride filled me, converting my scowl into a smile. "Nope. I'm a National Chess Master. Now tell me how to track my complaint."

"He slammed me against a wall in the bathroom and threatened me if I didn't throw the game!" I said low enough that only Meredith could hear me.

"Holy crap! Are you okay? Did he hurt you?" The Goth Princess crouched next to me as I packed my stuff. I glanced up to check on Bubbe. Rabbi stood with her, talking in excited animation as she arranged her knitting in a bright purple bag.

"Other than harboring a sudden and deep desire for revenge, and a mild headache when I stop to think about it, I'm fine."

"Aren't you going to tell?"

"I filled out the complaint form." Speaking of revenge. "It's all you can do."

"But he physically assaulted you!"

"His coach was in on it! He'll say that all the guys were with him before the game and I am lying. I have no witnesses, and they have an alibi. Nothing will come of it except I will get a reputation in the Federation as a troublemaker."

"You're a National Master now, doesn't that count for something?"

"I'm a fourteen year old girl in a man's sport. Did you see the face of the judge who handed me my trophy? He looked like his owner had just spanked him with a newspaper." She nodded. Meredith was many things. Stupid, thank god, was not one of them.

"What did Rabbi say when you told him?"

"He registered a complaint, too. That members of his team had been trash talked by the Saint Whoever's team."

"That's it?"

"That's all I told him."

"For a smart girl you can be majorly stupid," she said. "You should go over there right now and tell him the whole story. Remember when Jacob thought he couldn't tell us he was gay and tried to kill himself?"

"That's different."

"It's not! The secret ate away at him. This one could eat away at you! If Jacob had told us, we would have been like oh okay but in his head it was this big thing -- "

"Shh. Here they come."

Rabbi's eyes were lit like Hanukkah candles he was so happy. He chatted the whole way down the hall and to the elevators about what a wonderful job we had all done. I hugged Asa and told him he had gone over the top in his games today. Together, we had raised over $1000 for the

NYPAG. We promised to replay our best games from today in the final club meeting of the school year on Tuesday.

"Jewish Day School Team Picture everybody!" Meredith called holding up her fancy new DSLR camera. We all scrunched together under the US Chess Federation Banner. Someone shoved the team trophy at me to hold. Asa giggled as I set it down. It came up past my waist.

"Is it huge or are you just short?" he said smiling.

"I am officially five feet tall now, smart stuff," I said. "Rabbi, you hold it."

It didn't take much persuading. Rabbi hefted the trophy onto his hip and we all stood smiling beside the giant gold statue.

"It's like the chess Oscars," Meredith said as we all herded toward the elevator. There were stairs from the mezzanine to the lobby, but after the conversation in the bathroom, I wanted Bubbe nowhere near them. I put her in front of me as our team piled into the elevator, me bringing up the rear.

As I stepped through the elevator doors, a heavy weight slammed into my back. I lurched forward knocking into Bubbe. She smacked hard into the side of the elevator. She'd put out her hand to catch herself and avoid falling into the kid in front of her. Beside me, the click of a camera.

Meredith said, "I got that, you jerk."

"Sorry about that," said a foul, familiar voice.

Joseph Thornton smiled at me, a dirty, nasty smile showing small white teeth. His team stood behind him, staring in awe.

"Bubbe, are you okay?"

She gripped her wrist close to her chest. She turned as best she could in the packed elevator, looked Joseph Thornton in the face and said a phrase in Yiddish that means something so nasty I will not translate. I gaped in astonishment. The elevator doors were closing.

"We had words earlier," she said.

"What kind of words?" But I suspected I knew exactly what kind.

Rabbi looked at Bubbe's wrist when we unpiled into the lobby. She winced when he tried to rotate it.

"It is a bad sprain," he said. "Let's get you home and ice it. It's not a break or it would be bruising and you wouldn't be able to move it."

"How do you know?" I asked, worried.

"Former Coney Island EMT. I wasn't always a rabbi," he said. He looked over my head at one of our team's chess parents for a quick discussion on getting the other kids home.

Once everything was handled, Rabbi got a us a cab. Fifteen minutes later, we were all settling in at Bubbe's Upper West Side apartment.

"I'll be home in an hour or so," Meredith said into the phone. She explained to her parents what'd happened. "Dad you don't have to. She's fine." She looked at the phone and pressed the off button. "He'll be here in ten."

"Can we start from the beginning?" Rabbi Berman asked. "I feel like I'm in a vortex and have no idea why or what's happening."

I looked at Bubbe. She passed the plate of cookies I'd arranged to the rabbi and pushed the honey toward his tea cup.

"Do you want something stronger to put in that?" she asked with a sly look. "I won't have you starve to death or not have a celebratory sip on my account. We have a national master and a first place team win to celebrate!"

"Please tell me. What happened?"

She sighed. "When I was setting up dinner for the girls, the coach from the other team asked if he could talk to me. I said sure, he seemed friendly. He explained that this tournament was crucial for one of his players. I said, mine too. Then he asked if he could give me five hundred dollars to pretend to get sick and take Stacy home before the fifth game! I said certainly not, she was gonna win her title if she won. I was polite, Shayna pour me a glass of the red would you? He then upped his offer to a thousand dollars! Can you imagine? A thousand dollars to pull her out of the tournament! I said no and told him to go -- " she cussed in Yiddish again.

Rabbi's eyes got wide.

"My goodness." He turned his gaze on me. I shrugged.

"Nobody offered me a thousand bucks," I said.

"Joseph and two of his teammates trapped her and shoved her up against the wall in the bathroom so hard she hit her head," Meredith said. She stuck her hand on the back of my head.

"Ow!"

"Feel it, woman! There's a huge goose egg here!"

"There is?" I said. I reached around and sure enough a massive lump had raised on the back of my head. Mer stood up, talking and walking toward the kitchen at the same time.

"And then he threatened her! He said -- "

Rabbi held up one hand. "Let Stacy tell the rest."

Mer looked at me, eyes narrowed. "If you leave out any of the details, I will shake you till you see stars myself!"

Oh good grief.

Meredith came back from the kitchen holding something wrapped in a dishtowel. A baggie full of ice. She pointed to my head. Holding the ice to my skull, I told the rest of my story in gory detail. I left nothing out, including how I dumped over my chair and bolted for Rabbi right before the final match.

Rabbi and my grandmother sipped. No one said anything for a few minutes, absorbing.

"I'll do a formal complaint with the main USCF office on Monday. That coach has been a problem for years. This is one too much."

"He has?" I said.

Rabbi nodded and sipped his tea. "The Ohio branch of the Federation has had so many complaints against him, his team is banned from tournaments there."

We talked some more chess politics and I got up to dump my baggie. Its useful ice had transformed into useless cold water. While I was up, I got Bubbe a fresh bag of frozen peas to put on her wrist.

Our dads arrived. Meredith's first, yes, just a sprain and then mine, oh my god what happened freak out etcetera and the whole story got told again. After Bubbe calmed everyone down, and no, I did not have a concussion, she made my dad go into her freezer and pull out a secret something.

It was an ice cream cake with Congratulations Stacy and a chess queen drawn on it in fancy icing.

"I didn't want to jinx it, so I had it done a month ago so I could forget about it til today, in case you won."

I threw my arms around her and kissed her crumply cheek. "Thank you, Bubbe," I said. "I love it."

"Of course you do," she said. "It's your favorite." She looked at my dad, still in corporate casual from spending his entire Sunday at the office. "You should be ashamed of yourself for making work more important than your daughter today, Ernie." She fixed him with her serious mother stare. "If you had been there none of this would have happened."

"You're right. I would've taken the grand!" We all just stared at him. "Sorry," he said. "My stand up teacher said that playing into the stereotypes while being self deprecating is supposed to be funny."

Bubbe rolled her eyes and sighed.

"You're a wonderful lawyer dear. Be happy with that. Now, get the plates," Bubbe shook her head. "And cut the slices big!" Dad turned to the kitchen. He stopped and tuned back to us. "Did I tell you? Jill and I finally figured out the solution to keeping marriage fresh," he said. Oh god. Another one. "It's two romantic dinners a week. She goes on Tuesday and I go on Thursday." Meredith snorted a laugh. Her dad laughed for real.

"Thank you, Meredith, thank you, Saul," said Dad. "At least they appreciate me."

Bubbe looked at Rabbi Berman as my dad went into the kitchen.

"Thank God his father made him go to law school instead of being a comedian," she said.

"It didn't work," I said. "He's still totally repressed."

Dad came back with the plates. The glorious ice cream cake made its rounds.

"To Stacy Goldman, our faithful champion, undefeated by chess, bullies or pink paperwork," said Rabbi. "Mazel tov."

"Mazel tov," we toasted.

3.

Saturday, October 27, 2001. Richmond, VA

This is not my house, I said to myself as the heavy wooden door shut behind me. Cold struck my face in the open wind. Indignant, frustrated and sad, my chest tightened. Having learned to repress from the best, I shoved the uncomfortable emotions away. I had come. I had done everything they asked. I had given it a chance, like I had agreed to do. Two hours had been long enough, thanks. It was time to go home.

Make a plan. Stick to the plan. Be ready to change the plan. Keep your mind on the mate. Rabbi Berman's voice was close in my head as if he stood beside me, solemn and kind in his rumpled suit. Make a plan.

That was easy, get back to New York. If I went for a visit, I could maybe convince Bubbe I should stay. I could help her with things when I wasn't in school. I'd be useful at the temple, I could help her clean the sanctuary or manage the office.

The open space pressed against me. I can't stay here, I thought feeling slightly panicky. I have got to get home. Bubbe would understand.

I clutched the phone handset to my chest, hoping it would get a signal out here. Purple twilight filled the empty sky over the tops of wide, old trees as I dialed.

"Shayna, honey! I miss you so much already! How was the trip?" Bubbe's loud voice comforted me.

"I'm thinking maybe I can come back next weekend to visit you. What's changed since I left? How's your wrist?"

"Why are you asking about my wrist? That was months ago! And changed since this morning? Nothing."

Things *could* change, though. They could change in a second. Your life could be torn out from under you in the time it takes an airplane to crash into a building. And that is exactly what happened. On September 11, two airplanes crashed into the World Trade Center towers six blocks from our apartment and two blocks from my school.

This house, this twilight sky, this empty void of not New York was the result. The world changed in a blink. It was as if New York had evaporated and morphed into this unreal image of a city that wasn't a city, as least not as I knew cities.

"Why are you really calling, honey?" Bubbe said. "Is everybody okay? Is something wrong with the house?"

The house. God, the huge god-forsaken perfect house. Its charming stone exterior stared in pompous humility at me from under the too wide sky.

"The house is fine. We're all fine." I repressed a tidal wave of emotions. Hearing Bubbe's voice made me want to dissolve and wash away into the Long Island Sound. I could not wash this away, though. This was too big and I was too trapped in the role I had created for myself. Stable Stacy, the big sister, easy going and always responsible. I was a chess champion for crying out loud. No meltdowns allowed.

Summer after the tournament had flowed like any New York City summer, stiflingly hot days spent between apartments, The Met, and movie theaters accented by a couple weeks out of the city with Meredith's family in the Hamptons. It had been sweet and typical, an endless string of iced coffee runs, card games and late night conversations. Labor Day came and went. School started. The second day of school was September 11, the day that launched not only the biggest disaster in National and New York City history, but also the biggest disaster in Stacy history. Meredith argued it was the second biggest disaster and nicknamed it Disaster Number Two since I was so young when Disaster Number One happened. I might disagree.

Five weeks had passed since September 11. Five stunned, shocking weeks. Here it was, Saturday, October 27, 2001. I stared at an inviting bench swing hanging from a massive tree that overhung a cobbled driveway. I didn't even want to sit on it. Bundled in my wool peacoat and the gold scarf Bubbe had made and wrapped around my neck this morning, wind whipped my hair across my face. Bubbe had kissed both my cheeks, held my face in her hands and said to me, tears in her eyes,

"You are my Shayna maidel and you always will be. I am always here for you, don't forget that. And remind your no good father that I have to see you at least once a month or my cancer will come back and it will be all his fault. Tell him that."

"I'm sure you will tell me plenty yourself, Ma," he said. "I wish you would come with us. I could get you your own -- "
She held up her hand.

"I have lived in this city since I was fourteen years old and I will leave it like your father left it, God rest his soul. In a box."

"Trains are boxes," said Steve. My muppet-like six-year-old brother held hands with his parents, my dad on one side and Jill on the other. He had floppy brown hair, tucked under a Batman hat, wide eyes and a happy expression, kind of a cross between Barney the dinosaur and Big Bird with superhero gear. Jill on the other hand, looked like a picture out of a Macy's catalog, put together in her tan long coat and knee boots with a splashy matching hat and scarf. My father looked like he always looked, straight up and ready to catch his train to the office. This was not his normal train, though and not his normal office. This train would deliver us all, willing or no, to the new branch of his firm and the house it bought us. In Richmond, Virginia.

"Tell me about it! Do you like it?"

"Like what?"

"The house!"

Again, the house.

"It's bigger than Mt. Sinai Temple," I said. "The kitchen alone can fit our whole apartment."

"That's not saying much. What's your favorite thing about it?"

I reached, I didn't have a favorite thing. Two staircases, five bedrooms and seven (*seven*) bathrooms. Ridiculous. Dad had a furniture company come in and a designer do most of the furnishings calculated to be cozy and formal/ showy at the same time.

"Jill really likes the wall colors," I said. "They are beige. I mean, sand."

"Did they put in the red drapes she wanted from the catalog?"

"I think so."

"Pay attention, Shayna! Inquiring minds want to know. But I didn't ask what her favorite thing was. I want to know *your* favorite thing."

I scrunched my face up under my glasses.

"Jill says I'll be able to walk a lot of places once I'm out of the neighborhood."

"That's not terrible." The phone beeped a call waiting. My heart leaped again.

"Can I call you back, please, Bubbe? I think Meredith is on the other line and I haven't talked to her yet. I called you first."

"Of course honey. I love you. Make him buy you biscuits. I hear there's good biscuits in Richmond." She hung up and I clicked over to the other line. Meredith was already talking.

"Good grief, woman I'm dying over here! This is a terrible connection, can you go closer to the base?"

"I'm in the yard."

"Why? It's dark out. You were supposed to call me! Tell me everything! How's the house?"

"Why are you people obsessed about the house? And it's only twilight."

"Oh my God, of course it is! You can see the sky. Is the pool heated?"

"It's October! I have no idea if the pool is heated. My dad called my room the princess suite and I nearly vomited. It's stupid. Too big. I hate it."

"Stacy Rachel Shayna stupid head Goldman! Stop it right now! You will not ruin this for me. The only way I am holding my crap together at all is by thinking of what a wonderful new life and house you have that I get to come visit and that you are going to be happier there than here, so quit complaining! Now tell me something I can cling to to keep me from entirely falling apart, do you understand?"

A knot of guilt bunched in my stomach. I'd been so self absorbed feeling sorry for myself and thinking about everything that had happened that I hadn't even thought about how horrible this was for her.

"I'm sorry," I said. "I should have thought about that." Meredith fell quiet on the other end. She sniffed.

"If you cry, I'm gonna cry," I said.

"I'm not crying butt face," she sniffed. "Now tell me about the house." I wanted to ignore it. It wasn't home, so that made it bad.

"Jill keeps bragging to her friends about the seven-thousand square feet, built in 1925, historic home -- "

"Can you really see a river from your room?"

"Yup."

"It is beautiful?"

"I guess so. But it's not New York."

"Shut up. Did you get a fireplace?"

"I think so. I don't know."

"Go inside and look." Manicured grass sprung under my shoes as I crossed the wide expanse of lawn to the driveway. Dad's brand new car, forest green, gleamed in the light shining from square sconces on both sides of the front door. As I climbed the wide steps, Jill appeared wearing a puffy coat and sweatpants.

"You were outside?"

I pointed to the phone.

"Sorry! Meredith?" she said. I nodded. In her hands she held a Tupperware with a screw driver and a small plastic wrapped package. "Mezuzah," she said.

I walked through a wide open foyer with a staircase on the left, narrating as I went. I described some of the weirder details, like the potted plant in the hall, and the gigantic Chinese vase which made no sense except as an umbrella stand.

"There's oriental carpets."

"For your Dad."

"And big modern furniture."

"For Jill. Can totally picture it. A perfect marriage of G-old and new, I love it!"

"You are a dweeb."

"I love architecture."

"This isn't architecture, Mer. It's *decor*." I stood in the living room. "Fireplace, check."

"Good. I require a fireplace."

My scowl softened. Leave it to Meredith to make me almost smile, even in all this.

"Wainscoting in the dinning room?"

"What the heck is Wayne's coat-ing?"

"It's the paneling under the chair rail."

"I have no idea what you're talking about. It's just walls. Table is glass. The base is this big driftwood looking sculpture thing. It matches the cabinets."

"Sexy! Is the fridge big?"

"Enough to fit a body in. Why do you care about the fridge?"

I took her up to my room and went over every detail for about another forty minutes. My dad stuck his head around my door.

"Why didn't you answer me?" he said, irritated.

"I didn't hear you."

"Hello Meredith," he said, raising his voice. "Stacy has to come for dinner now."

I put her on speaker. "Hello Mr. Goldman! Congrats on the move!" she shouted.

"You're on speaker."

"Oh, sorry. Stacy gave me the tour."

"Very nice. Tell your parents I said hello, but she has to go now."

"K, bye!" she said cheerfully. "Call me tomorrow." I pushed the off button and got up from my new bed.

"You didn't hear me calling you? I shouted a dozen times."

"No, I didn't hear you. Have you walked this place from end to end yet? It's ginormous." I followed him down the stairs.

"What's your problem? Jill is very happy. Steve is very happy. I am very happy." I contemplated giving him a truthful answer for about a half second. I'd felt better talking to Meredith, but now the wave of homesickness washed back.

"Meredith is dying to come. Bubbe said she wants me to visit her later this month, so I thought maybe next weekend I could take a bus or the train and go home."

My dad turned to face me. We stood on a thick, red oriental rug half way across the open living room. I glanced at the floor to ceiling windows and saw the room in reflection, a wide screen tv, long coffee table and a sectional couch big enough to accommodate my entire chess team with room to spare. Dad fixed me with the litigation stare.

"No."

"Why not?"

"You live here now. You have to get used to it. Maybe closer to the holidays."

"We just had the holidays!"

"I mean Hanukkah/ Christmas, that whole thing. Maybe then. The city needs time to recover."

"I don't see what me visiting Bubbe has to do with the city needing -- "

"I said no, Stacy and that is that." I took a step backward in surprise. My dad wasn't particularly cuddly, but this was brusque even for him. Who are you? I thought to myself.

"Are you stressing, Ernie?" Jill said, looking over from the dining room. She stood unpacking little cartons of take out while Steve bounced up and down on a springy new chair. "The realtor said this was the best Chinese in Carytown," she said.

Dad turned away and walked to the table to sit.

"Carytown's one of the things the realtor said we'd love about this place. It's like we're in the best part of Connecticut, rural and peaceful, but everything we need to feel at home in the city is just a few miles away. St. Ignatius' is only three miles."

At home, the JDS was three blocks. I pulled my stiff, new seat toward the table. Resentment burbled under my skin.

I'll convince Bubbe she needs me at the temple, I thought to myself. She'll help me. I can do this. I've got a plan. Stay calm, stay rational. I looked through the glass table top at my legs.

Jill walked around the table to put a plate in front of Dad.

"I love you so much, Ernie. Thank you for this. It's a beautiful house and we are all going to be so happy here."

Speak for yourself, I thought.

"Mu shu or lo mein?" said Jill. She kissed Dad's forehead.

Under the table Steve waggled his fingers at me from his lap.

"Did you see the swimming pool?" he asked, eyes dreamy and excited. I scowled. Then I caught myself. I took a breath. Steve didn't need me to be a party pooper right now. He needed someone to enjoy the adventure with.

Lighten up, Goldman, I told myself. It's just Meredith's vacation home. You can leave as soon as you figure out how.

I sat up straighter and thought about home. Right. Good. I had a plan. Time to fake some happy for Steve.

"How about you show me when we're done?"

Monday, October 29, 2001

"This is the sanctuary," said Sister Tour Guide. She had been introduced to me as Sister Mary Louise, or Miriam Ruth or somebody. Sister Two Names Together I could not remember. I decided to call her what I would not forget. Sister Tour Guide.

"We have a gift shop," she said pointing back the way we came. "You can buy a St. Ignatius sweatshirt, sorry, 'hoodie', or a mug for your mother."

Ha, I thought. My actual mother hated the word "mug". I couldn't blame her.

Sister Tour Guide showed me around for another half hour. Jill had attempted to soften the new uniform up for me by tumbling it in the dryer, but it hadn't done much good. The navy skirt fell in stiff pleats above my knees and the matching (yes, matching) navy blouse felt dry and scratchy. I reminded myself to wear a tee shirt underneath tomorrow. We walked the flagstone corridor and beneath the border arch that divided St. Ignatius' church from St. Ignatius' school.

Lots of kids in the narrow tiled halls stared at me as Sister Tour Guide finished my tour. Something struck me as odd about the place, besides the obvious unfamiliarity of being a Catholic school, but I couldn't place it.

I started at Battery Park Jewish Day School in kindergarten and had been there, with Meredith, until last Friday. Isaac came in second grade, Sorrel in fourth. Jacob came just last year, but we liked him right away and adopted him into our group. Right now, my uniform clung to my back, damp with sweat. My breath came in shallow pulls and I felt headachy, a persistent press behind my eyes. I'd never been the new kid. Not once.

I headed to my locker after lunch to ditch my blazer and get a fresh notebook for AP Chemistry. I didn't pay much attention when the tall kid leaned up next to my locker.

"Listen up, new girl," he said scowling down at me, "We don't like your kind around here." He blocked me in between him and two other guys. It was such a classic bully move I nearly rolled my eyes. Was this guy for real?

My first day at St. Ignatius' College Preparatory Academy, the most academically aggressive school in all of Richmond, and I did not want to be late for class.

"What?" I said, standing as tall as I could and heaving my backpack onto my shoulder. "What did you say? Or are you just so stupid that you don't know you don't make sense?" I slammed my locker door so hard it made the shock of black hair that fell over his eyes blow back.

"We don't like people like you," he said again as if I hadn't spoken.

"And what kind of people am I?" It occurred to me I should maybe be scared of this idiot, but what was he going to do? Hit me in the school hallway? Over my shoulder, a nasty, familiar voice rattled off a long, offensive list of terms for People Like Me.

It ended with "Jews."

I froze. It couldn't be *him*.

"Welcome to Richmond, *friend*." I whirled. A thrill of horror rippled up my spine.

4.

October 29, continued.

I stood face to face with Joseph Thornton, the kid who'd attacked, threatened and pushed me into my grandmother at Nationals last June.

"You're from Ohio," I said in disbelief.

"I was," he said with that sour, small teeth smile. "My dad got transferred back here over the summer. Wants me to be at a school with an excellent chess team for my senior year." He held up his hands as if putting the hallway on display. "Mrs. Bason told me we were getting a new player from New York. I hoped it would be you."

He started to move forward.

"One step closer and I scream bloody murder. Don't think I won't," I said. He stopped. A murmur rippled through the gathering crowd. This was not good. One of Joseph's goons pressed toward me from the right, the other came in from the left. My locker had my back.

"I like your new stooges," I said. "I hope they enjoy attacking innocent people and cheating to win. Oh, except you didn't win, did you? You lost. To me."

"Oh but they aren't new, are you guys? We've known each other since elementary school. I grew up here, see? A few years ago my dad got transferred to Ohio and now we're back."

Around me, the goons snickered. The black-haired guy moved toward me.

"Touch me and your balls will never be the same," I said, glaring fire out of my eyes. I didn't even know this jerk's name. I think he was in my second period class, but I wasn't sure.

"Back off her, you pigs," said a warm contralto voice from behind Joseph. A tall, midnight skinned girl with the highest, thickest Afro I'd ever seen stood behind him. The gathering crowd went silent in her presence. "Move away, Joseph Thornton. And if I ever hear you use that kind of language again in the presence of an actual human, I will make it my personal mission to be sure you don't speak at all for at least a week." She smiled. A scary, sincere smile. "Were my words too big or did you miss my point? Get lost."

If only I had said what she said! Warrior Goddess Girl looked at me with mischief twinkling behind her eyes. She enjoyed threatening this imbecile. I enjoyed watching her do it. I decided I liked her.

Joseph Thornton pointed a finger at me. "See you in chess," he said, narrowing muddy blue eyes at me. He and his groupies made their way off down the hall.

"Disperse!" said Warrior Goddess Girl. The crowd scuttled like roaches when you turn on the lights.

I stood rooted to the floor. My heart pounded against my scrawny ribs. Joseph stinkin' Thornton.

"You held your own pretty good," she said to me. "I hope you didn't mind me helping. I despise that turd and couldn't resist taking a turn." Her voice caressed the clearing hallway, a deep and melodious voice, like a rock star.

"He called me Jewish," I said.

"He called you some other choice names as well."

"Yeah. but, no one's ever *called* me Jewish. You know?"

"Oh I know."

"I mean, I am Jewish, but he didn't have to say it like *that.*" I muttered.

"What's your next class? I'll walk you," she said.

I recalled the schedule I'd memorized last night.

"Religion."

Ironic, I thought.

"Ironic," she said, scooping up a backpack leaning against the lockers across the hall.

Interesting she had gone after Joseph without her backpack. What had she expected to happen? She cocked her head at me, regarding me like she could absorb who I was and judge me in a heartbeat.

"Gotta bolt or we'll miss the bell."

She had much longer legs than I did and slowed down twice to accommodate me. One sister called "No running!" out the door of her classroom as we flew by. My escort slowed to a fast walk.

The bell rang. She smiled and stepped aside so I could precede her. She followed me in. Was my class her class, too? I took the room in, book shelves along the back wall, long tables, no individual desks. I recognized a couple kids who'd been watching the scene in the hall. They looked at me.

Oh no. Joseph glared up from the back row.

"What can you do?" Warrior Goddess Girl thunked her books down on the end of one table. She patted the spot beside her. She gave me a sidelong look as we sat. "I made him wet his pants in fifth grade." She sneaked a glance at him over her shoulder. "I think he still remembers. He won't bother you again." Her confidence flowed like electricity. She smiled and winked at me.

Oh he will, I thought, though I smiled back. Maybe not today, but he will. I had humiliated him at Nationals with that win and he would not be forgetting it any time soon.

Round and rosy with a sweet expression, Sister Religion introduced herself as Sister Elizabeth. She had everyone in the class go around and say their names and something about themselves for me.

Warrior Goddess Girl went last before me. "I'm Layla Jackson," she said, "I go by my nickname, Finder. I have the highest GPA in the school, uncontested for the last three years. So don't get any ideas." She gave me a broad toothy smile. I raised my eyebrows. Had she just thrown down the gauntlet for a GPA challenge? Ha! I love a good contest. Finder seemed a worthy opponent. And then it hit me. The weird thing I hadn't been able to quite explain. Finder wasn't *a* Black girl at St. Ignatius College Preparatory Academy, she was *the* Black girl.

I took in the room once again, for people this time. Eighty percent blonde! It's not like I hadn't seen plenty of blond hair in my life, but I grew up at a Jewish Day School. You do the math.

I'm not sure what got into me in this next moment. It was like Finder's confidence was contagious. Standing to take my turn, I decided that I was not going to come here everyday afraid that some ignorant jerk was going to lord his opinions over me.

"I'm Stacy Goldman," I said. I looked straight at Sociopathic Joesph. "I'm from New York City. And I'm Jewish." The class let out an audible gasp.

"I'm a National Chess Master, and at my old school I was Captain of the Math Team, Chess Team, Treasurer of the Debate Club and I," I paused. I was out of impressive facts. I looked at Finder. "I accept your challenge. About the GPA." Finder raised her eyebrows. Her eyes twinkled. Smart *and* saucy. I liked her even more. I glanced around at the rest of the class. "Also I love coffee and chocolate."

A red head with glasses raised his hand.

"Were you there when the planes crashed into the Towers?" he asked. Ah. Everyone had stopped listening at the

I'm from New York City part. Sweat broke out across my back. My mouth got dry. My spine stiffened. You've got this, Goldman. Stay still. Breathe. Think before you move.

The whole room, including me, seemed to be holding its breath.

Sister Elizabeth Religion spoke in a soft voice.

"It's alright. You don't have to talk about it."

My face got hot. What was this reaction? I was fine a second ago! This would not do. I shoved every last emotion boiling up in me down into my shoes. I did not want to represent New Yorkers as weak so I stood straight and pretended I was my father.

"The South Tower went down before the first bell, so I was in chess club. Our classroom window faced the World Trade Center so we saw the plane hit and the building go up in smoke and fire. We heard the collapse from the gym where the whole school had gone to wait. It was like giant shaking thunder. The North Tower fell when we were evacuating. Because we knew what we had seen and it was mostly dust, we didn't believe the Towers had collapsed, even when we saw it on the news. It was like we couldn't believe it until we had seen it for ourselves."

Lots of hands raised. Sister Elizabeth Religion got me a stool to sit on at the front of the class.

Yes, we evacuated after the first tower collapsed. No, no one in my family died, but yes I knew people who did. Two fathers and one of the moms from kids at my school worked in the World Trade Center and didn't make it out in time. Yes,

I lived close. My apartment was declared a hazardous waste site and all my stuff was ruined by chemical smoke and debris. No, my dad didn't work in the Towers. Yes, it was scary. Yes, it was terrorists and yes the buildings had caught on fire.

"Did you have a near death experience?" That red head again. I wasn't sure how to answer. I mean technically no, but . . .

Sister Elizabeth jumped in.

"We have been having a discussion of near death experiences in class this year, Stacy," she said. "Joseph, may I . . .?" At the back of the class, he nodded in his sociopathic, nasty way.

"Joseph was in an airplane crash a few years ago and died for about 3 minutes."

"Two minutes and forty-eight seconds," he said.

"The rescue workers saved his life. We've been discussing God's will for us on earth and why certain lives are saved, and other seem unnecessarily lost."

Joseph interrupted. "Did your family run away from New York because you were scared?"

I looked at Joseph, smug in his question. I am not a violent person, but in that moment I would have pushed Joseph onto the third rail and been glad to do it. The phrase 'run away' stung.

My father *had* run away, and it twisted my heart.

"That's enough questions for Stacy, today," said Sister Elizabeth Religion. "Maybe she will share more about her experience as it gets a little farther away."

I gave her a grateful look, but said nothing.

Halfway through the Religion lecture, I realized I wasn't concentrating. Something was bothering me. I turned around. Joseph was staring at me. What was his problem? I passed a note to Finder.

You made him wet his pants? How?

Punched him in the mouth. Called my family names. Peed before I hit him!

Fantastic!

Not really. It smelled. She pulled the note back. What's up with you two? He keeps staring at you. He hates your guts.

I beat him at chess. I thought for a second, then wrote some more. *I'm leaving Richmond as soon as I can to move back to New York, hopefully next month, so it's only temporary, but would you like to be friends while I'm here?*

Finder whispered in my ear.

"Nobody asks to be friends. You either are or you aren't."

"It worked in kindergarten. Don't you remember asking people to be friends?"

She arched a doubtful eyebrow.

I drew a smiley face on the now rumpling paper. *Don't you like the clarity of it, me asking instead of assuming? Besides, if we're going to compete for the highest GPA, we might as well be friends.*

You're weird. But it's short lived, which is good for me. I accept.

Easy and open with her smiles, Finder offered me another one while turning the page in her faux leather hymnal-ish textbook. I smiled back.

Sister Elizabeth called on Finder to read the next passage. A glimmer of hope wafted across me and sunk into my chest. Southern Catholic School Day One and I now had Warrior Goddess Layla Finder Jackson as my temporary friend. My father would be so proud. I'd gotten it in writing.

Saturday, November 3, 2001.

My little brother jumped from behind my door for the hundredth time.

"Boo!"

"Get out, Steve! Go away!"

I felt unrecognizable. Black skirt, satin. Black boots, leather. Black shirt, fishnet. I wore a tee shirt, black, over the fishnet because I don't do the bra showing through the shirt thing. Meredith coached me on speaker.

"You look gorgeous."

"I look ridiculous."

"Boo!"

I threw a pillow at Steve. "Next time it'll be a hairbrush!" I shouted. He squealed and ran out the door.

"You can't even see me," I said to Meredith.

"I have a very accurate imagination."

"Is that why you smoked pot and got grounded?"

"I did not *smoke!*" she said. "Smoking is disgusting! I ate a brownie. None of us knew they were 'special'."

"Your dad told my dad that you did it on purpose!"

"It was a *brownie*. At a *party*, woman! Of course I ate it on purpose. Her cousin made them as a joke so Sorrel wouldn't turn sweet sixteen entirely innocent. None of us knew. Now, cheer up. The cousin got punished too so its all fair and square. Now, it's your birthday, I'm standing in a breeze that finally doesn't smell like burnt buildings and no one knows I'm on the phone with you. Life is good."

I started to talk but sirens blared in her background. I waited, then continued, "But you can't use the phone for an entire month! A *month!*"

I sighed. My birthday, so far from home without Meredith, without Isaac and Jacob and Sorrel and my school. I missed my grandmother, I missed Rabbi Berman and my chess team. I missed Sorrel's sweet sixteen, though maybe that wasn't such a bad thing. I even missed puny Asa and his nerdy, snorting laugh. I missed my job walking Mrs. Frankenfeld's dog. I missed my Starbucks. I missed the noise and the crush of the city and the hot subway air that blew up from the sidewalk grates. I missed the game of Dodge the Umbrella I played walking down 8th Avenue in the rain.

I missed the Twin Towers.

"What if someone you know walks by and tells your dad?"

"I'm at the phone booth on 86th by the park with the door open. Nobody is going to see me. I even have a little seat."

"Oh my god, don't touch that!"

"I know! I brought a paper towel. Next time I'm going to take the subway to the Plaza and use the fancy phone booths."

"The Met has good phone booths. And it's a lot closer."

"Who cares, woman? It's your birthday! You are dressed up -- "

"In *your* clothes! Jill's face when I opened the box was hilarious!"

"Was she confused?"

"Totally."

"Did you explain?"

"I'm not always a nice person."

"You should explain. She'll think I'm a jerk."

"Everything is Goth now."

"No complaining. Receivers of mail-me-downs do not have selection privileges."

"Next time save them til I come home."

We were quiet for a minute. She spoke first.

"Did you tuck in the fishnet?" I glanced down at the waist of the skirt. How did she know? "Pull it out! Goths don't tuck things in! You layer it over. Woman. Truly. What will you do without me?"

I paused. "I was thinking about emancipating."

"What?"

"I looked it up online. You can emancipate at sixteen in Virginia, but you can start the paperwork a lot earlier. It takes like six months. I have to live somewhere else, so I could come home and live with you or Bubbe. I need my dad's permission on the forms, which I think he would give if I got into Columbia. So I think I'm going to accelerate my program, graduate early, and come home at the end of next school year."

Meredith did not immediately reply.

"Sounds complicated."

"Don't you want me to come home?"

"I'm dying for you to come home! I just don't want your dad to hate me. He's going to think I gave you the idea."

"He is not."

"He is!"

I changed the subject.

"Can I wear sneakers with this?"

"God, Stacy! No! Look, your new black is the opposite of Mrs. Faber's black, got it?" I got it. Meredith continued, "She put all these lavender oil diffusers in her classroom to cover the burnt debris stench, and it's hilarious because everyone goes in all awake then we leave all sleepy and relaxed. Isaac tanked out, like snoring tanked out, on his desk yesterday."

"Did she pitch a fit?" I should be there, I thought.

"Nope. She wouldn't let the rest of us wake him up either. She said we'd all been under stress. If he needed rest badly enough to sack out in class, who were we to disturb him?" Meredith, queen of non-sequiturs. "I have to go in a minute.

I'm babysitting for the Furmans. Listen, have fun tonight, right?" She sang, "If you can't be with the one you love, honey, love the one you're with." Her voice cracked at the end. "Make cool friends because I don't want to hang out with dweebs when I come visit. Or rednecks. No rednecks! And find a cool boyfriend. No jerks."

"Got it. First boyfriend. Not a jerk."

"Email me in case I get to sneak in some email."

"What? They grounded you from email, too?"

"Yes! I'm grounded from *you*, Stace-a-licious! That's the point. They think if they take away my access to you, I'll never touch marijuana again."

"Are they right?" I looked in the mirror and wondered how to make my hair look less boring.

"Probably. This is pretty heinous. I kind of wish I'd at least been bad on purpose. Speaking of which, if you forget me or decide you love your new friends more than me, I'm coming to Richmond La Femme Nikita style."

"Won't happen. You're my best friend in the whole world and no power on earth could make me forget you."

She sighed. "Happy Birthday, woman. Don't eat any brownies."

5.

November 3, continued.

"They have a pick-up truck!" Steve trumpeted from the window seat in the living room. Hair now wet from his bath and wearing Superman pajamas, my enthusiastic muppet brother nearly knocked me over leaping up to answer the door.

He yanked on it, then yanked again. "It's stuck!" He put one foot on the door and the other on the frame, holding onto the handle and pulling and pushing at the same time like a monkey trying to loosen a banana. The doorbell rang.

"Steven! Get off that!" my father said before I could react. "It's just locked."

Finder and her boyfriend, Tully McCleery filled our entryway as my dad let Steve pull the door wide open.

"You must be Finder," my father said over Steve's head.

"Pleasure to meet you, Mister Goldman," Finder said, offering a handshake and her best prep school smile. She found me standing off to the side pulling on my coat. "This is Teulauren McCleery."

"Hello, sir."

She said his name Tull-LAH-ren. Funny I'd never heard it. At school everyone called him Tully.

As if on cue, my stepmother came around the corner dressed in a cream colored sweat suit and lamb skin slippers. She stopped cold when she saw my friends.

Steve turned to Finder and studied her like a beetle in his bug catcher.

"You're *really black.*"

"Oh my god! Shut up, Steve!" I said.

"Steven!" Jill exclaimed at the same time. "You know plenty of African American p-p-people!" she stuttered, flushing in embarrassment. "You'd think he was r-r-raised in the backwoods!"

"Don't worry, Mrs. Goldman," Finder said with a generous smile. "I got your little sprout." She crouched down to Steve's height.

"I am really Black, but are you really Superman?"

"Superman is a state of mind," Steve said under a serious expression. "Anyone can be a hero if they want." He touched the S insignia on his chest and straightened up to stand taller.

"My grandparents are from Kenya and Nigeria," Finder said to my parents. She indicated her skin. "Hence the very Black."

My grandparents are from Russia and Poland. Hence the very Jewish, I thought. But I couldn't bring myself to say that out loud. We all stood for a second in this awkward silence.

Jill started to speak but stuttered again. She took a breath, getting herself together. "I'm so sorry about Steve," Jill said, extending her hand to Finder. "He's only six."

"He's fine," Finder said, shaking Jill's hand.

Tully reached past Finder, took a few steps inside and offered Jill a smooth gift bag.

"Welcome to Richmond, Mrs. Goldman," he said. "Happy housewarming." Tully was over six feet tall, built like an athlete who occasionally sneaks an extra doughnut. Thick blonde hair flowed to his shoulders.

"Thank you!" Jill said, staring up at him then hurriedly looking down at the bag. "Bread and salt! Your mother is so thoughtful!"

Tully smiled. "It's not from my mother, ma'am. It's from me. From us." He indicated Finder with a gentle nod. "May you never go hungry and may your life be full of flavor, is that right?"

"Yes, it is! And look, Ernie, the salt is kosher! That's so sweet of you, thank you." Jill's cheeks flushed pink. She hadn't stopped staring at Tully. I didn't blame her. Both he and Finder were beautiful. Together they were eye stopping. My dad spoke.

"So tell me, Finder, how long have you had your driver's license?"

Way to change the subject and make things even more embarrassing, Dad.

"Say goodnight to Stacy and Daddy, Steven," Jill said.

"Nite, Stace." Steve held up his stuffed monkey for a kiss.

"Nite, Monster." I smooched the simian. "Thanks for my pet rock, Steve," I said. "It's great."

"It's a *frog* rock." He darted under Jill's arm and dashed back toward the enormous staircase. "I want Daddy to read my chapter! Please, Daddy?" he hollered as he ran off.

"I'll be up in a minute," said Dad. "We're reading Treasure Island."

"I love that book," Tully said. "Your son must be smart. I was twelve when I read it."

Finder glanced at me with a Do You Dare Me? twinkle in her eye. I smirked. She could kiss my dad's behind as much as she wanted. She wouldn't get anywhere. Unless she offered him a gig at a comedy club. That could maybe do it.

"Should I call you Counsellor?" Finder said, keeping eye contact. "Might go into law myself one day. My friends tell me I have an overdeveloped sense of justice." Her almond shaped eyes were large and direct, espresso brown touching black. "I might like to be a partner in my own firm one day." Respectful but equal.

"Well, that's certainly a solid goal to work toward," he said. A rise of interest climbed up narrow cheeks from under his five o'clock shadow to his eyes, dark and tired behind his glasses. "You'll have to be ambitious and motivated."

"Oh, I am," she replied. "Stacy says you're the best in your field."

I started to wonder what looked different about him, but then I realized . . .he was smiling? *Smiling?* My brows shot together in astonishment.

"Thank you," he said, holding his ground. "I'm flattered. Stacy speaks highly of you, too."

I stepped between them. "Okay, Dad. We gotta get going."

"Just a minute, birthday girl," Dad said, moving aside in that way parents do to indicate to your friend that it's time to come in and chat awhile. Finder winked at me as my dad shut the door. Winked! Wait. She had just played my dad! Finder didn't care about being a lawyer. She just wanted him to think that and now he was in the palm of her hand. I felt a warm admiration for her. That girl had talent.

In combat boots well-disguised under blue jeans and a slick, thigh length leather coat belted at the waist, Finder towered over my Dad. She had to be five nine, maybe taller. Add eight inches of afro held back from her face by a scarf, and she and Tully were easily the largest people to cross our threshold since the movers.

Finder turned toward my dad. "I've had my license for six months, sir, but Teularen's driving tonight."

Steve shot back down the stairs. "Can I see the truck? Please? Can I get in it? Can I? Please?"

"Your mother told you to get in bed."

"It's a *pick-up* truck!" he begged.

Jill looked worried at Tully. He tipped his head toward her. "I'd be happy to let him sit in it if it's okay with you, ma'am. I'm sorry it's not fancy."

My dad jumped in. "You go to Catholic school. Do you know how to make holy water?" Oh no. He'd probably been waiting all night to drop this one. "You boil the hell out of it!"

Bless him, Tully laughed. Not missing a beat, Dad launched into his favorite string of nun jokes as he, Tully and Steve vanished out the front door to do manly things with a truck.

"This is not my life," I said, shaking my head.

"We're used to kids riding the train, not being personally in charge of heavy machinery," Jill said.

"We weren't planning on joyriding bulldozers," Finder joked. "It's just a car."

"In Richmond it's just a car," said Jill. "In New York it's a death trap with 'steal me' written on the side."

Finder smiled. "You can assure your husband we'll have her home safe by eleven."

"He'll be happier if it's ten."

"I already told him when we'd be home," I said. "He said eleven was fine." This was not going as planned.

"I hear that, Stacy," she said. "I hear you want to enjoy your birthday and stay out late with your friends." Jill turned to me. "Your father will feel more comfortable and be more likely to encourage you to go out with your new friends again, if you're home well *before* the agreed on time."

Finder pressed her lips together, maybe trying not to laugh? Maybe being sympathetic?

I tossed Jill's reflective listening shrink speak back at her. "I hear you," I said.

Jill had been much easier to live with when she was just an actress.

Finder landed another successful prep school smile and said in a reassuring tone, "Of course, Mrs. Goldman. Ten is perfect. We'll see you then!"

If my dad hadn't been standing in the driveway, I might've run to Tully's truck.

Sitting in the back of the pick-up, two things occurred to me. 1. I had never been driven anywhere by a human of my own age, and 2. I should've worn pants. Meredith made Goth look natural. I did not. Next to Finder and Tully both dressed like normal humans, I definitely had gone in the wrong direction.

My Dr. Martens squeaked with newness. I'd gotten them right before we moved, on Mer's and my last shopping trip in Greenwich Village. I bought boots, she bought me a going away present; a thin, black leather bracelet with steel spikes. I'm not sure chess nerds can fall into Goth-ness, but somehow, I had.

"You weren't kidding about your dad," Tully said once we were down the driveway and away from my house.

"Nope," I said, shifting in the backseat.

"He's really short!"

"I thought he was going to whip out a camera and take a picture of your license," Finder said. "He is *definitely* an attorney!"

"I'm so sorry you got trapped with him in joke mode!" I said to Tully. The Southern Scotsman shrugged.

"One of his nun jokes was actually funny," Tully said. "What do you call the nun that lives upstairs? None of the above!" Finder giggled. I rolled my eyes.

"He sure liked you, Miss Partner in My Own Firm," I said to Finder. "I can't believe he smiled at you! The last time my dad smiled at one of my friends was like when I was four."

"Aw, he's sweet. Wound kinda tight, but not, you know. Evil." Finder turned around and locked her lovely African Warrior Goddess gaze on me. Her wide almond shaped eyes were lined with thick lashes and determination.

Behind me, the truck, which had a cover over the pick-up part, was packed with wood.

"What're all these logs for?" I asked.

"I help my dad with his firewood business," Tully said. "Keeps him busy when the landscaping isn't in season. I do a lot of deliveries."

"What's under my feet? I don't want to break anything."

"That's my fencing stuff. You're so small you probably could jump on it and not hurt it, but thanks for being careful." Tully's fencing gear took up the entire backseat floor, and though my legs aren't very long, in a skirt I do need somewhere to put my feet. Afraid to crush anything, I decided on sitting with my feet tucked under me on the seat. I resisted the urge to touch Tully's hair, a golden fall thick enough to braid into rope.

"Your hair is amazing, Tul," I said. "Viking hair."

"Highlander hair!" he said in a thick, put-on Scottish accent. Even from behind, sitting in the truck, Tully filled his seat with shoulders broad as a doorman's umbrella. Blue eyes sparkled in the mirror back at me. He wore a dark blue wool sweater that screamed Scotland, and a Dr. Who scarf that screamed Nerd. Meredith had asked if we could keep him, when I described him to her last week. He possessed a certain cuddly teddy bear factor, but as we turned onto the highway, I caught a different look in those sparkly eyes, a look with an edge. A strength and darkness flashed across his face that made me trust him. Can't explain why, but I relaxed.

Finder tossed me back a Kit Kat left over from Halloween. I tore it open and popped it into my mouth. She threw a Snickers over her shoulder that bonked me on the shoulder as I missed catching it, then a Three Musketeers that bounced off my reaching hand before landing in my lap.

"Candy rain!" She watched me with curiosity in the rearview.

"You could just hand it back," I said, raising an eyebrow.

"Why would I do that?" she said. "This way is more fun. Testing your reflexes," she smiled. "I see we have some work to do."

The bells tinkled on the door to the Third Rock Pancake House as the Southern Scotsman opened the door for Finder and me. Tully had traded his Impress the Parents sweater for a faded denim jacket with a painted back that looked more like it clung to him for dear life than kept him warm. Finder changed nothing. Heads turned to look at her as we waited at the host stand. I could've stood beside her in a giant french fry costume and not been noticeable. I thought about Meredith's assurance I would not look like a total poseur in my birthday Goth wear. I should not have believed her.

I slid into our booth as a server in a pink tee shirt with a galaxy on it tossed menus on the table. Across from me, Tully's tee shirt had a picture of a zucchini saying "Eat more fries." When the server returned with our food and, thank god, my coffee, I realized Tully planned to do just that.

I watched him organize three orders of shoestring fries around his other plate.

"No bacon?" I said. "What kind of southern man doesn't eat bacon with his pancakes and eggs?" I said, emptying another creamer into my cup.

"I'm a veg." Tully reached for the syrup.

"Huh?"

"Vegetarian," Finder said.

"Nothing with a face," Tully said.

"Why?" I asked, astonished. How had I not noticed this? We'd had lunch together at school.

"Contamination."

I stared at him, mystified. A man who specializes in sharp things and plays, of all violent sports, rugby, and he feared what? Salmonella?

"Feed lots use grain with a lot of additives," he explained, squirting ketchup onto a plate of fries. "Unnecessary growth hormones, preventative antibiotics to keep the animals from getting sick despite overcrowding, unsanitary living conditions. You know." I didn't. I never thought about it at all. As long as I didn't have to strangle the chickens myself, I was more than happy to eat them. They were yummy. "I don't even take aspirin, so why would I put all that junk into my body instead?"

"No drugs at all?" I said in amazement. I thought about my monthly relationship with Ibuprofen and about Meredith and her brownie. "What if you get a headache?"

"I meditate until it's gone."

"Come on."

"You asked." He shrugged then inhaled another biscuit.

"My mother thinks it's that no one in his family knows how to cook meat right." Finder smiled at her boyfriend. "They drove him to it, the bastards."

Tinkle, tinkle, tinkle! I looked toward the sound. The diner door slammed shut behind the most adorable Goth boy I'd seen in a long time. I paused, coffee cup halfway to my mouth. I had a lot of experience viewing Goth boys. At home they followed Meredith like rats follow a trash truck.

He bounded up to the counter and plunked himself down on a stool, trench coat flaring out behind him. The counter guy smiled and they did some male fist knocking handshake thing, then leaned across the counter to discuss something that made both of their shoulders rise.

"Earth to Stacy." Finder waved a fry in front of my face. "I said, what kind of music do you listen to?"

I sneaked glances over her shoulder at Adorable Goth Boy. "Bauhaus, though that's more my best friend's favorite band. I like Thomas Dolby, They Might be Giants," Adorable Goth Boy's black jeans were scuffed and worn. When he pushed up his sleeves to accept a steaming mug from Counter Guy, I noted that his spiked leather wrist-bands looked aged. I touched my own, still wafting that new leather smell. Poseur!

"Good lord, girlfriend! What is over there?" Finder turned over her shoulder to see what had caught my attention. "Fine boy alert!" She teased with a big, toothy grin. Tully ate another fry and looked over his shoulder, too.

"Oh, the Goth?" he said. A wave of emotion crashed over me. My heart felt all big and fat and juicy. Twenty feet away sat the first genuine Goth I'd seen since coming to Richmond. Tears sprang to my eyes. I wanted to run up and hug him. Don't get me wrong, Finder and Tully had been amazing since my first day at school, but they were a couple and had been since like fourth grade. They had a Past. How badly did I want friends here anyway? I was only going to leave as soon as I could and go home to New York.

"Right back," I said, scooting out of the booth. Launching toward the rear of the diner, I looked for the tell tale sign. By the time I pushed open the pink industrial door, my trapped tears were escaping.

Shutting a stall door behind me, I lost it. *What is wrong with you, Goldman?* I thought, wiping the renegade tears away. More just chased them down my face. I tried to get my breath, but only succeeded in crying more. *You have got to get yourself together*. I mopped my face with t.p. It didn't hold up well so I peeked out the stall door to look for paper towels. This bathroom had those awful air machines, handy if you've been caught in the rain, worthless for anything else.

I slumped against the stall door.

What am I doing here? I thought.

At home Meredith, Isaac, Sorrel, Jacob and I went for coffee and sushi at a little converted gay bar whose staff never cared how long we played chess or did homework. Something about the big mugs and the tiny, pretty food made the homework go down easier. On each of our birthdays they gave us a rainbow roll.

I started to cry harder.

Okay Stace, I said to myself, get control of yourself. Looking down at the porcelain, I felt dizzy and sat. My chest tightened and I struggled to suck in a breath. For a second I thought I heard a boom and there I was again, watching small things falling from the Tower. Small things that weren't things. Small things that had arms and legs and clothes that fluttered behind them as they dove from the death they feared to a death they chose.

"You are alive. You are safe. Nothing bad is happening," I said, forcing myself to breathe. I coughed as if the dust that had filled the city after the attack swirled around me. I said the mantra again.

"I am alive. I am safe. Nothing bad is happening." Three hundred and thirty-two point three miles from home, my heart hurt for Meredith. Even though I had just talked to her. I felt a cramping under my ribs and to the left that must be the pain people mean when they say heartache. Some part of me had had enough of this pathetic pity party. My mind went all logic-y, like when I'd answered questions about Disaster Number Two in front of my Religion class.

Splash cold water on your face so you don't puff and swell. Pee since you're here anyway. Wash your hands. Go introduce yourself to Adorable Goth Boy.

Once I got to the wash your hands part of the list, I looked in the peeling mirror at my red-rimmed eyes and pink nose. All in black, I looked like an albino rabbit on Halloween. I sniffed my last sniff, leaned over the sink and pumped bubblegum pink soap into an open palm. I scrubbed my face. It stung. I rinsed, pushed the big round button, stuck my face under the dryer, then looked at my still awful rimmed eyes in the mirror. I couldn't deny it: I looked like Steve on his first day of kindergarten; swollen, weepy, basically like crap. I think I must've been about to crack because I said out loud what I'd whispered in his five year old ear. I told him to say it to himself each time he felt scared or missed his mom or some bigger kid stepped on his foot.

"I am a brave and courageous hero." I still looked terrible. "I am a brave and courageous —" the floor outside the bathroom creaked. The waitress who'd served us pushed open the door. She paused, took in my appearance.

"You okay, honey?"

I tightened my jaw and pushed my self not to fall apart again.

"I'm fine, thanks." She closed her stall door eyeing me with outright skepticism.

I am alive. I am safe. Nothing bad is happening. I blew my nose a final time. Reentering the main restaurant, my eye went past Finder and Tully to AGB. Wait. AGB? His counter stool stood empty, his cup had been cleared. Frantic disappointment caught my breath in my throat. I scanned the restaurant. No Adorable Goth Boy.

"Where'd he go?" I demanded back at our booth.

Tully looked up from his food. "Who?"

"The Goth!" I hissed. Finder shrugged and stuck a forkful of omelette in her mouth. I swore under my breath. "Back in a flash." I walked as fast as I could without ripping my skirt. The door chime tinkled behind me. The cold November night hit me like a slap in the face. Fishnet sleeves, though comfy and warmer than you'd think, are not excellent winter gear.

I looked to my right, uphill. The side of the high brick building proclaimed its identity: the original Wonder Bread factory. Parked cars, several streetlights, no AGB. Downhill, the cobbled street crossed defunct train tracks and wound beneath a highway underpass. More parked cars, more lights, lots of highway noise. Still no AGB.

One streetlight illuminated an alley entrance beside the pancake house. Crossing my arms over my chest, I walked

Manhattan fast toward the alley. I could always ask Counter Guy where AGB went to school or if he came in regularly, and then try to intercept him later. One problem. How would I get here? I'm still amazed there are places in the civilized world, developed places like cities, which have no subway. Who doesn't need a subway? I mean, good grief.

I reached the edge of the alley and looked down, expecting to see nothing. Okay, maybe I expected to see a dumpster. What I did see froze my feet to the sidewalk and broke gooseflesh out over my whole body.

6.

November 3, continued.

I threw myself backward up against the building wall, hoping they hadn't seen me. AGB had some blonde girl wearing a white mini-dress and go-go boots in the clutch, pressed up against the exposed brick. She moaned and pulled away, letting her head fall back. Adorable Goth Boy traced the outline of her throat, then kissed it. And stayed kissing it and kissing it and alternately kissing and (eww) licking her throat for way too long. That'll be one mammoth hickey, I thought. He had one arm around her waist and the other, the one closest to me, on her leg.

I retreated a few steps back around the corner and slumped against the wall. Rats. Double rats. Of course there would be a girlfriend.

I heard a loud, encouraging moan. I know I should've walked away. I know peeking in on other people's business is wrong. I really do. Checking up and down the block to make sure no one spied on me spying, I flattened myself against the brick and peeped one eye around the corner.

Girlfriend's head was on AGB's shoulder, eyes shut. Her back rose and fell inside his tight embrace. I thought I saw movement at the other end of the alley, but when I squinted to see better, there was nobody there. AGB must've noticed it too, because he pulled his coat around his girlfriend and drew her closer into him, tipping his gaze to look down the alley.

He whispered in her ear. I listened so hard my ears hurt. She turned her face toward him and, I'm assuming, whispered something back. Then, he turned my way. Our eyes met across the distance. Crap! I jerked back around the wall. Should I run, I thought? A male voice rang out against the brick.

"Good luck," I heard. I couldn't help it. I looked. He stood back from her, wiping his mouth with the back of his hand.

"Please don't go!" Her voice was high and light, like a fairy.

"Give Aegisthus my message," he said, voice threatening. Without warning, he shoved her away hard. She kind of bounced off the wall, then fell back on it, sliding down to her knees.

"Hey Creep! Leave her alone!" My voice, loud and harsh. Barely aware of my actions, I stepped into the middle of the alleyway.

"If you belong to Glen Bacon, step away!" he shouted at me.

The girlfriend lunged forward to grab a handful of trench coat. He yanked the coat out of her grasp. She fell forward onto her hands. She reached again. "Please, Nicolai! Take me with you! Tell him to help me!" she cried to me.

Turning in my direction, she tried to stand. A dark stain ran down the front of the white dress. Whatever it was covered her neck, spilled up on to her face and down her arm. AGB stood frozen, arms open staring at me, a dark smear across his chin. I thought I saw movement behind him at the end of the alley. This time he heard it, too. He turned.

The streetlight caught the girl's dress illuminating the dark red stain. Blood? *Blood?*

"Help!" I shouted.

I charged down the alley toward the bloody girl. AGB ran in the other direction, toward the movement.

"Go!" he shouted. "Go!" He disappeared around the corner before I got halfway down the alley.

"Get back here!" I yelled. "Help! Somebody!" The girl swayed on her feet. "Oh my god," I said. "Do you need an ambulance? You need an ambulance. I'm going to go call you an ambulance. Will you be okay? Stay right here."

She pressed her hand over what I assumed was the wound.

"I'm okay," she said, trembling hard.

"No, you're not okay!" I said. I called again for help. Bloody Girl's eyes rolled up in her head and she fell forward onto me. I staggered back under her weight, but somehow kept my feet. Wrapping my arms around her, I lowered her first to her knees then stumbled and fell with her to the ground. A ripping sound as we hit the pavement and an icy breeze up my backside told me there was another casualty. She was much heavier than I expected. I guess that's what's meant by deadweight. I rolled her off me, leaning forward to keep her head safe in my hand. I slid it with as much care as I could onto the ground.

"Wake up! Wake. Up!" I shook her limp shoulders. Nothing. "Wait right here," I said like a dope. "I'm going to get you help." Meredith's antique satin skirt waved behind me like a pirate flag. I turned it to the side so the rip went up my leg instead of my rear end and pulled the tee shirt down as far as it would go. I bolted for the diner. Note to self: wear pants!

While the hostess dialed 911, and I gasped for air from the short sprint, Tully and Finder launched out the door. The mess on my hands and shirt where I'd caught Bloody Girl showed bright in the diner light. A crowd of diners stared alternately at me and the blood and the door. A few followed Finder and Tully to witness the commotion. Counter Guy tossed me a wet rag.

"Thanks." I cleaned up quick, then ran back out the door. Even the short distance at my maximum speed left a cold, closed feeling in my chest. Tully and Finder stood in the alley entrance, flanked by the crowd who had already started to wander back up to finish their meals. Sucking in a strained breath, I skidded to halt beside Finder.

Bloody Girl was gone.

"Yes, officer, I'm sure." I used my best attorney's daughter voice. Again, I wished I'd been dressed differently. One mustached cop nodded and listened intently to Tully, who hadn't even seen anything. Or maybe that was the point.

"She collapsed right here." I pointed to the spot. I gave the best description I could of AGB and Bloody Girl, but twenty minutes later the police were gone. They hadn't looked for blood or DNA or any of the cool things they do on crime shows. They just sort of glanced around swinging their flashlights, shrugged and left. The police in New York would've at least searched for clues.

"He attacked her! I saw the whole thing. What kind of crazy person *bites* somebody like that?"

"We'll look for her. For them," Finder said.

"He maybe came back for her." My friends exchanged a look. Finder glanced at me, then back at her boyfriend. They stood quiet together for a private second, like I didn't exist. "We'll figure it out," he said. "I'll get the truck."

Finder and I went back into Third Rock to take care of our bill. Our server handed me a go-box, a fresh, hot coffee and a pink Third Rock Diner tee shirt. "You didn't eat a bite," she said. "Thanks for helping that girl. Most kids these days wouldn't have bothered."

Tully drove below the speed limit all around the neighborhood as I told and retold what had happened. Finder and Tully were tense and quiet as we went, stopping frequently so Finder could jump out and stand, sniffing the air like a bloodhound. Tully's fencing bag gaped open at my feet. He had tilted it so the handle of some kind of blade was within easy reach of the front seats.

Driving slow with the windows down, we stopped at every corner, searched down every alley and after about an hour, had covered every side street in a five mile radius of the Third Rock Pancake House. No sign of Bloody Girl or her assailant. I sipped my cold coffee. My sense of urgency rose and fell with each block.

I noticed an absence. An absence of heavy traffic, of honking horns, layered conversations, shouting, doors opening and closing. No subway rumbled underneath us, no sirens blared in the distance. New York got in your face. Richmond offered a polite handshake. New York never shut up, but Richmond dozed off while you talked.

"What's the weirdest thing about New York?" Finder asked as if she had heard my train of thought.

Nothing is weird about New York, I thought. It's just home.

"Everything," I said. "It's New York."

"But is there anything over and above the regular weird? Like dangerous weird or unusual weird that maybe no one would think was real?"

"Do you mean like crime? Or like poker parties for transexuals? Because it's all there. New York has everything."

Finder shrugged. "I mean, is there anything," she took a long time coming up with the word she wanted. "Is there anything," she looked at me in the rearview. "Unimaginable?"

"The Chinese mafia is pretty unimaginable," I said.

"I'm being serious." She turned, laying her intense, judging gaze on me from over her shoulder.

"So am I." This line of questioning struck me as unlike Finder. I began to feel uncomfortable. Why was Madame Confidence uncertain?

"I think you're trying to ask me something without asking me something," I said. "What is it you want to know?"

A car passed us, and we all turned, noticing it. Who noticed *one car*? Where was everybody? Tully parked the pick-up at a corner bordering businesses and apartment buildings, and we piled out to take a closer look around.

The night felt gentle. The cold wind in the leaves sounded whispery and soft as I listened to my new boots thumping the cement sidewalk. Five story buildings held up a wide, starless grey sky. Trees marked even sidewalk breaks in front of the apartments as orangey light glowed from upper floor windows. Curtains alternated with gold leaking out behind blinds and the bluish glow of screens. I looked hard at the lit windows, hoping for a glimpse of a bloody dress.

Finder led the way into the alley and we searched behind trashcans and dumpsters. No traces of blood or Bloody Girl or Adorable Goth Boy, now a Total Criminal Jerk.

The night street felt both comforting and foreign as we exited the alley back onto the sidewalk. Windows lit just like in the City, but so few people on the street.

"Where are the homeless people?" I asked.

"Hospital," Tully's voice reminded me of cookies, soft and chocolate. "There's a shelter by the hospital and when they fill up, the homeless people try to get beds in the hospital."

"Some of these buildings are dorms," Finder said. "The college pays the cops to kick homeless people out as quick as they can. Keeps the parents from freaking out."

"Isn't that illegal?"

Finder raised an eyebrow. "Bribing police?"

"Moving homeless people against their will."

"We have a lot of laws about loitering," Tully said. "That's what they get classified under." He led us down another block to a busier one with restaurants and shops.

"Kids, too," he said. "The police run us off playgrounds at night for loitering."

"My cousin was a cop," Finder said. "He got offered a bribe of some kind or other every week. The senior officers teach the rookies on the sly. They tell them to take a bribe every now and then or people will think they're up to something."

"That can't be true," I said, outrage rising up through me as we walked. "Plus, forty-five percent of homeless people have some mental illness. Twenty-five percent have serious mental illness like schizophrenia. And if somebody gets out of prison with mental illness, there's pretty much no way they can get a job or take care of themselves so they end up on the street."

Finder reached over and patted my head. "You are very innocent for a big city girl." I wasn't sure if she was teasing me, or letting her guard down. "The world is a messed up place sometimes," she said. That was true.

"Was that why the cops basically ignored us earlier?" I said. "Could the Goth have bribed them?"

"Not an impossibility," Finder said. We crossed the street and took a quick look into the places that were open, a convenient store, dirty and small, and a Mexican Restaurant, smelled delicious with wide baskets of fresh tortilla chips on the tables, but still no AGB or Bloody Girl. We went another block and opened the door to a crowded bar filled with drinkers and dancers. Nobody carded us or stopped us going in and as we made our way through the crowd, I saw why. Most of these kids could not possibly be of legal drinking age. I saw a sturdy enough looking chair at an empty table covered with glasses and climbed up on it to get a scan of the crowd. No AGB. No Bloody Girl. We poked our heads in another couple restaurants along the next few blocks, but no sign of our quarry.

At one corner, Finder turned back toward the truck and said "It's 9:30 Tul. We gotta get Stacy home."

"No!" I said, even though my feet hurt from breaking in the new boots. "We can't give up. We have to keep looking!"

"It's not going to help," Finder said. "If we haven't found her by now, she doesn't want to be found."

"She was bleeding from her neck! Of course she wants to be found!"

"Well, unless she doesn't." Tully said. "I think we should get you home, too, Stacy, so we don't have parent freak out to manage on top of tonight."

"They're my parents, par-*rent*, and I don't care if he freaks or not. Jill is his wife and unrelated, so if she wigs, it's not my problem."

"It kind of is," Finder said. "You have to live with her."

I knew my friends were right, but I kept seeing the pleading look in Bloody Girl's eyes and worrying that she wasn't ok. If something bad happened to her worse than the attack, I wouldn't be able to live with myself.

"What if she gets hurt worse by us not finding her?" I said as we turned left to loop the block back to the truck. "What if she dies in an alley from blood loss?"

"We searched every alley!" Finder said. "Everywhere she could have gone on foot. If she went somewhere else, or got taken, it was by car and we have no chance of finding her."

"She also might live in the apartments. She might be home and safe, Stace," Tully said.

"What if she's not?" I cried. I felt sick leaving without knowing why she had vanished and if she was ok. "How can we go home knowing that jerk got away with it and might attack someone else?"

Finder and Tully gave each other another one of those loaded glances.

"What?" I said. "What are you not telling me?"

"We're done here." Finder said with a tone of practiced command that expected obedience. "There's nothing Stacy.

Nothing else we can do. Be glad you helped. It's done for now."

"It's not!" I retorted. "It might be done for the moment, but we *will* find whoever she is and make sure she's ok."

They stood outside the truck whispering after I shut my door. Finder's face adamant, Tully put his hands on her shoulders. He leaned down and said something in her ear. She crossed her arms over her chest. He let go and put his hands up like she was arresting him. She pointed at the truck, and our eyes met through the window. I knew with absolute certainty, that they were talking, arguing, about me. Finder crossed her arms again.

The truck was old enough that the window could roll down with a handle. It squeaked when I turned it. They stopped talking.

"Something is up with you guys." I said. "How about you tell me what's going on?" Something shifted in Finder's gaze. I winced, realizing. This Warrior Goddess Girl was not my Goth Princess Meredith. She had not known me since I ate glue and spat out play dough. She had an edge. She had put down her backpack when Joesph Thornton had threatened me and looked sorry he hadn't given her a full on reason to pummel him. I thought she did it to defend me, but maybe not.

Tully's brow rumpled, worried rumpled, when I looked at him. He took hold of Finder's hand and drew her toward him. He leaned down and said something to her that I couldn't hear. She took a big breath and nodded. He was her

Meredith, not me. I needed to remember that. Jacob had to earn his way into our trust when he came to school. I had to do that here. I couldn't just pass a note and then have years of friendship under my belt. Now, I had maybe just said something that would lose me the only two people I had met here that I liked. Even if we were only going to be friends til I moved back home.

I backpedalled. "I'm sorry," I said. "I didn't mean to interrupt. But if we should talk about something," I looked from Finder to Tully. "Then I can talk. Or listen." Shadows fell across their faces from the streetlight. I rolled up the window and sat back in my cramped little spot. I was not in a position or willing to lose even temporary friends.

We didn't talk much on the way to my house. I looked out the window and watched the hip University neighborhood blend into the wide mansion lined Boulevard and the neighborhood by the Museum of Modern Art. It stood lit up and pretty, tall Roman columns in front of a pale marble building. It's grounds took up the whole block.

"There's a big garden behind it," Tully said, slowing the truck down to play tour guide. "And a cool fountain that you see like the inside of a waterfall from the basement level of the museum. You should go sometime. If you like modern art. It's cool."

"I do like modern art," I said. "I like that you can see whatever you want in it. It's not just a beautiful picture of a chair or a girl with a dog or whatever."

"Sometimes it is," said Finder.

"My dad collects abstract art. That's what I think of when I think modern."

Finder made a humpfing noise. "Seems more like a traditionalist to me."

"He's weird. You think you've got him pegged and then he goes and does something totally random."

"Like move away from New York?" That girl might not be Meredith, but she understood me loud and clear.

"Exactly." Squashing a tide of emotions, I turned my attention back out the window to watch boring, snoozy Richmond for a few more miles.

"That's Maymont," Tully said indicating a big expanse of grass on our right. "There's a park, a house over behind that fence, and a petting zoo."

"Drive slow, Tul," Finder said. She opened her window and stuck her nose out. She looked like she had when we were searching. "You can see the Carillon from here," Finder said, pointing out a stone monolith I squinted to see from the traffic circle. We went around it a couple times, then, satisfied, she gave the okay to keeping going.

My neighborhood, Wilton, sat a few minutes drive west of Maymont, an easy maze of big houses comfortably tucked behind bigger lawns. Sidewalks appeared now and then and streetlights were nil. Each property had lights all its own and from the street you could see the houses illuminated like Christmas novel locations or murder mystery mansion settings, depending on the house.

Our place sat so far back on its bumpy cobbled driveway, you couldn't see it from the road. A lamp post style light stood by the mailbox, indicating a house lay hidden back there somewhere. Tully turned the truck onto the driveway and we bounced back until the wide lawn and house came in view.

"Where's the Jaguar?" he said as we pulled into the wide square driveway. Finder teased him about wanting to drool on it. I noticed for the first time that we had a garage. It stood by itself on the right of the driveway. "At least I have a car," he said. "Unlike *some* people who refuse to buy one."

"I'm not refusing, I just don't want the responsibility."

"You mean the insurance payments."

"Says the boy whose parents pay for his education."

I looked at my watch. 9:58.

"There's cake and stuff left over from this afternoon. Do you guys want to come in?"

7.

November 3, continued.

The bottom floor of the house made up a wide rec room with a giant screen tv, a pool table (why?), and another set of oversized casual furniture. It had a mini kitchen with a fridge, microwave, sink and counter. As a nod to me, my father requested a chess table be included. A comfy chair parked on either side of the low square table. Two more lingered close for zealous six year olds or, in my father's case, hecklers. The board was engraved into the table surface. Drawers held wooden, weighted pieces with a separate drawer for the clock, coasters, napkins etc. so the table could be used for social gatherings as well. Finder set her dessert on it. Relieved to have changed out of my ripped skirt into jeans, I handed them each an iced tea from the mini fridge. Tully read the back of the bottle I'd handed him, then set it down in favor of bottled water.

"You don't drink tea?"

"High fructose corn syrup," he said. "One of mankind's most addictive substances."

"Corn syrup?" I said, incredulous.

"Fructose," he said. "Engineered during World War II to be delicious, health destroying and a primary component of a master plan to fatten Americans up thereby increasing the financial dividends of both the food and medical industries."

"That's ridiculous."

"Look it up."

I looked at Finder for support.

"It's true," she said, but she drank her tea anyway. Good girl. "Snappy deck," she said, opening the sliding glass doors and stepping out onto the flagstones in her striped socks. We'd all taken off our shoes in the foyer per Jill's request. "Too bad the pool is closed."

"Too bad the hot tub is closed," Tully said, eyeing the raised stone spa.

"They talked about leaving the tub," I said shrugging. "Jill said close it. The whole thing stayed open until two weeks ago to help sell the house."

Finder shut the doors, then padded across the room. She picked up a pool cue, looking for the little chalk.

"Play me, Tul."

"I'm not as good as your dad," he said. "You'll beat me quick."

"Pick a cue," she said, lifting wicked eyebrows at me.

"I have played pool exactly once."

"You'll get plenty of practice," she said organizing all the balls on the table inside a plastic triangle. "What's in there?" Finder gestured toward the door next to the bathroom.

"Have a look," I said.

Finder put down her pool stick and threw open the door.

"Holy workout, Batman!" she said, beckoning to Tully. They ooohed and ahhhed, naming all the junk in there for me. Finder ran her fingers over every bit of it, the lifting bench, wall mounted weight rack, treadmill, kettle bells, medicine balls, stationary bicycle with a screen on the wall in front of it, machines for rowing and "GHD", punching bag, even the mats on the floor.

"Seriously swanky," she said, eyes aglow. "Not much room to move around, but you have all the gear." She faced the punching bag, hit it fast once with each fist, then did some fast turn thing and kicked it hard enough to make it sway.

"Righteous!" she said. She bowed to the bag then turned to me. "I'm moving in."

Tully asked if we could go outside and see the river at night. We collected our shoes and coats from upstairs and went out the front door to circle the house. A cold breeze whipped my hair across my face as we crossed the patio and went to the other side of the pool house where a set of stone benches glowed pale grey in the moonlight. Tully and I sat, Finder walked a few feet off toward the rocky slope that led down to the river.

"Jill said there's stairs down to a trail on the other side of the property, but I haven't gone to see yet."

"I know the trail," Tully said. "It winds down by Wilton Island and Park. Lots of people bike or run their dogs there."

"Have you lived here your whole life?"

He nodded. "Finder, too. You're our first friend from the outside world."

"Have you ever known anybody who graduated early at St. Ig's? Or who emancipated? I'm thinking about doing it so I can go back to New York and start college in the January semester when I'm sixteen."

"Ambitious. Nope."

We were quiet as Finder wandered back. Moonlight lit up the river below us, glimmering silver off the wavy sky mirror. A subway car length away, the pool house wall anchored me in this wide open space. Trees closed us in maybe a half block down the lawn, but the forest line felt far away. Sitting all the way back on the bench, my feet dangled well above the ground.

"So you know how I asked you about weird things?" Finder said. "It wasn't a random question." She paced back and forth in front of our bench. "Nobody can hear us out here, right?"

"I don't think so. Not from the house."

She scanned the grass and took another glance back at the trail beneath us.

"You saw him bite her. Then what?"

"I didn't *see* him bite her. I saw him shove her. Before that, they were making out and when she turned to me she was covered in blood."

"You said he focused on her neck," Finder said.

"Yeah, and she seemed enthusiastic."

"They usually do," Tully said, matter of fact.

My face flushed hot with embarrassment. What did he mean they usually do? I looked from one to the other of them.

"What we need to determine," Finder said, "is if what you saw was a human attack. Or. If you saw," she took a breath. She fidgeted with her hands. She took another big breath and wavered. "I can't do it," she said to Tully. "It's too soon."

"We don't want a second casualty tonight! We have to tell her." He met my eyes over his shoulder. "Sorry, Stacy. We shouldn't talk about you like you aren't here. This is hard for us." He looked Finder in the eyes and they stood together like that for a long moment. "She isn't going to betray us. It's time to trust somebody, Layla. Somebody besides me."

She turned away toward the river. Tully came back and sat next to me.

"Richmond is," he paused, searching. "Unusual." He threaded his fingers together in the moonlight and looked out at the river. "Things, live here. Creatures. Some won't surprise you. Some are," he paused, "unimaginable." He changed the link of his fingers.

Finder interrupted.

"We *strongly* suspect that what you saw tonight was not human. We think you saw something supernatural. Probably a vampire."

I snorted.

"I'm not kidding," she said.

"She's actually not."

"Well, except that you *are*."

"Stacy," Finder crouched in front of me so our faces were level. "I'm not playing with you." I looked back and forth between them. Warrior Goddess Finder in silhouette, river shimmering behind her, the wall of Tully beside me on the bench.

"And how is suggesting I saw a vampire attack *not* playing?"

"Forget it," Finder said. She stood up, turning on Tully. "I told you she wouldn't be one of us. I *told* you! I told you it was a mistake to tell her!" Tully looked from Finder to me.

"Who's us?" I asked. A disappointed ache filled my chest. "Why was it a mistake to tell me?"

"There aren't many regular people who know," said Tully. "Folks who aren't among the unimaginable themselves." He got up and took Finder's shoulders like he had outside the car. "Give her some time," he said. "It's not normal to have somebody tell you this. Is she just supposed to take our word for it?"

"Yes!" Finder's voice rose in frustration. "She is!"

"*She* is right here," I said, standing.

"This isn't helping, guys," Tully said.

Finder crossed her arms over her chest. "Run your mouth all day long Teularen, but you won't get anywhere."

"How do you know?" I said. "How do you know what I will or won't believe? You've known me for a week."

Tully took a long slow inhale, then exhaled closing his eyes. After a second, he opened them and fixed a clear gaze on me.

"I realize it's a farfetched suggestion, that you witnessed a vampire attack," he said, "but for us it's personal. We keep our involvement with the unimaginables secret because of moments like this." If he lied, he had practiced til perfect.

"And so we don't get killed," Finder said. "Don't you have something painful in your life that you don't like to talk about with just anybody?"

In fact, I did. Disaster Number One. Only Meredith knew the whole real story.

"You maybe noticed we don't hang out with a lot of people," Tully said. "It's not because we don't like people."

"It is for me," Finder said. "I don't like people."

"Trust issues," Tully said giving me a half smile. "I like people." He got back on track. "If you were acknowledged by a vampire, if you interacted with one, or with something else supernatural, and lived to tell about it, their society has become aware of you. So, you could be in danger." He kept his arm around Finder and turned her toward me. "Telling you makes us über vulnerable, Stacy. You could tell people about us, you could spread rumors at school, you could say something to the wrong person that could get back to Glen Bacon and, no joke, get us both hurt or killed."

"Wait," I said. "Who's Glen Bacon? The Goth said that name. He said 'if you are Glen Bacon's stay away'. The girl begged him to take her with him. Do you know what he meant?"

"What?! Why didn't you tell us this before?" Finder threw her hands in the air. "We are so screwed!"

"Layla! We can handle this. We just have to get Stacy on board and then we can make a plan."

Finder grabbed his coat lapels. She shook him. "She doesn't believe us, Tul-LAH-ren! Look at her face."

"Is that true?" His eyes searched mine. "Do you think we're lying to you?" An icy gust came up off the river and blew his hair and mine into tangles around our faces.

My mind swung in a thousand directions.

1. Is this the point in the movie where the hero gets informed that monsters exists and so she freaks out, denies it and then ends up in the hands of the monsters herself?

2. Are my friends sick or delusional?

3. Are Tully and Finder not my friends? Did Sociopathic Joseph pay them to play a nasty joke on me?

Confused, I put my head in my hands. Finder cleared her throat. She and Tully stared at me, waiting. Tully spoke.

"I said, are you cold?"

"Yes."

"Me, too." He looked at his girlfriend. "Are you cold?" She had her arms wrapped tight across her chest and had doubled up her scarf while Tully talked.

"Freezing."

"Would we plan to drop you off home, but then come in, hang out and make you bring us outside on a freezing night, that happens to be your birthday to talk in secret if all this wasn't," he paused, "true? Would we lie for a joke? Is that consistent with our personalities to you?"

"No."

"Okay, good." Tully looked at Finder but she didn't budge. She said, "What would be the benefit to us of fooling you?"

I shrugged. "Bragging rights that you tricked the new girl? Laughing amongst yourselves? Maybe Joseph Thornton paid you to do it?"

Finder snorted in derision.

"As if I would ever cooperate with that filth."

"Maybe you do this to all the new kids. Maybe some kind of Catholic school hazing to test my faith? Which," I added before anyone else could speak, "which I don't have, so it'd better not be that."

Finder threw up her hands again and walked away.

"The only reason he would mention Glen Bacon is if he was killing that girl, Tully!" she said over her shoulder. "Getting involved in this is bad! Very bad!"

Tully remained with me, calm and reasonable.

"Those nasty tricks are all possibilities," Tully said. "Would the payoff be worth it, though, humiliating someone who doesn't deserve it? Would we enjoy doing that?"

The wind left my resistance sails. I relented. "How can I believe you?" I said. "You want me to believe that vampires exist!"

"How about I just ask you to not believe that they don't?"

"What? Oh my god!" Finder rolled her eyes.

Tully stayed with me. "How about I don't ask you to believe in them full out, just hold off on your disbelief for now? Until we learn more."

Not an unreasonable idea. Maybe I could do some research and figure it out for all of us.

"You want me to just say I don't know if vampires exist or not, is that it?"

"Exactly! An experiment. If the experiment hasn't ended yet, we don't have a conclusive answer. Without a hard conclusion, we behave as if either outcome of the experiment could yet be true."

Finder paced around the clearing. "That's stupid, Tully! They exist and that's all! She has to believe us!"

"No, she doesn't! She does not have to believe us. You have proof. I have proof. Stacy doesn't and it's unfair to ask her to take our word for it."

"She has proof! He magnetized her!"

"*What?*" I laughed out loud. "I was not *magnetized*! I saw my first goth hottie since being here and I'm so homesick I can't even tell you! I just wanted to say hi!"

Finder fixed me with an unbending look. "And how often do you walk up to twenty-year old guys you don't know and said hi?"

Crap. She had a point.

"Right," she said. "Never. You felt *compelled* to go after him."

"Maybe I was, as you say, *compelled*, but not by some magnetic force. By my own free will!"

"Correct," Tully said. "You get the urge to go on your own."

Finder nodded her agreement. "We should've seen it when he pushed you into the bathroom. That had to be when he grabbed your mind. You felt really emotional right?"

"Well yes, but that was because -- "

"Experiment," Tully said with a pointed look to me. "Let's just say it's possible you were emotional *because he grabbed* your mind."

I sighed. "Okay, but I think it's because -- " Tully shook his head at me, waving a finger. He focused on Finder with a deep frown.

"We were relaxed, off our guard. We didn't see it. We should have." He looked back at me. "I'm sorry we failed you." Tully's sincerity and apologetic look tempted me to relent. Tempted, but not convinced.

"What if I'm just so stressed I'm willing to take more risks? Maybe he reminded me of my friends at home. The rubble gets transported on barges. Did you know that? There is a barge in the river across the street from my school hauling debris from almost two months ago that is *still burning*." The wind blew a huge gust of leaves toward us from the edge of the woods.

"Those thoughts aren't connected," Finder said. "See what I mean? How did you get from stress and friends to burning rubble? The unimaginable are devious," Finder said, nodding.

"They implant desires and impulses in your mind. They take connections away. It's how they survive."

"He did not implant anything in my mind!"

"How do you know?" she shot back. "Can you be sure?"

"The real question," Tully said, staring out at the river, "is whether or not you are in immediate danger."

I shoved my hands deep in my pockets. "I can't explain what I saw," I said. "And I can't explain why I went after him except that it seemed important. I didn't get near him so I don't know how anything could have gotten into my mind. If he's a big, powerful vampire," I repressed the heavier edge of my sarcasm, "why did he run away?   Why didn't he use powers on me? Or drink my blood, too? Or whatever?"

"It doesn't make sense for him to magnetize her, draw her out there to witness and then not come back for her like he did the victim," Finder said.

"Could he have followed us here?"

"No. I would sense him. But I can't be with her 24/7." She turned to me. "You need to take this seriously, Stacy, even if you don't understand why. Even if you don't believe us. You're not in New York anymore. This is the South. Things. . . exist here."

I shook my head. Things. There's no such *thing* as ghosts, no werewolves, no vampires, no Big Foot, no Loch Ness Monster. Actually, there is a Loch Ness Monster but it's just a giant lizard. Finder and Tully exchanged looks.

"How will you prove there's vampires?" I asked.

"It would be best if we don't," Tully's eyes narrowed, revealing that dark edge I mentioned back in the truck.

I needed friends. Even temporary ones. If I had to pretend to believe in monsters until I could prove they'd been duped, I guess I'd get better at pretending.

"We still have to find whoever she is and find out if she's okay," I said. "Meanwhile, vampires may exist, they may not. I may be in danger, I may not. What am I supposed to do about it?"

Finder looked me dead in the face. "You have to perform the ritual. Tonight."

8.

November 3, still, but not for long.

"Can Finder and Tully spend the night?"

My dad's face spasmed in astonishment.

"Please?" I begged. "It's almost midnight and Finder lives forty-five minutes away. And it's my birthday."

Jill and Dad sat tucked up in the living room watching late night TV, and, I assume, distance chaperoning me and my new friends. As if they could hear us.

"We wanted to watch a movie," I explained. "Tully can stay on the couch in the rec room and Finder can stay up with me or in the guest room."

"We have two guest rooms, Ernie," Jill said. "They're on the other side of the hall from Stacy's room so we have the space."

"They can call home and ask, if it's okay with you," I said. "Then you guys can go to bed and not feel like you have to be up with us all night. It's an easy yes, Dad. Did I mention it's my birthday?"

Dad scowled. "I don't like it. You're past the age where boys and girls can mix for sleepovers, Stacy. I don't feel comfortable. Finder can stay, but Teularen has to go."

I played the birthday card one more time, tried a little negotiation, but my dad was firm. No boys. Hmm. I didn't think I'd get a better offer.

Jill shrugged. She'd tried. Finder for the win. I went into the foyer where Finder and Tully stood side by side and announced the verdict.

"Well whaddaya know," Finder said. "The white man loses and the black woman wins." She grinned up at him. "I'll let you know how I like that gym on Monday."

In the kitchen, Finder used the phone to call home and get the okay from her mom. She told Tully what to look for and he rummaged in our spice cabinet til he found whatever ingredient we needed. Otherwise we'd have had to send him to the store and sneak down the driveway to get it from him.

"Where are you going to get pajamas?" he teased. "You can't even get half of one of those thighs into her Barbie doll clothes."

"I'm not that small!" I said. "I can loan her a tee shirt."

"You are that small," Finder said. She turned to Tully. "But don't you worry, son. I can figure it out."

He popped his head into the living room, thanked my parents for having him over and bid us goodnight. Finder and I stood in the foyer until we heard the truck start up and pull down the drive.

"You guys don't kiss much," I said, handing her a bottle of water.

"We don't," she said.

"Does that bother you?"

"No," she said. "He's Tully. Big on hugs, not so much the rest."

"That's kinda too bad. He's so cute. He looks like a good hugger." She nodded, smiling a real Finder smile for the first time since I ran like a crazy person out of the diner.

"He is the best."

We planned to watch a movie until my parents went to bed, wait another hour and then do whatever Finder had decided we needed to do. At one point during our film, Jill came down and took Finder upstairs to show her the guest room, towels etc. I changed into pjs and cleaned up our dessert dishes from earlier.

Finder returned in a brand new pair of men's flannel pajamas with the ankles rolled so they would look like capris, rather than just too short.

"Fresh out of the package," she said. "Lucky for me, your dad hasn't opened half of what your step-mom bought him."

Sunday, November 4, 2001.

We finished the film and watched half of another to be absolutely sure Dad and Jill were asleep.

Around 1:15, we padded upstairs to the kitchen. The stove light glowed a pool of yellow onto the professional gas burners. Finder opened the spice cabinet, took our ingredient and asked me for a piece of paper. She wrote a few lines and handed it to me.

"This is what you say. You focus your intention to make it work."

I blinked at her. I'd heard the phrase 'focus your intention' before but had no earthly clue how to do it.

"Can't you say it?" I whispered. I knew no one in the house upstairs could hear anything, including the TV we'd left on downstairs, but it felt weird to talk in full voice in semi-dark at 1:15 in the morning.

"It's your house, the intention needs to be yours."

"It doesn't feel like my house," I said.

"I'd trade you if I could!" she said. "Now I can help, add energy to you, but you need to do the bulk of this yourself."

Finder led me to the front door. The red warning light on the alarm panel blinked, letting me know if I opened the door without disarming the system, loud sirens would go off, the security company would be summoned and many embarrassing disasters would befall me.

I looked at the paper she had put in my hand. I read the little poem a few more times, making sure I knew it word for word.

I listened for noise upstairs. Realizing I held my breath, I rolled my eyes at myself. I rubbed a sweaty hand on my pants. I stared at the floor. I looked at Finder, close to invisible in the shadowy foyer. I imagined not going through with this. Finally, I took the lid off the container.

"There's no shaker top!" A mild panic rose into my chest.

"There isn't?" She took the bottle out of my hand. "How dumb is that?"

"Right? Who ever heard of garlic powder without a shaker top? Good grief." I shook my head. "Do I have to say the thingie out loud?"

"The incantation. Yes."

I started, then stopped. "This is embarrassing."

Warrior Goddess Finder took me by the shoulders the way Tully held her.

"What's your middle name?"

"Rachel."

"Stacy Rachel Goldman," her intense focus on me was stern. "It is possible that the lives of you and your family could be at stake. This is not a joke, and it is not a sham. Now say The. Stinkin'. Incantation!" She let go of me. "And mean it!"

I took a deep breath and said in the quietest voice I could manage, "By the power of three by three, this house is made safe by me. To cause no harm nor return on me. As I will, so mote it be."

Finder gestured toward the garlic powder. I took a pinch of the stinky granules and sprinkled an uneven trail along the edge of the front door. I said the incantation again, trying to mean it. Then I did the foyer windowsills, moving counter-clockwise, as per Finder's instructions.

"What're you doing?" behind us. I jumped and spun around crashing into Finder who had also turned at the sound. She caught me but the garlic powder sprung from my hand. Finder reached to catch it and missed. It spilled everywhere.

"Steve! What're you doing up?" I panicked. "Is your mom awake?" I whispered.

"I asked you first," he said, staring up at me from inside a snug pair of superhero pajamas.

"I'm older," I argued.

"I'll tell Dad." I loved him, I hated him. I tried to think fast. I failed.

"We're sprinkling the doors and windows with garlic powder to ward off vampires."

"Tell the truth," said Steve, cocking his head at me.

"I am!"

He sighed and shook his head.

"Okay, don't tell me," he said, "but I came down for a glass of milk." We trailed the kid into the kitchen where I proceeded to pour for him, then collect the mini-broom and dustpan. Finder grabbed the big broom. When we came back in, Steve had one foot on a chair and one on the table, and balanced over his glass, stood draining half a bottle of strawberry syrup into his milk.

"Whoa there, Superman!" Finder said, reaching for the bottle.

"That's not going to help you get to sleep," I said. He snatched the bottle out of Finder's range, popped the cap down, and jumped off the chair. "It's not for sleeping," he said, opening the fridge. I watched in fascination as he put the bottle exactly, and I mean exactly, where he'd found it. "It's for staying awake so I can save the day when the monsters come."

"And what monsters do you expect exactly?" I exchanged a look with Finder. Her face was somber. The dustpan of garlic powder weighed in my hand.

I looked into Steve's sincere little face and wondered if he knew or could sense or little kid intuit something that I did not or could not. Had I crossed far enough into the realm of adulthood that reality had begun to evade me at last?

My brother shrugged. "You never know what's coming," he said sitting down at the table. He picked up his too full glass and took a long drink. He didn't look at me or Finder. "But tonight it smells like teeth."

"Teeth?" *Calm down, Goldman. You're talking to a six-year old.*

When Steve finished his milk and I had corralled every stray grain of garlic powder that I could into a baggie, I left Finder in the kitchen and walked him back up to bed.

"Wait out here a sec," I said. I waded through an ankle deep ocean of Legos, action figures, hot wheels, and Nerf guns to get to his windows. I chanted, I sprinkled, I hoped that a) this was all a big hoax, b) if there was even a shred of reality in this, that it worked.

"Did you put garlic in my bed?" he whispered suspiciously when I emerged.

"It's on the window sills, dork. To keep the you know whats away." I leaned over and kissed the top of his head. "Now go to bed before we both get in trouble."

"Stacy," he whispered, standing alone amidst his toys, "Thanks."

"Nighty nite," I whispered back, handing him his stuffed monkey. "Monster will protect you."

The weird silence of our new house enveloped me as I went back downstairs. Arriving back in the kitchen, the dishwasher shut off with a buzzing click, the refrigerator barely hummed. Finder finished her own glass of strawberry milk, less than half the size of Steve's.

It took us about an hour to chant and sprinkle our way across the first floor and basement/ ground level.

"This place is huge, we'll be up all night," Finder said. "Give me the baggie." I kept the no shaker top container and we worked the rooms together each taking half. I'm not sure exactly when it happened, but somewhere in the rec room, I stopped feeling silly. Maybe it was hearing Finder's low warm hum of chanting and feeling her seriousness about the whole thing, or maybe it was Steve's weird prediction. Maybe it was just me. It was like the moment in my Bat Mitzvah when the rabbi blessed me. I got all teary eyed. I don't know why that happened, but I felt tingly and strange. Loved maybe? I know it sounds weird, but I felt *blessed*. Asking for protection for my house and family, that same feeling washed over me. Kind of emotional, kind of outside myself, but present. I don't know, it was weird. I will say that by the end of our little project I think I understood what Finder meant by 'intention' and a big part of me meant it like crazy.

🨅

November 4, continued.

Tully's phone call at ten the next morning found Finder and me at the kitchen table blearily watching leafless branches sway out bay windows. Wind howled outside. November had arrived. I nursed an oversized mug of whipped cream topped decaf into which I'd dumped four scoops of hot cocoa and a handful of chocolate chips. Finder's hands wrapped around a thick mug of Jill's specialty, chai tea.

Steve ran his train set across the entire kitchen floor. He hadn't quite adjusted to playing in such a ginormous space. When the phone rang, I didn't leap to answer it.

Jill held the cordless out to me.

"How'd it go last night? Can I talk to Finder?"

I passed the phone. "Tully."

"Great idea!" Finder said suddenly seeming awake. Her wide gaze fell on me. "Wanna go on a field trip this morning? To my dojo?"

"Dojo?"

"The studio where I teach."

"Teach?" I exclaimed.

"No one else will be there so we can show you some -- " She stopped mid-sentence remembering that we weren't alone. "Some of the neighborhood and you can see it."

I felt highly uncertain about a trip to a marital arts studio with Finder, but I had caught her drift. If I agreed to pretend to believe in vampires, I might as well pretend to have some self defense moves ready to use.

Even though Jill stood right there chatting to her son about the railroad, I hollered for my dad.

"He's still upstairs," Jill said, using that low tone psychologists use when they want you to speak more softly, too.

Right. He couldn't hear me. How long would it take me to adjust to not hearing each other at different ends of the house? At home, I could hear the Fabers at the end of the hall if they coughed loud enough.

I discovered my dad soaking upstairs in a bubble bath talking on his new cell phone, Eric Clapton cd in the player.

"I just want you to be safe and happy," he said. "We could get you a condo in Boca if you don't want to come to Rich -- "

"God, Dad, can't you shut the door?" I plunked down on the edge of his king sized waterbed, checking to make sure I couldn't see into the bathroom even if I looked in the dresser mirror.

"Hang on, Ma, Stacy just came in. It's my bathroom, honey," he said. "It's my bedroom. A man can do what he wants in his own bedroom. Talk to your grandmother. Tell her you want her to move to Richmond."

I closed my eyes and reached my arm into the bathroom.

"Tell your father to eat his shorts! I am not moving to Richmond!"

"She says eat your shorts, Dad. Hi, Bubbe! How's your wrist?"

"My God, Shayna, learn to ask a different question! It's fine. I miss you so much! I can't believe you're so far away! It's terrible, why don't you go get the toaster and drop it in his bath? I'm kidding, but I could clobber him for taking you away from me and for trying to get me to move! You know what they say about why Boca is so beautiful right? There's a Rosenblum on every corner." She laughed at her own joke. "Get it? Rose in bloom? Rosenblum?"

"I get it. I miss you, too."

"Good. Now remember it's your mother's birthday next week and she is going to call you."

I sighed. Oh great, the annual mother call. Not exciting. I wished I could tell Bubbe about last night. I hadn't told my dad or Jill yet. Part of me felt like keeping it a secret was wrong. What if the police called to follow up on my report, or someone called from missing persons to use me as a witness? The other part of me, the embarrassed kiss-witness part, didn't exactly want to be telling parents about how or why I'd seen what I'd seen.

"You have to help take care of her, Shayna, she isn't well and talking to you makes her happy. She can't help her condition, remember that. Your grandfather would always say that being Jewish means being generous. Helping people is what we do. Moses parted the Red Sea, Noah built the ark, even your father helps his clients. What're you going to do? You don't have to be Moses or Noah, but it's an important question, Shayna. How will you contribute to the world in a way that helps? And speaking of helping, I need you to carry a load of kitchen stuff I ordered to the relief center for the families." She meant the families who'd lost their homes on 9/11 and didn't happen to work for wealthy law firms who could buy them houses in new cities.

Guilt crawled into my chest and poked me with sticks. I had no business in Virginia. I belonged in New York. Where I could help. Where I could do some good for the people who shared my island.

"When are you coming to see me?" Bubbe said.

"As soon as they'll let me get on a bus," I said, loud. If Dad heard me, he gave no indication.

We caught up for a few more minutes as my father paged through a golf magazine and sang out loud to Eric Clapton. When we hung up, I tossed the phone onto his bed.

"You need to let me go see Bubbe. She needs help moving her donations to the relief center."

"Send Meredith."

"Dad. Bubbe needs *me*. She has nobody without us. I could live with her for the rest of the school year and come here to visit you in the summer. I want to go."

"No." His eyes stayed on his magazine.

"Can we at least talk about it?"

"No." He was infuriating.

"I could run away."

"But you won't."

"How do you know? Maybe I will. Would you at least look at me?" He raised his eyes over his reading.

"Get used to it here, Stacy. You live here now."

"Don't you miss the City even a little?"

"Of course."

"Then why don't we move back?" He looked at me hard.

"Do you want Jill to have another nervous breakdown? Do you want to deal with what will happen if she has daily panic attacks and can't take care of herself or Steven? Is that what you want?"

"No, but -- "

"Stacy! Enough! We are here and that is that."

Emotions rushed through me, guilt and anger and resentment and disappointment and utter bewilderment at how easily he could ignore not only his own missing of the City, but how cavalier he could be about mine. Jerk.

This conversation was going nowhere. I remembered why I had come up here in the first place.

"Finder invited me to go see her dojo this morning," I said. "Tully can pick me up and bring me home."

"Home work finished?"

Really, Dad? Homework is all you care about? I thought to myself.

"Will be by the time I go," I said. "I have religion reading and a page of calc left. Twenty minutes." Oh, and an essay to wade through for English. Except for the last bit, a piece of cake.

"Sure. Be home by six for dinner."

"I'll be home way before that," I said.

9.

November 4, continued.

"You have to slam it." Finder drew her arm back. She aimed and rammed the stick into the hay bale. We stood in the alley behind the Flying Eagle Mixed Martial Arts Studio in front of a rectangular stack of hay bales leaning against the exposed brick wall. Finder yanked the stake out of the hay and handed it to me. I hefted the heavy pointy stick. It had a smooth feel in my grip. I jabbed it forward with all my might but it barely went a half inch into the hay.

"It's not exactly cutting a peanut butter sandwich," Tully said, acknowledging my attempt. Finder put her head in her hands and rubbed her face.

"I think we have to start somewhere more basic," Finder said.

Over the next hour, back inside the dojo, she and Tully taught me correct positions for pushups, pull ups and some weird abdominal exercises I could do on the floor. She promised to come over after school one day and show me how to use all the machines in the home gym, but for now, she wanted me to be able to fend off an attack if I should get sneaked up on alone.

She had Tully grab me from behind and pick me up. I felt way too secure, even with my feet off the floor. His chest at my back felt solid and comfortable.

"You're so light!," he giggled, giving me a playful bounce. "I caught a Pokemon!"

"Except I can't electrocute you!" I said. His hair smelled like strawberry coconut shampoo. Not very manly, but quite nice. "Don't drop me!"

He gave me a squeeze. "Don't worry, I gotcha."

"When somebody grabs you from behind, you're job is to get them to let go. What part of him can you reach?"

I dangled in his arms, mine squashed against my sides. "Nothing."

"Reach back with your head." I tapped his chin with the back of my head. "Your skull is a weapon. It weighs about eighteen pounds and hurts when it hits. If you slam back when he's not expecting it, you can deck him. What about your feet?"

I kicked back. Tully moved his legs out of my way. "Where does your foot land when you bend your knee?"

I put my bare foot on his still leg.

"That's my knee," Tully said. Kick back at the right moment and you could wipe out my knee."

"Always remember you can scratch and bite," Finder advised. She walked me through a few drills where I had to break a grab, twist a wrist or find a tender spot to inflict as much pain as I could given my substandard strength.

Wrapping up, I laid flat on the canvas covered white mats sweaty, sore and breathing like a dog on hot pavement. "Your attackers will always be bigger than you," Finder said. "Unless they're twelve."

"You should show her how to take a fall before we go," Tully said. I groaned. I would never remember all of this anyway, I thought, but I said nothing. I hadn't been kicked out of their good graces for being weak and puny, or for being a klutz with a jar of garlic powder so better not open my mouth now.

Finder and Tully showed me how to land on my side instead of my wrists, and how to roll out of a shove from behind instead of landing on my knees. At one point, Finder gave me a front shove so hard I fell straight back on my butt. "You'll break your tailbone if you land like that," she said. She demonstrated the correct way. "As you feel yourself going down, you tuck and turn." I got it in theory, but that one would take a lot of practice.

"You can come to class if you want," she offered.

And let people throw punches at me on purpose? Yikes, no thanks!

"Let me get some muscle built up at home first," I said. I was ready for a nice jacuzzi tub bath, a nap and bowl of something chocolate. Combat was not as fun as the movies made it look.

I spent my afternoon, post bath, doing research. I finished my homework in record time, partly by pulling an essay I had written for my English teacher at home and recycling it (is that wrong?) and partly because the JDS was ahead of St. Ignatius' curriculum, so this week's calculus was, for me, review.

I wanted to see what the rest of the world had to say about monsters being real. Finder and Tully had hinted that vampires were just one of the local varieties, and was the most appropriate choice for AGB and Bloody Girl.

I typed in the most obvious search terms and read the low hanging fruit about vampires, werewolves, ghosts and Richmond until dinner time. Articles popped up detailing Richmond's famous vampire legend about a railroad worker named W.W. Pool. He was said to roam the city in bloody rags but the story was debunked by scientists in the 1920s. I was surprised to find articles about regular humans who drink blood, both human and animal, and call themselves vampires. Could AGB and Bloody Girl be in this category? Neither of them had displayed obvious supernatural powers, so maybe?

According to the web, some people drink blood for pleasure and some for medical reasons. Some of the medical reasons looked sketchy to me, but if you feel sick and then you drink blood and you feel better, and you can do it without hurting anybody who am I to judge? I found one page that astonished me. The New Orleans Vampire Association page. New Orleans has an actual organization for people who call themselves vampires! No joke. Anyone who identifies as a vampire may join.

I found exactly zero articles supporting the existence of/ science behind supernatural vampires, though I did find some interesting math evidence against them. Using the conditions that anyone bitten by a vampire becomes a vampire and a vampire must feed once per night, it doesn't take long til humans are extinguished. Do the math. It's fun.

The whole lot of it struck me as nothing to be taken seriously. Blood drinking humans, while gross and unnerving, didn't seem to be a big enough threat to freak out Finder and Tully. And what about the Glen Bacon thing?

I typed in more terms.

Interesting! Bacon was the last name of the couple that built Maymont, the mansion/ park /petting zoo place Finder had made Tully drive by so slowly. Hmm. I couldn't find anything about a Glen Bacon, but the house was a big deal in Richmond. A Gilded Age mansion, (think Carnegie and Rockefeller if you like that stuff,) it had been built in 1886 to show off the wealth and privilege of General Bacon and his wife Sallie Mae. They had no children and when Mrs. Bacon passed away in 1925, she left the whole 100 acres, complete with two barns, two carriage houses, a stone mill, several fancy landscaped gardens and enough money to keep it up for quite some time to the City of Richmond. It was made a museum almost immediately. Did Glen Bacon have some connection to this family? My guess was yes, but I'd have to ask.

After dinner, I went back to my computer. The other internet rabbit holes I went down led me to websites for a couple books about hauntings by local authors which seemed more historical than sensational, nothing connected to the word unimaginable and lots of links to monster truck rallies.

I sat back and stretched. It had gotten late. This was the first time I had been alone since Finder and Tully told me their secret. I didn't feel like I was in any danger. The new casa Goldman was creepy by virtue of its size and it's lack of proximity to neighbors, but it didn't feel unsafe. Maybe the silly ritual had worked.

I went to my window and looked out across the expanse of moonlit grass to the river. Six acres was a huge amount of space to me. My eyes searched for human shapes, found nothing. The lawn was not unlike my bedroom, wide and empty but for a few anchors, the pool, pool house and the benches where Tully and I had sat the night before.

The indoor anchors were my four poster bed floating on navy blue carpet, a broad dresser and small shelf with a huge oatmeal colored bean bag chair for reading. Off to the side was a second room, once maybe a nursery? It held a desk, a spinny desk chair and two tall (why?!) book shelves stocked with brand new copies of my favorites. I ran my fingers along uncracked spines on the shelves I could reach. Alexandre Dumas and Stephen Hawking would not see any action all the way up there, I thought. The designer had included everything but the ladder. The books had that wonderful new paper bookstore smell, yet I longed for my second hand library at home. I reached for the phone to call Meredith out of habit, and remembered that I couldn't. Drat those brownies! I guess her parents hadn't thought about how much grounding Miss Accidental Pot Eater would punish poor me.

Back in the main bedroom, I snuggled under my covers. Here is what I knew for sure:

1. I had witnessed a crime.

2. My friends asked me to pretend to believe vampires existed.

3. I did not understand why I needed to meet that Goth boy so badly when I have never (never) approached someone of the opposite sex like that in my life.

I opened the bottled water on my nightstand, drank half of it, then tucked myself back in. Why had I done that? It seemed like such a good idea at the time. How dumb could I be? Ugh. I rolled over. And over. And over. A la The Princess and The Pea, I couldn't get comfy no matter how I tried. Images of humans drinking the blood of other humans intermingled with images from the alley the night before. What had I seen? If there was nothing to worry about, why couldn't I sleep?

Eventually I got up, risked life and limb by standing on the swirly chair to retrieve the Stephen Hawking and the Dumas. I read over an hour of each before I felt drowsy enough to lie back down. Toss and turn, toss and turn. Werewolves and ghosts, maybe, too? Ugh.

"Good morning, Madame, I trust you slept well?"

Jeeves.

I rolled over.

"Good morning, Madame. It is time to begin your day." One solid hour of sleep and my Jeeves alarm clock's recorded British voice wasn't anywhere near as funny as I had expected.

Monday, November 5, 2001.

St. Ig's is an unusual high school in that you get a full hour for lunch and even lowly sophomores are allowed to leave campus. There is a park across from St Ig's and at lunch time, students are encouraged to go for walks, or take some time out of the building. Coincidentally, several clergy of both sexes are present in the park daily, walking for exercise, but everyone knows it's to chaperone. The park was not our destination.

We launched out of our third period classes, piled into Tully's pick-up and drove the twenty minutes to the VCU neighborhood, scarfing down our lunches in the truck.

"We have fifteen minutes," Finder said. Conspicuous in our uniforms, not to mention cold, Finder and I had both slipped on pants in the truck and left our St Ig's polyester in our seats. The Virginia Commonwealth University campus was mostly modern buildings centralized around a massive medical center. That wasn't where we thought we'd find our quarry though. We walked the small streets by the dorms, circled the library, went in (they had to drag me out) and then walked a row of retail heaven, taking turns going inside places to search. This block offered a taco place that smelled like cumin and onions (no AGB or Bloody Girl) and a second hand bookstore attached to a coffee shop called Chapter & Mercy. Finder gripped my hand to keep me from going in.

"Nope," Tully said. "You stay here." The rich scent of roasted beans rolled off him in a glorious wave when he came out, even though he had only been in there for a second. A little sushi bar occupied the corner. I jumped up and down on the end of Finder's leash like grip.

"Bookstore coffee sushi!" I chanted. "You people have been holding out on me!"

"Calm down freak," she said. "Nobody eats that. It's disgusting!" I stopped cold.

"You don't eat sushi?"

"It's raw fish!"

"Oh. Oh, poor misinformed Finder. It's soooo much more than that. Have you never tried it?"

"No!" She let go of my hand.

I looked at Tully. "You?"

"Nothing with a face."

"Oh. My. God. You people have not lived. Sushi is divine! The food of the gods! I will show you."

The three of us made the rounds of the neighborhoods around Third Rock Pancake House and the university every day that week. Rabbi Berman's words echoed in my mind. Make a plan. Stick to the plan. Be ready to change the plan. We had made a plan and stuck to it, but our game was not developing. No sign of Bloody Girl or AGB.

Finder and Tully did not let me near Godzilla Sushi or Chapter & Mercy again. Hmm. It was time to change the plan.

10.

Saturday, November 10, 2001.

Maybe she wouldn't call.

I paced from the kitchen to the dining room to the living room. Bright winter sunshine saturated the gold pattern in Jill's Oriental carpets. I watched my feet move through the warm light. Finding a spot where the sun had made the carpet hot beneath my feet, I paused, stared out the window past the pool to the river. Restless, I crossed the room. I turned on the sofa lamp, plunked down on the velvety couch and picked up a book my dad was reading. The Comedy of Politics. I opened it. My watch read 12:41. She was supposed to call at 12:40.

Maybe there had been an incident or an emergency or something. I hoped against hope the phone wouldn't ring. Maybe she wouldn't be able to call.

My dad's cell phone yelped the William Tell Overture. It rippled through my body. Maybe I had jinxed my luck by hoping.

"Stacy," Dad called from the kitchen. He spoke into the phone. "Yes, I understand. I give legal consent for my minor daughter, Stacy Goldman to speak to Sharon Goldman for no longer than ten minutes. You will need to cut the call off. Is that clear?"

He handed me the cell phone. It weighed like a brick in my hand. I wished it would magically evaporate. The stove clock read 12:42. I set the timer on the microwave for ten minutes. 10:00. 9:59. 9:58.

"Hi Mom. Happy birthday."

"Hi baby! Oh Stacy, it is so good to hear your voice. Happy birthday to you too, last week." Her voice, a cross between sultry movie star and over enthusiastic bank teller sounded cheerful and as normal as she ever got.

9:36.

"Bubbe sent a card. She told me you moved. We watched the Towers go down on the news in the day room. They don't let us watch the news, but this was like the Superbowl. So big they thought we should all see it. I called your father at work to make sure you were okay. Did you know that? Did you know how scared I was for you? Did you know I called?"

"Yes, he told me."

"Good. Good. I was worried for you. Very worried."

I heard her biting her nails on the other end of the phone, a tiny scraping and occasional teeth clicking sound. 8:52.

"How's your college going?" I asked.

"Good! Good. I'll be an LPC when I get out, can you believe it? Me, a counsellor! I might only be allowed legally to work with other ex-prisoners, but I'm very excited about getting out and about being able to help people."

Jill popped her head around the corner. She mouthed "Everything okay?"

I nodded as I paced, listening, trying to think of something else to ask when this topic ended. Jill pointed to the front yard. They always took Steve outside when my mother called.

"It's good to have a purpose for your life, don't you think? A way to help other people, a way to contribute. That was always my problem with your father, that he never wanted me to have a purpose other than being all day with you." 8:12.

I steeled myself against what I knew was coming. Bubbe loves you, I told myself, Bubbe and Dad and Steve and Jill. Jill had taught me what to do: imagine I was deep in a safe and beautiful forest surrounded by nature and peace and love. Jill had grown up in Ohio, so she knew about forests and felt safe in them. I did not. I imagined I stood in the middle of Times Square and that everything that made noise or lit up loved me.

My mother paused. It sounded like she was swallowing.

"He was very sexist you know, forcing me to stay at home with a child I didn't even want."

Times Square. The lights love me. The noise loves me. The traffic loves me . . .

"Stacy? Are you still there?" She swallowed again.

"Have you watched anything good on TV?" I asked.

"Lost, I love that new show Lost. And I love 24. That's really good, too. Do you watch TV? Maybe we could watch the same show and then have a phone call to talk about it."

I checked the clock above the stove. 7:23 to go. My mom kept talking.

"Did I tell you I have a dog now?" she said.

"A *dog*?"

"Yes! His name is Gable, like Clark Gable, he's an actor, you know, before your time. We're part of a new canine therapy program. He lives with me 24/7 and goes everywhere I go. They're teaching us to train the dogs, they're all rescue dogs, so that while we're in, we can learn to train them to be assistance dogs, so seeing eye dogs and differently abled assistance dogs. It's an amazing program. The sad thing is that once the dog is trained it goes to live with someone who needs it and we lose them! Of course we get a new dog, but still. It's kind of a Catch 22 you know? We're supposed to train them but if we do, we lose them. It's really terrible. But I love Gable, he's sitting here with me right now in fact. I wish there was such a thing as a video phone call so you could see his sweet little Heinz 57 face."

I didn't mind the dog talk and with just a few questions she told me everything about him. It was interesting asking questions. I had no idea a program like that existed. And it made for an easy, safe conversation. Maybe this one would end ok. 4:27 left. I started to get hopeful.

"Are you allowed to teach him tricks?" I asked. "Or does it interfere with his work training?"

"My mother asked the same question just last week." Oh no. Why did I have to ask the same question as her mother? This would be it.

"She wanted me to to teach him to give me a paw and then take a picture for her. Are you still writing to my parents? They haven't mentioned getting a letter from you in a while."

"Yes, but I haven't written since we moved. Do you want me to tell you about Richmond? My school is called St. Ignatius and the funny thing is I have a hard time telling the nuns apart. So I can't really ever remember their names. I just kind of make up names for them." Maybe if I could talk for three minutes we could skip what was coming.

"Oh of course, of course. They'd really like to hear from you. But I understand why you don't write to them, why you don't call. Especially since you are so neglectful of taking care of other people. You were always a thoughtless child and you still are as a teenager."

I looked out the front window. Dad threw a ball with Steve. Jill was taking pictures. Short of breath, my armpits got damp.

"Do you remember that year all you made me was a card for Mother's Day? Just this stupid little construction paper card? You're a rotten person, rotten to the core, just like him."

I put the phone on the counter. 1:32 left. She was shouting now. I was sweating. I walked away from the phone, but I could still hear. I thought about Times Square.

"I wish I *had* killed him that day! I wish I had! The fact that he gets to live free with all his crimes against humanity from that courtroom and I have to be locked up is wrong! It's wrong, do you hear me? Are you there, Stacy Rachel? Are you? He's an alcoholic and an adulterer! He deserves jail! He should be here instead of me! Do you know that? Have I ever told you what happened that day? Have I? Because you caused it. You. You were the one who betrayed me first!"

And here it came. The annual rehashing of Disaster Number One. I knew to say nothing. I only endured this once a year, but it hurt fresh, like we'd just done it last week. I started saying my mantra in my mind.

I am alive, I am safe, nothing bad is happening.

Underneath my mantra, my mother's rant raised in temperature.

"I'm glad I don't have to raise you myself, you rotten little witch! I'd say worse but we aren't allowed to curse on phone calls. Witch, witch! Witch is as strong a word as I can use. My freedoms are totally constricted here, even down to language! Do you know what it feels like to have someone else threaten you just for the words you use? It's *your fault* I'm here. *Your* fault we got divorced! *Your* fault I missed his head, too! If you hadn't interfered I would have done it! I'd be free right now because he'd be dead and no one would have believed your word against mine. If you hadn't been so attached to him and not me, we would have been fine."

I heard a voice that wasn't hers interrupt. Click. No goodbye, just the end of her sentence dangling in the silence.

I hit the end button and let out the ragged breath I'd been holding. It was over.

I sat down at the table and put my head in my hands. I wished I could erase every memory I had of that night, but the more I tried to force them away, the stronger the images became in my mind. I don't know how long I sat there. Eventually I heard the front door open. I didn't move.

"These calls can't be easy for you," Jill said, putting her hand on my shoulder. "Do you want to tell me what she said?"

I did not. I did not want to ever say those words or hear them again. I wished for one cruel minute that something would happen to my mother, some prison accident or riot and she would get killed or put in a coma or something so I would never have to listen to her again. I pressed my lips together, shoving emotion away. Resentment, disappointment, sadness all swirled. Every time I did this, some twisted little part of me thought that maybe she had finally changed. Maybe she'd gotten better.

Jill gave me the shrink 'em pause. She sat down across from me, a sympathetic yet neutral expression on her face. She waited. I said nothing. She waited a little more. Then she spoke.

"The main characteristic of people with Borderline Personality Disorder is that they turn on people they love. She can't help it, but you don't have to hear it. It is beyond kind of you to speak to her even once a year, Stacy. You know you don't have to ever do this again. We can just tell the prison no."

"Bubbe thinks it helps her."

"Bubbe is wrong," Jill said, adamant. She unfolded her hands. "I'm sorry Stacy, I know Bubbe means the world to you, and she has the biggest, most generous heart. But in this, she is absolutely wrong. If she had any idea what your mother says to you in these calls, do you think she would ask you to bear it?"

No. But she didn't know.

"Don't tell her," I said. "It's not her problem."

"And it doesn't have to be yours. I know the only reason you do this is to please her."

"Bubbe believes people are inherently good. I'm not going to change that."

"No, of course not. My point is, you're worth defending, Stacy. Your heart is worth protecting. Don't be so cavalier about letting someone hurt you. Even someone you love."

11.

November 10, continued.

"Why do you have to go out so late?" Dad said.

"Why do you have to have dinner at the club after you play?"

"You used to be such a nice girl." He shook his head. "Where did I go wrong?"

Teasing? Serious? Both? After the lovely lunch chat this afternoon with my mom, I just didn't have it in me to play. I gave him the straight answer.

"You took me out of New York."

I sat on the floor of Steve's bathroom, dressed for a night on the town. I leaned against his vanity, reading while he played in the tub.

Jill came in with wet hair and a new outfit.

"You both should join the DAR, like I did," she said in a not unrealistic southern accent.

"You're amazing, Jill," I said. "Is that your fourth or fifth outfit today?"

She smiled. "Fourth." It sounded like FOH-wah-th. "Y'all would be so much happier if you stopped resisting our new circumstances," she drawled, showing off her first career as an actress. She kept talking. I looked at Dad.

"Make her stop."

"If she goes all Stepford, it's your fault," said Dad.

"What are you talking about?"

"I got another call from the fundraising mothers at your school today," Jill changed the subject, returning to her regular voice. She dragged a comb through her hair.

"Like the tuition isn't enough?" I said. "Jesus."

"Exactly." Jill got stuck on a tangle. "They are asking for money because the classrooms need new crucifixions."

"Crucifixes," I corrected. "Crucifix*ion* is the verb. Art depicting Jesus on the cross is the noun, cruci*fix*."

"Are the old ones in such bad shape?"

I shrugged. "How should I know? They're the size of dinner plates." The wooden Jesuses, or is that Jesi? hung in every classroom next to the clocks. I figured the point was to capitalize on student guilt at counting the minutes until class ended.

The doorbell rang. I launched down the hall.

"Home by ten," my father called after me. I skidded to a halt.

"I took the SAT this morning!" I argued. "I technically don't need to do that 'til next year! Look. Dad. I babysat your son -- "

"Your brother," my dad corrected.

"For *six hours* while you played golf and drank martinis at the club and I have to be home by *ten?*"

"I did not drink marti*nis*, I drank marti*ni*. And fine, eleven."

"Midnight."

"Eleven-thirty."

I sighed in exasperation.

"Call me if you're worried," I said, patting the pocket where my new cell phone bulged. I grabbed my sweater and scampered toward the door.

The atmosphere in the truck was quiet. Maybe we were all just tired from getting up at five-thirty to be at the test center by seven, or maybe just because. Tully put Rusted Root in the cd player and my mind drifted.

I thought about what my father would say if he found out I'd witnessed a crime and not told him. I wondered if Whirlene, our rosy cheeked, yellow sweatered new housekeeper, had noticed garlic powder lining the doors and windowsills when she came this morning to clean.

We drove by a cozy stone church lit from the inside. A red, purple and gold gothic stained glass window shed colored light over the front steps.

"Do you guys ever go into churches?"

Finder turned her Warrior Goddess gaze on me like I was the truly dumbest person on earth.

"Not for school. Or regular church," I clarified. "but just to think?"

She shook her head. "Nope."

"Can't say I have." Sometimes listening to Tully reminded me of a retro TV show.

The light from the little church fading behind the truck reminded me of the tall, gold patterned panels in the Temple where my grandfather was rabbi. Beth Israel Temple on West 83rd smelled like flowers and the waxy lemon cleaner Bubbe had taught me to polish the pew benches with. The first time I went into St. Peter's Church downtown, I felt right at home because of that smell. Turns out they used the same cleaner.

"St Peter's Church is this cathedral in my old neighborhood," I said. "I used to sneak in on my way somewhere else and just sit in the quiet by the candles. And the most amazing thing was that nobody ever bothered me or interrupted me even though I was a kid alone."

"That *is* amazing," Tully said.

"You can be on a kneeler with your hands folded and eyes closed at St Ig's," Finder said. "The clergy will still be like hey are you late for class?"

"Rude," I said. "That's the one place besides the bathroom where people should get left alone. Do you guys do confession at school?"

"My mother would crap kittens if I didn't," Tully said.

"Mine would crap kittens if I did," Finder said. "Baptists don't do confession." And then in a loud, arm waving imitation of a gospel minister, she proclaimed, "In the true faith of our lord and savior Jesus Christ confession is between you and Gawd himself."

"Do you believe in God?" I asked. The cd ended and a moment of quiet settled over us.

Finder looked over her shoulder at me, her gaze bright and interested. "No. Why do you ask?"

"You don't?" I said, surprised.

She shrugged and smiled. "I don't."

"How about you, Tully? Do you believe in God?"

The Southern Scotsman sighed, a long, thoughtful sigh.

"Depends on what you mean by god." He clicked the blinker and we changed lanes to come off the highway. "Old man in the sky, no. Nature mojo, force like Star Wars Force that holds the energy of the world as one great, unified, divine intelligence thing . . . kinda, yes."

"I thought you were a seriously catholic Catholic, Tully!"

"Surprise," he said in that mellow voice.

"There's no way you can explain everything," Finder said. "But that's what church does. It tries to explain everything under one banner that doesn't always work."

"Is that why you believe in, why you can deal with . . .?"

"Unimaginables? Yes. Not because of church. Because they exist."

My next question was dangerous, I knew, but I decided to go for it. "I did some more research this week and I still can't find any scientific -- "

"It's. Not. Scientific." Finder's voice took on that closed quality, meaning if I kept going I risked her ignoring me. I decided to shut up and concentrate on having fun.

Walking the half block from parking to the club, I tingled with excitement and nerves. I labeled the grungy cafe next door a haven to run to if things went horribly wrong. Were my cargo pants and combat boots appropriate attire? Would guys look at me? Would I be able to hear Finder and Tully talking over the loud music?

Arriving at The Station, delight trickled down my spine. I had never been in a bona fide nighttime dance club, a fact I neglected to mention to Finder and Tully before we came.

We waited outside in a line of mostly girls wearing outfits I can only describe as small, smaller, smallest. Braver souls than I! Under my mail-me-down Elsinore Fencing Club tee shirt (Meredith is a total Shakespeare nerd) I had on a black tank top in case I got hot. I also wore my spiked wrist cuff and Meredith's favorite velvet jacket (not warm enough! When would I learn?) I'd pulled my hair back in a ponytail at home, but now took it out to keep some heat around my neck.

Finder? Well. I'm not sure if it's appropriate for one girl to describe another as hot, but with long legs dipping out of a fuchsia mini and landing in black combats lacing to her knees, Finder scorched. Her tight black sweater made her look somehow more tiny waisted and stacked than she already was, which was a lot. Mother Nature smiled upon Finder. Next to her, I stood scrawny and dull, but we were apples and oranges. What can you do?

Our Southern Scotsman sported a bona fide wool kilt. I'd never been out with a man in a skirt. I don't know why (again) I worried about people looking at me. Between him and Finder, I was invisible. Tully also wore a tee shirt: 'Hate you, hate Kansas, taking the dog. Dorothy', and red Chuck Taylor high tops. After all, what did he care what girls thought? He was there with Finder.

When we finally got into the alcove entryway, I shivered so hard my teeth chattered. I pushed my eight bucks through a hole in the glass to a tired looking, multiple pierced girl in a VCU shirt cut way down and way up. I think I'll be happy when fashion no longer dictates showing one's abdomen.

"I.D.?" she said.

I froze. I didn't have i.d.

"I don't have a driver's license," I said. No one told me I'd have to show i.d.! I began to panic. I felt people behind me in line staring.

"How about your school i.d.?"

"I just moved here, I don't have it yet." My heart thumped in my chest. She rolled her eyes.

"How *old* are you?"

"Fifteen."

"Yeah, right." She pushed my cash back under the window.

"I'm fifteen! I'm in tenth grade!" I put my hand on my money to keep it from blowing away. "I'll prove it! Ask me a calculus question!"

Finder popped her head over my shoulder.

"What's happening?"

I explained.

"Is Bolo here?" Finder asked Tired Girl.

Behind the sweaty glass, she picked up a phone, motioning for us to step away from the line. She nodded yes to Finder as the girls behind us paid. Glaring at me, they shoved past us into the pulsing, loud club.

After a few minutes of mortal humiliation as each person going past took a good solid look at me, Denied Girl, an enormous Black guy ducked and pushed through the curtain. My eyes got wide. This dude made Tully look small.

"Hey baby!" He grabbed Finder up in a bear hug and lifted her off her feet. "This your boyfrien'?" he asked, setting her down and sticking out a huge hand to Tully. "You a lucky cat, man. Every guy at our dojo wants a piece of her action."

"Except I can kick all of their asses," Finder said with a smile. Finder flirting? I stared. Oh my god. I looked at Tully. He looked pale and maybe nauseated, staring out at the line of incoming people imagining, perhaps, that he was on another planet where martial artists twice his size did not hit on his girlfriend.

"Stacy's from New York," Finder said by way of introduction.

"Oh yeah? I been to New York. My cousin live there."

"That's great," I said, squeezing to the wall as another couple shoved by into the club.

"Yeah! Where you live?"

"Battery Park City," I said. "Used to, at least."

"Whaaaaaat? You there when the Towers went down?"

I nodded. Small things falling. I didn't want to think about it.

Finder explained how I was new at St. Ig's and had no i.d. but I was a sophomore and in fact fifteen la la la.

"What's your Chinese Horoscope?" asked Bolo.

I felt small and, I'm ashamed to admit, scared being scrutinized by him.

"Your Chinese astrology animal. Pig, Dragon, Monkey?"

"I have no idea."

"Bes' question," he said to Finder. "People know or they don't, but when they know, I know if they tell me the right age."

"I was born in nineteen eighty-six," I interjected. Like at school, I felt compelled to answer.

"You a Tiger then."

"Okay." Rahr.

"When you coming back to practice?" Finder asked, sliding into a southern dialect that matched his. I had never heard her sound like that.

He slipped a tree trunk of an arm around her shoulders, walking us through the velvet outside, plastic inside curtain.

"Soon as we hire a new manager here. Don't worry baby, I'll be back." A warm breeze blew across my face as I crossed through the curtain. I suspected my tank top was about to get some air time.

"Have fun, y'all," he said gesturing for the bouncer to stamp our hands. "And congrats again on the win!" he said looking over his shoulder to Finder.

"Thanks!" she smiled, looking genuinely happy.

"Win?" I said, as the bouncer impressed a skull and crossbones onto the back of my hand.

"She won a huge tournament last month before you got here," Tully said. "State champion in her age group."

"I only fought other girls," Finder said as if that made it less.

"That's amazing! Congratulations."

She led the way into a room so loud it bounced.

"I didn't pay!" I shouted. "Should I go pay?"

"Forget it! Bolo walked you in," she shouted back. Not paying made me uncomfortable, like I had stolen something. However, I was relieved to not repeat my face off with Rude and Obnoxious Tired Girl. If I saw Bolo again, I would make sure to hand him the money.

The Station was exactly that, a converted train station where, I soon found out, the different rooms were divided by actual old tracks. I took a deep breath and stretched my arms in the open space, immediately comfortable under the super high ceilings and balconies that ran the perimeter of each room. Surrendering to the extreme decibel level, I followed Finder to the bar to get started on our free soda till midnight. I sipped. Watery, kind of sucky soda, but what the heck? It was free. Tully had to pay for his water.

After dumping our cups we followed Finder into a dark room filled with fog machine mist and music familiar in a Meredith sort of way, Sisters of Mercy, maybe? Nine Inch Nails? My bones vibrated, the music pulsed so loud.

I threw myself into the dance. Finder did this gothy twisty dance, moving her hips in ways I had only seen on TV. Tully danced a bashy version of the white boy shuffle, clumsy and a weensy bit off the beat. As the music changed, so did his dance and I realized that he was just as graceful as his girlfriend with every bit as concise a sense of rhythm. I have no idea what I looked like dancing, but I didn't care. A boy with long brown hair danced near me and smiled under his flailing. I smiled back, surprised he noticed me. I'm generally too small to notice in a big crowd unless you step on me.

I glanced toward the bathrooms and stopped dancing. Chills shivered from my face to my toes. Heading away from the bathrooms in white clothes and go-go boots gleamed a figure I had almost convinced myself I'd imagined. Bloody Girl!

12.

November 10, continued.

Grab her! I thought. Are you nuts? Run away! I thought a second later. I caught Finder's eye and pointed, reaching for her with my other arm. I found Finder's elbow, stopping her mid gyration. Tully, head thrown back to look at the light show on the ceiling crashed into my back. I fell forward onto my knees and in a second the Southern Scotsman scooped me under the armpits and lifted me off the ground, like flying. He stood me back on my feet.

"Sorry!"

"It's *her*! The *Girl!* The GIRL!" I caught a lung full of breath, pointing and shouting over the music.

Bloody Girl disappeared in a cloud of pale clothes and hair through an arched doorway. The arch filled in with dancers as soon as she went through. Losing sight of Bloody Girl, I snatched Finder's hand, pushing and shoving our way toward the throng. The beat, heavy and loud, carried us along on the bouncy wood. Frantic we'd lose her, I let go of Finder.

Turning sideways, I ducked through and in between the group clogging the archway. At last, an advantage to being small! The archway led into a wider room hung with disco balls. Video played across the ceiling. Air blew cooler across my face, chest and shoulders. A whiny singer on a narrow stage at the far end of the room covered some song I knew from the sixth grade skating rink craze.

I caught sight of Bloody Girl dancing with a group of other weird, overdressed girls. She stood out, taller than the others, wearing a lacy white tank top, satin gloves past her elbows and a tutu like mini skirt that sparkled with glitter. She'd smeared glitter on her arms, face and in her blonde hair. She wore the go-go boots I remembered over white fishnet tights. I craned my neck to see if her neck looked okay, but I faced the non-bitten side. Drat.

"Not 'missing'," Finder shouted, looking hopeful, as we shoved/danced closer to Bloody Girl.

Tully grabbed my other hand. "Be careful, Stacy. She might be . . ." Tully gave me a meaningful look.

"She's a *girl*, Tully!" I shouted. "Be right back!" He grabbed the back of my shirt.

"Not again!" he shouted. "Us, too!" I shook my head.

"She'll think we're stalkers!" I shouted back. I pointed to the ground, meaning 'stay here'.

I danced over to her group and waited for Bloody Girl to catch my eye. My heart pounded in my chest. My hands shook with nerves. I had played this moment so many times in my head. What I would do or say if I found her, when I found her.

"Hi!" I shouted over the music. She glanced at me. She looked away.

"Hi!" I repeated. She looked again. Her gaze lingered this time, turning into a flash of recognition. She leaned over and said something into the ear of one of her friends. Bloody Girl stopped dancing.

"I'm Stacy!" I shouted. "I just wanted to see if -- " Bloody Girl interrupted me.

"Grab!" she shouted. I thought I misheard her.

"What?"

"Grab! Grab!" she said, louder the second time. She grabbed my wrist with a cool hand. "I'm telling you I'm grabbing you!" she shouted. She looked at me like I was an idiot. I let her pull me toward the door.

We emerged into the club's backyard, a paved train yard filled with smokers and people who needed either air or a break from the noise. Out here, the music seemed distant. My ears rang with the quiet.

"What do you want?" she said, letting go of me.

"To see if you were okay," I said. "I came back and you were gone. "

"You didn't think Nicolai would just leave me there did you?" Pale blue lips pulled back in a satisfied smile. Unlike me, she hadn't even broken a sweat inside dancing.

"I didn't think he'd be back after attacking you," I said. I looked for a bandage on her neck or a bruise or some indication that the week before she'd been savagely bitten. Both sides were clear and uninjured. I examined her mouth. Fangs, no fangs? I couldn't tell. Lipstick, I was sure, pale blue lipstick.

Finder and Tully burst out of the club. Finder looked panicked, but her face relaxed when our eyes met. Bloody Girl looked over her shoulder to see what had distracted me. She paused, checking out the kilt wearer and his accompanying bombshell. Undisturbed, she pivoted back to me.

My eye level fell right at her chest. Like me, she was small breasted. Unlike me, she did not wear tee shirts over her see through shirts. I blushed. My legs trembled and I made a concentrated effort to look only at her face.

"I'm glad you're okay. I was worried about you after what happened and when I couldn't find you. But you seem fine." Time to go.

"Never better," she said a smile turning up one corner of her mouth. She reached out one long, gloved finger and touched the top of my cheekbone near my eye. She ran her finger in a silky line down to the corner of my mouth. I took a step back, giving her universal body language for 'gotta go'. She closed the space between us. The back of my knees bonked up against a bench, but I didn't want to sit. She leaned down so her lips were near my ear. I didn't breathe for a second, the threat of neck biting foremost in my mind. I banked on her not being that bold in public. I held my ground.

"I wanted him to take me," she whispered in my ear.

O-kay. Thanks. Too much information.

She trailed fingers along my neck.

"Sharing vitae with Nicolai brought me into a whole new world," she said. She pulled back just a few inches from my face and smiled again. This time she let her lips part and ran her tongue over sharp, pearly fangs.

"Life or blood?" My voice came out kind of squeaky. I didn't want to wet my pants. But I had to know.

"What?"

"Latin. Vitae means 'life's course' in Latin, so it could mean life or blood. Did you and Nicolai share life or blood?"

"Both. It's the only way," she said. "You know."

I broke out in a new sweat. She slid her gloved hand behind my neck, cradling my head behind my ear. Her eyes lingered on my mouth. I thought for a minute she was going to kiss me. I have never been kissed on the mouth by anyone, not even as a middle school prank and I did not want it to be her or now! My heart thudded against my ribs.

"You must be new. Don't worry," she said. "Aegisthus will make everything clear in time. Unless you're Glen Bacon's." She snatched her hand away and backed up a step. "Wait. Are you Glen Bacon's?"

"I don't know what you're talking about, but I do have one question."

"You don't know Aegisthus or Glen Bacon? That doesn't make sense. You defended me in the alley."

"I defended you because you were being hurt. People need to look out for one another. Just tell me one thing," I braced myself for the Big Question. Could I even ask it? I hesitated. Bloody Girl looked me up and down, taking in my ponytail, tank top, black cargo pants and combat boots.

"*People* need to look out for one another?" She parroted back, like she'd misheard me. Something sunk in because her eyes went round as Atlantic City poker chips. "Forget!" she said looking at me hard. "Forget!"

"What?"

"I want you to Forget we had this conversation! Do you need proof?" Expression urgent.

"Yes, I want proof! And I'm definitely not going to forget this!"

She suddenly dug in the tiny purse she wore at her belt. She cursed under her breath and emptied the tiny purse into her hand. She wasn't finding whatever she was looking for.

"Are you immune?"

"Immune?"

She stopped moving for a minute. Something clicked behind her eyes. She went from confident to terrified. Still looking at me.

"You must be a -- " She gasped, turned and fled back into the club. I lunged to grab her arm, but missed. Finder and Tully raced over to me.

"Wait!" I shouted trying to push my way through my friends to chase her. "I need to know if you're a real -- "

Finder clapped her hand over my mouth, wrapping the other arm around my waist.

"Leave it alone, Stacy!" Tully said anchoring my arm. I pulled against a tree trunk. Unmoving, Finder. Tully scrutinized my face. "Did she do anything to you?"

"What? No! Other than put her weird fingers on my cheek. What did she think I was? I must be a what?"

"A vampire hunter." Tully said as he drove. Angry they held me back from chasing Bloody Girl, I replayed the scene six times for them before they were satisfied they knew everything.

"Come on you guys. For real?"

"Stop saying that!" Finder glared at me over the headrest. "I know you're smart and from New York City, but you don't know everything, and it's annoying when you pretend you do."

Ow. That hurt. I did not say anything for a while. I sat in disbelief, taken aback. Is that how I came across? My feelings stung. Time to change the subject. We had searched the club three times, waiting about twenty minutes between each search to see if Bloody Girl would resurface, but she never did.

"There is no logical proof anywhere in the world," I said, "that supernatural vampires exist. I wanted her to tell me."

"I want to know about her use of vitae," Tully said. "Blood or life."

"She meant blood," Finder said.

"She meant both," I said. "Why would she think I hunt vampires? Are there for real people who do that?"

Finder smacked herself in the forehead, face palm.

"Just leave her by the side of the road, Tul. Nothing more we can do here."

"Remember what it took to convince you?" Tully reminded Finder. "It was no easy job." Sitting straight in her seat, Finder seethed with frustration.

"What more proof do you want, Stacy? Were you not scared at all?"

"Yes, but I don't have any actual evidence other than seeing her fangs which could be fakes! Is it wrong to want inarguable proof? Maybe she could turn into a bat, or erase my memory or just say yes I am a vampire and see here? My heart isn't beating. Proof which she was about to give me!" Before she figured out whatever she thought I was and bolted, I thought.

Back at my house, Tully and I demolished an entire half gallon of Breyer's vanilla ice cream while Finder worked off her desire to squash me in the home gym. Watching her alternate between lifting weights and rounds on the stationary bike, I visualized our next move.

"We need to know who Aegisthus is," I said, "and who Nicolai is to him and Glen Bacon."

"No we do not," Finder said. "We found your girl, she's full vertical. That is what we wanted to find out and now we know. It's over. We're done."

"I want to know for sure. I want one of them to tell me what they are and how they got that way."

Finder stared at me as if I had just suggested she eat sushi.

"What was she looking for in her itty bitty purse I wonder," Tully said, scraping the bottom of the container. "A vampire i.d. card?"

"I hate you, stupid Teularen." Finder said changing to do lifts with the kettlebells. "You're supposed to be on my side."

"I am on your side. I'm also fascinated by what people carry in little purses. It's a sporran thing."

"Sporran?"

"Scottish man purse," replied Finder.

Tully pointed to the hand sized leather pouch he wore on a loose belt. The belt hung over his hips in a way that made the purse/ sporran fall right over his- ah. His . . . I looked away, embarrassed.

"Look," I said. "I have lots of friends in New York, friends I've had basically my whole life. I only have two friends here. They both believe in something that I have no experience with." I chewed the side of my lip, reaching for how to explain.

"Unimaginables for me, are like sushi is for you. You can not conceive of sushi being delicious, because you have never eaten sushi. You only know what you know, which is that sushi is raw fish, and all the information you have about raw fish leads you to believe that sushi is basically belly poison.

"I have no experience with vampires or any supernatural creatures. What I know of them is that they are fictional. But I don't know what I don't know, right? You know some of what I don't know about the supernatural and so you know they are real. I do not yet believe you because I have never met a real vampire that I can prove is a vampire. You do not believe that sushi is delicious even though I assure you that it is, because you have not ever eaten a piece of sushi and therefore have no proof for yourself.

"Do you get it? I'm not trying to annoy you, or disbelieve you or whatever, I just need to eat a piece of sushi!"

Tully raised his eyebrows. "Makes sense."

Finder. "You are certain that sushi is delicious, right?"

"Yes."

"And I should take your word for it, because you have experience with sushi that I do not?"

"Exactly!"

She raised her eyebrows back at me.

I winced. It was so hard to make the leap.

"Vampires are real," I said, testing the waters. What did it feel like to believe in the unreal?

"If she and Nicolai are even vampires," said Tully.

Finder nodded. "Right. They could be something else."

"Werewolves," Tully put in before I could ask. It was my turn to face palm.

13.

Sunday, November, 11, 2001.

"I can't believe I lied to my father so we could do this," I said. I jammed my last safety pin through the garlic loaded envelope and the stiff kitchen curtain up where the rings traveled the rod. Achey and sore from reaching up so high over my head so many times, I was happy to climb down off the counter and call this project done.

"Better than finding him dead," Finder said, emptying her leftover envelopes into their little box.

"Or having to do the no shaker top garlic powder dance every time somebody vacuums." Tully opened up a baggie of carrot sticks and popped one into his mouth.

"It feels like fake-o-rama hocus pocus," I said.

"Sushi is definitely disgusting," Finder replied. I sighed and pulled a container of dip out of the fridge.

Dad and Jill had taken Steve to the club with them today since I'd made all kinds of crazy excuses about why I couldn't watch him. Having resorted to threatening words like calculus, chemistry and midterms, I eventually persuaded them that a six-year-old and a golf course could be compatible for one measly afternoon. I felt guilty for lying, but if I'd been telling the truth I never would've gotten Steve out, too. Words like vampires, garlic and victims didn't pack the same punch in my family.

"You should eat more vegetables." Finder pushed the last of the carrots toward me. "Lack of nutrition has stunted your growth." I futzed with the box of blessed garlic packets Finder had brought, stacking them up in columns.

"Ha ha," I said. "My maternal grandfather was 5'3." I looked up at my friends, both handing me blank stares. "Height comes from your mother's father," I said. "I didn't have a chance.." Inside the box, my garlic packet stack tipped and spilled. "Should any of these thingies go outside the house?"

We got up and headed for my front door, each swiping up a handful of packets.

Tully said, "This house is awesome. Having shared a room with two of my sisters for the last seven years, I love that it's so big." I opened the front door. The bright, cold sunshine made me squint.

"Two?" I exclaimed. "How many of you are there?"

"Six. I'm the oldest. I have three younger sisters and twin brothers a year younger than Steve."

"And how many bedrooms?"

"You do that side and I'll do over here," Finder said. "Use your intention!" She went left to bury packets in the dirt behind the boxwoods guarding the porch.

"Four bedrooms," Tully said as we went to the other side of the house. "I'll do the garage," he said, then finished his thought. "One for my parents, two split between us kids, and one for my grandma Addie who lives with us."

I thought of Bubbe, fierce and independent, refusing to live with us even though she now had no more family in the City. Until I go back for college. I shimmied through the shrubbery at the corner of the house and poked a dip in the dirt with my shoe. I held the little garlic bit in my hand and said the incantation only loud enough for me to hear.

"By the power of three by three, this house is made safe by me. To cause no harm nor return on me, as I will so mote it be."

Warmth swirled through me as the faces of Steve, Jill and Dad arrived in front of my eyes. A strong desire to protect them washed over me. A burst of love filled my chest and lungs with breath. In my mind's eye, light flowed from the sky into the top of my head. The sweet glow poured down through my torso and flowed from the ground up into my feet and legs. Energy from top and bottom met in the middle, spreading through my limbs. Lit from the inside like a road map of energy lines, love and protection traveled through me into the little packet.

I crouched and planted the warm envelope, a nickel sized lantern of love and protection. Standing, I wobbled backward and caught myself on the boxwood shrub, dizzy all of the sudden. Once I had my balance, I scooted behind the bushes under the next window, and poked another hole in the dirt.

This time, warmth and light surged through me so strongly my fingers tingled as I spoke the incantation. I buried the packet and went to my last stop along this side of the house, the narrow stained glass window by the front door. Finder stood a few feet away on the other side of the stoop. She used a piece of mulch bark to poke her holes in the dirt. I did my last packet. Again, the powerful surge of love and energy lit me from within. Dizzy again, I reached out and caught myself on the house. I knelt in the dirt. As I chanted, my ears rang.

Then, I wasn't alone. A tall, golden figure knelt both beside me and within me at the same time. Strong and iridescent, energy flowed around me like wings. A dream, I thought. Brought on by the incantation. I knew it was my imagination but it felt so real. I closed my eyes, deep and safe in the reassuring embrace, pretending for a moment that the golden being existed, that I was not alone. Clear as my own speech, a voice like pure adoration and simplicity said *I am with you.*

You are real? I imagined myself asking.

Y*es.*

Together, we buried the packet, full of love and protection. I sat back on my heels, hands cradled in my lap. Savoring. The feeling faded.

When I opened my eyes, Tully crouched on the stoop a few feet away scrutinizing me.

I just stayed there, unmoving, breath coming soft as I waited for the top of my head to stop buzzing. I just looked at him.

"Something shifted," he said. "I was finishing the far door in the garage and the crown of my head started vibrating. Like when I meditate and all my chakras open up, but it wasn't me doing it."

"I didn't feel anything," Finder said. "Wasn't me."

"I think it was me," I said.

"It was definitely somebody," Tully said. "Are you okay?" His clear blue gaze held mine.

My head still buzzed. I felt loose in my body, like my mind wasn't quite anchored. Tully sat down cross legged in the dirt in front of me. Finder stood over us, watching from the stoop. Tully faced me. "You need to ground," he said. "Put your right hand over your heart and your left hand on the top of your head."

The hand on my heart felt suffocating. The top of my head hurt in an instant mega-headache sort of way. I winced.

"Sorry, too much. Pull your hand away and leave it in front of your heart until it's comfortable to come closer. Lift the left hand. Feel the heat?"

My head stopped hurting when I lifted my hand. I could breathe fine as soon as I moved the hand from my heart. I felt heat under my hands like they were in front of an oven.

"This is weird."

"If you shut the chakras down too fast it feels like headache."

"What's a chakra?" He pronounced it shock-ruh. Emphasis on the shock.

"Later. I'll explain later. Let me do it for you this time. Do I have your permission?"

I had no idea what I gave permission for, but I agreed.

"Close your eyes."

I did. A weight came on top of my head, heavy and hot. I almost opened my eyes to see if he was going to drop a brick on me, but I heard that voice again.

Listen. Learn what he is doing. Pay attention.

I waited, listening, for what I didn't know, until the pressure lifted. The buzzing eased to a tingle. The sensation relaxed until just a tiny spot at the back top of my skull vibrated. I felt surrounded by a calm, loving presence, peaceful and balanced. It was Tully.

"Put both hands over your heart," he instructed. "Breathe into your hands. Good. Just like that. Press down a little on the exhale."

And just like that, like a tap almost, my head quit buzzing and my eyes popped open.

Tully held his hand floating over my head. He opened his eyes. Clear, blue, strong, powerful. Honest. His hair had escaped his pony tail in wisps and even though he was still him, sitting in front of me, he looked somehow different, like the man he would grow into had shown up and revealed himself.

"Feel better?" he said, smiling. I nodded. "Good." He touched Finder's leg. "Why don't you guys go inside so Stacy can have some water and maybe eat something? I'll do the back door."

Finder retreated with me to the kitchen. Sitting down, I told her where the stuff was for hot chocolate and she started the milk on the stove.

"What was that?" I said.

"Tully's the mojo master," she said. "I just track the nasties and kick ass."

"Do other people know about unimaginables, or just you?"

"A few people we know of know. Bolo, the guy you met at the Station, he knows. My cousin Christopher knows. Tully, me, now you."

"If the girl thought I was a hunter, more people must know. People who hunt them that we haven't met?"

Finder shrugged and put one foot against her knee like a stork. Leaning one hip on the stove, she stirred the milk.

"I don't ask questions I don't care about the answers to," she said. "I'm not known for playing well with others."

"You play well with me," I said.

"You don't have the small mentality of most of the people at St Ig's. Or even my dojo." She stirred, didn't look at me. "Doesn't feel like you're always aware you're hanging out with the Black girl. You're just hanging out with me. Sometimes when I'm with white people, or even the Asian kids at my dojo, it's like they can't see past the color of my skin. But other Black people think I act white. It's confusing."

Still feeling floaty, I imagined I saw Finder, too, like I had seen Tully. A vulnerable girl wanting acceptance. Craving permission to be who she was without pain, without needing to win, or prove anything, or be judged.

"I think we're kind of the same person," I said.
She raised a curious eyebrow.

"We're smart. We hate taking crap from people, we typically think we're right, we both have something to prove and we both have a parent we never talk about. My theory is we both have secrets we haven't told each other. You were forced to spill one of yours early because I went all crime stopper, but if it hadn't been for that, you would never in a million years have told me."

She slid a mug in front of me.

"Drink your cocoa," she said. "You're creeping me out." I smiled.

"So if a vampire's Jewish," I said, "does a rabbi have to bless the garlic for it to repel him?"

"Employ as much protective energy as possible," Finder said, sliding into the booth across from me. "Source doesn't matter."

"Maybe we should put a garlic in the mezuzah!" I laughed. Sometimes, I was funny. At least Meredith thought so. A footstep startled me. Tully padded in from the rear of the kitchen holding his shoes. "That freaks me out," I said. "You came in and I didn't hear you?"

"I locked the door behind me," he said, cheery. "What's a mezuzah?"

I knew something esoteric they did not? Ha.

I led them back to the front door and showed them our narrow brass mezuzah, a traditional Jewish blessing and protection rod you hang at an angle on the outdoor, right side edge of your doorway. Neither of them had ever seen one.

Finder reached up and gave it a tug.

"Don't do that!"

She looked at me.

"There's a scroll in it," I said. "A prayer. I was joking. You can't really stuff it with garlic."

"Why not?"

"It's blessed. You don't mess with it," I said, feeling oddly panicky.

"We scour your entire house with garlic and you're worried about hiding a teeny bit inside this stick?"

"It's not a stick!" I said. She brushed past me into the house.

Finder came back a moment later with her backpack. She dug in the front pocket and came up with a multi-tool.

"It's a holy object," Tully said. "Leave it alone, Finder. Tuck a garlic behind it."

"After the rabbi blesses it you don't handle it unless you have to. I don't know if it works once the thingy's been opened."

"I'll bet it's fine."

"I think leave it, Finder," Tully said.

Ignoring us, she started unscrewing the tiny object. A wash of anger rose in me. I stepped in front of the doorway knocking her hand away.

"Stop! You don't know what you're doing."

Finder raised her eyebrows. "Do you want vampires to get in your house and eat your family?" she said.

"I want you to leave the mezuzah alone. We can tuck a garlic behind it."

Her mouth tightened. I didn't even know why it felt so important that she not touch the mezuzah. I opened my hand for the multi-tool. Sighing in annoyance, she dropped it into my palm. I took the little packet from her, folded it in thirds around the tiny sliver of garlic pressed inside and tucked the whole thing behind the mezuzah.

"By the power of three by three, this house is made safe by me. To cause no harm nor return on me, as I will, so mote it be."

I looked at the multi-tool. I had used a screwdriver in science class once or twice. I resisted my urge to hand the foreign little object to Tully (sexist) or Finder (admission of inferiority) and took a deep breath. After a couple awkward jabs to get the business end of the tool to match up with the little X in the top of the screw, I tightened the mezuzah back to the doorframe.

"Are we done now?" I said, handing her back her tool.

"I hope you won't be this wimpy when it comes down to it, SG," Finder said. I looked at Tully for support. He looked away, took a step backwards off the stoop. Okay.

"Down to what?" I asked, defensive.

"Down to doing what needs doing."

My hackles rose.

"And what exactly is that?"

"Stopping it. Or them."

How did this happen? I thought. I made a joke about a mezuzah and here we were, arguing on my doorstep about legendary creatures I did not even believe existed? I wanted to say, could we stop now and blow this all back into proportion, but part of me wouldn't let go. She'd offended me on my turf and, whatever we were fighting about, I wanted to win.

"Stop it like stake it?"

She looked me dead in the eye. "Whatever it takes."

I imagined slamming a stake through AGB's heart. Even though he'd been all creepy and attacked Bloody Girl, his presence had given me a momentary sense of hope, like all was not lost in this southern industry town. I would not be doing any stopping of him if it meant killing. Even if he was technically already dead. Finder shot me a severe look.

"I'm not killing anyone," I said. The sound of a car caught our attention.

We dashed back inside and scrambled to spread out our calculus books in the kitchen. Finder still glaring at me, we made it just in time. Tully even had the wits to rip open a bag of chips and, holding his pen with his other hand, stuff his face as my family entered. Finder and my 'discussion' was over, at least for now.

14.

Tuesday, November 13, 2001.

There are good days, there are bad days.

Then, there is *that* day. The day where, on top of all the other things that go wrong, you forget that your body has an agenda. Ahem. And that agenda starts in PE class when you are out of whatever you use and discover yourself completely unprepared.

I looked at the clock hanging next to the dinner plate crucifix. Fifteen minutes left. Could I make it through class or was disaster imminent? I spent the next several seconds attempting to diagnose the severity of my circumstances. Fearing the worst, I stood entirely still, completely paralyzed with anxiety that I was going to bleed through my shorts.

Sister Mary Gymnasium alternated between blowing her whistle and shouting orders to the kids who could actually play. The chance of her noticing me even if I did go to her, was not good. I certainly wasn't going to ask her for supplies! The volleyball headed straight for me. It did not even occur to me to stick my arm out to thwack it. I just went on instinct and ducked.

The other team cheered. My team groaned. So much for not drawing attention to myself.

The Albino Atheist Chick's gym locker was next to mine.

"Excuse me," I said, desperate to get my uniform skirt in my hands before I went to the bathroom. She moved out of my way, but didn't speak.

"Thanks." I grabbed my skirt and bolted. Finder had told me about the Albino Atheist Chick when she gave me the run down of the school oddballs, herself and Tully included. According to Finder, this girl was so shy she barely even spoke to the Sisters.

I took care of my disaster as best I could. Arriving back at the lockers, AAC stood with her arms wrapped around herself, waiting for me.

"Hi," she said, barely above a whisper. "I'm," she took a big inhale, "Judy." She was taller than me, (not hard) and holocaustically thin. Her white blonde hair offset grey eyes more like an animal's than a girl's.

"I'm Stacy," I said, astonished she spoke to me.

"I know." Creepy much?

I said, "Nice to meet you," then rushed to stuff my no longer wearable shorts into a separate pocket in my backpack. We had some wiggle room to change, but we had to hustle to make it to second period on time. I had Calculus.

"Welcome to St. Ignatius'," she said in a whisper. "If you," she paused for a breath looking at the floor, "need anything and Layla or Teularen can't help you, you can ask me."

The wad of toilet paper in my underwear reminded me that I did need something. And I needed it now.

"I don't suppose you have any *supplies,* in your locker, do you?"

She looked at my anxious face, confused for a sec, then she got it.

"Oh, Sorry no. I don't get my period yet. There's a box of stuff over here though." Other girls pushed past us to get to the hall as (oh my god, I'd forgotten her name) led me to the custodial closet. "The lacrosse team keeps a stash." She jimmied the closet handle and I heard a snap and click, like she'd wrenched it open, but she'd turned it normally. She reached onto a shelf and pulled out a box of assorted of manna from heaven. I took two of what I needed and thanked her. She put the box back and pulled the door shut.

"You should run," she said over her shoulder as long, lithe legs carried her toward the door. "Sister hates it when we're late."

Two hours later, Sociopathic Joseph sat opposite me at the chess board. He aimed his balled up sandwich wrapper over my head to the trash can. I was in no mood to deal with his threats or shenanigans.

"I'm going to say this once," I said, my own lunch half eaten in my lap. I looked him in his hateful eyes. "I know what you are."

He started, and his brows shot together.

"You do?"

"You are a sadistic, sociopathic creep."

His face relaxed.

"I am not giving up chess because you're on the team. My dad put in a letter to the Head of School letting her know what happened at Nationals and in the hall the other day. If you come nearer to me than across a chess table or speak to me other than about chess, there will be a restraining order against you so fast your college career will be spent in Juvie."

"Got it," he said.

"Excuse me?" I wasn't sure I'd heard him right.

"I understand. I got it. I'll leave you alone."

"You will?"

"I said it before. I don't care about you at all. I care about winning, and about college and my team. Football. But you? Nah. I don't care about you. You were an obstacle in my way, that's all. I don't care if you live or die."

I crossed my arms over my chest. If he truly didn't care about me, why would he say such awful things to me? Why would he be violent? This did not line up in my mind.

"You agree to not bother me?"

"Absolutely."

"Not to speak to me unless it is about chess and there is an adult in the room?"

"That's right."

I eyed him with outright suspicion. I let the conversation end, ate my last bites, and looked at the fresh board. I needed a project so I wouldn't get bored and beat him too fast. I decided to capture his queen in fifteen moves or less.

The chess coach at St. Ig's was a thin, bent battle ax of a woman named Mrs. Bason. She said it all French like Bay-saw, emphasis on the nasal pronunciation of saw. She looked brittle and old, tottering over in her brown tweed jacket and skirt. Her blouse tied in an ivory knot at her throat. Her clothing marked her as a civilian, or rather, as non-clergy. Her eyes were runny and puffy underneath and her breath was halitosis central when she introduced herself.

I had a very hard time believing that this ancient crone had any experience in chess whatsoever. She watched as I tried to trap the queen.

"It won't work like that," she said as if she knew my plan. "Clear the c file and move the bishop so he isn't bad and then you'll get it in seventeen. Not fifteen. You moved this pawn too soon." She pointed a shaky finger at my e pawn. "You have to promote the pawn." She leaned over the board. "Once you get the pawn to the fifth rank here," she pointed a gnarled finger to a square about halfway across the board, "You use the knight to protect it. Avoid confrontation here and here," she pointed to two other pieces Joseph had used to try to trap me. "When you get the pawn to the eighth rank you promote it to queen and finish your plan with a quick, clean mate. Well done, dear."

How had she known what I intended?

Darn! She was right! I had moved the pawn before it was needed and now I was stuck with it away from its home square making it hard to defend across the board. If you get a pawn all the way to the last row of the other guy's side of the board without getting killed or captured, you can promote it, meaning turn it into any piece you want. In this case, I needed a queen. Pawn promotion is often the move that tips your advantage so you can win the game.

I did checkmate Joseph, but it wasn't satisfying. I did not capture his queen in fifteen moves, it took twenty-three because I couldn't promote the pawn once he knew about it and, I made another careless mistake. I played two other teammates, both guys, and won both games, but neither win satisfied. One I decided to win with five minutes remaining on the clock (I had three) and the other I wanted to capture everything but the white squared knight. I beat him with his black knight and one rook still on the board.

Mrs. Bason stopped me on my way out after practice.

"Miss Goldman," she said looking me in the eyes. At last, another short person. "I understand some kind of business occurred between you and Mr. Thornton at a tournament earlier this year. I want you to know that I will tolerate no nonsense on this team. He is my best player and I am pleased to have him back. You will not disrupt his education or practice in any way, is that clear?"

I stared at her, mouth agape.

"I understand that he is a desirable young bachelor and you are new here. I will not have you distracting him or any other players on this team with female ways. You are pretty and you are small and those can be very attractive qualities to eligible young men, but you will leave that outside of practice. If I become aware that you are a problem for any of my players, I will remove you from the team. Do you understand what I am saying to you?"

I swallowed, looking for words. Flabbergasted, I nodded.

"I expect, verbal confirmation that you understand me when I give you an instruction or request," she said, waiting.

"I understand," I said.

"Very good. You are a solid player, and titled, I understand. I see some gaps in your game we need to fill in. I hope you will enjoy the challenge. If you learn quickly we should be able to get you to National Senior Master or even FIDE Master at Nationals this year. Or if you prove to be more stupid than I anticipate, by the time you graduate. You are dismissed."

She turned her puffy, watery gaze away from me and walked back toward her desk. Her spine was crooked to the point where she went badly on her comfortable shoes, panty hose gapping at her ankles. She moved like she was a hundred, slow and labored, touching the desks as she walked past for balance.

"Goodbye, Miss Goldman," she said without looking at me. I turned and left.

♟

In Religion, I slid into my seat next to Finder, relieved to be with my friend.

"You won't believe this morning!" I said so only she could hear. She stared into her hymnal textbook.

Sister Elizabeth Religion stood erasing the board, her back to our noisy, entering class.

"How did you get here so early?" I pulled out my book and notebook. I looked at the clock to see if I was late, but Jesus' crucified arm pointed to the minute hand. Right on time.

Finder did not look up. I did the math.

"Still angry about the mezuzah?"

She said nothing. I had hoped that since we'd had Monday off for Veteran's Day and we hadn't talked, that maybe she had gone to her dojo and gotten all of her cranky bits realigned and would be fine today. Hope did not seem to be a successful strategy for me lately.

"You don't trust me," Finder said.

"That's ridiculous, of course I trust you. I trust you more than anyone here."

"You trust Tully."

"I trust you *both*. Is that a problem?" They were kind of the same person in a way. Or, rather they went together. Like peanut butter and jelly. Bagels and lox. Coffee and cream. "I just got nervous when you started talking about having to "do something" about Nicolai."

Finder shook her head. Sister Elizabeth started class like she always did.

"Good Morning, Young People. Does anyone have any questions before we begin the lesson?" This was her way of inviting the dozen of us to 'shape our own education in God's mercy' as she put it. Today, I raised my hand. Sister Elizabeth lit with excitement. "Yes, Stacy?"

"Would you please go over John the Baptist's relationship with trust and forgiveness?" I glared at Finder.

"Of course! John's view was that he could not forgive sin as a minister, but could direct his flock to a deeper faithfulness in God, who could forgive their sins. His practical advice was written in Chapter 1 verse 9 of the Book of John." She quoted, "If we confess our sins, he is faithful and just and will forgive our sins and purify us from all unrighteousness."

"Does that answer your question?"

"Yes. Thank you."

I scribbled a note. *I confessed, now forgive me, please so we can figure out our next move.*

Finder read my note and stuck it in her book.

Sister Elizabeth Religion started her lecture by reminding us that the purpose of the crucifix was to offer sinners the chance to accept protection and love from a being more powerful and loving than ourselves. At any moment, under even the worst circumstance we could turn to God for help and guidance. It was a symbol of our great faith in God and in His words, works, and will for us. I looked at the dinner plate crucifix hanging by the clock. It looked to me like poor worn out Jesus just wanted me to know when class was over.

Finder did not look at me for the rest of the hour. Ugh. Maybe she was on her period, too.

Tully sat between us in AP History. He and Finder passed notes through most of the class. My shoulders slumped. I hated being left out. At the end, he passed one note to me.

Are you free after school? Finder thinks we should take you back to the dojo.

So she can beat up on me? No thanks, I thought. I wrote: *We need to find the Goth and find out who Aegisthus is. If I'm in danger I want to know and if I'm not, I wanna forget about it.*

Tully read my note, passed it to Finder who rolled her eyes. She whispered in his ear.

He wrote: Where do you want to look?

Third Rock. We can go eat and hopefully talk to the counter guy who seemed to know him.

+ I'm dying for coffee and pancakes.

Tully passed my note to Finder who, by a miracle I can not name, nodded in agreement. I sat back to listen to the rest of Father AP History's lecture on economic trends during Reconstruction (yawn), surprised that for once today, something went right.

My peaceful feeling (translate: sleepy) did not last long. Finder did not look at me or speak to me en route to AP Chem, I nearly had to jog to keep pace with her. She continued the ignore Stacy treatment all through the class. At the end, I said to her, as we left and walked the same hallway toward our lockers "I don't know what's going on with you, but I'm not into people who have a dual personality thing. I'm sorry for the mezuzah and that you don't think I trust you. I'm trying to figure out who is in danger and what is real and what isn't and do the right thing. That's all."

Her shoulders shifted forward which told me she had heard me. That fact that she did not reply stuck in my chest the wrong way. I began to suspect I had picked the wrong friend.

15.

November 13, continued.

My final mistake of the day was not a small one. I called my dad instead of Jill to say I'd be home late because we were stopping after school for pancakes. Finder, Tully and I were going to hunt for Counter Guy.

I heard the buzz of Dad's office behind him.

"How did the math test go you were studying for this weekend?"

I hedged. "It wasn't my best."

"Maybe it'll be better than you think," he said. "When will you get it back?"

St. Ignatius' Prep had a state of the art new computer testing system for the AP classes and once a quarter everyone enrolled in AP took exams. The awesome/ horrible thing was that you got your score then and there.

My first instinct: self preservation. I opened my mouth to make an excuse. And then I closed it. I had lied to plant the anti-vampire packets. I consoled myself by thinking safety was a solid priority, and that an empty house would have been impossible to achieve telling the truth. Lying about this would only forestall the inevitable however, and I'd feel guilty.

"I got an 84."

"Out of 100?"

"Yes."

Other than office noise, the other line went silent. For a long time.

"Dad? Are you still there?"

More silence. Finally, he spoke.

"Could she have missed something and graded it wrong?"

"We took the test on the new AP computer system. It calculates your grade as soon as you're done."

"An 84 is not acceptable, Stacy."

"I know, Dad. I feel sick about it." This was not a lie. I'd felt queasy in my stomach since I'd gotten my score.

"You shouldn't go with your friends. You should come straight home and figure out where you went wrong."

"The Sister is going over the whole thing with us tomorrow. If I knew which formula I memorized wrong, I wouldn't have messed up so coming home doesn't do any good."

"School is the priority, Stacy! You can't afford to get 84s!"

"I didn't mean to do badly! I just made a mistake. I've only been here two weeks and they've done a few things I've only seen once or twice. It's what Finder and Tully were working on at the house on Saturday."

"This is an expensive education you chose! I only agreed to it because I knew you wouldn't waste it!" Yelling now, full voice. "Was I wrong? Are you more interested in that tall blonde boy than you are in your school work?"

"I know school is the priority, Dad! I know that! I never get Bs! Something just went wrong is all! It's only one test! I'll fix it! It was an accident!" Tears burned behind my eyes at the injustice. His entire office could hear his side of this. "And Tully and Finder are a couple! I just made a formula mistake is all!"

"You get home right now, young lady, and get to work on your homework! B students do not get into Ivy League colleges! They do not get privileges like going out with friends after school."

"You're over reacting," I sniffed, my face wet. "It's one test." Tully, being the most amazing human on earth in this moment tossed a box of tissues into the back of the truck.

"We will talk about this tonight." End beep.

I stared at my phone.

"Fathers are jerks," Finder said. Wait, did she just finally speak to me?

"Should we take you home?" Tully asked.

"No! My father. Just hung up on me. We have a date to eat pancakes and stalk Counter Guy," I said. "My dad won't even be home til after seven and Jill and Steve won't care. Let's go." I shoved my last tears away and blew my nose. Jerk.

Staring at the menu, I went for broke.

"Chocolate chocolate chip pancakes. With extra syrup. Please. And coffee."

"Fruit & egg breakfast with yogurt and sausage," Finder said. Tully's order was too long to mention.

Pardon me for a moment while I put my arm around some teenage angst and let it vent on my shoulder. Inside I fumed. How dare my father go all holier than thou on me like that, especially if he could be overheard.

Finder sat stiff beside her massive boyfriend on the other side of our booth. A tissue paper Thanksgiving turkey hung like a piñata over our heads. The door jingled open. Again, I looked over their shoulders to see who had come in. Surprise, surprise, it wasn't Counter Guy.

Our big hair server had started smiling at us in recognition after the night of Bloody Girl. Today she sat us at a table for six so we'd have room for homework.

"What's with women and chocolate?" Tully asked.

"Lecithin," I said, putting my aching head down on my open literature book. I wondered if I had a spontaneous concussion. "Your body dumps most of its lecithin during blood loss. Chocolate is high in lecithin."

"Gotcha," Tully said. "Fills a nutritional deficiency and as it contains lots of sugar, your body absorbs it quickly." The door jingled. I didn't even bother looking.

"Well braid my hair and call me a darlin'," Finder said, triumph in her voice.

I pulled my forehead from the page to which it had stuck. Counter Guy hugged our perky waitress hello! He bounced past us and held the employees-only door to the kitchen open for a server laden with chocolate and fries. Adrenaline shot through me. Counter Guy and food! Finally we could get this fanged fantasy over with and eat at the same time.

Twenty minutes later, we sat, still waiting for Counter Guy to appear at the counter. Had we missed him? Had he only stopped in to check his schedule and slipped out the back?

The pancakes, though delicious and satisfying on one level, sat like a lump of lead in my stomach. If he did resurface, what would I say? How would I come across? I had changed out of my school uniform and now had on black jeans and a turtleneck.

Counter Guy finally appeared behind the counter. "About time," Tully said, running his fingers down the pie list.

"What can I getcha?" said Counter Guy as I pulled myself up on a stool. He was cute in a long-haired college guy way. Looked more about literature than science so, not quite my speed. Not that I don't like fiction, I do. But there's no mystery. You keep reading and sooner or later the author tells you everything. Science on the other hand? Always something to discover.

Counter Guy's hair was brown with those blonde highlights that make guys look like surfers. He smiled when I ordered my shake, no fangs that I could see. I reached for a napkin from the dispenser so I'd have something to fidget with in my hands.

"May I ask you a question?"

He scooped chocolate ice cream into the blender, raising a curious eyebrow.

"Your friend," I said, twisting the napkin under the counter, "the goth who was in here two weeks ago-ish?"

"Ye-es?" He gave me a knowing smile. Oh no! How embarrassing! He thought I wanted a date! I blushed. I took a breath, trying not to appear as busted as I felt. Get the info, Goldman, I coached myself. "I think his name is . . . Nicolai?"

"Nicolai? Oh! Nicolai. Yeah. Hey, wait. Are you — ?" His brow furrowed.

"Am I who?"

"Nevermind." He smiled again, then slumped, leaning to the side. He picked up the pace of his speech. "What about Nicolai? Who wants to know?"

I checked over my shoulder to see if Finder and Tully were watching this odd little freak show. They were.

"I'm Stacy Goldman," I said. "I want to talk to him."

"Uh-huh. What for? What about? Nicolai is a busy man."

"I'm sure he is," I said, hoping I didn't sound as fake as I felt. Busy? Come on, as if anyone who has time to dye his hair, put on make-up and dress in full Goth-a-thon everyday has that much to do.

"This is important," I said. He squinted at me. His forehead was rumpled like an Alien of the Month on Star Trek. I repressed a laugh, but a giggle escaped. Counter Guy's expression shifted. The giggle lost me points. Meredith is the actress, not me. I took a breath and tried to get serious. It only made me giggle worse. I burst out laughing.

I looked over my shoulder. Finder had her head in her hands. She would never speak to me again if I blew this. Tully stared at me with a Get it together now! look. Maybe he was praying for psychic powers to bore some focus into my head.

"I'm sorry," I said. "I wasn't laughing at you, it's just I've had a rough day and talking to strangers makes me nervous. Sorry."

"It's okay," he said, straightening. "I had to get used to it, too." He kept my eye contact and smiled like he meant it.

"Are you ready?" he asked. Southern gentleman even in a diner.

"I am." I gathered what few pathetic wits I had left.

"You asked about Nicolai," he said, talking fast again. Weird, but okay. "What was it you wanted?"

"I need to talk to him."

"Who're you with?" Counter Guy said, suspicious. What happened to friendly gentleman boy?

"I'm not with anybody. I just want a conversation. Maybe give him my email?"

He dug around behind the counter then slid me a napkin and a pen.

"Thanks," I said as he turned away to finish making my shake.

"Yeah, yeah. No problem." He plunked a tall glass and a metal container with yet more chocolate in it onto the counter. "Good luck," he smirked. I looked over my shoulder. Finder had pulled on her jacket.

"Could I have this in a go-cup?"

"You gave him your *email?* Are you *crazy?*"

Finder was about to drive me over the edge. I stopped in my tracks, breath puffing out into the cold, twilight air.

"Okay, look," I said, turning to face her. I had to look up to get her eyes. "I don't know how you are used to treating your friends, but I am done with this treating Stacy like crap thing."

She stared at me.

"You sent me to do the talking. Now your cheese is sliding off your cracker because I didn't do it right? Is it not obvious that I am bending over backwards to make you happy?" I said.

"Is it not obvious that I am trying to protect you from creatures you don't even understand?"

Tully sucked down more milkshake and got in the truck. I wondered if he planned to help his girlfriend by running me over. Surely not. I'd just given him chocolate.

"You think you're better than us," she said.

"I don't!"

"Then why wouldn't you let me put garlic in the whatchamacallit? I wanted to *help* you!"

I felt lost for words. Then I realized she'd turned it around.

"I haven't done anything wrong," I said. "Why can't you say I'm sorry Stacy and be done with it? Good grief!"

Finder looked over my head toward the Wonder Bread factory. A tempting, yeasty smell drifted past on the breeze. Arms folded across her chest, she was a Warrior Goddess mystery. I grasped, trying to figure out what move she'd make. I admit I expected her to say *something*. Instead, she walked past me, reaching to open the car door.

"Hold on!" I shouted. I grabbed her arm. It was so fast, I hardly knew what happened. She had me on my knees on the pavement with my arm twisted behind my back in less than a second. My wrist hurt. A lot.

"Ow! Finder!" She let go. I fell forward.

"Don't grab me," she said.

"Don't worry." My hands shook as I brushed fine gravel off my knees. I looked in her face. Something cold had slid down across her eyes. I wasn't even sure she saw me.

Tully was out of the truck in a heartbeat helping me up. "Are you okay?"

He shot Finder a dark, angry look.

My heart beat fast in my chest. Finder had just attacked me. She scared me, too, reacting so fast and with such violence. Why did I want to keep this unpredictable, moody girl as my friend? Maybe I didn't.

A silence sat over us as Tully drove us to Wilton. I had gotten my heart rate back to normal, my breath was full again in my lungs.

Tully lowered his voice to Finder. "Don't do this again, Layla. Just apologize. It's not worth another friend."

"I'm sorry," close to inaudible from shotgun.

I had nothing.

Finder looked around the headrest. "I'm sorry, Stacy."

"You should be," I said.

"I shouldn't have grabbed you. I'm sorry. I," she paused. "I've been under some . . .stress."

"That makes me feel much better," I said, immediately regretting my sarcasm. A long pause sucked another mile.

"I don't always play well with others," Finder reminded me. She turned to see if I'd heard her.

"Well, I do," I said. "I like you guys, though now I'm not sure why because you're clearly lunatics."

"I chase people away before they can get close to me," Finder said. Her tone was simple, honest. "I get scared."

"Everybody does. I want to be friends with you, but there's no excuse for what just happened."

"I know. You're right. I'm sorry."

"I accept your apology," I said. "And, never. Again. No way. Maybe you guys can do that with each other, but not with me." I thought for a split second about telling them about Disaster Number One, then decided against it. They'd find out sooner or later. After tonight's events, it'd have to be later.

"I didn't mean to . . ." her voice trailed off. Didn't mean to what? Hurt me? Scare me? Make me not trust you? I thought.

Sitting feet up in the back seat, arms wrapped tight around my knees, I felt cold and hard, like I'd been sprayed with water and left to freeze.

I took a shower to thaw out and calm down as soon as I got home. I boiled some water in the electric kettle, made decaf and took two aspirin for my headache. Abandoned crayons and paper lay strewn across the kitchen table so I doodled Steve a picture of me kissing the frog rock and stuck it to the fridge.

Around 7:30 Jill came to find me.

"I got you something today." Her eyes twinkled with self satisfaction.

"*We* got you something," Steve said bouncing on his toes. "I picked it."

"Come see," Jill said.

Already in my jammies, but excited by the idea of a surprise present, I followed them downstairs. Parked in front of the rec room TV stood a blue bicycle. Oh no. Was this the surprise? My bicycle experience was limited to riding bike paths in Central Park a few times a year. What was I going to do with this on an actual road? Just the sight of it filled me with an emotion akin to dread.

A helmet, neon yellow traffic vest, matching wrist bands and a lock dangled from the handlebars.

"I thought you might like a way to get around when your friends can't come get you. It's not fair to you," she said, "having to always depend on someone else." Her smile was contagious. I smiled back. "I thought there'd be more busses and such, but nothing comes back here. It's crazy, right? How do all the house cleaners get to work?"

There's nothing quite like the let down of a gift you truly do not want. Jill was so sweet though, and so well-meaning I smiled and hugged her anyway.

"Thank you. This is a beautiful bike. Are you sure it's not for Steve?"

He danced around it. "I got one, too!" he said. "It's in the garage! It has Batman on it. I picked this one out just for you," he said. "It's called the Universal Blue Monster Mountain Cycle and I thought you would like that."

"I do!" I picked him up and gave him a squeeze. "Universal blue is my favorite color."

"It is?" He looked amazed.

"Yes, it is."

I checked my email both before and after my homework. I checked it after writing a long letter to Meredith about Finder and a PS about the bike. I indulged in an hour's worth of Steven Hawking and one last email check before sleep. Nothing.

The next morning, an address I didn't recognize topped my list. The message read:

Who are you? What do you want?

-N

Good grief, I thought, could you be ruder? Nonetheless, adrenaline pumped through my veins. I picked up the phone to call Finder, but an excruciating cramp stabbed into my abdomen. Why do ovaries have to hurt so much when they spit out the eggs? Meredith has never had a cramp in her life, her cycle lasts three days and it's irregular so she can go six weeks sometimes without one. Biology is so unfair. Despite the cramps, I replied immediately to AGB's email.

I'm Stacy Goldman, the girl you ran from in the alley behind Third Rock Pancake House. I want to talk with you.

Wednesday and school came and went. I checked my email three more times from the computer lab. The third time, it occurred to me that vampires are nocturnal. Duh. That evening, before dinner but after sunset, my computer beeped a message alert.

Chapter & Mercy. 9p. –N

I felt like I'd won the lottery. Perhaps against my better judgement, I called Finder.

"But Dad, we're going there to study!" I lied.

"Study here." He was adamant. I was desperate. I scrambled for an excuse.

"Dad, we *need* to talk with this guy. He has all the notes and . . ." I floundered. Dad gave me the litigation stare. I narrowed my eyes at him. Jerk. Fine. If this was how he wanted to play, I'd play. I'd listened to him practice arguments for years.

"I have his chemistry book. If he doesn't get it back to study for his exam, then his generosity in loaning it to me will be repaid with -- "

My father shook his head.

"He can come here and pick it up," he said. "Stacy, you got a poor grade on an important test. You may not be out at all hours." He pushed his chair back like the decision was final. I stared in shock.

"Why are you doing this?" I cried, abandoning reasonable argument me. "I get *one* B, *one*, and all of the sudden every other thing in my life means nothing?"

"Stacy -- "

"No, Dad! You tell me how important life is, how we left New York to protect our family, our way of life, and how September eleventh made you realize how much you loved us and how you weren't willing to risk our lives and happiness just for the sake of your career and how relationships mean everything.

"Did it ever occur to you that all of *my* relationships are in New York? How instead of staying and toughing it out like everyone else, we ran away? You made me abandon my relationships, Dad! My community, my friends. Now we're here and I have to work to rebuild some semblance of my life, make new friends *and* do well in a hard school where I do not fit in *and* be the daughter you expect me to be *and* the perfect big sister and this is how you help me?"

My face was hot, but there were no tears. I felt this rush of energy I had felt only a few times. Fury. When something builds in you and, for whatever reason, the flood gates open, sometimes you tell the truth and don't stop 'til it's done.

"Last night on the phone was it not obvious I felt horrible already? You could have said something helpful like it's okay Stace, you'll pull it back up, or don't worry honey you're a good student. One B won't ruin your life. But instead you accuse me of wasting my education, which I am *not*! You scream at me about how B students don't get into Columbia which, thank you, I *know*! I have known it since fourth grade! And you set a restriction on my time as if I haven't been managing my own life entirely on my own for the last seven years? How many nights were you at the office or out with Jill until one in the morning?" I paused for breath. He said nothing.

"If I got home at eleven, you didn't even blink an eye as long as my GPA stayed 4.0. Do you even know how often I slept weekends at Meredith's? Or that I walked Mrs. Frankenfeld's dog every single weekday morning at 7:00 without ever being woken up by you or Jill? Do you know that Meredith's father makes breakfast for their family every morning before he goes to the hospital unless he's on a night shift? Every morning, Dad. Want to know how often you have made me breakfast? How often you have even offered to get me a cereal bowl when you got your own out of the stupid cabinet? Never, Dad. *Ne-ver once in my life.*"

He stared, silent.

"In case you haven't noticed, which you haven't, I have led my own life for quite some time now and just because you're all of the sudden in the mood to play parent does not give you the right to take away everything I have. You took my home, you took my jobs, you took my friends. And since the day you announced we were moving for sure, I have not complained. I have done everything you wanted and on top of it, I've done a damn good job of getting back what I can and I'm not giving it up because you start pretending to be responsible for me!"

I took a breath. Dad looked stunned. Jill looked at her food. Steve looked ready to applaud. I stood up to clear my place feeling exhilarated, but disgusted at both of them.

"I am going to a coffee shop called Chapter & Mercy," I said. "You can call my cell if you need me. I'll be home by eleven. Thirty."

Adults. They think they know everything.

Time to figure out if I could still ride a bike.

The walls in the coffee shop half of Chapter & Mercy were painted this rich, red sponge-painty pattern pasted over with pages of largely handwritten script from the great works of world literature. In contrast, the bathrooms were wallpapered with photos and articles about the world's most horrendous atrocities and acts of kindness and justice. An unsettling juxtaposition, yes, but something about it made sense. I went into the bathroom wishing I had thought to bring fresh clothes. I had worked up a fine sweat riding the five miles from Wilton to VCU's neighborhood, and my shirt stuck to my chest. Once I got out of my neighborhood, I found my way because the route consisted of two turns that I had memorized looking out the window of Tully's truck all those days after school when we searched for Bloody Girl.

The best part about Chapter & Mercy was the coffee. I had a latte, the best I'd had since leaving the city; a rich dark roast with foamy milk and sugar served in a lovely fat mug aside a complimentary biscotti. Complimentary biscotti? Who does that? I loved it. I checked my watch. Eight-forty seven p.m. and something new was happening. Tully and Finder were having a fight.

16.

November 13, continued.

Finder stormed away from the counter with the Southern Scotsman tight on her heels. Should I be embarrassed to say I feared for her coffee? It sloshed over the cup's edge, dripping foam. I leaped from our cozy, arm-chaired nook to rescue it.

"My family does *not* think you're gay!" Finder protested as I took away her beverage.

"They *do* Finder! Your mother wouldn't lay off me tonight!"

"She thinks you're a nut because of what you won't eat, Tul, but she doesn't think you're gay."

I set Finder's cup on the scratched coffee table. It didn't look to have lost too much.

Tully plunked down on the purple velvet couch. "She blames me for a lot."

"She does not!"

Tully maneuvered his tea to a gentle rest on the table, then tore open a packet of honey.

"She asked me outright. She said, do you know why Layla acts so white, Teularen? Is it just that school? Or is it spending time with boys like you?" Tully's imitation of Finder's mother struck me as accurate even though I had yet to meet her.

"She was kidding!"

"I'm not gay, Layla."

"She was criticizing me, not you. She loves you. She just wishes -- "

"You'd date anyone but me and transfer to Jackson Heights Private. I know." He slumped forward, elbows on his knees. He sighed and a wide swath of blonde fell across his face. I resisted the urge to wrap an arm around his shoulder.

"She wants me to be in my own culture."

He raised his gaze through the curtain of hair.

"You are in your culture. You choose to be with me, you choose to go to St. Ig's. You've earned your way there for years. Why can't she accept that?"

"She thinks they renew my scholarship because they need to fill a quota."

"They renew it because you have the highest GPA in the school. Unless she beats you," he nodded toward me. "And because your mom doesn't earn enough to send you. You're an asset to that school."

Finder sighed and picked up her mug. "And I am the sole African American female on the campus. My mom is good with me being successful. She just wishes I'd do it with other Black people."

"I never realized she was so racist."

"She's not racist!"

Tully shot her a devastating look.

"Your father wants you to go to college in Scotland," Finder shot back. "What's the difference?"

"He wants me to go for *one year*. And to his school that's all. It's a family thing."

"And this isn't?"

Just then, Adorable Goth Boy (turned Total Criminal Jerk) swooshed through the door of Chapter & Mercy. My heart caught in my throat. Flanked by three other goths, AGB scoped the café. One of his boys wore a trench coat, one a leather jacket, and one, like AGB, layered both. I stood. AGB whispered to Just Leather who went to the counter. Spying me, the Adorable Goth Boy took a seat in a shiny red arm chair and opened his hands, like 'well?'

I walked between Finder and Tully who stopped fighting long enough (I think) to realize where I'd gone.

"You don't look very dangerous," he said.

"Neither do you," I said.

We'd spoken for five seconds and his manner already irritated me. He smiled, like he knew something I didn't. I hate that. Worse, he had an itty bitty lisp. My crush began dissolving.

I eyeballed Layered Jackets with a look I learned in chess club. It translates to 'get off your lazy behind and give the chair to the lady.' He stood. I am exceptional at that look. Helping fuel my entitlement to the chair, I had just ridden farther on a bicycle than I maybe ever had. Plus, I still had cramps.

"You wanted to see me?" he asked. I settled across from him. I'd practiced this in the mirror. I'd rehearsed in my head in the car. I'd even made Finder pretend with me once on the phone, playing him. Still the words wouldn't come.

He looked at me with curiosity. Just Leather came back with a steaming mug and set it in front of him. Smelled dark, like espresso, but in too big a cup. Maybe a double shot? He paid no attention. I noticed he had earrings in both ears. I love boys that can pull off double piercings. Maybe not enough to counter the attitude and the lisp, but certainly a step back in the right direction.

Out with it! I scolded myself. You didn't ask for this meeting not to get an answer.

I started to speak, but stumbled. I looked into soft, girlish green eyes rimmed in slight lines of eyeliner. I wondered about the color of his hair before he dyed it black.

Goldman! I thought. Focus! Daughter of a lawyer, ask the question! I can do this, I coached. I am alive. I am safe. Nothing bad is happening.

"Are you a vampire?"

"Of course," he raised his eyebrows in mild interest. "Aren't you?"

"No!"

He smiled.

"I hear you met one of my offspring," he said. "Looking to join us?" He eyed my neck like a snack.

"No way."

Gears turned behind his eyes. Trying to figure out my next move? I thought.

"Then what?"

I didn't know how to answer that. I should have, but I didn't. What did I want with him? Finder and Tully wanted to stake him. As for me, I wasn't so sure.

"Who's Aegisthus?" I asked.

"Why do you care?"

"Fine, be difficult." I shook my head in exasperation. His coffee smelled amazing. "You should drink that espresso before it gets cold."

"It's a double shot. I don't know anything about you, Miss Goldman," he said sitting back in a way that reminded me of the JDS's principal. "What reason can you offer me for answering your questions?"

I thought fast.

"You're here. That tells me you are not only prepared to answer my questions, but are in fact interested in doing so for reasons of your own."

"Pre-law?" he said.

Holy crap. He thought I was in college? I didn't want that topic going any further so I employed my dad's favorite distraction technique. I talked faster.

"Who's Aegisthus?"

"My mentor. My sponsor, perhaps you'd say."

"You said to the girl," I paused, "the girl in the alley -- "

"Angela."

"You said, 'Give Aegisthus my message.' What did that mean?"

"Aegisthus runs Richmond," he said with a casual wave of his hand. And still no move toward that coffee! "He's been sending me children who think they want eternity but are searching instead for entertainment. I bit Angela at her request, but sent her back to him unchanged to tell him to stop. I'm not a market for god's sake."

"But you did share blood with her?" I said. Emphasis on share.

"Eventually, yes. She is now my offspring."

This was so surreal. I couldn't believe this conversation. Why had he agreed to answer my questions, I wondered.

"She asked me if I was Glen Bacon's." I raised my eyebrows and shoulders in a query.

"Glen Bacon has many offspring," he said matter of factly. "The family has been in Richmond for a long time."

Ah ha! I was right about Glen Bacon being connected to the Maymont Bacon family. One point for me.

"How long have you lived in Richmond?" I asked.

"All my life."

"And your mentor?"

"Nearly as long as Glen Bacon. I'm surprised Bacon hasn't tried to take over our society's leadership," he went on.

"Your society?"

He smiled a wide smile. I had to look at his mouth twice. His canine teeth were long. And pointy. I shivered.

"The Hidden City."

"What's that?"

"Not all at once, my dear," he said. "State secrets, you know." He finally reached for his coffee. He sniffed, but didn't sip. It had to be getting cold.

"Why did you come tonight?" I asked.

"So few humans notice us, it's intriguing when one does."

"Thanks," I said. "This has been interesting." I rose to go.

"Oh no," he said, reaching out lightning fast to grab my hand. "How do I know you aren't going to betray me?"

"What? To whom?" I couldn't help but notice how soft his hands were, except for calluses on the pads under his fingers. Isaac got calluses like that after he started working out. Don't tell me vampires lift weights?

"I trust this conversation will remain confidential?" he said.

"Okay."

"Truth?" He still had my hand. "I want you to tell the truth."

"I am." I should be pulling away now, I thought. He smiled.

"You don't want to resist my command?"

I raised an eyebrow as best I could. "Don't be a freak. I'm not going to betray you."

He looked confused. I guess he was used to people like Aegisthus trying to trick him.

"I'm being honest," I said.

He smiled, confidence resumed, then leaned forward toward my wrist. I tensed, ready to punch him if he bared those teeth. He kept his lips together and, keeping eye contact with me, turned my hand over in his. Then, he kissed the back of my hand. His lips were soft and full.

"It's been a pleasure, Miss Goldman," he said. "I hope we'll meet again."

I tried to hold my face neutral. He let go of my hand. I turned back to Finder and Tully, one watching wide-eyed, the other open mouthed. I knew they were going to think he'd brainwashed me. Maybe he had. I'll never scrub that hand again, I thought, giving in for just a moment to girly stupidness. It was late. I was tired. My behind was sore from the bike seat. And I wanted my latte.

I'm not going to replay the gory details of the rest of the evening and Tully's merciful ride home because it basically consisted of forty-five minutes of us going around and around about whether or not to stake AGB.

Finder: Yes. There's nothing wrong with killing something that's already dead.

Me: No. Murder is murder. Murder bad!

Tully negotiated between us. The end of the day: I got home around 11:15 wired from coffee and adrenaline with no conclusions drawn about our next move. I wished my life went more like a movie where you can clearly see the next thing that has to happen in order to drive the plot forward.

Wednesday, November 14, 2001

The Richmond offices of my father's firm are in the historic district, in the opposite direction of St. Ig's. He leaves at exactly 6:40 a.m., same as me. At 6:20, we convene at the kitchen table booth by the windows, eat some cereal, drink some tea, say good morning then go our separate ways. Dad walks two miles to work or gets in his money-mobile depending on the weather. I walk to the end of our driveway and my bus stop. This morning Dad barely looked at me, or maybe I barely looked at him. I had peppermint, he had ginger ginseng. He ate corn flakes, I ate coco puffs, both freaky organic brands bought by Jill, but whatever. As long as it's chocolate, I'm not picky.

"I suppose we should talk about yesterday," said Dad.

I couldn't tell what lay ahead: the pre-punishment speech or the let's work it out speech. The clock read 6:37. I ate faster. My bus came at *exactly* six forty-two. If I missed it, this whole guilt inducing ordeal ensued. I already felt bad about hurting my dad's feelings last night, but I did not intend to apologize. I wolfed down my last few bites.

"Maybe tonight after dinner we could sit down for a while," he said, popping the plastic lid on his go-cup.

"Sure," I said. I slurped my leftover milk, then got up to put the bowl in the sink. I smelled his guilt. I tasted mine. Tonight would be about as fun as my first period class.

I made the bus. Part of me wondered why I bothered. It's not like the bus transported me to a chess tournament or a coffee shop. This was the bus to hell, the bus to first period gym.

Beginning one's day with involuntary participation in activities designed to bolster confidence in the large and dexterous while humiliating the small and clumsy is not my idea of a good time. No offense if you're an athlete.

I can walk, I can heft a backpack. I can run just long enough to make it down the stairs, duck under the turnstile and board my train before the doors shut. What more do I need?

Enough kvetching. Point is, my badassery in chess is balanced out by my hideousness in Physical Education. Thank God, Mary, Jesus, or Joseph or Santa Claus I have class with Finder second period.

Usually we have so much to say to each other that Sister AP Calculus has to call our names in order to start class. After a torturous hour of dodging the volleyball, I wanted nothing more than a comforting smile from my friend, but no smile arrived. Finder passed me a note fifteen minutes into class:

You don't even believe in them so why do you care if we you know what him or not?

I sent back:

So if I don't believe he's undead, then I must believe he's a person and ALIVE.

Finder: You have a crush on him.

Me: *Do not.*

Finder: Do too.

I knew this train of argument could not end well.

Me: *Believe what you want.*

Finder: Prove it.

Me: *What?*

Finder: No crush. Prove it.

Me: *This is so juvenile.*

Finder: Then stay out of my way so I can get the job done.

Me: *I will not. You know what-ing is WRONG.*

She didn't send the note back after that. She also didn't look at me for the rest of the class.

Arriving at the cafeteria for lunch, I parked at our usual table thinking that somewhere between Calc and English I'd maybe found a solution. Tully thonked down on the other side of the bench. Not the most graceful guy for a fencer.

"Where's Finder?" I asked. They had third period together and usually arrived in tandem. "I think I have a way to work this out."

"She's eating outside," he said, digging in his pack.

Not again. I thought we'd gotten past this.

"She talked to me last night. And in class today."

Tully opened his sandwich and began to inhale.

"It's forty degrees outside!" I said.

"She's angry," he said between bites. "She needs time alone."

"She needs therapy." I told him my brilliant solution.

"Won't go for it," he said, between bites. "I agree she's stubborn about this, but she has reasons." He looked around then lowered his voice and beckoned me closer with a crooked finger. "She has a vendetta."

"A vendetta?" I whispered in astonishment. "Against?"

Tully shushed me with a finger to his lips. He pulled out a sad, crushed bag of corn chips out of his backpack. I filed away 'lunch box' as a good Hanukkah present for him. Christmas. Whatever.

"She'll be furious at me for even telling you this much, but it's not fair of her to expect you to sign on without any explanation. I can't say more without betraying her trust for real. The thing is, Stace," he said, leaning over the table, "This is the closest she's come to finding someone to," he paused, looking for words. "To avenge herself on."

"That's disappointing," I said. He crooked an eye at me. "I thought you were going to say this is the closest she's come to finding a real friend except for you and she didn't want to wreck it."

"That's true, too, except the second part. I think she's trying to wreck it so she can stay safe in her messed up anti-trusting world."

"Tully, do you truly, in your heart of hearts believe all of this? Believe her?"

He sighed, but didn't break my gaze.

"I wish I didn't, but I do."

"You believe killing Nicolai is okay?"

"No, but she's too emotionally whacked about it. Genuinely unreasonable."

"Does she have a Borderline Personality Disorder?"

"A what?"

"Nevermind. There has to be another way," I said.

Tully shook his head.

"We've been best friends since second grade," he said. "I went to her first karate tournament when we were seven. I remember her mother when she was still thin. Much as I agree with you in theory, I have to keep her side on this one."

"But you think she's wrong!" I protested.

"Sometimes loyalty and friendship are more important than right and wrong." He picked up his backpack and headed for the door, the crushed chip bag in his hand.

I realized with an odd chill that right now, the only involved party who probably agreed with me was Nicolai.

That afternoon on my way to class I sent him an email from the computer lab.

Meet again. Important news and questions. C & M tonight. How early can you be there?

-Stacy

I went home on the bus, struggling the whole time with what to do about Finder. I'd done everything she'd asked me to do, short of stuffing the mezuzah. I'd even put my toe over the line of believing in supernatural creatures. When I got home I made a sandwich and parked at the dining room table where I could watch Steve build stuff with Legos as I dug into food and homework. Every half hour or so I popped up to my "office" to check my email. Just after sunset at 5:48 p.m. this arrived:

C & M. 7:30.

–N

17.

November 14, continued.

I told Jill my plan to go to Chapter & Mercy to meet a friend and study. Both true, just not in that order, and I'd be home by 9:00.

"Do you want me to drop you and come get you? I'm not doing much tonight so it's no problem." Tempting. Riding the bike was stressful. I considered, weighing possible options and outcomes.

"Thanks, but I'll ride. Can use the exercise." This was true, in part. I was sore still from earlier rides, but I hadn't been walking like I did at home. Mostly, I didn't want to "talk about it", meaning the conversation with my mom and my flip out at Dad, and I knew Jill would extend the invitation in the car. It made her feel valuable to be my confidante and I wasn't feeling particularly generous that way right now. I wanted to suss out the deal with AGB, clobber both Finder and my father, cure my mother, squash Joseph Thornton, put a sock in the mouth of sexist Mrs. Bason and wake up in my bed in our apartment in New York like this was all a bad dream about seeing a cute boy and finding out he was a monster.

I put on the vest and wristbands for night riding even though they made me feel like a total dork. The sun had set, but the sky still gave enough light to see. It would be dark by the time I got to VCU, though, and as I had found out last night, riding in the dark wasn't much fun. So better safe than sorry. I put my novel for English and a light notebook into my backpack, then loaded it onto the new rear seat rack Jill had picked up for me. I should do something nice for her, I thought. Maybe I would bring her a muffin. She had been going out of her way for me and I knew it. Helmet clicked and Docs tied so the laces wouldn't get caught in the pedals, off I went. I stood to pedal to save my behind the bouncy driveway ride, grateful that Jill had gotten mountain bike tires.

My neighborhood didn't have traffic so, headlight on, I rode in the road. Bubbe kept a bike at her place for me to use in Central Park. Meredith's dad taught me to ride when I was seven or eight. He used to take her and me on long rides from one end of the park to the other, buy us ice cream and then we'd all ride back stopping at all the good spots to play along the way so we didn't get exhausted. I hadn't ever ridden in traffic. Bikes were recreation not transportation. Tonight I closed my eyes for a second into the graying twilight. It wasn't as cold as it could have been, so I didn't have anything covering my face from the wind. The air felt cool, washing my skin with a scrubbing breeze. I dodged a couple potholes, but for the most part the Wilton streets were even and smooth under my tires, despite the hills. I rode a couple extra blocks to avoid the biggest dips and climbs since I hadn't mastered all the gears on this thing yet. Tully said he would show me this weekend after fencing.

I rode toward Carytown, then turned right on West Main Street. West Main was one-way going the wrong way so I rode the next mile plus on mostly empty sidewalks to the college neighborhood and Chapter & Mercy. I locked my bike at the rack on the corner and went in, got a coffee and three giant cookies (me, Jill and Steve) and parked in the nook I'd noticed last time. It was a table for two up a couple steps from the main floor. I hadn't gotten to sit here when Finder and Tully were with me, but the snug little nest had drawn my eye. Now, I deemed it a good vantage point as it afforded me a view of the door and most of the coffee shop. I couldn't be sneaked up on with the walls at my back and, to make sure I loved it, The Count of Monte Cristo text covered the walls.

I took a sip of an exquisite coffee. Rich, dark and aromatic, it coated my mouth in roasted luxury. I can explain in three words how my passion for coffee started.

Starbuck's ice cream.

My dad bought some, I ate it. The world opened up before me and that was that. Coffee became an established part of my vocabulary as often as I could make it happen. Dad refused to let me brew it at home afraid I would turn into some kind of fiend. I never would have taken jobs, neither my paper route, yes, apartment buildings sometimes have paper delivery kids, nor walking Mrs. Frankenfeld's dog if it wasn't for wanting coffee money. And sushi money. Mustn't forget the sushi.

AGB arrived a half hour later, on time and unaccompanied. My heart leaped as he walked through the Chapter & Mercy door. Almost six feet tall, and narrow framed, he carried himself with strength and grace like a dancer. He spotted me right away and sailed over, all of the sternness I'd seen in him last time, gone. He looked elated.

His lips had this sweet little curve I wanted to reach out and touch. Stopping at the bottom of my stairs, he smiled at me. Fangs in full evidence. So much for wanting to touch the curve.

"I have an idea," he said. "Would you care to accompany me on a short walk? I have something I'd like to show you."

I must have looked suspicious because he said "You have my word you will return here entirely unharmed."

"I just have something to tell you," I said, as if I wanted to cut this encounter short.

He came up the steps in one bound and scooped up my hand. He touched his lips to the back of it and kept my eyes in his, soft, green with gold flecks, lovely eyes. They sparkled with mischief. "Tell me while we walk. We won't get another night this warm til spring. Come."

I pulled my hand out of his. I slid my books into my back pack. He took it from me, zipped it and tossed it over his shoulder. He also scooped up my empty cup.

"I'll refill this for you when we get back." He went to the counter and handed my bag and cup to a short girl with a cute nose and barista cap. He said something to her and looked over his shoulder at me. She smirked and looked at me with a raised eyebrow. Then she took my bag and vanished into a back room. I pulled on my hoodie, a black Sisters of Mercy sweatshirt mailed-me-down from you know who.

"Jeanette is a trusted friend," he said. "She will keep your books safe so we don't have to carry them."

This was not a good idea. I knew it wasn't a good idea. Leaving a public place to go somewhere unnamed with a possibly supernatural creature who, supernatural or not, had bitten another girl in the neck in an alley not three miles away, was not a good idea.

But those eyes. I trusted those eyes.

"Where are we going?" I asked as we left the shop.

"You'll see." He twinkled. "Don't worry, it's not far. Ten minutes. Now that we are less likely to be overheard or spied on, tell me your news."

"I'd rather wait til we get where we're going," I said. It occurred to me that if he meant to hurt me, if he had magnetized me or whatever and I just couldn't tell, it would be to his advantage to get all my information first, so if he did do something bad, he would still have the upper hand strategically. He had left my bag, which I now realized had my wallet and phone in it, with his minion which means she could dispose of it, just like he could dispose of me. Finder will kill me for this, I thought. If I live.

We turned right at the corner, then made the next left onto a quieter street with minimal foot traffic. He had a long stride and I jogged a step or two to keep pace. He noticed and slowed down to a speed better for me.

"Apologies," he said. Not a fan of that little lisp though. "May I?" he smiled down at me, then slid his hand into mine. "It will keep me more mindful of my," he paused and his eyes flicked up away from mine. "Of how quickly I walk." I think he was going to say pace or speed, but changed it so he wouldn't lisp on the s. Interesting. Could he tell the lisp bothered me? Would he be considerate of me that way if he planned to bite me? I went through the list of self-defense techniques Finder had taught me. Kicking, biting, screaming all helpful, but also remembering to use my nails in the tender spot in his wrist to break a grab. I let him hold my hand because . . . why?

Because it felt wonderful. His hand was warm and strong in mine and the pace we walked now was perfect, easy and in step with each other as if we'd always walked this way. The side streets he chose got quieter and more residential. After about ten minutes he said, "Here it comes!"

He led me around the corner and I stopped walking. In front of me stood a cemetery so Gothic and so huge it could have been a movie set.

I pulled my hand out of his.

"This is not a good idea." Panic welled up in me and my heart beat so loud I thought he might hear it. I contemplated turning and running, but I might not have quite memorized the way back. His legs were a lot longer, it would take him two steps to catch me.

He looked puzzled. "You aren't afraid, are you?"

"No."

He smiled that lip curving delightful smile again. An expression of relief crossed his face. "Good. This is my favorite place in all of Richmond." Those eyes glittered with excitement in the waning moonlight. "Wait til you see the view." He led me toward the tall, iron front gate. Hollywood Cemetery. I had read about this place in my research!

"One of the gardeners leaves a back gate open every Wednesday so we can come and go without having to pick the lock. Thoughtful, no?"

We? *We??* I stopped following him. Play cool, Goldman, I thought. He thinks you know what you're doing here. Just like chess, don't give away that you don't have a solid plan. "How many will be here?" I asked.

"Likely no one. 7:45? It's early. Most don't wander up till around midnight. I have the place to myself a lot. I anticipate that this evening." He led me up a hill and onto a small dirt access road. We walked up to a line of shrubbery. He led me between two large bushes and with a quiet clank, undid the gate latch. "After you," he said bowing. "My home away from home."

I stepped out of Richmond and into Meredith heaven. Hollywood was no ordinary cemetery. It was old and beautiful and huge. AGB took my hand with confidence this time and took a long, deep breath. He closed his eyes and stretched out his arms, as if he could hug the place.

"Ah," he sighed. "Glorious, isn't it? The most peaceful place you will ever find."

The moonlight glowed bright enough that it was not difficult to navigate the winding paths up and down the cemetery hills. We walked together stopping to admire a particularly lovely angel statue tombstone, and one that belonged, according to Nicolai, to an old silent movie actor I didn't know. We came over a rise and paused. Nicolai let go of my hand. The lights of Richmond glittered to the left. Below us the James River rippled moonlight.

He led me to a spot and sat down on the grass.

"Now, what is so urgent?" He alternated gazing out at the view and turning those green flecked gold eyes on me.

A moment went by. What was so important again? And then I remembered.

I told him the entire story.

Everything pertinent, I mean. None of the personal stuff about 9/11 or Finder turning crazy moody or my assorted parent problems.

"So," I said, wrapping it up, "I truly need you to come clean about this whole vampire nonsense before something serious happens."

"Ah." He nodded and stretched long legs out in front of him. He stayed like that for a few minutes, thinking. Then he stood. He crooked a finger at me. I got up.

Leading me a short way down the path, I followed him off to the left. I searched the shadows. Was someone hiding, ready to jump out and attack?

AGB nodded at a low, humble tombstone with a rounded top. Nicolai Wilson Emrich. 1830-1849. Beloved son and husband. Served God and Country.

"Is this . . .you?"

My fingers touched the rough worn letters. I knelt in front of it. Son and husband? Well, folks did do things a lot younger back then.

Sombre, he came and knelt beside me. "I was the first person buried in this cemetery," he said. "It made it easy for my," he paused deciding. "For the person who made me what I am to do it."

I waited, saying nothing. "I'd rather not tell you the whole story right now, if you can forgive that," he said. "Honestly, I'm just enjoying this unexpected evening with you and I don't want to ruin it." In that moment he looked like any other nineteen-year-old college kid, sweet and hopeful and adorable.

I nodded. "We do need to make a plan though," I said. We knelt across from each other. He was close to me now. My hand was on the stone. So was his. The tips of our fingers touched. His gaze went to my lips and lingered there. A minute passed. Neither of us moved. Then Nicolai stood. We walked, not touching, back up the path to a bench. He gestured for me to sit.

Was it possible? Could he be a bona fide vampire? His teeth didn't look like the fakes Meredith had worn as Lucy in the JDS production of Dracula. His looked real. I realized I was staring at his mouth. His lips moved. Come to think of it, they had been moving. Uh-oh. I hadn't heard a word.

"-appreciate your concern and I don't mean to offend, but your friend doesn't have a chance of doing what she intends. She doesn't know where I sleep, she doesn't know what skills I possess. And even though I assume she's a student at St. Ignatius Prep like yourself -- "

"Wait. How do you know where I go to school?" Darn, my college girl ruse blown.

"Your computer lab. Emails come tagged."

Right. Duh.

"So though I assume she is as brilliant as yourself, I also assume that like most prep school students, her life experience has been somewhat limited to the realms of academia."

I snorted.

"You don't know Finder."

He stared at me, kind of deer in the headlights.

"Finder?" he said, emphasis on the question mark.

"Finder is *not* wealthy, she is *not* your typical Richmond girl waiting for her turn at cotillion, and she is determined, capital D. If anyone can find out what you can do or where you sleep during the day, it's Finder. If she weren't worth worrying about I would never have come." He paled. "She's also an amazing martial artist."

His eyes got wide.

"*Finder?*"

I didn't think he misheard me, so I stayed quiet.

AGB sat back, rubbing his hands through his hair. It looked soft as the long front of it fell over his forehead dipping across his eyes.

Stop thinking about touching his hair, I told myself. I leaned back onto the bench.

His brow furrowed.

"Finder. You're sure?"

"I'm sure."

He looked incredulous. Whole minutes passed in silence, a particular silence I knew well. He was re-strategizing. Happened to me all the time in chess when my opponent finally realized he wasn't playing just any girl. Nicolai sat forward with his elbows on his knees. He sat back and rubbed his head.

Soft hair. STOP.

He stood up, stretched and sat back down all the while his mind worked serious overtime. I expected he was hunting for a way around the curve ball I'd thrown.

"You're friends with *Finder the psychic?*"

Four and half minute of silence and that's your reply? You can do better.

"Tell me why this is a big deal," I said, attempting to cover my surprise/ignorance. Psychic? Huh? Now he really looked incredulous.

"You are friends with a girl who some supers say is only a legend and not even real, Finder the Psychic, and you ask me what's the big deal?"

"Supers?"

"It's what we call ourselves. It's short for Supernaturals."

"She's just a high school student," I said. I could see some kind of mystery unraveling behind his eyes, but what was it? Were they all in this together against me? I pressed my advantage by saying nothing.

"I admit, I pictured her older, but if she's just a kid, that explains everything. Her father's still missing, isn't that right?"

Missing?? She'd never mentioned her father. I had no idea. He must've read that loud and clear on my face because a sly smile crept onto his.

"Been here two weeks," I said shrugging. "Gimme a break."

"Explains the accent," he said. I scrunched my eyebrows together, bewildered. "Your accent," he repeated. My mouth formed an insulted 'O'.

"I don't have an accent!"

Kids from Brooklyn had accents. Kids from the Bronx. Even kids from Queens sometimes, but I was from Battery Park. If I had an accent, it was a dollar sign stuck to my butt from walking down Wall Street everyday.

"And I don't have fangs."

"Look, Nicolai. Whatever lies you're about to tell me about Finder won't make a difference. I know my friend."

"Not as well as you think. She's African-American right?" His expression was as earnest as I'd seen in the time we'd spent together.

I nodded.

"The entire occult community knows her, or of her," he said. He stared at me, I stared at him, each waiting for the other to give something away. I caved.

"Tell me."

Nicolai sat forward like a counselor at the campfire.

"The popular story is her brother or cousin or uncle, I forget which, shared blood with one of us, got HIV and died five or six years later of pneumonia. Her father set out for revenge and never returned. That's how the story spread. Missing persons signs and all that."

This was too much. He looked serious, but I didn't believe him.

"Anyway, since her father vanished, she developed this uncanny ability to locate us."

"Vampires?"

He shook his head. "All supers. Ghosts, vampires, werewolves, you name it."

"Not true. She would have told me."

Or would she? Tully kept secrets for her. I said so myself to her face on Saturday. I said we both had secrets.

And then something happened that could not have surprised me more. I took a big breath to accuse him of lying, but what came out was a giant sob.

"I hate this!" I wailed. "Things keep happening, things I don't understand!" Tears sneaked out of my eyes and rolled down my cheeks.

Long fingers entwined with mine. His nails were painted black. Meredith's nails were always painted black.

"Some days, I know exactly who I am and what to do, you know?" I squeezed AGB's hand and looked into his pine forest eyes. I thought, stop talking Stacy, you're about to embarrass yourself, but it was too late. My tongue and my brain just couldn't make the 'shut up now' connection.

"On other days I hurry to my next class just to avoid being in the one I'm in. And the worst part is that I shouldn't complain. I have a big house. I go to a good school. I have a family that loves me and a father who tries to make sure I get what I need. But what I need is to have my life back which is impossible. I need New York, Nicolai. I need it. I want to be home with people who need me. I miss my friends. I miss my grandmother. I miss traffic and tripping on homeless people and the subway. I hate Richmond. I hate the big stupid house and the ridiculous bicycle and the school full of Nobody Else Who is Jewish! I hate that the only people I like are crazy people who believe in vampires and werewolves and things that *are not real!* I wanna go home."

I ugly cried in the most embarrassing way.

Tears flooding down my cheeks, hiccoughing sobs. Super horrible.

"Come here." AGB slid next to me and pulled me close under his arm. He wore a leather jacket under his trench coat. It smelled faintly of old cars and the leather oil our neighbor Mr. Faber used to polish his sofa. He smelled safe. He smelled like home. I hid my face and shook, crying into his coats. Curling his other arm snug around me, he let me weep.

My father . . . cried today. In public. Even during the months that followed my mother attacking him, going into treatment, going on trial, going to jail, I had never seen him cry. He hugged me so hard when he saw me I thought I'd suffocate. By eleven that night, our apartment building had been declared a Hazardous Waste Site. I didn't know when we'd be allowed to move back in, but it hardly mattered. Our building still stood and I remember thinking at worst, we could move uptown, farther away from school.

What he and Jill decided to do in response to the terrorist attack on The World Trade Center would not in a million years have occurred to me. Ne-ver. My father gave me the litigation stare, pointed to Steve, and without even an apology, slammed an airplane into the side of my life and turned a blind eye as everything I relied on shattered in a cloud of filth and smoke and pain.

"It's gonna be okay."

"It's not," I sniffed.

"I know it hurts. I know. You miss your home so much," AGB said, stroking my hair. "I've lost people too, and it's awful. The worst kind of pain. Especially when you don't expect it."

I sniffed. "Maybe I should let you bite me. Do you get less emotional once you're dead?"

"Oh no," he said with a little half laugh. "Some would say it gets worse." I shook my head, wiping my eyes with my cuffs. He dug in his pocket and handed me a clean, folded black bandana.

"That doesn't make sense," I said. "Biologically speaking." I blew my nose.

"Neither do we," he said. Touché. "You are strong and smart and pretty and a great game player. You will be fine in this world, Stacy Goldman. Truly. Fine."

"I will?"

"You will." He smiled at me and put his soft lips on my forehead. He kissed me softly once right in the center and pulled away to look in my face. "I know you will. I am an excellent judge of character."

And swoosh, in a rush I felt dizzy and light and my head buzzed like when we were protecting my house. I observed from outside myself that this loving, thoughtful being whose energy seemed so clean and clear and relaxed was the creature we'd been protecting it from.

I closed my eyes and rested my head on Nicolai's chest as the energy flowed, warmed me from head to toe and settled. What had Tully told me to do? Put my hand on my head where the tingling was? I put my hand on my forehead, closing down whatever had opened. Like Tully had shown me. What had he called it?

"Death is a game, just like life," Nicolai said, looking out at the glittering river. "The difference is the things you're afraid of change. It's why knowing that Finder wants to stake me only sort of bothers me. I've already died once," he said. "I'm not afraid of death anymore. But what if I spend the next two hundred years alone? Or worse, what if I live that long with nothing to show for my lifetimes but a string of deaths?"

Still lightheaded, I asked, "Do you have to kill to live?"

His arms still held me close. Perhaps not the safest choice right now. Perhaps, in fact, a bad, bad choice.

"I don't," he said. "I do need blood to survive. It's just how it is."

"Sorry for crying on you." I pulled away and sat forward on the bench.

"No need to apologize. This is the most interesting evening I've had in a long time."

"Since the one where you bit Angela?"

"This is far more interesting than that." He brushed a stray strand of hair out of my face and tucked it behind my ear. He let his fingers linger on my cheek. "I think we should introduce you to Aegisthus," AGB said.

I gave him the 'are you crazy?' look.

"We'll introduce you to him as a vampire hunter gone renegade."

I liked the tone of that. Stacy Goldman: Vampire Hunter Renegade. It sounded so much cooler than I was.

"Why renegade?"

"Because you came to help me. I'm sorry if I was rude before. It's a nasty habit. I'm often on the defense these days."

I felt sad when the secret gate clinked shut behind us.

"Remind me next time to show you the grave of W.W. Pool, the infamous Richmond vampire," he said. "It's a spooky little spot. He's a myth of course, debunked years ago, by some science-minded vampire hunters like yourself. Still, I like to imagine that maybe the debunking is the myth and one day he'll just pop in on a Wednesday night and say hello."

We took our time walking back to Chapter & Mercy. We both kept our hands stuffed in our pockets, thinking, processing all we had learned about the other. Or at least that's what I did. Part of me wondered if he would turn on me and attack, but his body language was calm and familiar, like Meredith's. As if he was tuned into me beyond the boundaries of regular friendship and would know if I wasn't okay even before I said so.

As we came around the corner onto West Main, the door to Chapter & Mercy burst open. Two huge guys in suits scanned the street like Terminators, their gaze falling on AGB.

"Run, Stacy," he whispered. "Run! I owe you a coffee!"

18.

November 14, continued.

I should be ashamed, I admit, but I ran. I took off back around the corner. Halfway down the block, someone came off the steps of a neat, old fashioned row house and crashed right into me. I grunted in pain and staggered back.

The man grabbed my arms to steady me. A broad-brimmed black hat covered all but the bottom half of his face. I would have said something like 'watch where you're going,' but I couldn't get enough breath. Icy cold moved from where his hands gripped my arms down to my fingers. The freezing chill seeped into my chest and up into my face. Afraid, I tried to take a step back, but he held me fast.

The fear that rose up from my belly in that moment was not a logical fear. It was raw. And primitive. It was like the fear when I realized the buildings were falling. Only this fear recognized what was in front of me. It knew, so I knew with absolutely certainty. I was looking into the face of unfathomable evil.

And it did not mean to let me go. I stared at the exposed chin and mouth under the broad brim and blinked. It was morphing.

The man hummed as his chin flicked and slid from a clean shaven point to a round bristled chin. My breath froze in my chest. I blinked. His chin looked like an Asian with a goatee, it flicked and shifted again to a darker skin with a five o'clock shadow. I closed my eyes, unable to believe what I had seen.

He sniffed the air like a wolf, the hum paused and resumed. I wanted to scream, I wanted to run. My legs were rooted to the sidewalk as if his touch has frozen me to it.

"Re . . .sent . . .ment," in a dark, sibilant voice. It took him seconds to say it elongated as it was.

The Man leaned in closer, hat cocked to one side. He sniffed me again, long, slow, relishing. He spoke as if he had nothing but time and could go at the pace of the ticking clock itself.

"I . . . savor the taste of . . . resentment. It is . . . so . . . delicious."

He tipped his face so that a shadow from the streetlight covered all but his uncovered, morphing neck, now aged and sagging, now purple from strangled bruises. Behind the shadow was movement, a pulsing and flickering constant motion. Something under the hat shifted and grew.

A tongue, long, inhuman, snake-like slid out from the Man's mouth and reached across the inches to my face. I tried to scream, but no breath would fill my lungs. Was I going to suffocate? I was frozen, trapped. The serpentine tongue licked the edge of my ear. Run! I screamed in my head. I willed my legs to move, to rip out of whatever held them and GO!

Nothing. Paralyzed by the creature holding me still, the head of the snake brushed cool against the edge of my ear. It slid inside the opening, filling my ear with a dry, icy plug. An excruciating pain in my head blinded me. Somewhere in the distance I heard laughing.

When I came to, crumpled in a heap on the sidewalk, the Man had vanished. I tried to get to my feet, but my joints were stiff with an aching cold and my head pounded way worse than when Joseph Thornton slammed it against the bathroom wall. I looked at my watch. The numbers spun in front of my eyes. I sat, sucking in deep gulping breaths. The block was deserted. I moved to crawl and my gorge rose. Not wanting to vomit, I sat still again, for what seemed like a haunting long time. I pulled myself onto the steps of the house where'd I'd fallen until I could breathe regularly. I tried to stand up. I fell back onto my behind. What had happened to Nicolai? Was he okay? Why hadn't I stayed to help him? I focused on my watch. 9:15. I had told Jill I'd be home by 9:00.

I stayed on the stairs, too weak to move. My mind felt foggy. My headache grew more severe as I reached back for the details of what had happened and why I couldn't get my limbs to work right. I couldn't feel my hands or feet. I closed my eyes and leaned back against the stair rail.

Maybe I dozed. I came to myself, eyes fluttering open at 9:32. I could feel my feet. My head still hurt, but not quite so much like a baseball bat had hit it. I stood, legs shaky and made it a few steps. I reached for the railing of the next house's steps.

What happened? I thought. Dizzy, my knees gave out and I vomited into a little flower garden. I struggled to remember why I was where I was. Again, I threw up. I decided not to pursue that line of thought. Just get moving, I thought to myself.

One railing, shrub or small tree at a time, I made my way to the corner. I looked up and down the block but no Nicolai. No Terminators.

I staggered as I rounded the corner. In the same fashion as I had gotten this far, only using storefront walls and windows, I got to Chapter & Mercy. It's a miracle I got to the counter. I opened my mouth to ask Jeanette for my bag and only a croak emerged. I swallowed and tried again.

"Bag, please?" The back of my throat rasped against the air like something had sanded it raw.

"Did you see," I croaked. "Two big guys . . . suits?" I stammered.

"In here? Nah. I'd notice suits." She handed me my backpack like nothing was wrong. "Tell Nicky I said hi," she said.

Back on the sidewalk, I fumbled for my key and by some miracle got the bike lock undone. I struggled into my reflective gear and helmet, struggled harder to swing my heavy, heavy leg over the bike frame to get on. Fail. I lost my balance and fell backward. I landed on my side in the dirt square by the rack I'd locked the bike to. Sitting up took longer than it should have. I slid my backpack off. I pulled my phone out, then double checked to make sure my wallet and cash were still there. They were. I took a few breaths and practiced speaking.

Hi Jill, I'm sorry we ran over, I'm on my way home now. I got about half of it out the first time. By the fourth time it sounded almost normal. I said it a few more times and then dialed home.

Dad answered. "Are you okay? What's wrong?"

"I got knocked into," I blurted. So much for rehearsal. My throat felt raw and scratchy. "I'm okay, but I'm not sure I can ride."

"Where are you?"

"VCU," I croaked. "Chapter & Mercy on West Main."

"Just stay there. One of us will come get you."

I thought about getting up.

Don't sit here. Dogs pee here, said my common sense. But I truly could not get up. I scooted onto the sidewalk. I tried to remember what happened and a tiny sliver of memory stood out even as any other details began fading. There had been a man. Or was it a woman? He had on a hat. What kind of hat though? Was it a baseball hat? A straw hat?

I remembered the evening with Nicolai, all clear until when I ran and crashed into . . . what? Something? A tree maybe? A person? No, not a person. I couldn't remember for sure. I think a tree, but I wasn't sure. All I knew was that when I woke up, everything hurt and it took a long time to move. Why? Why and how had I been paralyzed? I didn't know.

By the time my dad pulled up in Jill's white SUV, I could barely remember getting my bag from the coffee shop.   I knew someone knocked me off my bike and that I had stayed on the ground for a while and maybe hit my head. Dad took me straight to VCU Medical Center Emergency Room and lucky for us it was a quiet night. We didn't wait too long and after a long list of questions and a few short tests, the doctor was confident I had no concussion. He was concerned about some bruising around my knees but it didn't look fresh enough or line up with a bike fall. Maybe from working out with Finder and Tully at the dojo Sunday, I said.

As we left the hospital, a homeless woman came in demanding she was sick and needed a bed for the night. She turned to me and her eyes went wide.

"*You*!" she screamed. "He has marked you! I smell him on you! *Evil!* Evil shall rain down on you! The wicked one has touched you and you smell like snakes!"

My dad got between her and me and whisked me out of the sliding glass doors muttering about mental illness and how somebody should do something about people like her. I was exhausted.

"There is a beautiful cemetery here," I said and zonked out sound asleep in my seat.

I staggered into my room and turned on my computer. I felt like a truck had hit me. Maybe one had. I turned on the shower and went back to the office nook to send Nicolai an email. One waited for me.

Miss Goldman,

Thank you for a spectacular evening. I hope you got your bag and made it home alright. I'm fine. Inconvenienced. Annoyed, but fine. I've never been blackmailed before and I confess it's quite unpleasant. Hope you're feeling better after our talk. I owe you a coffee.

-N

I'd put Nicolai on my instant messenger list. Since he was still online, I IMed him.

Me: Who blackmailed you? For what?

AGB:. GB. Angela. Apparently, I'm not supposed to make offspring without permission.

Me: I thought Aegisthus gave you permission?

AGB: Correct. GB disagrees.

Me: But Aegisthus is the one in charge. Glen Bacon should take it up with him.

AGB: I was told, 1. Aegisthus lied to me, 2.GB is the real Senior here, 3. I've been a bad boy and, 4. If I do it again, I will be burned til truly dead. Oh and that I must destroy all four of my offspring by week's end.

Me: That's not blackmail. That's threats! You could press charges.

AGB: Except I can't.

Me: Oh. Right.

AGB: I'm meeting Aegisthus tomorrow night at midnight to discuss. Can you make it?

Me: Why? Need an attorney?

AGB: I need my new friend, Stacy Goldman the renegade vampire hunter. But now that you mention it . . .

Me: Where should I meet you?

What was I thinking? Tomorrow night. Thursday night. A school night. I signed off with AGB and climbed into bed.

That night, sleep was not my friend. I alternated between the dreamless torpor of exhaustion and recurring nightmares of being stuck under the Twin Towers as they fell. I would have my kindergarteners, one on each hand and be heading toward Fulton Street to get across the bridge to Brooklyn when a deafening boom followed by smoke and dust consumed us and then a rain of heavy debris fell, crushing us all to death. I woke up in panicked sweats three times from this nightmare before I just decided to stay awake.

Technically, Thursday, November 15, 2001.

I turned on my computer and wrote Meredith an email on the off chance that she'd get to read it telling her everything from Day One to the bike accident with many assurances that I was fine and my real problem was what to do about Finder wanting to stake AGB. After that, I searched Hollywood Cemetery and read all I could find. When it was close enough to time, I got dressed for school and, starving, went down to the kitchen. My father was there, also early. It was 6:03.

"Sleep well?" he asked.

"Nope."

"Me neither."

I wondered if my father stalled because he hadn't found a good way to punish me yet for my outburst. A stray fortune cookie lay unopened on the counter. I pulled the crinkly wrapper open then snapped the cookie, popping half into my mouth.

I read the fortune: Truth hurts.

"What kind of fortune is this?" I said out loud. "They should say something like 'you will be successful in business' or list my lucky numbers and colors."

I handed it to Dad.

"Ouch."

"Right?" I opened the fridge and found leftovers. No cereal for me today. I was ready for Food.

My dad is a horrible conversation maker when you're not a stranger. Most people have the opposite problem. My dad could chat like your best friend if you were the guy at the next table or sitting beside him in an airplane, but heaven forbid you should be someone he knows. Ask him anything beyond the news or weather or his golf game and if you're related to him, it's prying or being nosy. If a stranger asks him, its interested conversation.

"Stacy," he began. "What you said the other night. It surprised me."

I dumped a container of lo mein into a bowl and stuck it in the microwave. I said nothing, figuring I'd better be quiet until he was done. I didn't know what he wanted me to say.

"I was under the impression you were happy about the move. I thought you liked your new room, your new school. Your friends here seem like good, sensible kids." He floundered. I had to stop him before he said something unrecoverable. Happy about the move? Was he crazy?

"New York is my home, Dad. Big difference."

"I know," he took off his glasses. Then, as if the counter wouldn't accept their weight, he put them back on. "I know that when your mom left -- "

"After she went over the edge in a Borderline Personality Disorder flip, tried to kill you and kidnapped me to her parents house? Yes, I remember."

He shrugged. "After she left, I threw myself into work because I needed something I could count on, something stable to hold onto," he paused, watching me to see if I was grown up enough to handle this information. Like I hadn't already figured it out ages ago.

"I also knew you could take care of yourself."

"I was *nine*, Dad. No nine year old can take care of herself."

"You did. You made your breakfast, you did your homework, you took your own books out of the library. You walked home by yourself when your after school program was over every day. You were amazing."

I thought back to then.

It had seemed normal. Didn't every kid make her own bed and return her library books on time? I scrambled my own eggs. I set my own alarm clock. Didn't everyone?

"You made my lunch," I said. "I couldn't have done it if you hadn't made my lunch." I smiled. He didn't see. His shoulders were slumped, face dragging. He looked miserable.

"I haven't been there for you, Stacy," he said. "I see that now. I thought that coming to Richmond would give us more time together. I thought you'd want me to be involved in your life, but from what you said last night, my plan backfired."

"I do want to spend time with you, Dad," I pulled my food out of the microwave. "And, you can't just jump in and start making rules and doling out consequences where you never have. It's not fair."

He put a mug of hot water in the microwave.

"You should use the electric kettle," I said. "Hot water from the microwave can over boil, explode and burn you."

"That's a myth."

"Isn't. We talked about it in Chemistry. True fact." I glanced at the clock. 6:11. "Look, I'm playing chess and you're playing Settlers of Catan, Dad," I said as he met my gaze. "No one wins if we aren't even on the same game board. I get you want to be all King of the Hill and parenty, but it's sort of late for that, you know?" He broke eye contact and opened the cabinet to pick his tea.

I didn't know what else to say. 6:13. I felt bad that he felt bad, but at the same time, he'd made his choices, you know?

He made his bed and now he had to lie in it, as Bubbe would say.

Spooning honey into his cup, he shook his head, slow and sad.

"I'm sorry, honey." His voice shook. "I didn't know."

Part of me felt hard, almost outside it all, as I watched him agonize over choices he'd made years ago and now couldn't change.

I didn't ask him to work all the time. I didn't ask him not to work all the time. Who knows to change what we do until it's too late?

The worst part was that right now, when he needed my love and support, I felt nothing. I didn't feel guilty for him, angry at him, ready to leap into his arms and accept the attention I'd missed out on as a child. I felt nothing.

I got up to put my dish in the sink. My father's eyes landed on me, his expression looking for forgiveness, or maybe some kind of lovey-huggy reward for his brilliant flash of honesty and insight. I looked at the fortune cookie fortune crumpled on the counter. Truth hurts.

I'd been so overwrought, spilling my guts in the arms of someone I barely knew only hours before, and now, when a mild display of affection might have done some good, it seemed my emotional piggy bank had all been spent.

I thought about AGB and our midnight meeting tonight. I had time to figure out the logistics after school.

"I love you, Stacy," Dad said in the foyer as we put on our coats.

"I love you, too," I said, but it was as emotionless as a litigation statement.

I didn't even put down my backpack before logging on and sending Meredith an update email from the St. Ig's computer lab. Two minutes later, my phone rang.

"I'm on Isaac's phone and I'm in the bathroom." She'd seen my email last night and had been thinking.

"Get a cross," she said. "Wear it the next time you see him and look for any reaction. I know he showed you his grave, but he could have been making that up. You've gotta get some bona fide proof, Stace, for your peace of mind if nothing else. Get him to show you his powers. Make him - what did you call it? Magnetize? Make him magnetize someone for you so you can see it's real. I mean, wouldn't it be amazing and cool if he was a vampire and you were his friend? That would be so awesome! The point is, you need to know the real story behind this guy before you go back to crazy Finder and talk death and destruction. You need to prove he's human, or if he's not, that he's a good ghoulie."

"What if he's not a good ghoulie, though?" I said fast. "What if he has me snowed somehow? Finder and Tully think he magnetized me and I couldn't tell."

"Oh. Well there is that," Meredith said with a long pause. "Then the burden of proof is on Finder to get you on her side," she concluded. Meredith can be a very sensible girl.

"I miss you," I said. "Nothing's the same here."

"There's no place like home, that's for sure," she said. "But if what Finder and Tully say has even a matzo ball of truth in it, you'll be having some way cool adventures that sure beat sushi and comic shopping."

"Nothing beats sushi and comic shopping."

"Except living the stories in the comics! Listen woman, I gotta go. If I get caught my goose is cooked."

19.

November 15, continued.

It occurred to me as I changed into gym clothes that maybe the real thing bothering me was that I didn't know how to make the midnight meeting happen. I had to get through my school day, acquire holy objects to use as weapons, and concoct some reason that would allow me to go out late and return home in the wee hours of the morning on a school night. Recipe for a major fail. The first thing I considered was if I could sneak out after everyone else went to bed and then sneak back.

Problem 1. The house alarm system had panels on every floor and made a loud beep (read: loud enough to wake up Dad and Jill) anytime a human turned it on or off, so disarming it and rearming it to get in and out would destroy secrecy. Attempting to convince Dad or Jill that we should go a night without the alarm on would require explanations I was not prepared to give.

Problem 2: Should I sneak out and anything bizarre happen, like the house catching on fire and them looking for me, I would be gone which would a) cause family panic resulting in my lifetime of guilt for scaring them and b)undermine my argument about Dad trusting me and not needing to monitor my every move.

I could check to see if the alarm had a volume button. I didn't think it did, but muting the alarm and sneaking in and out could be the simplest solution, though also not without risk. If Jill got up and checked the alarm and saw it muted, she would, of course, adjust it. I'd investigate when I got home, but I expected muting or even turning down the alarm would not be a viable solution. Overall, the sneaking out plan had too many possibilities for failure.

Enough is enough, though. The time and opportunity had arrived to get the truth. Meeting another alleged "super" and maybe stopping him from bullying Nicolai would convince me one way or the other just how deep this sham (or not) had gone.

If I refused to take action for Nicolai, to stand up against Finder as well as Aegisthus in his favor, I'd be running away. If I had learned anything from moving to Richmond, it was that the shame of running away after 9/11 was something I would live with for the rest of my life, even though the decision wasn't mine. It had taught me that no matter what, I did not want other people making my decisions. Not now, not ever. I would not be caught like this again.

I might not do any good tonight, I thought, but at least I would be there to help if I could. Oh, how the tables had turned. I had decided to protect a possible monster from the person who I had thought was protecting me.

I made my way out of the locker room and into the gym. I stood in the back, hoping to get overlooked. Darn. Sister Mary Gymnasium caught my eye and poked Michelle Longwarder. She rolled her eyes as she called me to her team.

As far as I could tell, Nicolai had done nothing deserving of threats or punishment and it made me angry Glen Bacon or Finder could presume to waltz in threatening to wipe him like a mafia capo.

Someone had to make sure this Aegisthus knew his job: defend your people. Once you commit to bossing someone, you commit to a certain loyalty Aegisthus neglected, and that was not okay.

The volleyball hurtled my way. Sister Mary Gymnasium screamed for me to punt. I dodged. Michelle Longwarder glared at me. Whatever.

Determined and worried deep down in my stomach, I dodged my way through the rest of the period. Getting yelled at by a nun somehow seemed the least of my concerns.

♟

"Please, Tully?" I begged at lunch. "I'll slip in the back door, sleep on the couch. No one will even know I was there!" The fencer regarded me over his tater tots with a mix of apprehension and curiosity. Desperation must've shown all over my face, I'd barely touched my lunch. I felt desperate; I'd never asked to spend the night at the home of a male friend.

"My mom won't go for it," he said, pouring ketchup. Oh yeah, some people weren't in the habit of lying to their parents.

"Could you ask?" I pleaded. He shook his head and forked his iceberg and tomatoes.

"If you were a guy, I could maybe ask, but . . ." He shook his head. I sighed. I'd lost this one. "Why don't you ask Finder?"

"I can't."

"Why not?"

I nibbled a piece of cheese.

"You're doing something with Nicolai," he said. I pressed my lips together. He put down his fork. "Okay, Stace, 'fess up."

"Promise you won't tell her."

"Can't do that."

Daughter of attorney versus stubborn Scotsman. Not an easy fight, but I had his curiosity on my side. He caved, promising not to tell. I gave him the update.

"So both Aegisthus and Glen Bacon both claim rights as Senior?" Tully said, brow furrowed. "One encourages Nicolai to make offspring while the other threatens him because of it?"

"Bingo."

"And this concerns you how?"

"He asked for my help, Tully. He hasn't done anything wrong."

"He's a monster, Stacy! He drank a girl's blood until she died!"

"She wanted him to do it!"

Tully looked at me with his jaw open, speechless. I took a bite of my sandwich.

"He said no at first," I said through the food. "It wasn't his fault she insisted. Did you know he was the first person buried in Hollywood Cemetery?"

Tully stared at me. "You've lost your mind," he said. "He's addled your reason."

"Not true," I said, taking another bite. Then, I had an idea. "Why don't you come with me?" I suggested. "It'd be perfect! You can see for yourself he's not evil, then *you* can talk Finder out of her crazy murderer phase! Come on, Tul, please?"

"Forget it." He pushed back his chair. "I have done what I can. You're a good person and a nice friend, but I'm not going down this road with you." He shouldered his backpack and took his tray. "I have few rules," he said looking down at me. "No thieves, no drugs, and no unimaginables."

"They call themselves supers!" I called after him. I watched his back shrink across the room toward the trash cans and tray return. A sensible, loyal person, I thought. Maybe this is for the best. If I don't have friends here, I'll be more motivated to graduate early and get home.

I finished lunch alone and early, getting up from the linoleum table in quiet denial. Time for some retail therapy at the St. Ignatius Church gift shop.

"I am alive. I am safe. Nothing bad is happening," I chanted down the hall to Chemistry, with my purchase tucked into my backpack. I could still prove to them that AGB was not evil.

When I walked through the door, Finder had her book open, reading at our lab table.

"I saw Nicolai last night," I said, unpacking next to her. "I was alone with him in an isolated location and he did not hurt me. He is not evil and I will not stand by while you stake him."

Finder stared at her text book.

"I am sorry if we can't be friends anymore, but that's how I feel."

The chemistry classroom radiator sat beside our table, hugging the wall. It creaked and the heat blew so strong I started to sweat. I took off my blazer. Finder glanced at the movement and her sharp, intelligent eyes went wide. She reached over and poked me in the arm.

"Ow!" I looked at where she'd poked me. Four long bruises wrapped round my arm. It looked like fingers. She grabbed my collar and jerked it aside.

"Stop!" I whispered. Sister Mary Chemistry shot us the Vatican Glare. Finder got up and went to get our experiment kit from the other side of the room where Sister supervised the distribution of items.

Where had I gotten those bruises? My other arm had a matching set.

"I was in a bike accident," I said as she put our equipment on the lab table.

"Did the bike grab you?" she said.

"He never touched my arms! They aren't from him."

"How did you get them?"

"I don't know." I didn't. I knew AGB hadn't grabbed me, nor was his one embrace rough in any way. His hands never even touched my arms.

Finder pulled tubes out of the kit and set them in the holders.

She looked again at my throat.

"He didn't bite me!"

"Show me."

"What?"

"Move your collar and show me."

Fine. She'd see. I moved my collar aside, so she could inspect my neck. She poked me in the side of the throat under my ear.

"Ow!"

My hand flew to the spot.

"Go to the bathroom and look," she hissed. I grabbed my blazer and put it back on. Finder muttered under her breath as I walked away. She was still muttering as I asked Sister Mary Chemistry for a bathroom pass.

Confused, I half ran to the girls bathroom. I hadn't noticed any bruises when I showered last night. I pulled my collar aside and inspected my neck. Sure enough there was a deep green and purple bruise running from the inside of my ear down the side of my throat. It curved like a snake. The hallway felt long and the lights too bright on my way back to class. I handed Sister my pass. I had no idea why I had left.

"So he didn't bite you?"

"What are you talking about?" I said.

Finder squinted at me. "Did you see the bruise?"

"I just had to pee, Finder. What bruise?"

"Are you kidding?" She stopped, vial mid-way to pouring.

"What is with you today? I told you he was kind and thoughtful. Sweet, even. I'm going to see him again." I thought of Nicolai and our conversation on the hill in Hollywood Cemetery. I remembered his sparkly eyes and the feel of his hand in mine.

Finder reached out to poke me again. I swatted her hand away. "Stop!" Why was she so obsessed with my neck?

"Ms. Jackson! Ms. Goldman! Do we need to have a conversation?"

Finder fell quiet for the rest of the class.

I arrived at History to find Finder and Tully already seated beside each other whispering.

Sister AP History handed me an empty exam book. Oh no. The Constitution. In my obsession with AGB, I'd forgotten completely. The Albino Atheist Chick (what *was* her name?) took the desk beside me, trembling in fear. Her thick glasses steamed with panting breath, her veins showed blue under white, white skin. Were the glasses new? I didn't remember her wearing them before. Her greasy blonde hair clung to her scalp in a ponytail so tight, little hairs frayed straight out around her face. As mean as it sounds, I said my mantra. I am alive, I am safe. Nothing bad is happening. After all, I could be her.

On my way to the bus, Sister Elizabeth Religion walked across the lawn struggling to carry a box far too wide for her to manage. The ground must've been uneven because she tripped and the box went flying. It hit the ground hard spilling its contents all over the ground. I dropped my heavy backpack and jogged the short distance to the rescue.

"Are you okay?" I said, offering her my hand.

"Oh yes." She accepted my hand and climbed back to her feet. "I'm just so clumsy! I tripped."

Her white habit had grass stains on the knees.

"Well that's disappointing," she said, regarding her clothes. "Now I'll have to go change, too!" She smiled in her rosy way and sighed.

"I'm glad you're okay."

"My pride is wounded knowing you saw it, but otherwise I'm fine."

She must've seen me try not to smile because she said, "Was it funny?"

I giggled.

"Now that I know you're okay."

She laughed. The trip had been spectacular with her habit whooshing around her as the box flew from her hands.

I crouched to help her clean up the debris. I looked twice at what lay scattered on the ground before me. The breath stuck for just second in my throat. I blinked. All around us in the manicured green grass lay large, dinner plate sized crucifixes.

"These poor things are so worn out," she said. I looked down at the greying wooden face of one Jesus and the peeling arms of another. "They were old when I came here fifteen years ago! The PTA just purchased new ones which arrived this afternoon, so these get to go to peace."

"Go to peace?"

"Oh! Of course! When a religious object that has been blessed gets retired, we bury or burn them out of respect. Assuming I don't scatter them all over the lawn again, that is. These are headed to our little cemetery. We have a spot to bury sacred objects."

My gift shop purchase was tiny compared to these. Some of these crosses measured as long as my forearm. I helped Sister Elizabeth collect the last few and helped her heft the box to the cemetery gate. If I lingered any longer to try and see where she put the box, I would definitely miss my bus.

She thanked me. Wishing I had the guts to ask for two of those crosses, I walked fast back across the lawn to my backpack. As I reached it, Joseph Thornton and his cronies came out the door.

I had a lot on my mind. I did not need to deal with any nonsense from him.

"Hi Lesbo," he said passing me. I scowled at him. He flipped me the bird and continued on his way, crossing toward the athletic field. God, I hated that kid.

Now, I needed to come up with a believable story about why I had to go out later without Finder or Tully.

See, I'd thought we were playing Bughouse. Bughouse is four player chess. You play on two boards in teams of two who sit beside each other. One plays white on one board and one plays black on the other. When you capture a piece you hand it to your teammate who can use their move to add the captured piece to their board and strengthen their game. It's fast and loud. Players shout I need a rook! or Get me a bishop! The first person to checkmate or capture a king wins the whole game for their team. I had thought Finder and I were playing Bughouse as one team with AGB and Aegisthus as our opponents.

I glanced at my watch. My bus would leave in about 30 seconds. I had to run if I wanted to catch it. My lungs already felt tight from the short jog. No choice, I had to bolt. I ran as fast as I could toward the side of the school that lead to the bus ramp. My leaden backpack thunked against my back.

This was the middle game. The opening had occurred when we met AGB in person the first time Chapter & Mercy. Finder wanted to skip the rest of the game and go for a premature mate by attacking AGB right away.

It was clear now that my role was to help AGB, not Finder. AGB and I were playing the same side. We developed our position last night at the cemetery, assuring our alliance. I had made an unexpected decision agreeing to go with him to his meeting with Aegisthus tonight. I was abandoning Finder to take his side, or was it just defiance? Either way, how could I not defend him when she wanted to kill him?

I turned the corner, wheezing cold fall air into my lungs. Make a plan. Stick to the plan. Be ready to change the plan. Keep your mind on the mate. This was the change the plan part.

Helping Sister Elizabeth had taken just a minute too long. My bus, number 36, turned the corner out of the school driveway and onto the road. I waved, but our driver, Mrs. Angelini didn't see me. Drat. Well, it wasn't raining or snowing and the walk home would give me more time to think. I was not walking three miles with this weight, though. I turned back to the building to ditch some of the books at my locker. I overpacked homework supplies just in case I needed them. And, there was one more thing I could get done while I was still here.

The sanctuary of St. Ignatius' Church was tall and wide. When the whole school gathered for assembly, the 500 of us took up less than half of the space available for seating. The oldest Catholic establishment in Virginia, St. Ignatius' had been a Jesuit monastery before it became an all boys school in 1875. Women were permitted to attend as a post war effort to educate young women in 1947, a short couple decades before Black students were permitted in 1965.

Sister Tour Guide had given me the history on my tour. I was surprised I remembered it. The school had only opened to people of all faiths in 1974. I'm not sure why the progression of monastery to school to gender integrated school to racially integrated school and then lastly to a faith integrated school struck me as interesting, but it did.

Jewish schools in the reformed tradition had always been open to everyone. People who weren't Jewish didn't tend to want Jewish school, but we wouldn't turn them away if they came. Jewish religious law was simple enough. Don't hurt yourself, don't hurt anybody else and don't take what's not yours. Help, if you can. The 'Help, if you can' is why anybody could attend school. Help if you can is also what separates Jewish people from other religions according to my late grandfather. Sometimes I think that my dad is the way he is because he grew up with a rabbi for a father.

I walked into the small side chapel dedicated to St. Michael. Pictured in bright stained glass, gold robes with a red sash, he stabbed a dragon with a spear. A white stone basin filled with water sat beneath with instructions on how to scoop your dipper of holy water. I had nothing to carry holy water in, but I pulled my fresh bought crucifix necklace from its package and dipped it. About as long as my pinky, this cross was the biggest silver one the gift shop had.

I dangled it in front of my heart. Time for some improvisation.

"By the power of three by three, this cross is to protect me," I paused and thought, then focused my intention on what I wanted it to do, I whispered, "this cross is to protect me, to scare off any vamps I see, as I will so mote it be." The top of my head tingled. Dizzy, I sat in the pew behind me and breathed long and deep to steady myself. The top of my head continued to buzz and my heart area buzzed. I let the cross fall into my left hand and on instinct covered it with my right. As I did so, I remembered an Old Testament Hebrew blessing, the only one I remember well.

I hummed it like a cantor. "Ateh malkuth ve geburah ve gedula le olam, Amen." My head buzzed harder, like I'd super charged it. I thought my version of the incantation a couple more times as well, then packed the cross back into its baggie and put it in my pack. My head still felt buzzy as I entered the school to cut through and save myself a few minutes of outside cold. As I passed Sister Elizabeth Religion's classroom I noticed a box sitting on the floor. Could it be?

"Sister?"

No reply. I peeked in. No Sister Elizabeth. The box and two others were full of giant, worn out crucifixes. I didn't even think. I unzipped my back pack, snatched two off the top and stuffed them in my bag.

"Thank you, St. Michael! Thank you, thank you!" I chanted under my breath. "And please forgive me!" I thought. With a grateful step, I headed down the hall and outside for the long, cold walk home.

20.

November 15, continued.

My phone rang eight blocks from school. I hoped for Meredith, or maybe Tully calling to say I could sleep at his house tonight.

"Everything okay?" Jill asked. "The bus came and went and you weren't on it."

"Oh my gosh, I'm so sorry!" I said, remembering her dentist appointment. "I completely forgot!" I told her I had a project I'd needed to work more on (not a lie) and had stayed after to do a few things on it (also not a lie.) "I'm walking home now."

"That'll take too long, but there's still time for me to make it if I come get you. Keep walking this way and I'll find you." I told her what street I was on and noticed my phone was nearly out of battery. I reminded myself to charge it and kept my eyes open until I saw her white SUV coming toward me.

"How are you feeling?" she asked as I got in.

"Fine. Sorry I forgot about the dentist."

"Are you still sore from the fall?"

I wasn't sure what she meant.

"Off the bike last night," she said. I didn't remember falling off my bike. She looked concerned though so I wondered how to respond. "Your dad took you to the emergency room."

If she thought I didn't remember something she thought was important, she would definitely not let me go out tonight to meet Nicolai, so I said, "Sorry, I thought you meant something new today. Yes, I'm feeling pretty good."

The rest of the way back to the house I wondered why everyone thought things that hadn't happened to me yesterday had happened. Finder thought Nicolai attacked me, which he did not. She thought I had bruises which I didn't have. I remembered going with Nicolai to the cemetery and that some goons went after him. I had run away and my dad had picked me up. I remembered going to the hospital but not why. Jill just said I fell over on my bike. I searched my memories. Was that true? I didn't remember falling off my bike. Come to think of it, I didn't remember anything between Nicolai telling me to run and getting my bag from his barista friend at Chapter & Mercy. I think I just ran around the block from him to the shop and got my bag. Yes, that felt right. That's what happened. He told me to run and I had, all the way around the block back to the bookstore/coffee shop. Then why had Dad taken me to the hospital? That had happened. I remembered a homeless lady had shouted something nasty at me and going home to bed. I woke up this morning fine, but I hadn't slept well. Bad dreams, I think, but they were foggy now, too.

Why had Finder been so adamant that Nicolai had attacked me? Is that what she wanted to have happened?

I fixed dinner for Steve and me. I made grilled cheese sandwiches and tomato soup with some chopped vegetables and dip. As I flipped the sandwiches, I came up with a story I thought would work to get me out of the house tonight. Chopping the veggies, I practiced in my head. I popped a slice of sweet pepper into my mouth. I even made myself a second grilled cheese.

"I like your friends," Steve said as he ate. "I like that they are so tall. And I super like the boy with the truck."

"I think you just like the truck!"

"I do," he said, "But I also like the boy." He took a big bite of sandwich and said, "Youshoomphhhimmphmmphhm."

"What? Don't talk with your mouth full."

He swallowed.

"I said, you should make him your boyfriend."

"He's Finder's boyfriend."

Steve's face fell. "That's disappointing."

"Why do you care about who I have as a boyfriend?"

"You need someone to protect you," he said. "From the monsters."

I leaned my hip against the counter. "What monsters?"

"The ones chasing you."

A trickle of fear spilled down my back. "There's no monsters chasing me, Steven," I said.

"Oh, there are. I can smell them."

I sat down across from him.

"Are you joking? Can you seriously smell monsters? For real?"

"Yup." He slurped his soup.

"How do you know?"

"The man with no face stands at my window sometimes. He smells like dead things."

"What man with no face?"

"Will you tell my mom?"

"Tell her what?"

"That I can see the man with no face? You've seen him. You had his smell on you last night. You won't tell her I can smell the monsters, will you? She'll make me go to therapy. I don't want to go to therapy. I just want the man to leave me alone. I kind of like the other monsters. They're interesting."

Something stirred in my belly at the mention of the man with no face. Something unpleasant and thick feeling. But then I forgot about it.

"Why are they interesting?"

"They were all regular people once, that's what one of them said."

"You've *talked* with the monsters?"

"With one of them, yes. It was a teeny tiny squirrel that came up to me in the yard and brought me a nut."

"A squirrel?"

He nodded. "She was super cute. She was in a car accident and died, but then she came back to life. She says she lives in the woods by the river and can turn into a person."

"Squirrels can not turn into people."

"This one can." Another big bite.

I crossed my arms over my chest.

"Did she show you?"

He nodded. "Can I have strawberry milk?"

"A squirrel turned into a person in front of you?"

He bounced in excitement as I got a cup and the syrup. "She is only five though so she made me promise to not tell any grown-ups about her and to not tell the man with no face. She wanted me to know he was bad and she had seen him coming to the house to visit and decided to warn me. She's my friend now."

I knew I was repeating myself but I had to get this straight.

"A squirrel changed into -- "

He cut me off, eyes went wide. "It was super cool! She made me turn around and I heard this weird suction sound and air blew all around us and nearly pushed me over, but then she said turn around and poof! There she was! A girl not a squirrel! She did it three times so I would believe her. It was so cool."

I put my head in my hands. What was happening?

"Did she call herself a super?" I asked feeling so tired, weary in a deep way like I should go to sleep right this second

. . .

Steve poked me back to consciousness. "Wake up! Wake up, Stacy!" I lifted my head groggily off my arms on the table. "I smell something bad. It smells like cat pee." He danced from one foot to the other, nervous, scared.

Out the window dark had fallen. The clock on the stove said 5:45.

"Let's go to my room," I said.

"No. I want to make a fire. They don't like fire."

"Steve," I said waking up, "I have no idea how to make a fire."

"Daddy can do it. He flips the switch on the wall. I'm not allowed."

The switch for the gas fireplace had several settings. I picked up the phone.

"Hey Dad, how do I turn on the fireplace?" I followed his instructions and in five seconds the fire danced in the stone setting like it had been burning all day. "Oh, and I have to finish a project tonight so I'm going out later. I'm going to spend the night at Finder's." I said it.

"Why doesn't she come to our house?"

"She teaches karate til 8:30 in her neighborhood. She asked if I could stay with her so I said ok. It's no big deal. Just a chemistry project."

"That's awfully late. You won't even get to work til nine."

"We only have the last bit left to do. It's just too much to get done in the morning before class. We need like two hours."

"Are you sure you'll be on time for school?"

"Dad, she gets to St. Ig's on a school bus, same as me. She just leaves earlier."

"I guess it's fine. How are you going to get to her house? Surely not another night ride on the bike."

I thought fast.

"Tully can take me over. I'm meeting him at the Starbucks in Carytown."

"Just call me when you get to her house so I know you made it okay."

Just then Jill walked in the door. Steve went straight to her for a hug and then beelined for the DVD cabinet. He pulled out his new favorite DVD and put it in for the eight hundred and forty-second time that week. Shrek. A movie about an Ogre with a Scottish accent. I would have to ask Tully if he'd seen it. I sat down with Steve on the gigundo couch. He snuggled up under my arm and opened his hand for the remote. He pushed buttons until he landed on the track where the the three little pigs complain about the wolf.

"It's where I left off," he said. While the movie played and Jill made a vegetable smelling dinner for her and Dad, we whispered.

"Do you still smell it?" I asked.

"Yes, but not as bad. I think it's leaving."

"What is it?"

He shrugged those little shoulders under my arm. "Dunno."

Steve doubled back to the conversation before I dozed off. He said he hadn't heard his friend call herself anything yet, including the word "super". That was a new term for him.

"Does your friend have a smell?"

"Apples," he said.

"So you can tell if the super is good or bad by the smell?" He shrugged again. "Steve this could be really important. If I had a . . . friend . . . stop by, could you smell him for me?"

"That's weird."

"No, I mean a friend who is . . . special. Like your Apple Squirrel Girl."

"Oh. You mean a monster friend. I don't know, I guess so. I don't know if I can do it on purpose."

I gave him a squeeze. "I guess we'll find out."

I left Steve sitting on the massive couch wrapped in a blanket half watching his movie, half listening to his mom talk to a friend back in New York on the phone. I wished I could do the same thing. I missed Meredith so hard it hurt.

As I got dressed and packed for the evening, I acknowledged I had no idea where I'd be spending the night after the meeting. A park bench looked like a serious possibility. I wondered if I could stash a sleeping bag in the pool house? Did we even have a sleeping bag? I went to the alarm panel on the landing to check and see if it had a mute button. It did have a volume control, but it didn't go all the way silent. I trotted downstairs to see if Jill was off the phone.

Success. I told her I had permission to sleep over at Finder's but just in case we were done quicker than we thought and Tully brought me home, could she leave the alarm off so I could get in?

"You have thirty seconds to turn it off, after you come in with the key," she said. "It only does the one short beep when you use the key. We usually don't fall asleep til midnight, so you won't wake us up. I don't arm it til we go to bed, anyway. Besides, it's a school night. It's not like you'll be coming home after midnight."

"Right," I said.

I'm not meeting AGB until midnight and I have to walk at least an hour home so I won't get in til 2:00 a.m., I thought. Risking waking them might be better than the alternative. Maybe just coming in wouldn't disturb them. And if it did, at least I'd be home safe and could think of some excuse as to why I'd gotten home so late.

"Okay, thanks."

The pool house was locked but I found the key under the mat. An over head fixture glowed to life. As cold inside as it was outside, the pool house was basically a glorified mini kitchen/ changing room.

This wasn't going to be much help, but if I ended up in a serious emergency, I could make it work. I found an air conditioner, but no heater. Drat. The most useful feature was a wide empty closet that ran along one wall. I stocked it with a pair of pajamas and a fresh uniform as well as my toothbrush, toothpaste, deodorant and a towel. I also moved the two couch blankets and a big pillow from the rec room into the bottom of the closet.

If whatever we were doing went til the wee hours and I had to pretend I'd slept at Finder's, I could come home, take a nap in the pool house, get my stuff and walk to school before my dad left for work. The bike trail between the house and the river gave a path on and off the property without triggering the motion sensors on the driveway.

When we first got here, the backyard sensors kept going off because of deer. Jill complained that the lights woke her up, so she shut them off. According to the map of the neighborhood stuck to the fridge, using the bike path to get to St. Ig's made the walk longer since I had to go around Wilton instead of through, but it would work just fine.

After completing my emergency set up, I dressed and packed for the real night. Meredith's point about vampires and religious symbols stuck in my mind.

I pulled my Star of David necklace out of the new jewelry box I'd picked out to replace the ballerina one I'd had since I was six that got smoke damaged.

The last time I'd worn this was the tournament I'd earned my title at. Doubly special, it was the only item I owned that my dad had taken from our apartment after 9/11. Being gold, and kept in a box, it was undamaged.

Tonight I was Stacy Goldman, Renegade Vampire Hunter, I thought, staring into my closet. What would Meredith make me wear? I decided to go practical. I put on black jeans with leggings underneath, a snug, long sleeved tee for warmth under a turtleneck, and sweater. I decided on sneakers instead of boots because they were more comfortable for the walking, which tonight could be a lot. I looked less cool, it's true, but in the dark with a coat on, how cool could I look?

I emptied my backpack of school stuff, including my now dead phone. I plugged it in to charge and stuck it on my desk. Oh, crap, I needed to leave all my school stuff in the pool house. I packed it all, except the charging phone into a tote bag and sneaked it outside via the rec room door. My father arrived home as I came upstairs.

"Hi honey," he said. "Still here?"

"Leaving at 8:00," I said. "We're meeting Finder at 9:00. She needs time to shower after class."

He nodded, hanging his coat on a peg near the door. Jill came out, hugged him and they disappeared into the kitchen to eat.

Though I saw no alternative, lying to my father bothered me. What bothered me more was that it had gotten easier.

It's not like I was off starring in dirty movies or getting addicted to drugs, but I still felt guilty. I consoled myself with the logic that as long as he continued to think I slept at Finder's, Dad would be fine. He'd eat a good dinner, spend some time with his wife, sleep well. Were a few lies to help someone else so wrong?

I clasped my silver cross necklace around my neck over the turtleneck, positioning it to be easy to pull out on top of my sweater or coat. I gave each crucifix a once over before packing it in my backpack. Jesus' gold face peeled revealing the surface underneath. The second Jesus had turned nearly gray with wood age and his crown of thorns had all the tips broken. He looked sad. Poor Jesus, all crucified. Just a good Jewish boy who meant well and tried to help.

I ran my finger along the satiny spines of my new old books. I wanted something lightweight since I had to carry it, but distracting enough to keep me from worrying.

The conversation with Steve played over in my mind. Before I left I knocked on the door of his room.

"Come in."

Fresh from a bath, he had a tower of Legos happening on his nightstand as Jill got him ready for bed. When Jill ducked out to get his laundry from the dryer, I checked all the little garlic packets pinned into his curtains, then gave him a damp bathrobe hug.

"Anyone still here?" I asked.

"No, they left." He grabbed my sweater sleeve. "Be careful, Stacy," he said. "I don't know where you're going, or what for, but be careful."

I thought about saying, I'm just going to Finder's but I didn't want to lie to Steve.

"Thanks. I will." I kissed the top of his head and the top of mine started to buzz.

"Can you feel that?" I whispered.

"Feel what?"

"That buzzing."

His face scrunched in confusion.

"Nevermind. Love you, Muppet. See you tomorrow."

I said good night to Jill and Dad, got my backpack and slipped out into the cold November night. My watch read 8:05. "Hey Stacy," Dad called after me. "Let me give you a ride. This neighborhood is so dark, I'm worried about you walking."

Sipping my second latte, I shifted in my chair and checked my watch. 10:30. An hour to go. I'd gotten bored of the novel and had turned back to schoolwork because, well, because I have no life.

The guys behind the counter glanced at me and whispered, but not in a good way. I recognized the look in the hot barista's eye as he came over to my table. He had glossy black hair and chiseled Latino features. His chest filled out his snug tee shirt and his compact body drew more eyes than mine.

"Are your parents picking you up soon?" he asked, in a soft Spanish accent.

"Nope," I said with a straight face. "Are yours?" He looked alarmed. "Joke. I'm fifteen. I'm allowed to be out by myself."

"You're not fifteen," he said.

I flashed my prep school smile. "Ask me a calculus question."

He got a sudden twinkle in his eye. He crossed his arms over his chest and leaned into one hip.

"What's the relationship between the derivative and the integral?"

I smiled.

"They're inverse processes."

He held out his hand for a high five.

"We close in half an hour. Just making sure you were okay."

I planned to head over to the rendezvous when they closed, a good twenty minute walk away, find a place to stash my bag and maybe see AGB for a few minutes before Aegisthus arrived at midnight. I put my head down on the table, just for a minute.

I woke up to Hot Calculus Boy trying to sneak a broom under my table without waking me. Bleary, I took in the situation. Chairs up, music off, water running as someone cleaned the machines.

"Sorry to wake you," he said. "You looked so peaceful sleeping there, we decided to not bother you."

"What time is it?"

"Almost eleven thirty."

Eleven *thirty?* I'd slept through clean up for nearly half an hour? I leaped from my chair. I swept my notebook into my bag. "Thanks for the nap," I said, trying to return what he'd thought was a huge favor with a tinge of gratitude. I started for the door, but after all the coffee I needed another stop. "Can I use the restroom?" I said.

"G'head. Knock first so you don't scare Jake if he's not done cleaning."

Oh great. Providence was with me though and the restroom was empty. Soon I was on my way thanking Hot Calculus Boy a last time as I bolted through the front door. It shut blowing warm air behind me. I walked as fast as I could up the last groovy block of Cary Street toward Boulevard. My watch read eleven thirty-six. A sudden realization churned the late coffee in my belly and dropped my heart into my sneakers.

I'd forgotten to call my dad.

21.

November 15, continued.

Even now, weeks later, I can barely think of a way to describe the sudden and overwhelming panic that grabbed me by the throat and shook me down right there in the middle of the wide Boulevard sidewalk. I had Forgotten. To Call. My Dad.

I dropped my bag, tore open the zipper and rummaged for my phone. He's a sensible man, I coached myself, trying to calm my panic. He would've called your phone. Just check it and see if he left a message. I dug. I sorted. No phone. I dumped the contents of the bag out under a street light so I could better see the little loaf-like phone. Nope. It was too big to fit in my pocket. And then I remembered the last time I'd seen it. Plugged into the wall at my desk to charge. My phone was at home. Maybe he would call it, hear it ring and not panic because he knew I had left it home? Or maybe he would call from downstairs and not hear it ring because it was half way across the house.

I am alive. I am safe. Nothing bad is happening. Well, I thought, unless it is.

I repacked my bag as fast as I could. 11:51. I walked downtown fast until the wide pillars of Richmond's Modern Art Museum loomed ahead in the cold. One of the Boulevard houses, the street is called just Boulevard, by the way, not Something Boulevard. I think it's weird, a street with no name, just a title. Anyway, one of the houses a block or so from the museum had a plethora of rough wooden spikes shoved in the dirt on the street side of the lawn. They were foot long narrow construction stakes people paint bright orange tips on to indicate where the water main is or whatever and, in a blazing moment of paranoia, I yanked one out of the dirt. Rough and splintery to the touch, I peeled a smoothish spot to hold as I walked the last block to the museum. Not that I had the upper body strength to shove it through a Cornish game hen, but holding it made me feel more prepared.

11:57. I searched the wide expanse of museum lawn for signs of people. Seeing no one, I exhaled in relief, and half jogged around the side of the white marble building.

Boxwood bushes lined the Museum's sides. I knew what boxwoods were because there's a maze of them in the garden at the Metropolitan Museum of Art. One summer my grandmother had made me go there with her every day til we had read every single placard in the garden.

I found a spot where no one but a seriously determined gardener or desperate homeless person would stumble across my bag and stowed it. I thought for a second, then left the lawn stake, too. Was I going to show up to a formal meeting carrying what looked like garbage from a road project?

I tucked my two ex-classroom crucifixes (they're not really stolen if they're garbage, right?) into my belt then pulled the cross necklace and my Star of David from under my sweater. I laid the cross over top of my coat.

Sister Elizabeth Religion had said the crucifix's purpose was to remind people to accept the protection and guidance from a being more powerful than yourself.

Okay Jesus, I thought. Help a fellow Jew in her time of need?

The Star was on a short chain and wouldn't reach over more than my sweater. I snapped on my leather spiked wrist cuff from Meredith so it showed just below the sleeve of my coat. Re-buttoning my pea coat, I rounded the grassy corner. The museum's wide Grecian steps extended out in front of me.

I whispered my Hebrew blessing. If God was real or the Force or whatever did exist, it was possible I would need it tonight. I pulled my black mugger cap down over my ears. The worn out Jesuses dug into my ribs. What would I do with them, I wondered, if I decided to use them? Look, Goldman, I told myself. You don't have to believe Jesus is God to use a crucifix against a vampire. It's like bishops. You don't have to believe in bishops to use them for those amazing diagonal board hits that they were meant for.

That didn't make as much sense as I wanted it too, but it was the best comparison I could muster.

The air felt below forty already, my breath coming in crunchy white puffs. I followed the long, columned museum porch toward the steps.

A few feet ahead of me, someone stepped out from behind a column. I jumped back and gasped, managing not to scream.

Friday, November 16, 2001. 12:03 a.m.

Nicolai's leather and trench coat guy, the one I had nicknamed Layered Jackets and ousted from the seat back at Chapter & Mercy, smiled at me, flashing fangs. "Walk this way," he said, in a soft voice.

"Wait," I said. "Are all you guys vampires?"

He led me across the museum front to a set of stairs hidden from view of the road. Nicolai perched on the railing with his two other guys, Just Leather and Just Trench. Below them glowed a sculpture garden lit by a couple large outdoor lights. I felt like I was walking into an album cover for a Goth boy band.

"Excellent!" AGB said, seeing me. "I wasn't sure you'd make it for sure." He hopped off the railing, bowed and extended his hand. His lips were super warm when they touched the back of my hand. I have to say, hand kissing should be brought back into fashion. "Aegisthus will be here soon," he said. "He's always late. This is Mike." Just Leather jacket guy waggled his fingers and grinned showing fangs. "Aiden," Just Trench coat, "and Slim." Slim, the bulkiest of the boys, had been my escort in the layered jackets.

"Angela coming?" asked Just Trench.

"She can't. She has a -- " said Just Leather, glancing at me. "An engagement."

"What exactly do you want me to do here?" I said.

"You'll know." Nicolai smiled that sweet lipped but yucky, fangy smile.

Just Trench cleared his throat and jerked his head toward the building. AGB and his three guys all stood. I had already forgotten their names. Nicolai offered me his arm.

"Shall we, madame?" His eyes twinkled like they had before we left for the cemetery.

I shivered, my nerves prickling.

Up ahead, figures melted out of the shadows. First one, then two, then four. The hair raised on the back of my neck. I glanced over my shoulder. Two men dressed like Goth mafiosos, fell in behind us at about twenty paces. I nudged Nicolai; he nodded the tiniest of tiny nods. In front of the museum doors, the shadow melters made way for a couple to pass.

A wiry man with hair to his shoulders walked arm in arm with a woman. Her mini dress clung to a strong, petite frame, shimmering violet in the museum light. Tall black boots and a wide black belt echoed the bowler hat topping her outfit. On some girls bowler hats looked so cute. On me they looked like Orthodox headgear.

His outfit had more poetry: a blouse-y man shirt tucked into leather pants, assembled with a spiky belt. No jackets. Good grief, people! Weren't they cold?

"Well met, friends," the wiry man said in a commanding voice.

"My liege," Nicolai said.

They shook hands like men in a King Arthur movie, clapping hands around each other's wrists.

"Lady Matilda," Nicolai said. "A fair beacon of light as always." She offered her hand. He kissed it. An inappropriate surge of envy ran through me. I reproached myself. Do not get attached to people here. Right. I was going home to New York as soon as I could. Meredith had told me to get a boyfriend but that was not an option. No need to get involved with anyone past the surface here in Richmond. I should be grateful Finder and Tully had decided to ditch me over this.

"Allow me to present to you three of my four offspring and a new ally, Miss Stacy Goldman, Renegade Vampire Hunter." Aegisthus stepped forward and took my hand between both of his. He studied my face, drinking me in with eyes blue and bright over a sharp, rugged nose.

"Always a pleasure to meet mortals who choose to support our Hidden City," Aegisthus said leaning on the word 'hidden'. I got his point. He leaned in to kiss my hand. I pulled it away.

The woman, Matilda, stood close enough I could smell her floral perfume. I was impressed I remembered her name. She met my eyes and blinked. I liked her. She was pretty. She reminded me of Meredith, pretty and funny and smart. And my best friend in the whole wide world. I reached out to kiss her hand myself. Nicolai grabbed my arm. He lowered it back to my side. I elbowed him in the ribs. Matilda shot him a sharp look. Then her gaze eased. I wanted her to look at me, not him. Her wide features were dramatized, made harder yet more lovely by make-up. Tight, curly hair fell below her shoulders. She noticed my cross and winced.

"Tuck that in." A voice like bells.

Nicolai grabbed my hand. I yanked it out of his grip.

"You don't just have to do what she tells you," he said. "You can resist." I unbuttoned the two top buttons and tucked the cross back under my coat.

Aegisthus stood too close, but I didn't want to step back. It would take me further away from Matilda.

"It's all right to fear us," he assured me. I wanted to kiss pretty Matilda. How could I get closer?

"Your hands trembled," he answered as if I'd spoken aloud. "Your coat looks quite warm so I made an assumption. Pardon me if it was inappropriate."

Nicolai took a step forward.

"Don't touch her again," he said in a low voice I hadn't heard him use before.

"Don't worry," Aegisthus said squinting into Nicolai's face. "I have no intention of hurting your friend."

"I know you won't dare hurt her," Nicolai said. "But don't touch her again, either."

Irritation flashed across Aegisthus' face.

"Nicolai, what's the purpose of this?"

"Glen Bacon had me . . ." Nicolai gestured with open hands, "borrowed, shall we say, last night. As in, escorted into a car against my will and taken to the Bacon family headquarters at Maymont."

A police car cruised by the museum.

"I was informed that you were not Senior. I was informed my children are illegitimate under the auspices of a usurper, namely you, who had no right to govern my actions or give me permission to make offspring. Furthermore," Nicolai summarized his blackmailing. Matilda smiled at me. I blushed.

The police car cruised past again, much slower. Panic rose like vomit in my throat. They're looking for me, I thought. My father didn't hear from me, he panicked and is having the city searched.

"Let's relocate . . . to a less conspicuous area?" I said. Aegisthus nodded. I took several long, cold breaths to regain my composure as we headed around the side of the building. A routine patrol, I thought. If you were a cop and you saw a bunch of oddly dressed people on the steps of a major public building filled with valuable items, wouldn't you slow down to look?

Aegisthus led us into a grove of trees surrounded by shrubbery at the back of the museum. A small brass sign gleamed on one of the benches, but it was too dark to read. No one sat.

"I should not be involved in this, Aegisthus," Nicolai said. "I am the offspring of none still in Richmond and you have no right to use me as a pawn in a power game between you and Glen Bacon."

"You're more like a knight," I said. True fact. They had him jumping.

Matilda made an unladylike sound I would call a snort. She put her hand to her mouth. The corners of her eyes crinkled in mirth. I wondered why I could see her so well in the dark. A special light glowed from within her making even her tiniest mood and glance stand out to me. It was comforting. I liked Matilda. Maybe I could do something for her. The guys kept talking. I could maybe make her dinner, or do her laundry, or do anything she wanted me to do. Yes, that would be nice. Her eyes were bright and blue. Yes, I could do anything she wanted me to. I took a few steps away from Nicolai toward Matilda. I noticed Just Leather and Just Trench also gravitating toward her.

"Miss Goldman," Nicolai said, voice sharp, "As an outside voice, what's your conclusion?"

Annoyance rippled across me. How dare he interrupt me deciding how I could serve Matilda? He took my hand and turned me to face him. His green eyes glittered in the moonlight. A fog of some kind cleared from my head. I felt confused. What had I been thinking?

"I'm sorry," I said. "I lost the conversation at the end. Summarize?"

"Aegisthus claims he will not defend me to Glen Bacon even though all of my offspring were sent to me by Aegisthus. I thought I was cooperating with the Senior, but instead it turns out that Glen Bacon is Senior and I have been in violation of the local laws. Aegisthus will not take any action with Glen Bacon in my defense and Glen Bacon now wants my offspring dead. If I don't kill them within the week, I will be killed for violating the local law."

Aegisthus held up his hand. "Absurd," he said. "Bacon has no right to claim your life or the lives of your children. I am the Senior. Bacon knows it."

"This problem is between you and Glen Bacon," I said. "One of you is right. We simply don't know which one. How are these matters usually resolved?"

"Death," Aegisthus and Nicolai said together.

"Sometimes they duel for it, for Seniority," said Layered Jackets. Aegisthus' guards shifted their weight. One stuck his hand inside his jacket.

"I see. Well, before we go to dueling and death," I said, eyeballing the Guard Guys. "We need to get clear on some information." I shot them my Give the Lady the Chair look and the one took his hand out of his jacket. Good Guard Guy. Simmer down. "What evidence can you or Bacon produce to legitimize your claim to Seniority? Nicolai and," I looked at Just Leather and Just Trench, searched for their names in my memory . . . nope. "And his offspring, are not implicated or involved in this conflict at all. You and Bacon have to work out your differences and then whomever is the actual Senior, hopefully you, has to deal with any reparations due to the actions and threats made by the other."

Aegisthus looked about to retort. I held up my hand.

"The real problem, Aegisthus, is that no matter what the situation with you and Bacon, there needs to be a zero tolerance policy for him molesting your people. Nicolai is clearly loyal to you. Bacon has no right to scoop up one of *your* people and threaten him! It's your job to defend him. It's your job as his leader to respond to the threats Glen Bacon made on Nicolai and his offspring and stop it. You should be ashamed of yourself for just letting all this happen while you stand by doing nothing."

A heavy fluttering in the trees above snagged my attention. Nicolai looked up, too. So did Aegisthus. Matilda watched Aegisthus. Half a dozen pigeons beat their wings against the branches. No, I realized. Not pigeons. Bats. Matilda grinned.

22.

November 16, continued. 12:18 a.m.

A foreign, yet familiar sensation: like watching a movie and being in it at the same time. Frigid wind struck my face as the bats descended. They circled, then landed. One little bat landed on each of the five benches just inside the tree line of the grove.

I felt the suction first in my arms. When the nurse takes off a tourniquet or blood pressure cuff, the fluid in your arm rushes around for a minute then rises to the surface. My feet and cheeks felt feverish. Blood raced to touch my skin. My face hurt, liquid pulsing hard against muscle. Then my legs, belly and chest caught the feeling. In a blink, the air sucked out of our circle. Out of my lungs. Like being crushed. Nauseated, I closed my eyes. In a rough burst, the air refilled me. I staggered back from the force, coughing once air inflated my chest. Wind rushed around us, whipping my hair sharp against my face. When I opened my eyes, the bats were gone. In their places, surrounding us, stood five men.

Two of them were the Terminators from last night! All five former bats, now men in suits, surveyed us and then looked to Matilda.

We turned around to face the Suits. Matilda and Aegisthus were at our backs half a car length away. Leather Jacket, standing right behind his boss, crumpled to the ground in a faint. Matilda giggled.

"That was so much fun!" she exclaimed, clapping her hands together like child. She laughed a real laugh. "Your faces! Oh! priceless!"

AGB grabbed my hand and pulled me close beside him. His fingers shook. "How did you do that?" he said, turning us in a slow amazed circle landing back facing Matilda. "That was incredible! Mike, get up!"

Behind us, Mike did not get up.

No one spoke. Aegisthus' arms were slack. He stared at the suit guys open mouthed. Imagine being surrounded by Secret Service but not knowing where the President stood. My skin tingled in an uncomfortable under the surface way, feeling like it wanted to come off and crawl away. I couldn't stand the silence another minute. My voice rang through the garden with all the irritated Manhattan-ite I could muster.

"What is going on?"

The suit on my left stepped toward me. He wore a silver tie. I didn't mean to, but I stepped back, bumping into AGB. He wrapped his arm around my waist.

"What a sweet question," came a soft, clear voice. Matilda. "What is 'going on' is called a set up." Her eyes were so beautiful, wide and sapphire blue. Her voice sounded different than other Richmonders. Was it a British accent? Meredith would know. "I decided that these adorable pretenders needed to be taught a lesson. And so I," she giggled in a conspiratorial way, "Get to teach it!"

I liked learning. This sounded fun. Part of my mind tapped, to get my attention. Like when you forget a name or a word and your mind itches til you remember it.

"You, however," she said to me, "are not pretending. It's flummoxing. I'm not quite sure what to do with you."

Silver Tie glared at me. I took another step back.

"Gentlemen," she said to the former bats, now men in suits. She inclined her head. "This is Aegisthus. That is Nicolai."

AGB moved me to his side and put himself between me and Silver Tie. He slipped something into my hand. A tiny laminated card with one word on it. Resist.

"What business does Glen Bacon's brute squad have with us?" His voice didn't even shake. He looked excited. I was impressed.

Aegisthus' six minions, the four who had melted out of the shadows ahead of us when we arrived and the two that had tailed us, formed a defensive line around the grove, lining themselves up with the Bat Suits. One of them had an arm across his body hand inside his coat, like he might draw a weapon.

"Boys." Aegisthus guards all looked at Matilda. "Sit," like to a pack of puppies. They did. She snapped her fingers. "Sleep." They all fell onto their sides.

Aegisthus, shouted "Get up you idiots! Aren't you even going to resist?"

Matilda touched his face and pressed her body into his. "It doesn't work like that, love," she said, sliding her silky hand across his chest. "You'll see."

AGB had asked me the first time we met in Chapter & Mercy if I wanted to resist. I slipped the card into my pocket. Thoughts were scrabbling for purchase in my mind.

Terminator Suit from Chapter & Mercy, not the bald one, looked AGB up and down. He turned to Matilda. She inclined her head ever so slightly. Yes.

This next part happened lighting (I mean *lightning*) fast. Terminator Suit grabbed AGB's arm, pulled him away from me and snatched him up off the ground. AGB faced out, his back glued to the Terminator's chest.

A little card fluttered to the ground as AGB shouted, "Stun!"

The Terminator looked confused and Matilda laughed. "Stun!" AGB shouted again.

"He's trying to use his pretender powers," Matilda said, bursting again into laughter. "This is so much fun!"

Just Leather moaned behind me. I turned to help him stand. Just Trench beat me to it, yanking his friend to his feet. I spun around unsure of where to look.

Aegisthus reached to grab Matilda shouting something I didn't catch. Matilda caught Aegisthus' arm, twisted it behind his back, then put her boot to the back of his leg. She kicked out his knee. He fell with a cry.

My attention went back to AGB. "Stop!" I shouted at the Terminator. "Leave him alone!" I tore a crucifix out of my belt and held it out before me.

AGB's expression changed. Realization dawning with a gasp. "Run!" AGB shouted. "Stacy! RUN!"

In a bizarre slow motion moment, Terminator Suit opened his mouth and sank long fangs into AGB's throat. AGB cried out, eyes wide in astonishment. Blood bubbled and ran in dark streaks down his neck. He kicked backwards. Terminator Suit fastened his mouth over the bite. AGB's three guys stood confused, unsure if they should fight or flee. I brandished my cross. Red Goatee Suit looked away from me, and started toward the boys. The one in Layered Jackets pulled out a gun. Just Leather and Just Trench did, too. Orange guns with blue stripes. I'd stepped on that same gun on Steve's floor! They opened fire, little foam darts flying. Matilda shrieked with laughter. Goatee Suit snatched the toy out of Layered Jackets's hand. Aimed and shot. The kid screamed and dropped as if a real bullet hit him, his two coats flying theatrically around him. Goatee Suit emptied the clip into the trees then tossed the plastic gun on the ground.

Goatee Suit raised his arms over his head, curling his fingers like a child playing monster games. He roared. AGB's other two guys ran, Goatee Suit chasing them across the lawn. Matilda howled laughing, applauding.

Aegisthus rallied, pulling himself to his knees. "I am Senior here!" he rasped. "Obey me!" A brawny, Bald Suit, one of the two Terminators, grabbed Aegisthus' shirt and punched him in the face. Silver Tie tossed a set of handcuffs to Bald Suit. He bound Aegisthus' wrists.

AGB thrashed, scrabbling to tear out of Terminator Suit's grip. Terminator Suit jerked a bloody face away from AGB's neck. This was not stage blood. I smelled it, metallic and ripe. Thicker and stockier than AGB, he shook AGB like a rag doll, muttering something. AGB went slack.

"No!" I shrieked. Terminator Suit tossed the limp AGB over his shoulder and trotted out of the garden. I screamed. Was he dead? Could I stake Terminator in the back with my cross? I ran after them. Bald Suit had AGB's Layered Jackets guy struggling in a strangle hold. I hadn't seen him stand. They careened in front of me, cutting off my path. Layered Jackets gasped, then went slack. Bald Suit dropped him in a heap right in front of me. Lamp light shone off Bald Suit's scalp.

I stared. Dead? I pushed the cross in front of me, keeping Bald Suit an arm's length away. He winced, but grabbed for me. I dodged (thank god for volleyball), but dropped the cross. The wood bounced off Bald Suit's arm. He missed.

A familiar voice behind me shouted, "Stacy, go left!" I threw myself left and rolled out of the way. Above me, a huge figure, blonde hair flying, dove into the melee. He swung a long heavy broadsword. Tully! Bald Suit stepped back to avoid the blade, but not far enough. The Southern Scotsman landed a solid blow to Bald Suit's side, slicing deep. Bald Suit doubled over, dropped to his knees. A smell like rancid meat filled the air. I expected gore.

Tully raised his blade. The metal was clean like it had cut through stuffing.

Tully attacked again, going for a downward chop to the neck. Bald Suit dove for Tully's legs. Tully leaped back, and the heavy broadsword fell across Bald Suit's back. Tully pulled his weapon, leaving the jacket sliced clean in half.

In a split second between attacks, Tully shouted, "Stake!" I lunged for his legs and grabbed one out of his boot. I crawled to my feet and stood, waiting. Tully and I were the last two definitely human people standing. I held the thick wood dowel out in front of me, then screamed out two words louder than I have ever screamed.

"Help! Police!"

A hand clamped hard over my mouth. I hadn't seen or heard the Suit come up behind me. I bit and missed. Not enough flesh to grab. I screamed behind his hand, elbowing him. I smacked at the Suit over my head with the stake. Silver Tie stepped in and plucked the wood neatly out of my hand. He gave me a disdainful, pitying look, dropped my weapon on the ground and walked away.

Tully turned, seeing. I whacked my attacker's chest with my elbow. It bounced off his chest, a pigeon pecking a sidewalk. He pinned both my elbows to him with an arm like a subway rail. He felt remarkably scrawny behind me, not that much bigger than myself. I threw my head back and butted him in the face, like Finder taught me. My head rang with pain, but something in his face crunched. He grunted. He stank of strong, bitter, man cologne.

"Get off!" I shouted behind his hand. "Get off!" I wriggled for my second cross, but couldn't get my hand under my coat at the right angle to grasp it.

The air became noticeably colder. All of the Bat Suits and Matilda went still, stopping all movement in a unified instant of awareness. My breath caught in my lungs. Tully also stood unmoving. Matilda sniffed the air. Everyone listened to the quiet night. I did too, but I didn't know what I listened for. Matilda's expression shifted from confident and amused to something else. Fear fluttered in her face.

"Hurry!" said Matilda, brusque and bossy. "Get them. Start the car!"

She looked at me, no, not me. Disappointing. She locked eyes on the Stinky Suit who held me. "Finish quick."

Just feet away, Bald Suit got up. He snarled, squaring off with Tully.

"Keith! Leave it," Silver Tie shouted to Bald Suit. "She said leave it!"

Abandoning his fight with Tully, Bald Suit scooped up the knee wounded Aegisthus and jogged off in the same direction Terminator Suit had carried AGB. In the grass something stirred. AGB's Layered Jackets guy was coming to. He crawled toward the trees. He used a tree to scramble to his feet and run back toward the street. Through the trees, Bald Suit loaded Aegisthus into a long black car and opened the passenger door for Matilda.

Stinky Suit yanked my head to the side. His breath came dry on my neck.

"Put. Her. Down."

Stinky Suit laughed. Laughed! Tully swung, a side cut like the one he'd used on Bald Suit meant to wound the smaller man in the ribs. Stinky swung his arm, the one not anchoring me to his chest, and backhanded Tully's stroke away like a baseball bat deflecting a fly swatter. Tully staggered backward.

I struggled to bite his hand again, missed, then stomped hard backward, aiming to mash Stinky Suit's feet. "Get *off!*" I shrieked. He spun me around hard. He pinched that spot high on my shoulder that Mr. Spock uses. I cried out in pain. It hurt. A lot. I looked into his face, eyes red rimmed and black.

"No eyes!" Tully shouted to me too late.

"Be quiet," Stinky Suit commanded in an accent I couldn't place. My outcry cut off mid shriek. I took a deep breath to scream. My voice would not obey.

Stinky Suit's breath came close in my face. It reeked. Minty and wrong. My brain short circuited. He started to sniff me, but my head butt had mashed his nose. No blood, but it definitely looked crunched. Go me.

Tully climbed to his feet. Behind Stinky, he pulled back for a shoulder cut. I had forgotten about Silver Tie. Now, he launched into action. Moving fast, crazy fast, inhumanly-like-a-blur-I-could-barely-see fast, Silver Tie jumped between Tully and Stinky Suit.

I tried to warn Tully but again, no voice. Silver Tie's back blocked my view of my friend. The Scotsman's blade flashed in the garden lamplight, once, twice, then stillness. My eyes widened with panic. Had Silver Tie hurt Tully? If so, how badly? Silver Tie brushed his hands off. I cast a desperate glance toward the sword, but I saw only empty nighttime lawn. I tried to shout Tully's name. I failed.

Stinky Suit grabbed my face. Small, red rimmed eyes regarded me like prey. He leaned in, smiling a long-toothed Wolf to Little Red Riding Hood smile. I did not like it one bit. I spat in his face.

23.

November 16, continued. 12:26 a.m.

"Be still," he said, shaking me hard enough I heard my neck crack. I wanted to scream, to punch him, to hit and run. My body refused. I bore down, willing my body to follow my orders. It did not reply.

Stinky Suit pulled off my hat. Grabbing my hair, he yanked my head to the side. Since I couldn't move, he let go with the other hand. He reached up and tore down on my turtleneck. It ripped, exposing my throat fully. My necklaces slid icy against my skin. Stinky Suit jerked me toward him. He leaned over my neck. Two hot forks broke my skin and sliced, pulling down. My neck burned. I tried not to wet my pants it hurt so much. Food rose in my stomach as he devoured blood out of my neck. The sound of rushing liquid filled my ears. And then time slowed, his feeding drawing out something else. Something untouchable and precious within my heart. It tore inside me, ripping off and vanishing into the creature that held me. It hurt worse than the blood. I cried out, a wounded animal sound I had never made. My voice rang in my ears. Stinky Bat Suit swallowed.

His teeth ripped my flesh in a long arc. His fist on my mind let go. Shrieking like his mouth was on fire, he shoved me away harder than I have ever been shoved. I fell flat onto my back.

I scrambled like a crab, using my elbows. I slid in a patch of damp grass.

He clutched one hand to his chest, curling over it. He screamed, shook his hand and held it out in front of him. His face contorted in pain and disgust. He spat several times in the grass, clearing his palette.

"You're a Jew?" He held out his hand. A Star of David smoked in the flesh of his palm. My Star of David. Burned. Into his skin. An expression of revulsion clung to his features. An expression of revulsion I've never, and I mean never, seen on a real person's face. Not even Sociopathic Joseph looked *revulsed.*

I crawled backward toward the heap I thought might be Tully.

"You will never beat us," Stinky Suit said, voice a sinister version of the three pigs in Steve's movie. And poof, I placed his accent. In a split second, the air sucked from the world around me and I lost my breath into its void. Blackness opened from inside the monster, a hole where his heart should've been. His man body sucked into the hole and out popped the bat.

Wind blew back into the space. It forced air into my lungs. Stinky Bat Suit flew away. Choking and wheezing, I laid exhausted on the grass. I rolled over and pushed myself to hands and knees. I scanned the garden and lawn for more suits. None in sight. Through the trees, a car engine started up.

"Tully?" I croaked. A dark pile of what looked liked leaves groaned. I crawled to it. Blood ran down my neck, hot and sticky. Tully lay dazed in a pool of his own vomit.

"Tully," I said. I touched his shoulder.

"I'm okay," he rasped, groaning. "No worse than rugby." He tried to sit up, but immediately lay back.

"Did he bite you?" I asked, panicked. An uncomfortable stream trickled from my wound. The spot where blood pooled in my shirt already felt cold.

"Kicked me. In the spine." He drank in a long, deep breath. He rolled to all fours, then after another long slow inhale, pulled back to a sit. His sword had been planted upright beside him, stuck two feet deep in the frozen dirt. Tully finally looked at me. After a second, his eyes went wide. He saw.

"What do I do?" I said. My voice shook, cracking at the end. I pressed my hand over the wound. Blood flowed between my fingers. Tully yanked off his scarf and pressed it to my neck, a few inches in front of and below my ear. Saying nothing, the Southern Scotsman took my clean hand and helped me to my feet. Not letting go hands, we went to check on Aegisthus' ineffective guards.   Each one lay were where Matilda had put him. Everyone else was gone.

I leaned down next to a bearded man who looked more like he should be selling computers than guarding a vampire lord. He snored. Snored? I went to the next guy and leaned down next to his face. Breathing.

"They're asleep," Tully said in amazement.

I shook the shoulder of bearded one. "Sir?" I said. "Hey! Dude! Wake up!" Snoring. Out of his coat pocket fell a stack of laminated cards. Stun. Mesmerize. Sneak. Hide.

Resist.

Tully and I just stayed there for a second. I pulled the card from my pocket that Nicolai has pressed into my palm. Resist. It didn't match these. Same size card, but different font, different paper under the lamination. The toy guns were a big clue, but Holy Crap. Homemade cards. They'd been playing a game.

We tried in vain to wake up all six guys. Their coats fell open to reveal a collection of weapons, all toys. Some painted black with colored tips to look more real. Three of them had plastic stakes with foam tips tucked into their belts. None of them seemed hurt, and nobody but me appeared bitten.

"We should leave them," Tully said. "I don't think anyone's coming for them. These guys might not even remember what happened when they wake."

"The Suits were . . . real. And so was she."

"Yes."

"That's why you came. In case," I paused, absorbing.

"In case they were all real."

I allowed myself to absorb what Tully said. In case they were *all real.*

"Why did they leave us awake?" I looked for my big Jesus in the grass.

"They didn't care about us. We aren't important enough. We're kids."

Something about that lit a fury in my belly. Oh you'll care about us, I thought. Maybe not this minute, but you will definitely care about us soon.

"We have to get Nicolai and Aegisthus back," I said.

"Did they know?"

"That they were playing with real ones? I don't think so. Right before the fight, Nicolai gave me this."

I opened my palm to reveal the card. Resist.

Tully turned it over in his fingers then gave it back to me.

I found my is-it-really-stolen-if-it's-trash cross and tucked it back into my belt.

"What did Matilda see that scared her?"

Tully shrugged. He regarded his sword. Bracing it against his shoulder, he squatted and yanked up on the hilt. Nothing happened. Watching Tully yank and wiggle the blade to free it from the dirt, this occurred to me: the Suits left us alive on purpose. It wouldn't have taken much to have left Tully under that blade instead of beside it. Those guys weren't sent as assassins. They were messengers. That meant Nicolai and Aegisthus, whatever their real names were, for now at least, were alive. It took a few tries and a good bit of grunting, but

Tully unearthed his sword. Silver Tie's message was clear. Butt out.

"Car's there," Tully said. We picked up our pace toward the street.

"Wait," I said. "My bag."

"We'll drive by for it."

I felt safer but kept looking out the rearview once we were driving down the wide tree-lined Boulevard, away from the museum, away from Carytown and away from Wilton. I didn't have to ask where we were going, or to whom.

Tully parallel parked on a street populated by neat, single story houses that reminded me of my aunt's in New Jersey.

"Finder's mom knows?" I said, still pressing the scarf to my throat.

"Taught Finder everything." He turned off the ignition.

"Finder's *mom* fights vampires."

"Fought, yes. Finder does it now."

I could not in a million years, light years, or all the digits of pi imagine my father fighting off a subway rat, much less another adult, only with fangs and, depending, wings.

"Does she know about the bat thing? Did you know?"

"They told me." He got out, shut his door, then came around and opened mine, "But, you know," Tully said, giving me a brief, wry smile, "There are some things you have to see for yourself to believe."

Appreciating his irony, I thought about Steve and his Apple Squirrel Girl. I would have to make sure he knew I believed him.

Finder's mother opened the door as if she'd been expecting us. In under a minute she had us settled at the small round kitchen table with steaming mugs of strong black tea laced heavily with honey and cream. The bloody scarf went straight to the laundry. A plate of hot biscuits and a tub of soft butter appeared soon thereafter. Mama stood as tall as her daughter, but where Finder was buff and athletic, Mama was statuesque. She wore her hair slicked back in a bun. Her royal blue sweat suit matched the checks on her curtains and dishtowels. Her pink terry slippers were as pristine as her countertops. I hadn't been in her kitchen more than two minutes before I loved Finder's mother completely with all of my heart.

After making sure we had enough hot liquids and carbs, she went to wake up Finder, returning alone, but with a basket of rumpled first aid supplies that looked about as old as I was.

"We don't get hurt much," she said by way of explanation, "but gauze is gauze whenever you use it, eh?" She smiled just like her daughter, all teeth, and turned to wet a washcloth in the sink.

"Take off that sweater, baby." She cleaned my neck, washing the wound several times until all the blood was gone. She advanced to dipping cotton balls and Q-tips in at least four different solutions, one of which smelled like rotten fruit, and dabbing, pressing and squeezing them on my wound. During all this, Tully doctored his own minor cuts and scrapes and told Mama his version of the whole story.

I listened closely despite various degrees of stinging, burning and jabbing moments of pain. There were an algebraic number of differences, Tully solving for X while I solved for Y. Mama seemed non-plussed. She nodded and um-hmmmed, and even once exclaimed "He didn't!" when he told her how the Bat Suit who'd bitten me recoiled with a Star of David burned into his hand.

My forehead relaxed. Bat Suits. Funny.

This Goth girl I knew from New York - mid-thought, pain-fire burst in my head like someone smacked the back of my eyeballs. I finished the thought. This Goth girl I knew from New York would say that Bat Suits would go along with the Bat Cave, Bat Mobile, Bat Phone, etc.

Pain-fire splintered behind my eyes. It grew in intensity spreading through my face. I dropped my head into my hands.

"You okay, baby?"

I described the pain. Mama's forehead scrunched in concern.

We were going to have to hurry if we meant to save Nicolai and Aegisthus from whatever the real vampires had in store for them.

After a minute, the pain dissipated. By the time Finder came into the kitchen fully dressed and armed, Mama, who'd introduced herself as Letitia Jackson, had Tully and I scarfing down fresh scrambled eggs with extra biscuits, gravy and home fried potatoes heated up in her microwave.

"Sweet Jesus, Layla," she said, appraising her daughter. "You can't go see Glen Bacon dressed like that."

Tall, Gorgeous and Cranky wore fatigue pants, a black turtleneck, and her field jacket. She held two thick dowels that matched the ones Tully wore in his boots. Around her waist hung a tool belt stocked with a rubber mallet, flashlight and some other things I couldn't see because of the coat. She looked wide-awake, something I didn't feel at 1:30 in the morning.

Finder came over and without asking peeled back my bandage for a peek. She looked me in the face.

"God you're stupid," she said. Then she leaned over and put her arms around my shoulders, hugging me hard. "Promise to do what I say tonight or I'm leaving you here."

"You can't stake him," I said, suspicious of her sudden change of heart and not at all sure I felt ready to go anywhere near those Bat Suits again. She shrugged.

"I will stake him. He left all those bruises on your arms!" She grabbed my arm and shoved up my sleeve. Sure enough, there was a massive bruise on my upper arm. That's weird, I thought. How had that happened?

"See the bruise down her neck?" Finder asked her mom. "That's not from tonight. She *went out* with him, the one she wants to save, last night. By herself! Says he didn't hurt her. Didn't feed on her, didn't attack her, no. But she shows up at school today covered in bruises with absolutely no idea where they came from! I'll tell you where they came from!"

"Finder. Nicolai's human," Tully said. The voice of reason. "He and Aegisthus both are."

She stared at him in disbelief.

I told the last part of the story.

"Nerf guns, homemade cards." I put mine on the table.

Finder picked it up and inspected it. Resist. She put it in her pocket.

"These must have been what Angela was looking for in her purse!" Tully said. "These little command cards."

"Nicolai gave this one to me right before the fight started. I think he thought the guys turning into men from bats was some kind of effect. He never seemed scared til he got bit."

Finder shook her head. "He endangered you by inviting you. He had to have known who was playing."

"He didn't. And he never meant for me to get hurt. He kept himself between me and them," I said. "He tried to defend me."

Mama nodded. She leveled her head with mine and pulled my eyelid up with her thumb. She looked first in one eye than the other. She sat back and regarded me, then spoke to Finder.

"Glen Bacon is the real problem."

"Speaking of real problems," I said, apprehensive. "Did my dad call?"

"I covered for you," Finder said scowling.

"Ohmygod. Thank you!" Then I paused. "Why?"

She shrugged. "Dunno."

"You must have some kind of magic, Stacy," Mama said to me. "Layla doesn't like anybody except Teularen. But you, she likes." She smiled.

"Yeah," Tully said. "Enough to call me at quarter to midnight and send me over to make sure you didn't get killed. In my own defense, I was walking out the door to do just that when she called."

"How did you know where I was?" I asked Finder, then realized that was a stupid question.

"I called Tully as soon as I hung up with your dad."

I looked at Tully. "You are a terrible secret keeper," I said.

"You're welcome," he replied.

"And I wouldn't want you to break your no-friends-but-Tully habit on my account," I said, looking up at Finder. I warmed my hands on the hot mug. "I'm not staying, anyway. Three years at most, then I'm out. So don't get too attached."

"Don't worry," Finder said. "You're still stupid."

Mama cleared her throat and surveyed her daughter.

"I'm not going to a graduation, Mama," she said.

"Ain't the point, Layla. Glen Bacon is a person of society."

"Glen Bacon is evil."

"I'm just saying you'll get a more positive response if you look nice."

Finder made this gravelly sighing sound and stalked out. Mama put more food on our plates. She sat down and absently buttered a biscuit.

"Layla says you're new to Richmond?"

"Yes, ma'am." I don't think I've ever said ma'am in my life, but it seemed natural and appropriate with Mama.

"And how do you find it here?" Her face was open, interested. I didn't know how to answer that question without insulting her home.

"I'm getting used to it," I said. "Except for this." I gestured to my bite.

"Hazard of the South," she said, propping her feet up on the empty kitchen chair. "Don't worry, it didn't get you good enough to do any real damage."

Real damage as in turn me into a vampire? Or real damage as in send me to the hospital for stitches or surgery? Mama went to the stove. She poured steaming mugs of something that smelled like apple pie, setting them down in front of Tully and me, then bringing two more, one for Finder, one for herself. I sipped. Spiced cider.

"Mrs. Jackson, I think you're my hero."

"Call me Mama." Convert her initial mugs of tea into lattes and I wanted to be just like Mama when I grew up.

"You sure must miss home, don't you, baby?"

I nodded.

"Shocking what happened. I couldn't believe those buildings coming down like that. All those poor souls. I prayed for them, I tell you. We all did." She looked at me like I was supposed to say something.

"It was scary," I said. The understatement of the year.

"When you going home to visit?"

I thought of my grandmother and my Goth Princess friend. Pain-fire smacked me behind the eyes. I gasped. My hand shot to my head.

"What's the matter?" Mama said.

I caught my breath. "It's this weird pain," I said. "I've never felt anything like it. It keeps sneaking up on me out of nowhere."

Mama got up and stood beside my chair. She took my forehead in one pink palm and the back of my head in her other hand.

"Breathe, baby."

I did, long and slow and deep.

"It goes away fast," I said as the ache subsided. Her hands were comforting, like pulling a heavy blanket over your shoulders.

"Did I teach you how to do this, Teularen?"

"The crown polarity thing? Yes."

"You can do it with any of the chakras. You just have to put your hands on or a few inches above the physical body."

My head cooled as Mama let go.

"You have a lot of God in you, Stacy," she said, voice full of something soft and relaxing. Love? Affection? She looked at me as if she'd known me a long time. "Do you know that?"

"I'm not sure I even believe in God."

"You do. It's okay if it's unacknowledged, but you do."

"Your energy is forceful," Tully said, raising his mug for a sip. "It's raw, but clear and honest. Maybe it's why you can handle Layla. She's forceful too, but in a different way than you." He looked at Mama. "I think divine connection is how she burned that vamp," Tully said as if I wasn't sitting right there. "We did a protection at her house and her chakras started vibrating as soon as I opened mine up. She's very resonant."

"I can see that. She doesn't have a lot in the way," Mama said.

"I have no idea what you're talking about," I said.

"Teularen will teach you."

"I will?"

"In time. Tonight all you need to know is that your friends need you. That should take care of everything."

"Assuming I survive the night?" I asked.

"Don't worry. Layla knows what she's doing," Mama said. "Now, look at me and let me ask you some questions."

She asked me a lot of questions about last night. I told her everything that happened. I told her about the Terminator Bat Suits and AGB telling me to run. I told her about the trip to the hospital and the crazy yelling lady and my night of nightmares. At one point she stopped me, made me retell a couple sections, one about Nicolai and my conversation at Hollywood Cemetery, and one about not being able to climb on my bike.

My neck wound had turned to a dull ache under its bandage. The image of Tully lying in a heap next to his sword blazed fresh in my mind. I knew why the Stinky Bat Suit had dumped me as his next meal, but I couldn't think about that right now. Not on top of everything else. I was lucky it was him who'd grabbed me because anyone else might've killed me. We had to get Nicolai and Aegisthus out of there. This was not a game.

It all seemed so normal here in Mama's kitchen. Yes, child. Come in, get your wounds cleaned and have a hot, midnight breakfast before going out to fight the vampires. I wanted to ask how she had found out, why she knew what she knew, but when I opened my mouth to ask, it felt wrong. The taboo around asking personal questions felt as thick as with my father, even though I sensed Mama was a much more open person. I decided to try something new. I minded my business and ate.

Finder came back into the kitchen wearing black dress pants and a matching long coat with velvet cuffs and collar. The tool belt was fastened around her waist, with the mallet and other big things mostly covered by the long suit jacket. She spread her arms for Mama's approval.

"Much better," Mama said, leaning forward to pick a bit of lint off the jacket. "Don't get blood on it. Sit down, baby." She pushed Finder's cider mug in front of her. "I think we may have a bigger problem here." She leaned forward resting her forearms on the checkered blue and white tablecloth. "I believe Stacy is telling the truth about Nicolai. He is obviously human and did not hurt her."

"Are you kidding?" Finder said, pushing her chair back so hard she almost dumped her cider.

"Common neuroscience, baby. She didn't blink, she kept my gaze, she didn't stumble or even look down and to the right, which liars usually do. If she is lying, she's a master."

Finder stood, outraged. "But the bruises!"

"I think something happened between when she left Nicolai and when her dad came and got her," Mama said. "I don't know what it could have been, but her memories are inconsistent about that time. Like you say, she has bruises we can't explain. I say an attack doesn't fit the profile of the boy she describes, plus, her pupils dilate when she tries to remember why she went to the hospital. Something's missing. Something important."

"How do we find it?" Tully asked.

"We don't. We just notice. We avoid making assumptions without proof. We ask Glen Bacon to release the prisoners."

"Is there any other way?" I said. "Other than marching in with demands? Those bat guys, suit guys, they're powerful. I mean, I couldn't scream or speak or even move when he told me not to. No way will we win a fight against that!"

Finder thunked her mug on the table.

"I now induct thee, Stacy Rachel Goldman, into the hall of believers, for one must be truly terrified before the truth can be seen."

"How bad did it hurt when he bit you?" Mama asked.

"Bad," I said.

"Did he take more than blood? It hurts a lot worse when they take more than blood."

"What do you mean?"

She looked at Finder and Tully. "Did y'all not tell her?"

Finder looked sheepish.

"How many times do I have to tell you, Layla? Withholding information is dangerous! It's worse than telling nothing! You either give the whole story or you give none!" She shook her head and looked at me. "You can only do so much with teenagers, you know? Think they already know everything." She shot her daughter a glare so dark Finder flinched. "In movies, vampires suck your blood." Mama squared her face with mine. "In real life, they also suck your soul."

She got up and poured me another cider from the pot. "They are capable of just sucking blood. It keeps their physical form alive, if you call it alive." She turned back to me and put the mug on the table. "But they need essence, they need something to fuel their consciousness so they aren't just zombies.

"Some do become zombies, those that won't or, for God knows why, can't suck souls. No one has figured out which it is. They become walking animated corpses who drink blood and leave bodies in their wake. Very nasty critters, them. Vicious as a werewolf, but in a more direct and mindless kind of way. Eat this last biscuit before you go. Teularen's waistline doesn't need it." She winked at him. "What you're up against, they use your soul to maintain consciousness, cuz theirs disappeared when they died."

"How do I know" I said, voice trembling, "if it sucked my soul?" My breath came in short pants.

Stinky Bat Suit could take an actual part of me? Not just my blood? What part did it take?

The room around me got smaller. A weight came on my chest, heavy and suffocating. I couldn't breathe well and I couldn't stop it. Jill had described this to me, the inability to breathe, feeling like a piano sat on your chest, feeling trapped and helpless.

"I think I'm having," I choked on my breath and coughed. "A panic attack."

"Nonsense," said Mama. "Get a hold of yourself, girl. Eat that biscuit."

I took a bite. Mama pulled a chair across from mine and turned my chair sideways to the table. She put her hands on my knees. "You're a fighter now. Chew and swallow. Does it need more butter?"

I shook my head.

"Teularen, get me the Rescue Remedy." She turned her attention back to me. "Look at me. Imagine you have a big golden ball at your heart. Close your eyes. Picture it." She took the biscuit out of my hand.

I did, big golden ball at my chest. Got it. My chest immediately began to feel warm and spacious.

"Now pull that ball into your body. Imagine it soaking into your skin like it's a real thing. Good." She paused. "Now pull the golden energy out of that ball. Draw it like electric current to a socket. Bring it through your arms and legs to your hands and feet and up through the top of your head. Open your eyes."

I felt warm and awake, but relaxed. My breathing was normal and the room stopped shrinking. I felt strange. Strong and capable in a different way than usual.

Mama took a little spray bottle from Tully. "It's flower essences," she said and gestured for me to hold out my wrist. She spritzed. It smelled good. She put her hands back on my knees. I didn't know when she had taken them off.

"That is how to get God to help you, baby. You take His energy into you and give yourself over to being an instrument for Him. You can call it what you want, God, Divine Intelligence, Nature, it don't matter. What matters is that you surrender and let it help you. Listen Stacy, belief is irrelevant. That vampire sucked your blood whether you believed in him or not, right?"

"Right."

"What you believe and what is real are often two different things. You saw those bad creatures, right? They exist?"

"Yes."

"Then by the law of nature, doesn't the opposite also have to exist? Like I said, you're a fighter now. Fighters don't get panic attacks. Layla said you wanted to help people? This is how you will do it. You will be whatever that boy called you. Stacy Goldman, Renegade Vampire Hunter? Well, that's you now. It's not a role you're playing and it is no game. These things are real and you have stumbled into their world because it is God's will that you do, do you understand?" Her eyes glowed bright and intense. "This is your destiny. You. And Layla. And Teularen. So finish that biscuit, get over yourself and go tonight and do your work." She put her hand around my arm and squeezed. "This won't do, Layla. She's skin and bone. You need to get this child in the gym."

I finished the biscuit. Mama's talk hadn't made me feel any more confident in what we were doing tonight, but it had made me feel secure in myself. Strong and real and grounded in a new way. Still, as I finished eating I worried, what part of me had Stinky Bat Suit stolen?

I hugged Mama goodbye at the front door. She hugged me back and shoved an extra sweatshirt into my arms.

"Thanks so much," I said, "for the food and cleaning me up," I rambled on.

"You're welcome, Stacy. Come back anytime." She patted my cheek then turned to Tully. "Don't you come back here boy," she said affectionately, "until you're ready to eat some meat." He smiled.

"Oh I'll be back before then, Mama, don't you worry."

"Not if I'm at the door," she said. "You aren't crossing this doorstep without a T-bone between those teeth, do you hear? Vegetarian . . ." She shook her head.

"Bye Ma," Finder said. She held a tool box in one hand.

"You listen to me, baby," she said, reaching up to straighten the jacket collar. "They. Are. Evil. They'd rather bring you with them then send you home in pieces. Shoot first, ask questions later. And if they try to bite you, poke 'em in the eyes. It's the eyes have the power anyway." She turned to me. "And I'm not bandaging you twice in one night so you stop looking in their eyes in the first place. Pretend your daddy's a janitor, not a lawyer."

I must've looked confused because she clarified.

"Pretend you were raised not to look anybody in the eye, baby." Righto. She squeezed me one more time then kissed my cheek. She shooed us all out the door.

"Ready?" Finder said.

"Will we ever be?" Tully replied and unlocked the truck.

"Hey Finder," I said, getting an idea. "Do you have your multi-tool?"

24.

November 16, continued. 3:01 a.m.

We went over Finder's plan one more time on the way from my house to Maymont. I didn't like it. We had stopped to sneak my overnight and school stuff out of the pool house and on the way I had tried to convince her that her strategy needed more to it than Walk In, Make Demands, Fight Our Way Out. I was scared of those Bat Suits and there was no way I could fight my way out if things went wrong. Tully had barely fought his way out of the museum and who knows what would have happened if Matilda hadn't called off her Bald Bat Suit. Before getting out of the truck, I pushed the little light button on my watch. 3:04. Ugh. School started at 7:25.

I got out and an icy wind cut right through my clothes. I shivered. I knew I'd regret leaving my coat in the truck, but it's weight would slow me down if/ when I had to fight or run. Or both. Besides it served a safety purpose. It covered my uniform, backpack and overnight stuff we'd retrieved from the pool house.

On went the loaner hoodie.

I held my stake in one hand then the other trying to get comfortable holding it. They'd shown me the basics at the dojo and reviewed them on the ride over, point and shove, but I had no confidence in my ability to successfully stake anything thicker than a piece of toast. My neck ached. I'd seen enough blood for one night. On the bright side, my dad believed me snug in bed at my new friend's house after an evening of academic pursuits. I couldn't think about how I'd explain my vampire bite right now. Hi Dad, I've got a big bite wound on my neck, I'm missing an unnamed piece of myself and I was late for school? No. My brain might explode.

Frosty grass crunched beneath our shoes as we headed for the Maymont Mansion entrance.

"Nicolai said you're a legend," I said trying to keep up with my friends. "That you can track supers of any kind."

"Supers?"

"What supernatural beings call themselves. According to him." I jogged to catch up to my walking friends. Long legs vs. short ones. Size does matter.

"He was playing a game. Everything he told you was fake."

"He knew you. He told me that someone in your family got sick and changed into a vampire. Your dad went missing looking for him. Is that what happened?"

Finder stopped and looked at me. "He knew that?"

"He said you developed your ability to find supernatural creatures after that. You're a legend."

"But he's just a gamer."

I shrugged. "Was he telling the truth?"

She was silent.

"There's more to it than that," Tully said. "But the main points are accurate enough."

We approached the wrought iron gate. Easily almost twice my height. And locked.

"You're sure they're here?" I said.

Tully laced his fingers together and bent his knees.

Finder put her boot in his hands, looked down at me and said, "They're here." Utter confidence. Okay, then. And I still wanted to know what happened to her dad. Right now, though, I wanted to know how Tully planned to get me over that fence. Finder hoisted herself up from the boost, pushing up on the top cross bar with her hands. She swung a leg up, catching it firmly on the bar. Holding the fleur de lis, a French leaf/spear looking symbol that topped each post, Finder upped and overed with the ease of a cat burglar.

I stared, impressed.

"Eight years of gymnastics," she said.

Great. I'd had eight years of chess. How in heck was I getting over that fence? Pawn promotion?

Tully basketed his hands like he had for Finder.

"Is there another gate? Like a lower one somewhere? Maybe around the back?"

I eyed Finder hoping she would agree that hoisting me over this fence was a bad idea. She put one hand on her hip.

"Boot in the basket, Goldman."

No more Warrior Goddess friends for me, I thought. I had other friends.

"Ow!" Pain-fire behind my eyes. It blistered. My shoulders hunched and my chin fell to my chest, eyes squeezed shut.

"What happened?" Tully reached out to steady me.

Nicolai was in danger. I needed to get over this fence.

Pain-fire faded.

"Sorry. That headache thing again. I'm okay now."

Stepping one foot in and grabbing the iron, I held on.

"You have to jump kind of," he said.

"What do you mean?"

"I mean it's not an elevator ride. You have to boost yourself."

Oh.

He gave me another lift. I grabbed for the top bar. Missed. Tried again and got it. I braced my right foot on the vertical bar while Tully pushed my left up high as he could reach. I lost my balance and grabbed for the fleur de lis.

"I think I'm stuck," I said, muscles trembling as I braced my foot against the bar.

"Tully, keep her left. Stacy, squeeze your abs and pull up hard."

I did and got my other hand to brace on the cross bar.

"Pull your knee up and get it on the bar."

Grunting, I did.

"Good. Now, swing your left foot over." To my own utter astonishment, I managed it. The freezing iron burned my hands.

"You could just jump," Finder said as I got my other leg over and looked at my options for descent.

"Nope." The drop was just too far.

It took Finder another minute to coach me the rest of the way down, but she did, catching my legs as I eased myself toward the ground, hand over frozen hand.

Tully gave himself a short running start, jumped and ran a few feet up the fence to grab the cross bar. His climb over the top was surprisingly graceful for such a big guy. The enormous expanse of lawn in front of Maymont Mansion was dotted with shadows as clouds passed over the moon. Halfway up the lawn, Finder stopped in one of those shadows, closed her eyes and rubbed her thumbs across her finger tips.

Why were we stoping? Bat Suits might already be on their way to mesmerize our minds. Or stake us, or turn us into juice boxes. No. Thank. You. The only thing I wanted was to get Nicolai, Finder, Tully, Aegisthus and myself out of here alive so I could walk away from monster world forever and get home to sane, peaceful New York.

I'd tell Finder and Tully it had been nice knowing them, then find some normal math nerds to keep me company for my stay in Richmond. I might just ditch people all together. If I refused to speak, I'd get ostracized like Albino Atheist Chick. Just survive so you can get back to New York, I thought. Home to the real world, the City. Beautiful New York. Sweet New York. Where monsters like this did not exist. Or if they did, they had the decency to get out of the way of your umbrella when it rained and ride the subway like everyone else. Early graduation was becoming a must.

The top of my head began to buzz in what was becoming a familiar way.

"What's she doing?" I asked Tully. "It's making the top of my head tingle again."

"She's finding," he said. "It opens up her energy. Probably opening your chakras, too."

Chakras. What were they? He hadn't explained the first time I'd asked. Tully surveyed the area, glancing at Warrior Goddess Finder every few seconds. "Watch behind us," he said to me, keeping his gaze on the wide stone Victorian mansion. It hovered, a three story mini-castle in front of us.

I turned to eye the fence for Bat Suits. "What's a chakra?"

"They're everywhere," Finder said, an edge in her voice I'd never heard. "The house, the barn. The greenhouse. The gardens."

Vampires 'everywhere' was not covered in Finder's strategy. Her plan relied on them being in one place.

"Crap."

"How many in each place?" Tully asked. "Can you find just Glen Bacon?"

Her current plan would not work. We needed to stay out of groups of them. It was in Glen Bacon's best interest to out number us. And we were way too vulnerable out here in the middle of the yard. Glen Bacon had no guarantee we would come to the rescue of Nicolai and Aegisthus, but it was to his advantage if we did.

Any place we could get to here, he defended more times than we attacked. Three of us to how many Bat Suits? And did I even count in a fight? Attacking a square with more defenders than you had attackers was a recipe for losing material, material being in this case, our lives and the lives of our friends. Our arrival alone gave him more potential Bat Suits or offspring or whatever, or just increased his/ their food supply. In chess terms, developed his material. If he was manipulating the mortal world, our arrival also developed his position, gaining him possibly more influence. Worst of all, we gave him fuel for tactics. He could use us as bait to entrap the others into doing whatever he said, or he could do the same to us. Deeply not good, from my perspective.

He had chosen an aggressive opening at the museum, capturing our pieces and wiping out pawns. No subtlety. I knew players like that. If I knew anything about chess, this predicated a game where he wouldn't hesitate to capture as much as possible or just plain kill until we were so underpowered that he could move in for an easy mate. It would be a direct game, and carnage would not be out of the question.

Playing black, we had to reply with strength, also not fearing carnage. The most important thing we could do was surprise him. Not in the opening, but in the middle game if we could, and definitely in the endgame. We couldn't prevent our weak army, we'd already lost a tempo because of my injuries and the actual kidnapping. We'd added a rook, Finder, and a knight, Tully. Unless I could figure out how to force Glen Bacon's moves and trap him, we were done. I had to use his own pieces against him. I had to block his development and squash his potential for action in a classic smothered mate. If I couldn't do this, we could kiss our lives goodbye.

"We have to smother him," I said out loud. "We have to force or block his moves. It's the only way."

Finder and Tully looked at me.

"Game theory," I said. "Glen Bacon is playing a game. It's not the same one that Nicolai and Aegisthus were playing, but it's a game nonetheless." They came a little closer. "Matilda laughed through the whole fight. At one point she applauded! This is fun for them. Glen Bacon's aggressive. Aggressive players are bullies. They take straightforward action with the intent of inspiring fear and crushing you. That's where they're strong. Glen Bacon has Bat Suits. He's already captured two of our pieces. Nicolai and Aegisthus. Aggressive players, even smart ones, have a weakness. They overlook the small pieces. They get so involved in capturing material and wiping out your obvious strengths that they underestimate how you can trap them.

"That's how we can gain advantage. We have to push on his weakness if we want to win. Right now, his weakness is that he wants something from Nicolai and Aegisthus and maybe from us. So we have to make him think he's going to get it while we block him from developing any more strength.

I predict that Finder is going to be the target. She's the strongest fighter," I looked at Tully, sorry. He nodded. "So he's going to go after her first, you'll be next and I'll be either ignored or wiped out if it's convenient to get me out of the way."

"Those are different things," said Finder.

"Yes. We have to be prepared for both. The way we do that is stop him from moving his pieces. We need to block his actions. How can we do that?"

"We can't," Finder said. "That's crazy."

"It's not! We just have to figure out how."

I know this seems like a lot of thinking, but from Finder stoping to do her Finder mojo and the end of that last sentence was less than two minutes. I talk fast.

That's when we heard the singing. Off in the distance, it came carried to us on a cold gust of wind.

"Laaaay-la do de de de de da do badadobedadada . . ." Glen Bacon was not going to give us a tempo or a free move. We had made it over the fence. Our move. Now, someone was coming. His move, advance. And he knew it was us. How did he know Finder was here? Should we attack, defend or retreat?

I yanked the mirrored sunglasses Finder had given me from her toolbox off my collar where I had tucked them and put them on over my regular glasses. Not fun, but necessary. The moonlight, shadows and everything in between got a few shades darker. Finder and Tully did the same. Mirrored glasses wouldn't defend us from mind control powers if we looked in their eyes, but anything to help prevent eye contact was welcome.

The vampires had powers we did not have, they knew we were here and they had two human captives. Three huge advantages. Most likely, the majority of Bat Suits would be guarding Nicolai and Aegisthus. They may have already been killed or turned. Their capture could be an elaborate plan to lure us in and get five Bat Suits for the price of two.

Keep your mind on the mate. In my minds eye, Rabbi Berman put his hands together and blessed my game.

Finder started walking. Toward the singer.

"Where are you going?" I hissed. I didn't grab her arm. Tully did.

"Wait," he said to his girlfriend. "We should listen to Stacy."

Finder turned to him. "I can't avoid this."

"Just wait until we have a plan."

"We have a plan," I said. "Block his moves, smother him for mate. What would he expect us to do right now.?"

Finder scanned the lawn. "Run."

"From the singer?"

"Trust me. He thinks I'll run."

"Then there's an ambush in the direction we'd run. You think the house?"

Tully nodded. I had his full attention. "We'll go to the singer instead," I said. "Will Bat Suits be waiting? Will we have to fight?"

"Bat Suits?"

"Sorry. It's what I call the," my voice trailed off as Tully snorted.

"Bat Suits," he said. "Like the Bat Cave. That's funny."

"Now is not a time to be funny!" Finder scolded. The song came again, louder, still far away, but closer this time. "Fight or not, we have to move!" She started walking. Tully and I kept up.

The trouble with more than one mind at work, we couldn't plan moves ahead. I didn't know Glen Bacon's board or how many pieces he even had. I didn't know if this game was one of many, meaning part of a larger game or collection of games like in a tournament, or if this was his big one and only. Finally, I knew what checkmate was for me, but not what mate would be for him. What was he playing to win? I had to use what I knew, my mate, and get creative. I was going to need a surprise ending. To get that I had to identify one thing: the most direct path to mate.

"Can you find humans?" I asked, keeping up to them. "Have you ever tried to find people?"

Finder said nothing.

"What exactly do you do?" I asked as we walked. "How do you know you're right?"

She sighed. "Can we just take care of this? I have a Latin quiz first period."

I promised myself to get Jill to shrink her. ASAP. Assuming I survived the night. And kept Finder as a friend after this. The girl had issues. I didn't know what they were, but they were definitely there.

"Can you take us straight to Nicolai and Aegisthus?" I said.

"I don't. Know where. They are." She walked faster. I jogged to stay beside her.

"Have you ever *tried* finding regular people?"

"No!" she hissed. "No, I haven't and no I can't, so get off my back!"

"How do you know you can't if you've never tried? What if you can?" Tully touched my shoulder, message clear. I got it, back off, but now was not a good time for backing. Lives were at stake. Including ours! We needed every tool, every and any advantage we could get.

"I want you to try."

"No, Stacy."

"Your idea to negotiate isn't going to work! He has way too much man power for us to defeat. Your mom's strategy of negotiate and fight our way out, won't work either. This guy is a bully! He wants a body count! I know how these people think."

"He's not a person."

"A bully is a bully, supernatural or not." I ran a couple paces to get in front of her. Even just that little bit made my lungs tight with cold. I gulped in a breath.

"Can't you trust me? I beat Joseph Thornton. I beat his friends. I'm telling you! Glen Bacon is afraid to lose his power. That's why Nicolai playing a pretend game about being a vampire is a threat. He feeds on fear, including yours!

Come on Finder, please try! He won't expect us to go straight to the prisoners!"

She picked up her pace jogging toward the voice, singing again, louder now. A lot closer. She had a stake in each shadowy, moonlit fist. I stopped and put my palms on my knees, catching my breath. Tully stayed at Finder's side but checked on me over his shoulder. Was I coming?

I was not. I had to get some air.

In front of me, my friends jerked themselves to a halt.

One Bat Suit, a tall, forty-something Black man stepped into the light opening his arms in welcome.

"Can I have a hug?"

Finder stiffened, flipping a stake in her hand.

"Hi, Dad."

25.

November 16, continued. 3:16 a.m.

Hi Dad? My jaw hung slack in shock. I closed it. *Hi Dad?*
The silence was thick.

"I'm happy to see you, Layla." He was handsome in a traditional African way, wide nose, broad smile, skin like hers. Dark darker darkest. "You look good."

"Can't say the same."

"Come back to the house please, Darcy. Bring your daughter with you." A voice I had heard before, floating on the breeze. Attached to nothing.

"He has no influence over me," Finder said, not taking her eyes or the aim of her stake off her father. "You won't win this way."

"Ah, my dear," came the sweet voice, "It's not if you win or lose, but how you play the game."

"You here for the game?" Finder's father's face fell. "I thought maybe you had a change of heart." He held out his hand. "Maybe came to see me. To make a deal for my soul."

"You don't have a soul anymore, Dad. It's too late for that."

Finder's father took a step closer.

"Stay where you are, sir," Tully said, leveling the point of his blade.

"Why don't you take off those glasses? I miss seeing my baby's beautiful eyes." Finder's dad spoke only to her. Tully maintained the aim of his steel. He stepped forward sliding the sword in between Finder and her dad.

Finder's father raised his hands, backing up a step.

"It's nice to see you, too, Teularen," he said. "You've always been such a good friend to Layla."

"Thank you, sir."

"I hope you wouldn't really chop me to bits with that."

"Wouldn't hesitate, sir," Tully said. "Nothing personal."

I couldn't grasp it. Finder's *dad* was one of Glen Bacon's Bat Suits? Finder's father edged closer.

Tully's height and mass made him intimidating. At home with steel in his grip, his muscles engaged, he looked confident and ready to sweep and strike. I held ground on Tully's right, standing tall as I could, squaring my shoulders to look like I meant business. I held Finder's stake with both hands.

"Come on, baby," Dad/Bat Suit said. "Just one hug?"

As if on cue, the air sucked out of the space pulling the three of us apart with force. I fell backward onto my behind, Tully's hair clung as if glued to his face. Finder ducked her head and stood, stakes out, unmoving. And then whoosh!

The air refilled our lungs with a painful burst and the Bat Suits arrived. I recognized four of the, counted quickly, seven Bat Suits. Bald Suit, Terminator Suit, Goatee Suit, and Silver Tie. Matilda linked arms with Finder's father and kissed his cheek.

"Darcy dear, I told you to bring her to the house. You know I loathe waiting." Seven Suits plus Finder's dad, and Matilda. Three to one.

I said there would be an ambush. I said Finder would be the target. Should've listened to me! I scrambled for a solution. Retreat? Nope, they had too much muscle. Attack? Nope, again too much muscle. Defend was our only option. Unless I could create a diversion.

"You are much prettier than I was told," Matilda said as if only Finder stood before her. Finder tipped her chin up, looking over the petite woman's head. I searched for a place to hook my gaze so I could avoid Matilda's mesmerizing, but still see her shift her weight for an attack. Where I landed was too embarrassing. I adjusted my eye line thinking shoulders, shoulders.

"Layla, is it? Darcy your singing is excellent but your descriptive skills are woefully incompetent. She's stunning."

"My business is with Glen Bacon," Finder announced.

"Oh! That's so sweet! Are you in this little play, too?"

"It's no play. Two humans are hostage here and we've come to get them back."

Matilda laughed and clapped her hands. "This is more fun than I've had all century. Are you pretending to be one of us as well?"

"I am not!"

"Oh, too bad. I love these little cards." She pulled a handful of the homemade cards out of her pocket and rifled through them. "This one is my favorite. Magnetize. Wouldn't it be so cute if I had to actually wave a little card at the people before they came and asked me to eat them? It's given me some ideas about how to introduce myself at the Richmond society parties, though. The absolute tastiest children show up there. They're kind of one shot deals, and I never get to finish the meal, but they are so adorable. My mother taught me a lady always leaves some food on her plate so she doesn't look greedy. I only get to go once every fifty years as my own granddaughter and great granddaughter and so on. Otherwise, some clever elf might figure out how long I've been here and that would never do."

At last, a weakness. She fears being found out by society. It set the wheels whirling in my mind.

"So do we fight or trade or negotiate or what?" Finder demanded. "We have school tomorrow, I mean today, and it's time we got on with this."

"Is she rushing me?" Matilda asked Darcy. "Oh sweetie, no rushing Mother Matilda now. Didn't your Daddy teach you manners? Never insult, or rush, someone in her own home." Matilda shook back her curls. I noticed she looked a little older than I had originally thought at the museum. Maybe somewhere in her forties. "Now, let's be clear about one thing, Glen Bacon is the sir name of my family. You clearly did not do your research before coming over. Another manners no-no!" She wiggled her finger at Finder like she was a naughty puppy. "I am Matilda Elizabeth Glen Bacon, my daughter is Sallie Mae Glen Bacon and so on and so forth. Our genealogical chart is in the city records because we are such an important family originally from England but I'm afraid my Queen's English is faded and I sound almost American now. So sad. All of these little pretenders believing in someone named just Glen Bacon amused me so, I have allowed the play to go on.

"I play the hapless beauty and Darcy here plays the lead, guess who? Glen Bacon!" She laughed, weird hysterical laughter. "My darling gentlemen butlers are the supporting cast."

It occurred to me Matilda might be throwing a false lead, but I think she feared being alone. She might just be talking to bask in the attention. I filed that away.

"Don't you want to visit with your father?" she said. "I brought him over especially for you. You should get his advice. Did you know he is wonderful with stocks? Told me to buy this little thing with the most attractive name, Starbucks! Have you heard of it? They sell addictive drugs legally and he was so right! I make money hand over fist on that stock. And this other new company named after a rainforest.. I think they're going places. You should see my portfolio. I truly do rely on my sweet Darcy."

"I want Nicolai and Aegisthus released."

"Why? They will be far more useful to me. And they love pretending to be like us. Think of how much they will enjoy being able to," she read the skills of the cards "Stun, freeze, hide, speed, truth, and magnetize without having to wave these little cards?"

We couldn't beat the seven Bat Suits closing in on us in a fight. We were so going to end up eaten unless Finder could talk us out of this. I did not doubt her as a fighter, or as a chemistry lab partner, but her ability to talk us out of this without bloodshed? Unlikely. Leaning forward on her toes, Finder looked eager, maybe even hopeful this chat would come to blows. Tully also looked excited, entirely prepared to swing his dragon slicer. I saw my chances of survival as slim if fists flew and I didn't relish the idea of becoming a blood and soul milkshake. I had to act before Matilda got bored and launched the melee. I tucked the stake in my belt and pulled out the worn crucifix. God help us if I fail.

"Call off your bats, Matilda, and no one gets hurt," I said. Finder shot me a glare. Matilda arched an eyebrow.

"Is she threatening me, darling?" She nuzzled Darcy.

"I'm telling you the truth."

Goatee Bat Suit on my right sneaked forward. I brandished my cross at him. He stopped.

"What truth? That three mortal children can defeat my gentlemen butlers?"

"Did I say that? I said, if you let the prisoners go, no one gets hurt."

"Namely yourselves." Matilda laughed.

"No. I meant you." I pulled aside my hoodie to display my neck bandage. "One of your gentleman butlers bit me tonight, Mrs. Bacon."

"Mrs. Bacon! Oh, a true southern touch, dear," she said, delighted.

"If I start publicly praising the Lord, with this mark of the devil on my throat, every fundamentalist, evangelical and superstitious vampire loving yahoo below and above the Mason-Dixon Line will leap on board to hunt Satan spawn. And," I added, "I don't know how familiar you are with fundamentalists, but they believe it's an honor to die for their cause."

"How about you?" Matilda asked. "Will you die for your cause?"

I shrugged my shoulders. "I'm fifteen. What else do I have to do?" In my head I said, *I am alive, I am safe. Nothing bad is happening.*

"So why again shouldn't I just eat you all?" Matilda asked. It was my turn to laugh out loud.

"Have you heard of police? Of missing persons? The internet? Three top students at Richmond's most prestigious prep school vanish on the same night from a popular public park and mansion? This place will crawl with law enforcement by daylight, all looking for you."

"You're serious, aren't you?"

"I am."

"I thought you might be playing," she said. "I see I," she paused, searching, "underestimated your level of commitment."

"Give us your prisoners and we'll keep your filthy secrets," Finder demanded. "Keep the prisoners and we'll do whatever we have to do to make you miserable for as long as possible."

Matilda considered for a moment. Then a happy expression brightened her face.

"In honor of my prisoners, as you call them, and your foolish but courageous rescue attempt, I think it's my turn to start a game." Finder, Tully and I stood silent, glaring at the thirsty Bat Suits, waiting for their leader's suggestion. I waggled my cross at Goatee Suit who had again edged closer. He winced and stepped back. I wonder how the cross made him feel. Matilda spoke.

"If you can find your friends before my gentlemen butlers capture you, then you may all go free with my congratulations. If we catch you, you become mine. To do with as I wish. Assuming you'd be killed may not be accurate," she said. "I could use a few good mortal servants, and one of you is already somewhat in the family." Matilda smiled. I shivered. Finder's spine stiffened and Tully made his sword practically growl at delighted looking Bat Suit Dad.

"Teams and time?" I said. Her eyebrows shot together. "It's a game right? Everyone starts a game on equal ground. Same number of pieces, same amount of time. Same amount of Monopoly money, whatever. There's three of us -- "

"Technically five," Darcy said.

"Shut up, Dad."

"Two of them don't even know they're playing," I said.

"Oh they know they're playing," said Matilda. "Just not this game."

"That's not fair!" I leveled my cross at her.

"True," she said, "And it is too bad, but I could just kill you now instead."

"Wouldn't be as much fun," I said.

"That's true, too. Then let's play five to five." She clapped her hands together in delight. "Like that game with the basket!"

"Basketball," said Darcy.

"You know the territory," I said. "We don't. An unfair advantage as you challenged us."

"Fine," she said. My eyes stayed on her feet, but I imagined her rolling her eyes. "Four on five."

"And you sit out," Finder shot in.

"What?" she said. "No! Why should I?" She sounded pouty.

"We're starting with only three players," I offered. "If you sit out, we both have three players to begin." Matilda pressed a finger to her lips. I looked back at her feet. Careful, I thought. I remembered the feeling of being magnetized to her at the museum. It was hard to resist the comfort of it.

She tapped her lips. I knew that pause. That was the bully making a decision pause, when the aggressive player can't decide whether to smite you then and there or save your smiting for later. I didn't trust that pause. I didn't want her having too much time to think. I needed to distract her.

"I'll sit out," she said, letting her hand fall from her mouth. "For an hour. But then I join the game."

"So for the first hour it's three on three," I said.

"Not exactly," she said. "If our strongest player sits out," she sighed and though I stared hard at her feet, I thought I heard her smile. "Then so does yours."

Faster than Tully or I could react, the seven Bat Suits descended on Finder. She landed a stake in the shoulder of Silver Tie. He grunted and cursed. Her foot flew to kick Terminator in the face. Tully drew his blade. I snatched a stake in one hand and a cross in the other. Before we had even completed our actions, Silver Tie yanked out the stake and threw it on the ground. The rest of the Bat Suits upped off the ground and hovered over our heads in the sky. And then whoosh! Still in man form, clutching Finder, they flew off.

When we tore our gaze from the sky, and from Finder being dragged across it fighting and shouting, Tully and I were alone.

It was one of those moments. You're astonished, but not surprised. Holy crap they can fly and holy crap they're fast and get out get out right now! It was a frozen moment, but so heavy with internal movement that there aren't words.

We didn't say anything at first, we just stood there.

"Know your way around this place?" I asked. "We're safest searching now while Finder has them occupied. Some of them at least."

"She doesn't have an infinite Bat Suit supply," Tully said. "Maybe that was all of them."

"One was missing," I said. "At least."

We'd been standing listening to Matilda's weird monologue for so long my joints had gone stiff. I could no longer feel my feet or nose from the cold.

"She'll expect us to chase them," I said.

Tully looked stricken. "How can you be so calm?" Desperation crept into his voice.

Keep your mind on the mate.

"We underestimated her. I won't make that mistake again."

"We're not getting out of here alive," he said. "None of us."

"Oh yes we are! I am going to die in my sleep on my hundredth birthday in a swanky apartment overlooking Central Park. Put your blade away. We have to run."

"We can't leave her!"

"We're not leaving her, you dolt!" I wanted to thwack him in the head. "We have," I checked my watch, 3:24, "fifty-six minutes before Matilda joins this game. We need to find the guys and Finder, too, before that happens. Once Matilda joins, it's over." I wrapped my arms around myself for warmth. "Tell me the layout."

Tully sheathed his sword, but was shaking so hard he missed the scabbard on the first try. I think he thought Finder was invulnerable. They both had. It's why they ignored me when I told them 1. Matilda was a bully and bullies love carnage, and 2. Finder would be captured on the first attack. I know I'm small, but people should listen to me.

Tully calmed down as he explained the layout of Maymont, the park, petting zoo, barn, green house, gardens, paths and mansion.

"She'll want to wear us out before she lets us make any head way," I said. "She might move them or put some kind of hiding magic on them if we get too close."

"Hiding magic?"

"If they can *fly? Fly* in man form, then I'm not limiting my imagination as to what else they can do."

Or how we can be squashed like roaches on Ninth Avenue. Stop! Not gonna think about that. Rabbi Berman had drilled it into me: *Don't think of how you can lose. Make a plan. Stick to the plan. Be ready to change the plan. Keep your mind on the mate.*

I went back to the plan. We're going for a smothered mate. We're going to block or force her moves, occupy her pieces and use them to block her action. We have to keep her guessing.

"The place is big, we can't cover it all in an hour," I said. "We have to force her moves. She captured, and now it's our turn. What do we want her to do?"

"Let Finder go."

"That's the new checkmate. It's premature. If we go for mate too soon, before everything is set up, she'll crush us.

She's still excited about her capture. We have to take advantage of that. She has to gloat for a move. She'll want to threaten Finder or maybe try to convince her to come over to the vampire's side of her own free will. She knows we won't just leave her. But we can't rescue her yet. We have one move to spend. We need to get closer to freeing the guys." I thought for a minute. The addition of material, if the guys were okay, was as likely to be a hindrance as a help, depending on how freaked out they were, but we'd come here to get them and that's what we would do.

I stuffed my crucifix back inside my hoodie. I'd forgotten I still held it. I jammed my frozen paws in my pockets for warmth.

"Cold? Here." Tully opened his hands, I put mine in them. He was like a toaster! Tully rubbed his square palms together over mine. He was *hot*. I felt immediately better. He pulled me in, like for a hug, and rubbed his hands brisk and strong up and down my back. His heat melted through my sweater and hoodie soaking into my skin.

"Better?"

"Yes. Thanks."

"No problem. I'll teach you how, but not tonight."

I pulled my hat down over my ears to keep in the heat. "So think, what is Matilda going to do with Nicolai and Aegisthus?"

Tully's face scrunched in discomfort. "Turn them. Into Bat Suits. Or eat them."

I shivered.

"Where would she put them for safe keeping? Is there a dungeon here?"

"It's a house, Stacy."

"I'm from Manhattan, Tully. I have zero experience with big houses."

"I did the tour with school. No dungeon."

She will turn them into vampires or eat them, I thought. Where would I dump a project or store food I was saving for later?

"What about a kitchen?"

26.

November 16, continued. 3:24 a.m.

The mansion loomed ahead at the top of a low rise, three levels, wide stone exterior, columns in front and behind holding up the porches. A mini-castle, not unlike the one in Central Park. Under any other circumstances I would've thought it beautiful, but running toward it tonight, it was another enemy in a long list of foes.

Running/ wheezing the last few yards, part of me wondered why I was here, away from my bed at three in the morning rescuing fake vampires from real ones? I was just a kid, a kid who wanted to get back to New York as soon as possible. And graduate with honors into Columbia University with Cornell and Stanford as backups. I'd do my four years, maybe five so I could graduate with a Bachelor's and a Master's at the same time, get recruited by NASA or a well -funded research institution and spend my life making interesting discoveries in math or science. I wanted to rank up to Grand Master in chess, maybe have a dog. I maybe even wanted to take a luxury vacation somewhere I could see my feet through the blue water. What did monster fighting have to do with any of that?

Nothing, I told myself, trotting up the steps, my lungs burning with cold air. You aren't like Finder and Tully. It's not about occult phenomena or revenge or lore. I was here to help a friend, to find some justice for a person who'd been wronged. Now that the question of supernatural creatures being real had been answered, I admit I was curious. How were these creatures possible? They couldn't exist beyond the realm of science, so what science made them work? How long could they exist and by what means?

As for Matilda, why had she gone to all the trouble to stage this, what with kidnapping the guys and now stealing away Finder? Could it truly be that she was bored and this was pure entertainment? Why did she need more Bat Suits? I counted nine so far including the missing one and Finder's Dad. (Still working through that one. Her *Dad?*)

I pulled out my crucifix and made sure my Star of David was visible over the neck of my hoodie before Tully touched the door knob.

"Good luck. Be careful," Tully whispered.

"You, too."

"Stay behind me." He tried the handle. I gripped my stake.

The heavy wooden door swung open onto an industrial carpet runner lined with stanchions and velvet ropes. An admissions desk sat to the left. Brighter than outside, the wide wood paneled foyer held the light from an antique crystal chandelier.

Tully stepped over the stanchion ropes, stake held like a warning in front of him. Staying behind him, I ducked under. My feet sank into an oriental carpet. Ahead and to our right swept a broad staircase leading up to an L shaped balcony that ran the rear width of the room and the length of the right side. The balcony emptied into hallways, one right and one left. Ancestor portraits hung over display cases along the left wall. Three doors were on our level. One behind the ancestor wall in the far left corner, one behind the admissions desk and one on the far right near the stairs. Matilda's Suits could be anywhere.

A bat peered at us from its perch on the back of the leather admissions desk chair. It had cute little ears, translucent wings, a dense, venti sized, furry body with teensy clawed feet. I looked around for others. Nope. It was alone. Two to one in our favor.

Tully thrust his stake back at me. I grabbed it as he drew his sword. He swung at the bat. Pamphlets and bright colored papers fluttered from the desk. The bat flitted out of the way. It dove at my head. I waved my stakes and smacked it. It landed on the banister. Tully turned around and launched toward it, swung again.

A dark spot opened in the bat's chest. First, a pinprick. That's when we heard it, the rushing sound of air or flesh or evil or whatever moving through that minuscule hole. I braced myself and held my breath. Tully staggered as the air left his lungs. The aperture grew to match a dime. My blood rushed to the surface of my skin like getting into a too hot shower. When the hole reached the size of a quarter, I broke out in a sweat. The bat body vanished into the blackness of the spot, and the human form of the vampire stepped out. The rushing sound stopped. The void was filled.

This time, I could breathe at the end instead of having the air slammed back into my lungs. Ah ha! There was a technique to being around morphing supers! Hold your breath and brace yourself. Not getting knocked on my butt was a victory and a first. Maybe I had a future in this monster hunting business after all.

My victory evaporated as I recognized the Bat Suit. The one that bit me in the museum garden. A hot wash of outrage flowed from my face to my feet. My neck burned in sympathy. His suit looked rumpled. I hoped being crammed into that bat body felt horrible.

Tully staggered, recovering from the air sucking morph. He got his balance and swung at the suit. Stinky Suit ducked, catching the blade's flat side on his bicep. Tully hefted the sword and hacked downward. The shoulder blow struck Stinky hard from the front. He crashed backward into the railing. The Southern Scotsman seized his opportunity. He yanked back his blade and lunged forward like a fencer. The dragon sticker sank deep. Stinky Bat Suit howled, sword protruding from his chest.

Tully leaned forward, ramming the sword deeper. He jerked upward to make a diagonal cut at the same time.

"Stake!" he shouted. I ran forward, coming in on Tully's left. Stinky writhed, pinned to the railing. Tully's sword stuck on a step. Its blade anchored the Bat Suit at a diagonal, hilt up, point down. The wide meat of the sword skewered him through flesh and rails. Tully leaned his shoulder into the hilt. His face scrunched in effort as he fought the struggling Suit. I aimed the stake at Stinky Suit's chest.

"Do it!"

"Where are the prisoners?" I cried. Stinky Suit spat at me. The spit splattered like hot oil, burning my face. I shrieked and jumped back, dropping the stakes and wiping my cheeks with my sleeves. Stinky swung his working arm, missed me and clocked Tully in the head. Tully grunted, his feet giving way on the soft carpet.

I grabbed up a stake, again. I aimed it at Stinky's chest and flung myself toward him with all the force I could muster. Stinky Suit swung his open arm and it hit my shoulder like a baseball bat. I screamed and crumpled. The stake fell useless. Stinky Suit anchored his good hand on Tully's shoulder and pushed.

How could I get that stake in him? My arm throbbed, like it might be broken.

Tully let out a resounding man-fight noise as he shoved the sword hilt upright, slicing through Stinky's shoulder. Stinky screamed. Tully kept pushing. Stinky reached out with his open arm and sank his fingers into Tully's throat. My friend gasped for air.

"Lie down!" the Bat Suit commanded. The power in his voice touched me like fingers on my neck.

"Lie down, boy!" Stinky shouted again.

Tully choked, air not making it to his lungs.

I staggered to my feet, snatched a crucifix from my belt and walked forward. I took a breath, picturing that golden ball of light traveling from inside me into the worn out Jesus. I stepped closer. Stinky looked at me.

I jammed the cross in his face. He winced but it didn't do what I hoped. He sneered, not letting go of Tully.

"You fool!" he hissed. "You have to believe in what you use!" I pulled more light and pushed it into the cross. He gasped and flinched, but the energy wasn't strong enough. My faith wasn't strong enough. *I* wasn't strong enough. Stinky squeezed Tully's throat tighter. His nails sank in and drew little half moons of blood. He ignored my shoving his head with the cross. He pulled Tully's face closer. Screaming "Tully, no!" I saw their eyes meet.

"Be still," he hissed. Tully froze for a second.

I remembered that second. The second when my fear turned inward and I became my own enemy. My mind had screamed no, but my body had obeyed.

Still leaning into the sword and the Bat Suit's torn body, Tully went limp.

A vibration boiled up in me. Fear and rage exploded out of my mouth.

"Get off him! Get off him!" More adrenaline kicked in, a surge of energy and heat. I was the only one standing.

Stinky opened his mouth, aimed his face at Tully's throat and bit deep. Tully gasped as his blood flowed into Stinky Suit. What could I do?

The vampire was still pinned to the railing. When a piece is pinned, you capture it. I dropped my cross and grabbed the stake up off the floor. I ran around behind him up a few stairs until I was taller, above him. The angle to stake him was wrong. My arm throbbed from where he'd whacked it. I didn't believe I could push the stake hard enough to penetrate and get him off Tully. I needed another move. Back here the depth of damage was visible. Tully had sliced from the low ribcage up to separate the shoulder. Rancid meat smell filled the stairwell. The only sound was slurping. Ignoring the pain in my arm, I gripped the stake with both hands and swung as hard as I could at his ear.

"Let go!" I screamed, bashing over and over at the monster's skull. "Let go!" Stinky did not let go. Tully's eyes were wide in terror and pain. I knew what was happening. Stinky was sucking Tully's soul. And healing.

I may never know what got into me at this next moment. I dropped the stake, grabbed Stinky's hair with my left hand and shoved my right hand under his jaw. I yanked his head left. He did not let go of Tully's throat. I dove forward toward the side of his open throat and bit Stinky Bat Suit harder than I have ever bitten anything in my life. A nasty, bitter taste filled my mouth, strong men's cologne. Ignoring it, I dug my teeth deep into the divet just under his ear where a thick muscle diagonals from the jaw down to the breast bone.

I grabbed that little strip of muscle in my teeth, clamped my jaw as hard as I could. I jammed my teeth together with all my strength and wrenched away from his head. A snap, like the breaking of a pencil. A sour mouthful of flesh came loose in my mouth. Stinky suit yelped and his mouth came away from Tully's throat.

I spat out the disgusting mass of undead flesh. Getting grossed out was a luxury for people who weren't fighting for their lives. A luxury I didn't have.

The monster started back toward Tully's bloody neck.

I couldn't let him get there. In a frenzy of panic, I wrapped my arm around Stinky's throat and grabbed my own wrist just below the cuff. I yanked back hard, digging my spiky wrist cuff into the flesh above his Adams apple. It sank in and a pop broke the skin. I jerked my arm back toward my face as hard as I could. Bat Suit let go of Tully. He gurgled. Liquid spilled over my hand and wrist.

"Stake him!" I shrieked. "Tully! Stake him!"

Bat Suit thrashed, fighting to get his head out of my grip. My arm where he had clocked it earlier seared in pain as he battered it with his fist. I would rather he rip it off than kill Tully. I screamed and pulled his throat back with all my might. I was not letting go.

I held him trapped between my arm and the bannister posts a long time, him thrashing, me gouging my wrist cuff deep in his throat skin. At long last, a thump, and something sharp stabbed me, ripping into my thigh. I cried out and fell back as Stinky Suit went limp. Tully stood above him, hands still on the stake, panting, blood soaking his shirt.

I almost didn't dare breathe.

In my eyes, a question.

Tully gave a half nod.

I looked at Stinky Suit, head lolling in a very unnatural way.

"You're sure?"

"It's dead."

Over the mangled corpse, I met Tully's clear, blue eyes. I knew better than to ask if he was okay. In that moment, we were alive, aching and gasping air. But neither of us was okay. Tully came to the bottom of the steps and held out his hand. I stood, saw what had stabbed me in the thigh. Tully's stake protruded through the back of Stinky Bat Suit.

"Sorry," he said, seeing my torn jeans and blood.

I looked into his clear ocean gaze and took his hand.

At the bottom of the stairs I stepped past the stanchion and walked around to the front of Stinky Bat Suit. We had done it. His body was wrecked by the sword and stake. His throat bore a raw mass of rips from my cuff spikes. A chunk of flesh was missing from the side of his neck. A dry, blood stained tongue lolled out of his mouth falling toward the Oriental carpet. His fangs were sharp and long. The putrid smell was overwhelming, but no gore spilled. No blood or guts or liquid anywhere, except on his face. And the blood was Tully's.

I shook some dead flesh chunks off of my wrist cuff. My hands were wet with Tully's blood that had spilled out of Stinky Suit's mouth as I strangled him. The alcohol aftertaste of Stinky's cologne stuck to my tongue. I wiped my hands on the leaves of a potted plant that hadn't gotten involved in the fight then spat into it's dirt. Not successful at either job. I wiped my hands on the carpet and licked my sleeve in desperation to lessen the foul bitterness.

I didn't have that sensation you read about, that oh-my-god-I-just-killed-a-person sensation of shock, regret, grief. I felt triumphant and fascinated, like we'd just squashed a colossal, revolting bug. Even with the stench and corpse sitting there, I sighed in relief. Amazed at their tenacity, I took off the stupid sunglasses.

In the city, we occasionally encountered enormous cockroaches. The kind that chase rats in the subway and glare at you if you run them off the dog food. I went out of my way to murder them. If it's a mammal, trap it and set it free, but if it's a cockroach, squash it, smash it, kill it dead. It's how I felt about Stinky Bat Suit. Do what you have to do, but make it die.

"Time is it?"

I checked my watch. "Three thirty-six." Twelve minutes? All that Finder stealing and running and killing our first Bat Suit happened in twelve minutes? Yikes.

"We should throw it outside," Tully said. "Dead ones disintegrate in daylight."

"I'm not touching it," I said. "We have to find the others."

"Maybe we should hide it?" Tully said, sliding his blade out of the carcass. He wiped his blade on Stinky Bat Suit's clothes.

"Teularen!" I said, not unlike Finder. "Matilda joins in forty-six minutes! This," I pointed to the corpse. "This was player *one*. There are at least *two more*, unless she cheats again, which she will. We have to keep our minds on the mate!"

Tully's throat was torn. He had some bruises. I felt damp blood soaking my own neck bandage. I had a gash in my thigh, and an arm so weak and sore, I could barely move it. My face had tiny burns that still stung from the vampire's spit.

Hurt isn't dead, I told myself. Dead is dead and it's a solid possibility that you all will be dead by morning if you make a false move. *Mind on the mate.* To get Finder back safely, we needed more strength, more pieces. We had to recover our material.

Where were Nicolai & Aegisthus?

I remembered.

"Show me the kitchen."

Tully peeked in first. He flung himself back around the corner, looking faint and kind of green. He stepped out of the way so I could nose around the doorway and see into the room.

My overall impression was of a pristine professional kitchen, white, tiled and chrome. The lights were on, but my sunglasses made edges and details fuzzy. Nicolai and Aegisthus sat tied to chairs. Chrome kitchen chairs, like from a 1950's retro diner. They sat across from each other, their forearms lying on the counter like they'd been arm wrestling. Nicolai's jackets were in a heap on the floor.

Both Nicolai and Aegisthus had sleeves rolled up and held something upright in their hands. Their ankles were tied to the chair legs with rope. Kitchen towels knotted around their heads gagged their mouths. They were blindfolded. And alone. Their heads lolled like they were asleep.

Tully pressed himself against the wall. His eyes squeezed shut. He took long slow breaths. Finally he whispered, "Are they dead?"

I held my second big cross out in front of me with both hands. The hurt arms was barely able to grip. I couldn't, wouldn't answer that question. I stepped into the kitchen. On cop shows they check all the doors and say "clear" if there's no one there. This kitchen was a giant booby trap of closed doors, cabinets, windows over the sinks, and two other door ways.

"I'll open the cabinets. Be ready," I whispered. He nodded, gripping a stake. I stood to the left of the first door, located on our left in the corner of the kitchen. Holding my cross in the weak hand, I yanked the door open in front of me so Tully could see inside.

"Servant's stair," he whispered. I did the closest large cabinet. Empty. We went along the kitchen wall to the far doorway which led to a butler pantry and then into the

formal dining room. Also clear. I turned around to come
back into the kitchen to search the other cabinets and then, I
saw it.

Nicolai and Aegisthus were not holding things in their
hands. Each of their right hands was skewered, palm up, to
the chopping block counter. The daggers pinning them were
thick and wicked. Each forearm rested limp, smeared red with
blood. A series of words had been roughly tattooed into each
of their forearms.

The position of the tattoo ran chills up my spine. My face
got hot in a surge of powerful, powerful hate. I ran to AGB
and reached to yank the dagger out of his hand. Blood from
the bite inflicted by the Terminator Bat Suit at the museum
saturated his shirt. My vision spun for a second, black, white
and red with chrome as my brain processed the mouth-sized
rip in his throat. We were dealing with real vampires. And this
boy was *not* one of them. Hand hovering, I read the tattoo.

Ich bin eine Fälschung.

What did it mean? My attention flew back to the hand.
What if it had split a tendon or something? Just jerking the
knife out could hurt him worse. What would Meredith's
father - pain fire blinded me and I knocked forward into the
table. Nobody else moved. What had I been about to think?
As if my brain got tuned to the survival station, I forgot
about whatever it was and the agony receded. I pressed my
good hand to my forehead until I could see without the little
pain lights flashing in my vision. How could I get the knives
out safely? Straight up, I thought. Less variables on a line

versus on a curve. I tucked my cross back in my belt, pressed my belly into the table and braced myself. I took hold of AGB's dagger hilt with both hands and pulled straight up. Frozen for a moment, I held the knife as blood burped up from the wound. Fury filled me. I threw the blade as hard as I could across the room. It skittered off the wooden cabinets.

"Napkins," I demanded. Tully opened drawers. I recreated the process for Aegisthus' hand and flung his knife so hard it cracked a pane in the window. Tully gave me a handful of stiff, linen napkins.

"Wake up, Nicolai," I said, lifting his hand out of the bloody pool. "Wake up." I slid off his gag and blindfold. Tully did the same for the older man. I shook AGB. No response. A dread so deep that they were dead filled me almost to inaction. How did Mered-

Again, pain-fire behind my eyes. It dropped me to my knees. I cried out in pain.

Tully was right there. "What is it? What happened?" He lifted me up under my arm pits and stood me back on my feet.

"This . . . pain. It keeps coming," I said with a gasp. Tully took me into his arms and squeezed me. The arm where Bat Suit had hit me was almighty painful. He rested his head on top of mine. I breathed into his chest.

"Why are people so awful? I don't understand why the world is like this!"

Get ahold of yourself, Goldman! I said in my mind. You have to get these guys out of here! You can't meltdown now. I took a shuddering breath and looked up into Tully's bloody neck. Come on, girl. I thought. Mind on the mate.

I stuck my hand under AGB's nose. Warm moisture touched my fingers. Alive. I looked at Tully, he did the same with Aegisthus. Relief flooded his eyes. Using the wretched daggers, we sawed and hacked away at their restraints.

I shoved my emotions away as I sawed at the rope. "And just so we're clear," I said, leaning over AGB's bound hands, "I'd rather be dead than have something tattooed on my arm there."

It took longer than I thought to hack through the rope. The knives were not as sharp as they looked which must've meant that the impalement had been incredibly painful. I worried.

"This was too easy. Finding them unguarded. And all organized like a movie set. It's a trap. It always is."

"What do you mean? The Suit upstairs was the guard. I think maybe we just got lucky."

"No. That was no guard. It was an offering. A test to see if we would run or fight. You never get lucky unless the other guy makes a mistake." Hands, done! I wiped my forehead. Sweat trickled down the inside of my shirt. I started sawing his ankle ropes. "I don't think she made a mistake. It's a tactic. I can't figure out which. Fork, pin or skewer." I said more to myself than Tully.

The frayed rope split at last. Together, we lowered them each to the floor.

I wet two napkins and we used them to clean Nicolai's bite and the tattoo wounds.

Ich bin eine Falschung. I am a 'Falschung'. False thing?

"Is there any alcohol?" I said. Tully searched. Except for three drawers of different knives and two cabinets of glasses, pitchers and various vessels to hold liquid, a drawer of napkins and one of towels, the kitchen was empty.

I searched the butler pantry. On a top shelf I couldn't reach, I recognized an unlabeled bottle shaped like a swan peeking out from behind a silver tray. My dad's favorite.

"Tully! Get that, please. It's vodka."

He reached and retrieved, an obvious question on his face. I poured vodka over each of the tattoos and into the puncture wounds. We cleaned them with napkins and wrapped each hand in a dishtowel.

We did everything to wake Nicolai and Aegisthus. We shook them, moved them around, flicked water in their faces. A low voice startled us.

"Would you like help with that?"

27.

November 16, continued. 3:51 a.m.

Silver Tie spoke from the doorway behind us. Player number two. Where was three?

I turned around to check our backs and our escape path. Number three filled the doorway to the butler pantry. Finder's father propped himself at a jaunty angle against the doorframe.

Smiling, he waggled his fingers at Tully.

And then I understood. A fork. We'd have to divide our combined power to defeat just one and who could tell which was the right one to pick? No way could we could take on two of them. And would Finder be grateful or furious if we did manage to kill her father? Silver Tie was inhumanly fast. And in this moment, Tully and I were both on the floor on our knees.

This was it. We were going to die. I had fallen into Matilda's set up: a forked attack. She was attacking Finder, AGB, Aegisthus and us all at once. I had been suckered to save two lives that were now also going to be lost. Stupid, stupid, stupid.

Bat Suits would feed on me while adding Tully to the ranks of Terminator minions. Matilda and Darcy would turn Finder into a vampire just for fun. Nicolai and Aegisthus might become human servants, or just blood and soul snack packs like myself. So many ways we could lose.

Stop! I told myself. Stick to the plan. Be ready to change the plan. Keep your mind on the mate.

They hadn't moved to eat us yet. She would expect us to attack, but with two incapacitated, it was two on two. If we were at full, we could maybe make it a piece trade, but we were down in material. We would lose the exchange. The only possible way out of this fork was to force her move. I had to make sure we didn't have to fight.

I stayed vulnerable on my knees. "Can you wake them up without harming them?"

"Of course," said Silver Tie. "I'm the one who gave them the command to sleep. I came by to see how my associate got on with Matilda's little art project. His sloppy job was torturing them." I swallowed. "I have no problem with torture, but not when it's inflicted as a side effect of shoddy workmanship. Torture," he said with a gleam of joy in his voice, "is for fun."

These vampires were awfully chatty. Maybe eternity had bored them all? I needed him to be curious enough about me to not kill us right off.

"I agree."

"You do?" Silver Tie said.

"The temptation to torture your friend," I began.

"Associate," he corrected.

"The temptation to torture your associate," I continued, "was great, but it would not have been enjoyable. We killed him."

"You certainly did. Not very tidy though."

Careful, Stacy, I told myself. No eyes. Silver Tie spoke again.

"If I were to make you my child, I could teach you much more efficient ways."

Child? Yikes. Bad train of thought, bad. Distract him.

"Thank you for waking them."

"Yes, of course." Silver Tie snapped his fingers. "Awaken."

Nicolai and Aegisthus came alert with a pop, not like real sleep where you're groggy for a few minutes. I held my finger to my lips.

"You're awake and alive. That's all for now. Try not to move your hand." They were both ghost white. AGB glanced down at his arm and his eyes went wide. Aegisthus trembled.

"Sir?" I said, pulling myself up to my full height and stepping away from Nicolai. I felt Tully and the other two tense. The other door out of the butler's pantry led to a gentleman's parlor. If I'd glimpsed what I thought I had, maybe we had a chance. I looked at Silver Tie's tie.

"Sir, do you play chess?"

The Bat Suit's brow furrowed. Too close to the eyes! I scolded myself. I looked back at his tie.

"Why?" His voice took on a sly quality. Confused, I hoped. Suspicious and confused. Nice change from smug and patronizing.

"I'm not much of a fighter," I said simply. "We need some information. So maybe if you'll play me at chess, we can work something out."

He resumed smugness.

"Speaking of information," he said, "My mistress requested I deliver a message."

I did not look at his face.

"She wants you to know that since you found these two so early, she is changing the rules."

Of course. Bullies.

"She will give you the remaining time to find Mr. Jackson's daughter. If you fail, the previously agreed upon terms apply."

"Until she changes them," I said.

"She will not. They are very favorable terms for her and quite disadvantageous to you." A cell phone ring from behind made me jump, startled. Darcy Jackson held up a finger and pointed behind him toward the butler pantry as he pulled out his phone. Silver Tie nodded. Finder's dad stepped out and shut the parlor door behind him.

"Yes! I said five hundred shares. *What* is the confusion?" I was surprised we could hear him so well.

"There's a secret window in the cabinet," Silver Tie said as if reading my mind. "Darcy wasn't here when it was in use so he probably doesn't know. So the servants could hear the conversations and serve refreshments on time." I opened the cabinet door. Sure enough, a slice of white canvas covered where the wooden cabinet wall belonged.

"Where did Matilda take Finder?" I asked Silver Tie. Offering your opponent a chance to make a random, obvious mistake is part of chess. He held up a finger, head cocked, eavesdropping.

"Sell the Blockbuster," said Darcy. "Yes, I said sell! As soon as the exchange opens in the morning. Buy that new one. What's it called? Yeah. Buy that. As much as you can get. Yes. I know. Renting movies on computers won't ever work, I get it. Just buy the shares. Thank you."

Darcy came around the corner. He fixed me with eyes like his daughter's. I looked away fast. That was close.

Speaking of random careless mistakes.

I adjusted my mirror sunglasses.

"Sorry about that. Important call. Are you guys going to play chess?"

Sloan turned to face me.

"We were about to discuss the terms." In other words, what each of us gets if we win. I looked at his polished leather shoes and listened to him think. I hate having the inferior position. It's a rotten place to make an offer. Either I would suggest too little and he would refuse and kill us for fun, or I would give too much and he would kill us because I agreed to it. Holding my ground and worrying, I waited silent. Let him go first, I coached myself in my head. He's going to ask for blood. Don't over offer because you are scared.

I was scared. He had supernatural speed and mind control. We had sticks and stones.

"You need information," he said, feeling his way. "I need blood. The question is, how much of your blood is the information to save your friend's life worth to you?"

His utter arrogance rubbed me the wrong way. Before I could stop myself I blurted, "How sure are you that you'll win?"

He folded his hands. "Interesting question. How sure are you that Darcy and I aren't just having a little fun before we kill you? What if I have no intention of playing your little game at all?"

"That's possible," I said. "Likely, in fact."

Sloan chuckled. "If this one is anything like your daughter, Darcy, you are going to have your hands full!"

Finder's father smiled.

A chill of realization shot up my spine. Wait. Was Finder's capture more than a strategy to remove our strongest player? I did not like them talking about Finder as if she was going to stay here. What if the threats with Nicolai and Aegisthus were not about their game at all? Was the blackmail and midnight museum kidnapping an elaborate ruse to lure Finder here so her father could change her into one of Matilda's filthy vampire Bat Suits? It couldn't be, could it? How could they have known that I would show up at the museum, that Tully would jump in to rescue me and Finder would get involved at all?

How do they turn into bats and freeze your body on command just by looking in your eyes, stupid Stacy! I wanted to smack my head. How had I not seen this? How could I miss such an obvious play? Goldman, you are an idiot, I said to myself.

I intended to wait for Sloan's offer, but that was no longer an option. If they jumped us now, with Finder snug in Matilda's hands, Tully, Nicolai, Aegisthus and I would definitely get eaten or enslaved and Finder would die. We had to avoid combat. Time to make Sloan an offer he couldn't refuse.

"If you win, you can drink my blood for thirty seconds."

A human female of 100 pounds, in other words, me, has about 3.7 quarts of blood in her body. The mean blood speed through the main aortas in your heart is twelve centimeters per second. It takes less than five minutes for a human to bleed to death. My offer was not only generous, it was dangerous. And no fun. Thirty seconds is a *very* long time with a vampire sucking your blood, believe me.

Sloan's eyes got wide. I kept talking.

"And if I win, you tell me where Finder is and guarantee our safety to her location. So no chasing, no biting, no mind commands, nothing." I eyed Finder's dad. "You *both* leave *all of us* alone."

"What about soul?" Sloan. "How much of that do I get?"

I paused. Panic filled my belly. The soul sucking had hurt.

"None. No soul," Tully said. "Too high a price for information and action that cost you nothing."

Blue circles dipped beneath the Southern Scotsman's eyes. Had Stinky Suit taken some soul from Tully, too? Fierce and haunted looks clashed over my friend's face. I knew the answer.

Silver Tie looked past me at Finder's dad.

"What say you, Darcy? Shall we eat them?"

"I say play the girl at chess, Sloan. It'll give Layla and Matilda a chance to talk." Oh great. Just what we needed. "You're Layla's best friend, Teularen. How she's been doing? Play me at pool and talk with me while they play and I'll agree to leave you alone."

"Leave *all* of us alone," Tully clarified. "And we all stay together."

Darcy nodded. "Seems fair."

This wasn't shaping up as I'd intended, but it did get us out of mortal combat, at least for now.

I remembered the feeling of the dead vampire's teeth breaking my skin a few short hours ago. Eight seconds with one of those things latched onto you felt like an eternity. Thirty would be a lifetime.

I knew anything Sloan told me was likely to be false, but it seemed better to do this than let him and Finder's dad attack us outright. The time playing would give me time to think up a new, new plan.

"Won't you even look me in the face, Teularen?" Darcy said to the Southern Scotsman.

"Not a chance, sir," Tully said.

"Come on. I used to buy you peppermint ice creams."

"And I greatly enjoyed them. Thank you."

Sloan led the way to the parlor and flipped on a light. First in, I blinked into the brightness around the edges of my sunglasses. Aegisthus, still trembling, eased himself into a chair by the butler pantry door. Nicolai, silent since we'd woken him, stayed behind me. Tully went around the room opening every door, poking his sword into every closet. He checked all the windows, which ones opened, which didn't. We didn't want the Bat Suits morphing and escaping, or worse, trapping us in here.

How must it have felt, being trapped in the tower, knowing there was no way out? The choices were bad. Get crushed to death as the building collapsed in a death you couldn't control, or to jump to your death? Which would be faster? Less painful? What had been the last thoughts of those people I saw? Not fictional people, real people. Mothers, fathers, sons and daughters. People who were in love, who had dogs, who had stood in front of and behind me that morning in Starbucks.

I lost my air. The room swirled back into my vision. Dizzy, my knees started to give. I stumbled backward and Nicolai caught me. He eased me down into a chair across from Sloan at the chess board. He pressed a hand to my shoulder, said nothing.

I felt Tully more than I saw him, though his height hovered in my peripheral vision. Taking a spot at the far side of the pool table, he stood sentry, watching out the opposite door, monitoring every movement in the room. The pool balls clicked as Darcy Jackson racked them.

I took a long, slow breath in. Exhaled. I am alive. I am safe. Nothing bad is happening. I could do this. I had to. Finder was in danger, and so were we all. Thirty seconds being fed on? Not an option. I took another long breath and nodded that I was ready. I had to win.

Across the chess table, the über smooth Sloan Silver Tie slid out of his jacket and made himself comfortable. His gaze on me chilled, like standing with the freezer door open knowing ice cream is there. His presence called to me like dessert, bad for me, but still I wanted to have it. I wanted to look up and release the pressure by looking into his eyes. Just one spoonful. No Stacy, I said to myself. He is evil! He is not ice cream! Just play chess. I stared at the board. Looking into Sloan's face would end it all. Sloan picked up two pawns and switched them behind his back. I chose the fist on the right. Black. The defender. How apropos.

I reached for the old-fashioned analog chess clock, friend or foe when you play depending on how you handle noise. I liked having my time announced, tick by tock.

I turned both sides to an even twelve o'clock.

Behind me, I heard Tully slide a pool cue out of the wall rack.

"Just like the old days, Mr. Jackson?"

I negotiated with Silver Tie: the victor wins two out of three five minute rounds. We each had two and a half minutes to play per game. I adjusted the clock. My watch read 4:03. Minus fifteen minutes made 4:18. We'd have nine minutes left to locate Finder before Matilda joined the game at 4:24. Nine minutes.

It was risky, using fifteen minutes to buy nine. I had no guarantee that Sloan knew where Finder was, or would tell the truth if he did. Still, if it meant we didn't have to fight anyone and could have those nine minutes unmolested, the time and risk seemed worth it. If I won.

Darcy Jackson's voice was soft as he grilled Tully on Finder's life. Better talking than staking, I thought. My brain tapped a memory. The pain behind my eyes tapped back. Just a slight ache and burn. It hurt. I didn't need to look for that memory. As soon as I quit reaching for it, the pain faded. The surface information was there, and not painful to get. I'd had some school friend whose Dad was a doctor. I had liked him. That was all. I still didn't think I could stake him, even if he did get turned into a soul sucking supernatural monster. I could probably stake my mom. Maybe not, but probably.

Time to focus on the chess. Sloan Silver Tie used a standard King's Pawn opening, moving the King's pawn up two spaces. I copied. He played fast, tapping the clock hard like a Russian, not wasting time in his opening. He played to dominate, to keep his opening move advantage by developing knights and bishops to maintain control of the board's center.

His first mistake was moving his queen out early to threaten my back rank. I castled Kingside, then after his next move, a pawn move as an afterthought to protect his queen, I captured her with my white squared bishop and gained both a tempo and a material advantage. Sloan shifted in his chair and muttered a curse under his breath. His pawn captured my black bishop on his next move, after which he relaxed. Capture always soothed the aggressive players. We danced around for the next two minutes cleaning each other off the board.

Then I made my mistake. I advanced my knight to capture a pawn. Sloan took advantage.

"'Mate," he said.

I stared at the board in disbelief. What had I done wrong? Then I saw. The knight I'd moved had abandoned its position keeping his rook stuck the whole time. Sloan laughed and smiled wide, clicking his fangs against his bottom row of teeth. Gloater. We set up the board again, him keeping white as winner's privilege. I took two deep breaths. I could not afford another defeat. Anger at my mistake pumped my adrenaline.

Stay calm, Goldman, I coached myself. Resetting the clock, I realized I hadn't gone in to the last game with a plan. Fact of chess: you need a plan to win. He opened his second game like the first, Ruy Lopez if you play, bishops and knights moving ahead of the pawns to control the center if you don't. I struggled for a plan.

He's a dominant center, aggressive player, I thought. Get control of the center yourself and don't let him get a foothold. Worry about endgame when you get there. And capture his rooks. I made a mantra: hold the center, kill the rooks. I chanted it in my head. Hold the center. Kill the rooks. In three minutes and thirty seconds, I checkmated him by capturing his remaining rook with my queen.

Relief flooded me. One to one. I had a shot at winning this. I looked up. Finder's dad was lining up a shot on the pool table. Tully was focused on me. He raised his eyebrows. Can we do this? I gave the tiniest of nods. I had to win. I had to. Tully needed Finder like I needed — who? A face flashed before my eyes but erupted into a volcano of colors then black. An excruciating pain in my head made me shut my eyes and clutch the table as Sloan reset the pieces.

"Stacy? Are you okay?" Nicolai's voice was hoarse.

I nodded. The pain was fading already. What had I been thinking about? Tully. Tully needed Finder and if I didn't win this game he would lose her and I would lose both of them. And my life. I had to win.

The third game: Playing white, I opened with my knights and a plan that echoed my Matilda strategy. Crush his development. Every time he moved a piece, I thwarted it. I gained a tempo more than once by forcing his moves. I did lose my black squared bishop and three pawns, but as the carnage flew across the board, my knights leaped to block, counter and attack. Sloan Silver Tie shifted in his chair. He tapped his fingers on the board. Drumming his heel on the floor, he didn't notice my rook development via castling to the Queenside and the one small pawn push it took to protect the square I needed.

I hung my white bishop and hit my clock. Four seconds left in the game. Sloan gloated as his c file pawn captured my helpless piece. Then, I snuck my queen in to take his pawn. Three seconds. The move unblocked an entire file. Sloan Silver Tie brought in his last piece to defend. Two seconds. I struck fast, sweeping my castled rook down the open file for the checkmate. His king faced my rook, trapped, surrounded and immobilized by his own pawns in a classic smothered —

"'Mate!" I tapped the clock.

One second. My chest pounded with adrenaline, the thrill of victory! I'd used every trick and trap I knew and they had worked! It had been a long time since I'd played this well. Then again, the stakes had never been so high.

Looking up, I stuck my hand across the board to shake hands. Tully shouted a warning behind me. AGB dove and grabbed hold of my shirt. Before I had time to react, Sloan Silver Tie snatched my wrist, front lip curling back to expose long, razor-like fangs. He yanked my arm so hard and so fast I flew out of AGB's grip. A sharp pain stabbed through my wrist. I cried out. I slid over the board and onto Sloan's lap. Chess pieces clattered to the floor. Small things falling . . .

My shoulder slammed into Sloan's chest. The iron armed Bat Suit pulled me across him like a shield. As my back smacked into his chest, I kicked out, my feet scrabbling for purchase. My mind scrabbled, too as I lashed out, balling my fist to pound the hand that gripped my other wrist.

I fell toward remembering, remembering that day like today. A day that changed everything. A day where I learned something true that I didn't want to know, didn't want to believe. Like today, September 11 had been a day I couldn't imagine being real, until it was. Like every other New Yorker, I had watched the buildings fall unable to change the course of events. Today though, I could change the course of things. I already had. I had bought Finder time, if nothing else.

Rage erupted inside me as I realized for the first time that the intensity boiling under my skin since September 11, was not only rage for the victims, it was for me. A scream of fury boiled up from my belly, fury at feeling helpless against a bully attacker who left me only two paths: flight or flee. A lighting bolt of realization shuddered in dark sparkles up my spine as Sloan Silver Tie held me pinned to his chest. I heard the echoing clang of my mother's voice, and in an instant, I put it all together. Of course I hated bullies. Of course I hate being made to feel helpless. Of course.

Sloan squeezed me so hard my ribs creaked.

He was going to drink my blood and kill me.

"No!" I shrieked, my epiphany bursting out of me in a fit of frenzy. I kicked out for the table anchoring my boot against its edge. I rammed my other boot forward against the heavy table and shoved back against Sloan. Astonishment ripped through me as the table tipped over, crashing to the floor. AGB jumped back to avoid being hit by it, then dove forward, reaching for me over top of the mess. Sloan did not loosen his grip as he stood up. He landed a hard, fast kick in the center of AGB's chest. AGB staggered then crumpled to his knees. Panic surged up in me. I kicked, encountering only air. Tully had a stake in his hand. His hair flew as he sought wildly for an opening. My body covered Sloan Silver Tie's chest. Fear of being bitten again made me desperate.

"No!" I shrieked again. I thrashed my head back toward Sloan's to maybe break his nose and get him off me. Whacking my skull on his hard collarbone, I gasped in pain. The flesh ripping was coming. The thought of it terrified me. I screamed. And thrashed. I would not make biting me easy for him. I screamed more. Sloan Silver Tie made no attempt to stop me screaming. Something hard poked me inside my pocket. OMG, my pocket!

Sloan hoisted me up to biting range. He released one of my arms. Maybe he thought it was pinned under me? He pushed my head to the side. I slipped my hand into my pocket. I wrapped my fingers around its contents. Opening a spot to bite me, Sloan leaned in. The wind of his movement brushed my sore skin.

I took a big breath. Weapon clenched in my fist, I arced the mezuzah up like a stake, across my body and behind me into Sloan Silver Tie's cheek. He screamed. The acrid stench of burning flesh filled the air. Sloan threw me forward with enough force that I flailed airborne over the toppled furniture. Tully dropped his sword to avoid stabbing me. I crashed into him. We tumbled backward into the pool table, wind knocked out of me. Tully grabbed me with both arms, then set me on my feet. He gave me a look - you okay? I caught my breath, nodding a quick yes. Sloan writhed, still on his feet, trying to yank my mezuzah out of his face. Letting go an ear splitting howl he dropped to his knees. His hand smoked where it had touched the holy item.

Air moved behind me. AGB anchored his long pool cue just left of Sloan's shiny, silver tie.

"Don't look in his eyes!" Tully shouted.

"I won, Sloan!" I gasped, snatching hold of the pool cue. "You owe me my information!" A movement in the corner of my eye caught my attention. Finder's father was creeping up behind AGB. Darcy reached for the Goth's shoulder.

"Watch out!" I cried. AGB turned to smack away the older man's arm. Tully snatched the second stake from his belt. The towering fencer lunged for Darcy. AGB dodged. Tully missed as Darcy slid sideways. Sloan took advantage of my distraction and ripped the pool cue out of my hand. He swung it and clocked me hard in the ear. I cried out, the shock of pain turning my whole torso numb. My ears rang with the impact.

"Sleep!" Darcy commanded. Clutching my head, I glanced up to see Aegisthus dropping a pool cue and crumpling to the ground.

"Stop!" I cried. To my astonishment, the combat paused. Heat rose in my body. In my mind's eye, golden light filled me. I stepped toward the kneeling Sloan, my hand out stretched. One step. Two. The mezuzah started to glow. Rays of burning light carved charred veins through his cheek where the narrow rod punctured his flesh. Sloan roared, an animal shriek of pain and fell forward onto all fours. On my left, Finder's father shrank back. Tully brandished the stake, getting AGB behind him. Sweat dripped down my forehead. I leveled my gaze on the mezuzah.

"Tell me where Finder is and I'll stop it," I said, though I had no idea if I could do that or not.

Sloan Silver Tie arched back up to his knees, screaming, shaking his head in a furious attempt to dislodge the holy item. Both of his hands smoked from where he had grabbed it. "Greenhouse," he choked out. I let up on the golden light. The burn slowed across the monster's face. "She has her there."

"No!" growled Finder's father. "Layla is mine! Only mine!" The air shifted. I sucked in a deep breath and braced myself. The oxygen sucked out of the room in a whoosh as Darcy Jackson morphed into bat form and shot out the parlor door.

AGB coughed as air rushed back into his lungs. "I know where!" He aimed his pool cue at Sloan Silver Tie's chest. "Will he warn Matilda?" AGB choked out.

"Will she move Finder?" Tully, also gasping, demanded of Sloan Silver Tie.

"*One piece* of information," snarled Sloan.

"Tell us where she'll take her!" Tully shouted.

I knew the rule about playing a bully in chess. Capture when you can, or your opponent will make you regret it.

AGB looked at me. This was my decision. Capture or not. Life or death. If I didn't capture, if we didn't kill Sloan, he would come after us again. The bully would make me regret it. I just stood there.

Sloan dove forward onto his belly. He grabbed for Tully's ankle and sank his fingers deep. Tully screeched in pain. He lost his grip on the pool cue. AGB grabbed it and slammed the makeshift stake into Sloan's back. It bounced off his shirt. Sloan rolled onto his side keeping his grip on Tully's leg.

"Look at me!" the Bat Suit commanded as AGB raised the stick for another go. I felt the pull to obey, but squashed it. AGB was too close.

"Nicolai! Here!" Tully shouted, hand open for the weapon.

AGB ignored him, caught in the lure of Sloan's gaze. Crap.

"Look at me!" Sloan commanded again.

"No!" I shouted, scared out of my frozen moment of indecision. AGB didn't blink, zeroing in on Sloan. I shoved Tully out of the way, ducking under his arm to get next to AGB. I drew back my hand and slapped the Goth as hard as I could.

"Ow!" I yanked my hand to my chest. It stung!

AGB dropped the pool cue, wounded hand flying to his face. He held his cheek and spat something solid into his good palm.

Tully dove for the dropped stake. Snatching it up, he let out a Highlander worthy battle roar. The Southern Scotsman slammed the stake down through Sloan Silver Tie with a thud. I turned my head away. He'd been a worthy opponent. I know he was a monster and wanted to eat me, but I felt bad killing him nonetheless. I'd played him at chess.

Stacy Rachel Goldman! Now is not the time to get philosophical! I shouted to myself as the flesh on the monster crackled, my mezuzah smoldering in his cheek. Right. Lives at stake. Time to move. The stench of cooking flesh filled the room as Sloan's corpse decomposed in front of us. Thick, dusty smoke rose from the body, caking into my eyes. Thick and dusty like running from the towers . . . I staggered back. Coughed. Covered my mouth with my sleeve. One of the guys grabbed my hand and yanked me out the parlor door into the foyer.

We all three stood for a second, catching our breath.

AGB looked at Tully with awe. "How'd you do that? I couldn't even get it through his shirt!"

"Have to put your back into it," Tully said letting go of my hand. "It's easier with two whole hands."

"Where's Luke?"

Luke? He must mean Aegisthus. Darcy had put him to sleep. AGB started toward the parlor, blood dripping fresh from his palm.

Tully put up a hand.

"I'll get him." In two strides he was gone.

AGB touched the red slap mark on the side of his face and rubbed it. Blood got on his cheek.

He held his injured hand away, realizing.

"Can you get the bandanna out of my pocket?"

I stepped in close to him, close enough to smell the New York in his jacket and the warm fragrance of him on his clothes. "Left inside."

I held his trench coat open and reached into the left inside pocket of the leather jacket underneath. It was warm from being next to his body. My arm brushed his chest. The bandanna was folded into a rumpled square and easy to find. Good thing or I might have left my hand warm next to him, tucked into that pocket.

He looked down at me as I paused. Green forest eyes flecked with gold . . . we both stood very still. His eyes flicked to my lips and hovered.

A noise from the other room startled me and I stepped back, handing AGB the bandanna.

He licked a corner of it and rubbed his cheek.

"Did I get it?"

I nodded. He shook the square out and folded it over his arm into a messy triangle.

"Can you please tie this?" He stepped in, closing the space between us again.

"I'm sorry!" I said, tying the little fabric around his palm. Seeing the wound close up made me wince. "I didn't mean to hit you that hard." I didn't know I *could* hit somebody that hard, I thought.

"No worries," he said, pronunciation clear and precise. "I appreciate the save! And I won't be using these for a while, if ever." He opened his good hand. Two shiny, realistic fangs lay on his palm. "Besides," he said. "They make me lisp."

"Does your neck hurt?" I asked. His bite wound hadn't been cleaned by an expert. It looked painful.

"Does, but I can't do anything for it right now, so I'm trying to ignore it. It's not gushing blood, right?"

"No." In fact, it looked like it was already scabbing over.

Tully emerged a second later, coughing, but with Aegisthus slung over one shoulder. AGB helped ease his friend to the floor. Using his good hand, AGB gently shook the man awake.

Quickly as it had come, the smoke cleared.

"Let's go," Tully said arranging his sword back into its sheath. "We have to find Finder."

"Wait," I said. "They don't have any weapons." Aegisthus got to his feet.

Tully put his stake back in one boot.

Behind us, the body of Stinky Suit slumped mangled by the stairs. AGB and Aegisthus recoiled from the mess. Sloan had been right. We had killed him, but it was not a tidy job. On the floor by Stinky Suit one of my big crosses lay discarded. I picked it up. The other must've fallen out in the fight with Sloan.

"She's at the greenhouse?" I asked. "Where is that?"

"Other side of the property," AGB said still staring at the dead vampire. "Volunteered at Maymont last summer instead of going home."

Navigation, check. Plan, check. Find Finder & don't get killed.

"Can we find anything for these guys to use as weapons?" I asked Tully. "I'll be right back."

I stepped back into the parlor. Chess pieces lay scattered. The black king rested on its side in the pile of smoking ash that had been the vampire Sloan. I picked up my other cross from where it had fallen by the overturned chess table. My shoe hit something as I stepped forward. The white queen. She lay at my feet, cold marble. I picked her up and used her to drag my mezuzah out of the cremated Sloan. It radiated heat like a mug of too hot coffee. I ran back through the pantry door and grabbed a clean dishtowel. I picked up my mezuzah with the towel and wrapped it. In a bizarre moment of triumph, I stuck the cold, white queen in my pocket.

The chess games had taken less time than planned. even with the fight, we were up a tempo. We had thirteen minutes left.

"We're rescuing Finder? *The* Finder?"

AGB and I kept watch at the front of the house. Tully had taken Aegisthus to find weapons. AGB touched the side of my face. I winced.

"That's gonna be black and blue for a while," he said. "Too bad you won't be able to brag about it. Oh yeah, this vampire hit me upside the head with a pool cue after I kicked his butt at chess. But don't worry, I burnt his face with a mezuzah and he exploded in a pile of ash. It was no big deal."

My arm ached where Stinky Suit had whacked me, my split lip stung, though I didn't even know when that had happened. We were all wounded somewhere and two of our party were not only inexperienced like me, but also unarmed. Not good odds heading into the endgame. Darcy and the other six bat suits were alive and unharmed. Matilda, I assumed, was at full strength and had Finder captive. Finder's condition was unknown. Sloan Silver Tie said Matilda had her in the greenhouse, but then Darcy flew off, presumably to warn Matilda that we knew where they were and were coming. Would she settle in because her stronghold was set and she could sit out and watch as her Bat Suits killed or captured us? Or would she castle at the last minute, hiding Finder and buying herself the remaining minutes she needed to get in the game?

A bully would hide Finder to scare us, make us think we had no chance. Maybe even lie and tell us she was dead to get us to surrender. A bully would enjoy doing the final decimation on her own. Letting her minions do it would be a disappointment. I needed my surprise endgame.

Make a plan. Stick to the plan. Be ready to change the plan. Keep your mind on the mate.

My plan to smother Matilda, trap her behind her own pieces would no longer work. She had too much strength still in the game. Without Finder to do damage, we just hadn't destroyed or incapacitated enough of Matilda's men. And the men we got back were broken, reduced to fighting one handed. I had failed. Each individual skirmish had come out okay, but I had secured no true advantage. My army was trashed, my strongest piece captured. I needed to get a pawn across the board and promoted to a stronger piece in order to win. I didn't how that could happen though. In real life you couldn't just become something that you weren't, even if you did travel far at great peril to do it.

How could I pose a great enough threat that she would back down and flee, or hide letting us retake our Finder? I had maybe surprised her by not chasing Finder's captors, and had pinned and captured one piece, Stinky Suit, guarding the trap. I'd fallen headlong into the trap of rescue, which accomplished an important positional goal but cost a lot of time. I'd avoided her fork in the kitchen, meant to be a physical fight that killed or incapacitated us, with the chess game. Still, I had been so busy reacting to her moves that I'd only forced one, the one where Silver Tie gave me information.

A smothered mate would take a miracle. I needed a new plan.

I unwrapped the mezuzah. It had cooled enough to go back in my pocket. I chucked the dishtowel. I struggled to discover the new better plan. AGB watched me intently.

"You're beautiful when you think," he said.

Part of me started melting into a girl with a crush.

Stacy not now! I scolded. MIND ON THE MATE. Well, that sounded wrong.

Ignoring his compliment, I asked a question.

"You know what a mezuzah is?"

"I'm from Florida," he said. "You know what they say about why Miami is so beautiful?"

"Yeah. There's a Rosenblum on every corner."

He smiled. That sweet touchable curve of his lip was deeply distracting. I asked a question that had been bothering me. An important question.

He answered.

"Nick."

"No, your real name."

"Nick! Nicholas Richard O'Malley, at your service," he said. "I loved the headstone and decided to make Nicolai my character name so that when people said it, I would be less likely to stare into space and be like, what? Who, me?"

"And Aegisthus?"

"Luke Whitehall. His brother John owns the game store in Carytown. It's how we all met." I had a thousand questions, but I had to stay focused.

"Can you use your arm?" I looked at the one with the hacked tattoo. He opened and closed his fist, testing the pull on the skin.

"It's just a flesh wound," he said.

"My dad loves that movie," I said.

He looked at me, confused. "I mean it's just skin damage, nothing too serious. It hurts, but I'm not actually *hurt.*"

"Right. Sorry. You said flesh wound and I thought Monty Python . . ." My voice trailed off. It clicked behind his eyes.

"Oh! Sorry. Holy Grail. Of course. This, on the other hand," Nick said, holding up his punctured palm.

"No pun intended," I said. Oh god, could I just shut up now?

Blood oozed from the puncture. Nick knelt and picked up my discarded dishtowel. He wrapped it around his hand, then offered the thick bundle to me.

"Would you?" he said. "It'll help, and shouldn't bleed through."

He laid his hand on mine and showed me how to put pressure on the puncture from both sides to stop the bleeding.

Aware of him watching me as I pressed on his hand, his heavy, warm hand wrapped in terrycloth and held carefully in my palm, I kept my eyes on the towel. A long minute went by where all I could hear was my heart thudding in my chest and both of us breathing. The proximity of him rippled over my skin.

"Did they hurt you anywhere else?" I asked, eyes still on the towel.

"She wanted to humiliate us. And I think she planned to . . ."

"Eat you."

"Yes. I think."

Behind us something shuffled. I turned, dropping AGB's hand and whipping out my cross. Tully and Aegisthus each held a pool cue. The stake Tully dropped in the parlor was tucked in Aegisthus' belt. Aegisthus handed AGB the dagger that had pinned his hand. It had been washed.

"Better than nothing," he said.

Aegisthus stepped up beside me. Closer than he had come yet. He smelled bad. Bad like when I used to help change Steve's diapers.

AGB puffed air out of his nose to clear it. He raised an eyebrow at his friend.

"Luke. Did you — ?"

"Having my hand crucified was very scary," the older man said, cutting AGB off. He looked at his shoes, cheeks brightening red. "I don't want to talk about it."

Right.

28.

November 16, continued. 4:13 a.m.

"Catch Tully," I gasped. My lungs ached with cold and exertion. I stopped and put my hands on my knees. Nick ran ahead.

Freezing air rushed into my cramping chest. In the city, I'd walked forty sometimes fifty blocks a day, fairly average for a New Yorker. I could walk and walk and walk. I didn't get tired, I didn't hyperventilate. I didn't choke from car exhaust. In the clean Virginia air, however, I couldn't run from a house to a barn without needing 911. If I lived through the night, I needed to start paying attention in PE. Or using the new home gym. Being unable to breathe while running felt both ridiculous and embarrassing.

Half a minute later Nick arrived back, Tully on his heels.

"What? Did you see something?" Tully said.

"This is what Matilda wants us to do. We're losing time chasing. I think she took Finder back near the house. Aren't you suspicious that no Bat Suits have attacked us out here?

She isn't scared. She thinks we've already lost, and if we keep," I tried to get a bigger breath but my lungs were so tight. "If we keep running we will."

"You think we should go back?"

I nodded. "Not the house."

"Maybe the stone barn?"

"She'll want us enclosed but in a space easy for her Bat Suits to attack. And clean for when she kills us," I said. "She'll want a place where we can see Finder, but not get to her."

Tully started back up the hill.

"Tully! Wait!"

He turned, frustration building behind his eyes.

I explained the short version of my theory.

Tully clenched and unclenched his fists. "If Mr. Jackson told her we were coming, would Matilda move Finder or just set Bat Suits to run us down on the way?"

Nick looked back toward the mansion. "I'd say both."

"No," I said. Ugh! I had just explained this! "She's a bully. She wants to watch us lose, or kill us herself. There's only eleven minutes til she joins the game. It's in her best interest to keep us busy so we don't track Finder in time."

"So she's moving her?" Tully asked.

"Yes. Or killing us, but I'm not as worried about that. She didn't get her hands dirty at the museum."

"She didn't mind practically breaking my arm," said Luke/Aegisthus.

"She was just having fun," I said.

"We're losing time!" Tully said. "We have to get going!"

"She'll bring her close. She's sure we'll just start running and searching! What's closest?"

"You can see the garage and carriage houses from right there," Nick said nodding toward the front steps. "My guess would be the Stone Barn, it's on the other side of the garage."

The stone barn was empty. Something on the floor caught my eye. A tiny laminated card.

Resist.

"They were here! Crap! She must've just moved her!"

I'd made a classic mistake. I'd decided I was smarter than my opponent. Tully looked at me.

It makes sense to have taken Finder far at first. Matilda thought we'd chase them and then have to run back across the gardens to find the guys. But when we didn't chase, she changed her plan. Kept Finder right here, under our noses.

I held the little card last held by Finder and closed my eyes. Where are you, Finder? I thought? Where?

"What're you doing?"

Despite the time crunch and the rush, I slowed my breathing and took three long deep breaths. In my head, I pictured Finder. I imagined her hands on my shoulders back at her house. Her eyes, wide and determined and espresso black. Silently, I said *By the power of three by three, help me find . . . the girl I seek. To cause no harm nor return on me, as I will so mote it be.*

The top of my head tingled, a light flickering on in the back of my brain illuminating an image of a building with a turret at the top.

"She's castling!" I turned to Nick. "Is there any building here besides the house that looks like a castle?"

We raced back into the frigid night, Tully in the lead, Luke just behind him. I was flanked by AGB/ Nick, who frequently checked to see if I was okay. We had six minutes to locate Finder. Maymont was *big*. I hadn't realized, but it had been nice to be warm. The house may not have had the heat on since the museum closed for the day, but sixty degrees and no wind feels toasty compared to a gusty outdoor thirty

The downhill part of the run went okay. I managed an initial sprint, then slid, but didn't fall in the frosty grass. The temperature had dropped while we'd been inside transforming the dew to ice. Tully ran ahead, passing the barn and skidding onto a gravel path. I forced myself to keep going. My lungs tightened, accepting less and less air with each lunge forward.

"Go that way!" Nick called, pointing to Tully's left. "Shortcut through the Italian garden!"

I was so bad at running. My sneakers slipped again on the slick grass. Nick took my hand with his good one and helped me go faster.

"Breathe slow," Nick said. The cold rammed into my chest like an ice pick. Cramps started along my sides.

Tully and Luke disappeared down the hill, through a gap in the high, stone wall. I staggered, gasping for air. I slowed to a walk. I coughed. I looked at my watch. 4:19. We had until 4:24 before Matilda came after us.

I forced my legs to go, trying not to concentrate on how my lungs felt like collapsing ice cube trays, but on the feel of Nick's strong hand in mine and the sound of our feet on gravel: crunch, crunch, crunch.

Nick ran backwards watching me. "Have you always had asthma or did it come from an illness?"

I tried to say "I don't have asthma," but I couldn't get enough air. I slowed to a walking jog.

Keep going, I told myself. Crunch crunch crunch. Like they say, could you do it, crunch crunch, if your life depended on it? We made it, me gasping with each burning breath, to the wall where the others disappeared.

My entire torso hurt. I hated running. Or maybe I just hated feeling like an elephant sat on my chest. It struck me, passing through the dense trees and through the wall's wide gate, that this would be a perfect place for an ambush. In their bat bodies at least, the Suits could easily negotiate the trees, dark and cold.

"Looks like an 'all my life' asthma if you ask me," Nick said. "Not that I'm a professional or anything." His eyes twinkled green gold.

Tully and Luke disappeared over the hill's rise, way ahead of Nick and me. I struggled to breathe as Nick and I climbed. We crested the top. I stopped again and put my hands on my knees. Our vantage point overlooked the garden below. The Stone Mill, a square building turreted at the top with a rook-like silhouette, glowed eerie gray in the moonlight. A castle.

"She's there," I said, hoping I wasn't wrong.

Two running figures melted out of the downhill shadows. Tully's blonde hair whipped below us like a banner in the wind.

"Tully! Wait!" I shouted.

The noisy breeze scattered my voice into nothing. Tully and Luke disappeared inside a doorway. A collection of shadows coalesced from outside the doorway into three more figures. They followed Luke & Tully in.

Crap.

Whether I was wrong or not, that was where we were going.

"Another interruption?" Matilda exclaimed as we burst through the narrow stone doorway. "God, I hate being interrupted! Hold!" Matilda raised her hand and I took in what was happening.

The wide mill room, lit by electric fairy lights strung from the rafters, was set up like an old-fashioned boxing arena. Barefoot on the white mats, Finder and Bald Suit stood across from each other in fighting stance. The arena edges were marked by corner posts and ropes. Inside the ring, blood had spilled. I smelled it, strong and metallic. Bald Suit kept his eyes on Finder. He wore rolled up shirt sleeves and no tie.

Dread filled my belly. Finder bled from multiple cuts on her face. She had stripped down to her tank top and dress pants with bare feet. Her arms were dark with bruises, but she was standing, defensive, fists curled in front of her. I squinted to see in the dim light. Finder had bite marks on her neck and arms.

Matilda looked at her wristwatch.

"Thirty-nine seconds? You beat me by thirty-nine *seconds*? Are you bloody kidding me?"

Goatee Bat Suit sat next to Tully on a bench, a thick arm draped over my friend's shoulders. The Southern Scotsman's elbows were anchored to his torso by thick rope. His ankles were tied together. Luke sat on the other side of the bench untrussed but dazed and still. A Bat Suit I didn't recognize sat next to him.

"Darcy Elvis Broadmoore Jackson! You told me, you assured me, you *convinced* me they would never find us down here. You were wrong, you dolt!" She leaned over and open palm smacked him upside the head. "How tragic is that?" she moaned. "What a wasted night! And you brats ruined two, *two* of my perfectly good gentleman butlers. Do you have any idea how *long* it took me to get those two to behave as I expected? Now, I am irritated. You should know that. I bet you think you're going to ruin the rest of my fun by ending the tournament! Well, you are not!" She snapped her fingers and the shadows around her materialized into Bat Suits. Most of them wore rolled up shirt sleeves like Bald Suit and several were bloodied. Fury boiled in my belly. Dead things didn't bleed. So all of that blood belonged to a person. One person.

"First of all, I am keeping those two in exchange for the ones I lost," she said pointing at Luke and Tully. "It is *unfathomably* rude to come to someone's home uninvited and damage their property!"

"You can't keep them!" I pulled my hand away from Nick as I stepped forward. I stared at her feet. "The agreement was that if we found our people within the hour you would let us all go!"

"Well that's boring and I'm changing the rules. Now sit down and watch the fight or I'll have you trussed up like those. Well, like that one. I have had quite enough games. Darcy is making his daughter one of us tonight, but I wanted to see what she could do before the change enhances her abilities. I admit, she is impressive. Don't you agree, gents?" The various bloody Bat Suits muttered reluctant agreements. Matilda turned back to us. "Sit!"

Four Bat Suits slid behind us, next to the stone mill wall and herded us toward a long wooden bench. We sat. I did not like having Bat Suits at my back. It was disconcerting. I cast around, desperate for an idea. How could I get us out of this? Tully was incapacitated, Luke sat mesmerized. Nick and I were weaponless except for my holy items, Nick's knife, two fake fangs and the pool cue he had failed to impale with earlier. Wait. Where was the pool cue? I caught Nick's eye and he nodded toward the door. He had stuck it in the door frame and in the dim light no one had noticed it. Hmmm.

Terminator Bat Suit rang a bell. The round started. Bald Suit circled Finder who moved opposite him in response. He attacked, fist to her face. She ducked and kicked him in the belly. He didn't react. He bounced on his feet like a boxer, Finder stayed soft on her toes. They danced around each other swinging and dodging. He threw another punch to her head and hit. The sound of bone on bone sickened me. Skin split over her cheekbone. She punched his face and spun with a swift kick in his groin that would have collapsed any human man. They went at each other hard and vicious. Finder's blows were targeted, intelligent. She kicked his knee hard. He fell to the mat. She stepped closer, but he grabbed her leg and yanked. She landed flat on her back. With inhuman speed, he reached for her. Matilda rang the bell.

"No special skills!" she shouted. Finder took her opportunity. She kicked Bald Suit swift in the jaw. He reeled back. She hopped to a crouch. And punched his face again. And again. He stayed down.

Goatee Suit stepped in as the referee.

He held up Finder's arm as the victor.

She had hardly a moment to rest before the next challenger stepped into the ring. It was the Terminator Bat Suit who'd rung the bell for the previous match. Stripped to his shirt sleeves, he towered over Finder and was twice her girth. Darcy Jackson hit the bell to start. I didn't want to watch but I was afraid not to. How long had she been fighting? How much longer could she keep it up before she got exhausted and made a mistake?

She ducked Terminator's first blow. Dude was huge. This one could not end well. I closed my eyes. I listened to the grunts and sounds of the fight as I scrambled for a way out. What could I do? We weren't playing chess anymore. There were no rules to this game. It was Do Whatever Matilda Wanted. How did she have a never ending supply of Bat Suits to do her bidding? I counted. Four behind us, two with Luke and Tully, Terminator in the ring, Goatee, Bald Suit and Finder's dad. Ten. There had been twelve. Were there more? The sound of a heavy thud stopped my mental count. My eyes shot open. Terminator reeled back from, I assume, a head punch. Finder leaped into the air, a badass marital arts kick spin thing. Terminator caught her leg and threw her to the ground. She lay still. Goatee came in and pronounced Terminator the victor. He poked Finder who didn't move. He poked her again. Nothing.

"Victory prize!" Announced Matilda clapping her hands in delight. Terminator leaned down and bit Finder. Her body jerked and spasmed. The Bat Suits chanted, "One one thousand two one thousand three one thousand" and on to eleven. Finder stirred with a moan. The Bat Suits all applauded, hooting and shouting encouragement. Terminator let go. He dragged her upright. She swayed on her feet, but did not fall.

"I think she's ready, Darcy," he said, voice like gravel. Blood dripped off his chin. He reached a finger to wipe it and licked it off his fingers.

Clad in clean white shirt sleeves, rolled up to the elbows like the others, Finder's father entered the arena.

The room went silent.

"I don't want to fight you, baby," Darcy said and opened his arms. "Come to me."

"No."

"Please." He stood arms open. I glanced at Tully, all tied up. My God, where was a highlander with a stake when you needed him!

"Won't let you take me, Dad," she said, not very loud. "I'll break my own neck first. I know how." Her eyes were steely on his chest.

Finder limped as she bent her knees and came into fighting stance. Had Terminator broken her knee? She bled from her face. Her fists were slick with it.

Father and daughter stood opposite each other, neither relenting. Neither moving. Finder's breath labored in her chest. She wheezed when she inhaled. Did she have internal injuries?

"I think she's bleeding inside," Nick whispered as if he was in my head with me. "See the angle of her ribcage? She has broken ribs."

Darcy Jackson finally put his fists in front of him. He drew back for a blow.

Across the room a Highlander wail.

"No! You'll kill her!" Tully's voice, cracked and desperate. "Mr. Jackson, please! Don't!"

"This is no fun at all!" said Matilda. "She's too badly hurt. You'll take her in a second Darcy. It's not a win if she's helpless." Matilda leveled her gaze at Finder. "I don't suppose you'd tolerate me licking those bite wounds for you, would you?"

"No, ma'am, I would not."

"I could give you some of your father's blood to drink. That would make you feel better and maybe get you back on that knee. It would also make you emotionally inclined to do what he wanted so maybe that's not a good idea, either."

Matilda clapped her hands together. "I've got it!" She whispered to one of her Bat Suits and he reappeared moments later with a thick wooden stake.

"You'll accept a weapon? That will help even the odds!"

"A stake, Matilda?" Darcy shouted. "Are you crazy?"

"It's life or death for her, Darcy dear. It's only fair." She nodded toward her servant. "Give it to her."

Finder took the stake.

Matilda rang the bell. It didn't take long to see how Finder had gotten started in martial arts. Together, she and her father danced, fluid and beautiful in their violence. It was like watching her fight herself. Finder wielded the stake like a wooden sword or knife, depending on what kind of attack Darcy used against her. He struck at her hands trying to force her to drop the weapon. She held it like it was an organic part of her arm, inseparable. She jabbed forward, trying to catch him off balance, but failed. He kicked. A sickening crunch as he swept her hurt knee out from under her. Finder yelped as she fell onto her back. Darcy dove for her. Clutching the stake to her chest, she rolled. Darcy caught himself before he hit the ground and lunged, landing on top of her. She slammed her head into his nose. He cried out and she shoved hard, rolled on top of him. She pushed up to kneeling, crying out as she put weight on the damaged knee.

An icy wind blew through the stone mill. The fairy lights flickered. Finder raised the stake above her head like a samurai.

A chill shook my spine. A voice, a voice I knew but couldn't place, slithered into the space silencing everyone. Finder froze, arms overhead.

"Delicious . . ." the word hissed through the room, long and sibilant. The doorway to our left filled with a dark shape. "Fear . . . and greed . . . and fury . . ."

Nick shuddered beside me. Matilda slid off her chair and dropped to her knees. The shape said nothing else, but moved to her. Its dark coat and hat held its face and body in shadow. Beneath the coat something writhed, lumps lifting and shifting beneath the material.

Matilda fell forward in prostration.

"Up . . ." said the voice.

"I am sorry," she whimpered. "I did not mean to draw Your Greatness' attention. I did not mean to -- "

A long, too long, snakelike tongue emerged from beneath the hat.

"No," she whispered, leaning back. She shielded her face with her arm. The coated creature grabbed her just below the shoulders, pulling her to standing.

"Please, no!" she begged. The snake-headed tongue slid into her ear. The vampire queen's face went white, her eyes filled with terror. Her expression contorted into one of pain. A long green bruise raised on her neck. Around us the Bat Suits stood frozen in horror. I tried to reach for Nick but my body felt heavy and thick. What was happening? Was this the creature Steve had called the Man with No Face? A nasty aroma caressed me, ammonia, strong like cat urine. I tried again to reach for Nick. The air itself pressed on me with a force so strong I couldn't lift my arms. Not wanting to draw the attention of the being in the coat and hat, I stayed still and did not try again.

It fed for a long time. Minutes. As it fed, some of the Bat Suits began to pant and moan. In the arena, Darcy Jackson pushed against the leaden air and reached for his daughter. Finder, straining against the impossible weight, brought her stake down like a club on her father's head with a resounding thump. The Man with No Face kept feeding. Something beneath the coats grew fuller, the coat clung tighter. The creature dropped Matilda into a heap on the rough stone floor. The air immediately lightened.

As I watched her crumple, conflicting emotions battled for dominance. She was cruel and deserved to die. But eaten by the Man with No Face? No one deserved that. Maybe she wasn't dead. Did I want her to be dead or did I not?

The sensation of falling filled me and I grabbed the bench to stay upright. A feeling of heaviness, being pulled by gravity to the ground . . . falling discarded into a heap just like Matilda. Recently. I gasped, my mind suddenly spilling images, blurry and sparse, but images I recognized as memories. The morphing chin, the tongue with the little snake head, waking groggy and confused on the steps of a house. What I couldn't place was when. When had it happened?

As if I had called his name aloud, the Man with No Face turned. The shifting, morphing chin and mouth beneath the hat tipped my way. Nick gasped.

"Hello again . . . resentment . . ." It stepped once, twice, three times closer. I felt it looking at me and shifted my gaze to its feet. "No need to look away . . . angry resenter . . . I do not do those mind tricks with my eyes . . ." It took nearly a full minute to utter the words. After a moment, it tilted its chin toward Nick.

"I . . . have seen . . . you, too, of late. Still disappointed you have . . . no power?" It approached our bench.

The Man with No Face came toward us, locking his invisible gaze on Nick. Next to me, AGB went stiff.

I opened my mouth to protest, to defend Nick, but it felt like hitting a wall. No sound came out.

"Taste . . . it," offered the Man with No Face, sliding still closer over the stone floor. It lifted an arm and passed a hand, a shifting, morphing hand, first the square hand of a working man, then a wrinkled, long nailed claw of a crone over Nick's head. I reached out and grabbed Nick's arm. I tried to speak, to tell him to snap out of it! To not let the fiend take control of him! I failed, my voice not emerging. Silent, thinking *No NO NO* to Nick as loud as I could, I shook his sleeve instead.

"Take . . . it," the Man said to Nick, its voice a croon, an invitation and a demand all at once. My skin itched. It ached to come off me, painful in the creature's presence. I let go of Nick's sleeve. I put my hands on his cheeks and turned him to look at me.

Snap out of it! I screamed in my mind. Nick's gaze was blank, preoccupied, unaware of my touch or pleading eyes. Desperation to bring him back shook me. I shook him. He didn't react.

The Man with No Face ignored my actions as if they were utterly irrelevant. If I could move, why couldn't I speak? Was it controlling me, too?

"Take . . . what you . . . crave," the creature purred, holding his hand steady over Nick's head. I reached out to smack it away. A jolt of electricity shot up my arm when I got close. I cried out in pain and yanked my hand back.

"No, no . . . little resenter. You . . . may not . . . interfere." The Man turned back to Nick. "You are my creature . . . do not ask . . . If you crave . . . take."

Nick squared his shoulders to the creature, then slowly, like a predator tracking prey, turned to . . . me. His arm shot up from his side and before I could react, grabbed my wrist. His gaze caressed me, dark and hungry. This was *not* Nick. It was his body, but not his sweet soulful self. Not the Nick that held me in the cemetery, that called for my help, that didn't finish his coffee.

Not Nick started to pull me toward him. I backed away as far as the length of my arm would allow. I pulled. Not Nick held on. I slid my backside as far away from him on the bench as I could. None of the Bat Suits moved.

Nick, this isn't you, I thought as loud as I could. As if calling out in my mind could make him hear me.

"It is . . . still him . . ." the Man with No Face said as if hearing my thoughts. "It is his . . . shadow side . . . my side . . ."

I wanted to speak, but again could not. Not Nick edged with me as I backed closer to the end of the bench. I hadn't realized how much bigger and stronger than me he actually was. He could overpower me in a second. It scared me. I slid to the edge of the bench and put my feet on the ground to stand. Not Nick stood with me, holding tight to my wrist. I unfolded to my full height, my nose even with his shoulder. His fingers dug into my skin.

No doors on this side of the room. I'd have to go past him and past the Man with No Face, whatever he/ it was, to escape. I wanted to speak, I had to, to maybe save both my life and his. I reached out with my will, that part of me that could see multiple moves ahead by deciding, *deciding* to do so. I closed my eyes. Extending that deciding part of me, the Man with No Face surfaced like a physical wall. My mind bumped against it.

Players build walls in chess all the time, barriers made of pawns, rooks, a queen. In every wall, I could find a weak spot, a peephole. Sometimes it took more than one move to break through. Sometimes I had to create the hole by finding the weakest spot in the wall and leaning on it hard. The right amount of pressure and the right piece at the right time could do it. All I needed was a glimpse of opportunity.

I pulled my mind back from the wall and searched for the gap. There was no board, there were no pieces, but I knew what a weak spot felt like. The fragility of an unprotected square, a hanging piece, doubled pawns undefended in the midst of battle. I had to meet this creature on the board he played on, a field of energy and mind and space. I opened my mind to *feel* . . . I imagined slipping unnoticed through his wall, through a crack the Man with No Face might have missed. I took a deep breath, creeping hushed mind energy along the creature's solid, evil wall. One unprotected square was all I needed.

And then I felt it. A tiny breeze touched my mind as the Man's attention to Not Nick wavered. Something moved in my peripheral vision. Behind the creature, Finder had dragged herself to the edge of the boxing arena and was using the cords to pull herself upright. In a gasping second, the Man with No Face saw her. A crack in his wall opened.

Summoning all my courage, I pushed against that chink and broke through. A furry feeling rose into my throat. My voice came out thin, quavering.

"Nick. It's me, Stacy. I'm your friend." Not Nick gripped my wrist so hard I winced. He took his time backing me toward the stone corner.

"Rage . . ." the Man with No Face purred at Finder. "Beautiful rage . . ." It moved to grab her arms.

"Don't touch her!" I cried, throat raspy. "She's hurt!"

A laugh unlike any sound I had heard reverberated off the stone walls. It shook me. Too much bass and to shrieking sharp a high note at once. My hands flew to my ears. The movement jerked Not Nick, still locked onto my wrist, closer to me. My back bumped up against the wall. Trapped. Not Nick hovered over me, green eyes menacing. He licked his lips.

"She is ripe for me . . . so angry . . . and so sad . . ." hissed the Man with No Face.

Not Nick pushed my hand down to my side, pinning me between him and the wall. I wrapped my free hand around the mezuzah in my pocket. Would it even do anything? What if it did? I didn't want to hurt real Nick. Letting go of the mezuzah, I saw the knife used to puncture his hand sticking out of his pocket. Could I reach it? What would I do with it if I could? Not Nick leaned in and touched my hair. I smacked his hand away. I realized my mistake. If I let him touch me, I could maybe reach the knife.

I pulled my hand back to my side, closer to his pocket and the knife handle. He reached for my hair again. The soft looking lock of his hair fell forward into his face. He lowered his face like he might kiss me. Fear rushed up and over me making me sweat and shiver at the same time. Turning my face hard to the side, my hand dove for the knife. I snatched it from his pocket and pressed the tip of the blade into his belly. I didn't think I could push it in.

"Back up," I whispered. "This isn't you."

As if someone opened a freezer door next to me, the Man with No Face's gaze landed on me.

"Do it," breathed the fiend. "Do it. I will reward you . . . little resenter . . . his life will feed me . . . I can give you my gifts . . . It hurts . . . you to be here . . . You want . . .to go home. I can visit . . . your father and change . . . his mind. I can . . . convince him . . . with his own thoughts . . . to send you back . . . to New York. To live with . . . your grandmother. I will even return to you . . . what my creature stole . . . Memories . . . of your precious . . . friends."

I squinted into the darkness under the brim of his hat. What memories? What friends?

Pain-fire behind my eyes. And then like a dam breaking open in my heart, I realized what had, for the last hours, been missing. What the vampire had fed on and stolen, what my mind had reached for and found pain instead. Pain ripped at the wound of what had been cut out. Meredith! The memories of her pushed at my mind, but a convulsive spasm of blistering fire shot through my body, leaving our past and full relationship just out of reach.

"Not yet . . ." The sibilant voice spat. "Not until you do it . . ." The knife warmed in my hand.

I would remember Meredith. I would go home.

"Take the life . . . give me the life . . ." encouraged the creature. He murmured the request over and over. "Kill him before he kills you . . . I will not . . . stop him. . . . if he bites you, he will take everything . . . blood . . . soul . . . everything."

The dim fairy lights reflected in the green flecked eyes. A person who had been kind to me was trapped behind that hungry expression. Nick was in there. Someone I could trust. He was not a killer. Neither was I.

Not Nick opened his mouth in a rictus smile. Fangs.

I bolted to the side. Nick grabbed my hood and jerked me back toward him. I dropped the knife and yanked the mezuzah out of my pocket. With a wild yelp, I mashed it into his face. Skin sizzled and I let go. The mezuzah clattered to the ground. Not Nick screamed and shot away from me. His hands flew to his face cowering from the tiny, blessed bar. I ran to the side, but the Bat Suits that guarded Tully and Luke blocked my way. I backed away. The Man with No Face waved its arm and Nick snapped back up, as if the mezuzah had never touched his flesh. He came toward me, cheek blistered and still smoking. His mouth hung open in fury and desire.

"What is your choice . . . little resenter . . .?" The Man with No Face's voice echoed against the walls.

Everything I wanted, he could give it to me. I could go home. I could get away from this rotten, monster-infested town and go home. Home. Rabbi Berman, Bubbe. Meredith, Isaac and Sorrel. And my father would think it was his idea. It was all I had wanted since before we left the City. But I had to kill Not Nick.

My rescued crucifixes jabbed my side where they stuck in my belt. I reached for them.

Not Nick lunged for me. I dove to the side but wasn't fast enough. He caught my arm so tight it made me cry out.

"You aren't a real vampire!" I shouted as he spun me toward him. "You're a fake! This. Isn't. You!" Nick moved toward me still, his mouth open to bite.

"Nick! I cried. "Nicholas Richard O'Malley! Look at your arm!" I cried. I reached for the crosses, but couldn't get them. "You're not a real vampire! You're a fake!"

"He is real . . . I helped him . . ." said the thing. "For now."

"It's lying!" I grabbed Nick's sleeve and shoved it up his arm. The tattoo glowed red and angry, still so fresh. In German: I am a fake. *Ich bin eine Fälschung.*

"See?" I said. Nick who wasn't Nick grabbed my other arm. He squared me to him. He dove in to bite. I stomped hard on the top of his foot and thrust my knee into his groin. He howled in pain and fell forward slamming me back against the stone mill wall. Winded, I shoved him off, nearly slipping on the floor. I lurched out of his grasp. I yanked the crosses out of my belt. I held them out like a shield in front of me.

"Get off him!" I cried to the Man with No Face. "Let him go!"

"Why . . . would I . . . ?" it said in that slithery voice. "I can transform anyone . . . even you, little resenter . . . Do you . . . want to feel . . . your darkness . . . your power . . . take you over?" The Man with No Face walked forward. The tongue, that over long tongue with the tiny, sniffing head arched and closed the distance between us. The space between the Man's collar and the low brim of its hat shifted and morphed. A slender woman's neck became an obese throat then blended into a black neck beard. The creature raised its hand toward me, like it had over Nick, though it was still a body length away.

"No!" I screamed! "Don't touch me!" If my resentment was going to turn me into a monster, I did not want it.

Anger rose in me, my fury at this creature for threatening me, at Matilda for hurting my friends, fury at the people who attacked my city, at the adults who had attacked my life and forced my moves. Forced me to abandon my home and friends when we needed each other most. Forced me to betray my mom.

My rage, my resentment drove my will toward the horrible thing raising its hand in front of me. Even though I knew it was wrong, dark emotion curled to the surface of my skin. Nick had lied to me, put me and my friends in danger. Who was he to risk our lives? Who was my father to tear me from my home?

I rose to the creature's call.

I imagined Not Nick breaking in the grip of my hands, strong hands, powerful hands. Not the little helpless hands that moved chess pieces. In my pocket, the white queen weighed.

Rabbi Berman's voice echoed deep in the back of my mind.

Keep your mind on the mate.

The mate. I had come here to save lives, not take them. Matilda lay crumpled, still unmoving. Finder slid in front of her and behind the creature, limping and bloodied. She was heading for the doorway. I didn't have half the injuries she did. My dad may have taken me from New York, but he wasn't trying to kill me and make me undead. She slid closer to the entry. Wait, was she running away? Leaving us to die here while she escaped? A surge of angry desire pulsed through me, pulling my attention back toward the Man with No Face and his offer. I could ditch all of these selfish people. I could go home . . . I would be a murderer. I kind of already was.

I pulled my hand out of my pocket, ready to reach for the injured Not Nick. A tiny, laminated card fluttered to the floor.

Resist.

As if a fog cleared from my brain, I saw what the Man with No Face was doing. How it manipulated me in service of its will. *Its* will. Not mine.

I would not give away my will. I reached deep inside of me, desperate for the opposite of my fury, for the opposite of what the Man with No Face called to in me. I did not want the future this creature offered. I had made a choice when we moved here, a choice to live furious. If I didn't want this thing to control me, I had to make a new choice. Right now. Hands empty except for the worn wooden crosses, I reached for the only weapon I had left. My will.

The Man's serpent-like tongue licked the air inches away from my face. In a flash, I understood that true prayer did not plead, it demanded. It made your will clear and true and alive. For the first time in my life, I prayed.

"By the power of three by three, heal the thing that's harming me, to cause no harm nor return on me, as I WILL, so mote it BE!" Something tingled in my chest. The tongue came closer. A word came to my mind.

Forgive.

Mama's golden ball of light appeared my mind's eye.

Inside it, I saw my dad. "I forgive you," I whispered. I saw my mom as she was when I was little. "I forgive you."

"What . . .?" the head at the end of its tongue reared back, hissing. It prepared to strike.

I saw the towers on fire. "I forgive you," I said louder. And small things falling. The golden cloud grew. My heart was breaking. How could I live without anger? How could I not feel fury at these people? At injustice? At all the cruelty that existed? "I forgive you," I said. I meant it.

A switch flipped inside of me. Forgiveness wasn't about not feeling anger, it was about not hurting myself with anger. Forgiveness was a demand for growth. The realization you could become more than you had been. Forgiveness was pawn promotion.

"Stay away from me!" I rooted my feet into the stone floor. I smacked the tongue with the crosses in front of me. "I don't know what you are," I cried to the thing, "but I know what opposes you." I took a breath pulling my will from everywhere in my body and mind. "I KNOW WHAT OPPOSES YOU," I said in a voice I didn't know could come from me, "AND I. WILL. BECOME IT!"

The snake tongue thing came forward as if my crosses meant nothing. It curved toward my ear.

A vision of the St. Michael basin where I blessed and bathed my crosses popped into my mind. At the top of my lungs I screamed, I demanded, I prayed. "HELP!"

And in my head all the fear and noise and knowledge went quiet. A heat, a blush colored heat rose from my feet and came down from above me drawing power from the earth and the sky. The crosses in my hands began to blaze. The Man with No Face paused as if surprised. It stepped back one small step. And shrieked. An unthinkable, unearthly sound that knocked everyone to the floor. Matilda and the Bat Suits writhed and screamed.

Finder leaped forward with a last draw of strength and slammed the pool cue Real Nick had left in the doorway into the Man with No Face like a stake. He looked down and yanked the cue through his chest. He turned to Finder with inhuman grace and slammed the stick across her face. Her eyes rolled in her head. She buckled and fell.

I did not fall. I stood. My whole body flamed with energy and light and faith. Two words blew through my mouth as if I were an amplifier.

"BE GONE!"

The creature screeched and threw something at me, but I felt nothing. It attacked again, but whatever it threw burned in the fire from my crosses.

The words again boomed from within me.

"BE. GONE."

The Man with No Face shuddered. A shriek of anguish and demonic fury filled the stone mill, shaking its very stones.

"BE GONE!" I cried again. A whoosh of air lifted me off my feet. The fire in me blazed hot as an ear splitting pop filled the mill. The Man with No Face vanished.

Energy flowed through me for one last moment. Still airborne, I slammed into something. And everything went black.

29.

November 16, continued. 4:56 a.m.

"Stacy? I think she's waking up."

My eyes fluttered open. Finder was leaning forward. Nick reached to take my hand. I jerked away. He backed off, scared.

"Did I hurt you?"

Finder slid her arm behind my shoulders and helped me sit. My tailbone killed.

"You blew backwards as the angel left you," she said. "You hit the wall then landed right on your butt. It might be broken."

"An angel?"

"Your tailbone, stupid."

She pressed something into my hand. My mezuzah.

"Wouldn't want to lose that," she said. Astonished, I closed it in my fist. I'd have to check with Tully later, but I believe that for Finder, that was an apology.

Speaking of Tully, his voice echoed from across the room.

"Watch it! That's real skin there."

Luke knelt in front of the Southern Scotsman, knife in hand. "Sorry!"

"No worries. Thank you!" Arms now free, Tully rubbed his wrists. Luke started to go for the ropes binding Tully's ankles.

"I'll take it from here, chief," Tully said opening his hand for the knife.

"I'll be more careful this time," Luke said, but handed Tully the blade. Tully bent over and started sawing at his own ropes. Finder saw the other knife glinting in the fairy lights near the bench where I had dropped it. She picked it up and went to help Tully.

"They're gonna wake up soon," said Finder. "We gotta jet."

Around us in various poses of collapse, lay the vampires. Matilda lay in a heap at the far end of the room from us, the end closest to the door we came in. Her Bat Suits lay all over, depending on where they had been when they fell. I now saw that Tully and Luke had been in front of not another wall, but sliding barn doors.

"Let's use those," I said nodding to the wide wooden panels.

"It's not waiting for us, Goldman. You banished it. You summoned an angel and banished whatever that was. But we don't know for how long."

I looked at her, one eyebrow raised. I didn't think I had heard her correctly. Angel? Banishment? This was very confusing. There were no more cuts on her face, though she was bloody as hell. "Why is your face healed? Your ribs were broken. You had internal injuries. Your knee . . ."

"You are the densest brainiac I have ever met," she said, standing. "Can we please go?" Finder said to Tully. "I don't want to be here when my dad wakes up. We can explain what happened to Smart Stuff on the way."

Tully stood, stretched and offered Finder his stake. She looked at it, at Tully, hovering for a moment in his gaze. She walked over to where her father lay. She crouched over him and raised the stake high in front of her chest. She took a big breath. She dropped her arms.

"I can't do it."

"Do want me to?" Tully said in a voice so tender, I knew he would do anything for her.

She brushed her hand lightly across her father's face. "No. If it has to be done, I'll do it. But not tonight. Not when he's helpless."

One of the Bat Suits stirred.

"Guys," Nick said, indicating.

I crawled to all fours. He offered his hand.

"May I help you?"

"Are you sure you're you? Open your mouth. Say ah." He did. No fangs. Permission granted.

I took a step. Excruciating pain shot down my legs and torso. I yelped.

"And that's the sound of a broken coccyx," said Nick. "Looks like I'll be carrying you."

"I'll carry her," Tully said, coming over to us. "I'm used to carrying heavy things." He looked at me. "Oh wait, that means you don't count." Tully smiled. He was teasing me! Tully had never teased me. Maybe this meant that we were now really and truly friends.

"I think I can walk," I said. I took another step. A jolt of pain made my head swim. Fail! I made an embarrassing noise and Tully caught me on my way to the floor. Okay. Walking was not an option. "I want her wrapped in my coat in case she goes into shock," Nick said.

They bundled me into Nick's coat, so long it dragged on the ground. Tully said, "You should be a doctor."

"That's the plan," Nick said.

Finder opened the mill door still in her tank top, the suit jacket slung over her arm. She looked like she'd been in a slasher movie: blood had dried on her face and arms and had soaked her shirt. She had promised her mom she wouldn't get blood on the suit jacket, but it was cold and she shouldn't be out in just a tank.

"Wait." I shimmied out of the coat and took off the extra hoodie. I held it out. Finder put it on. The guys helped me rewrap and Tully scooped me up. Nick's coat smelled wonderful. Warm and comforting, like him.

My worn out wooden Jesuses lay scattered where they had fallen.

"Nick?" I asked. He saw what I was looking at and picked them up.

"Thank you."

He nodded, then spoke to Tully. "I can carry Stacy, too. If you get tired. It's a long walk."

As we tiptoed past the unconscious Bat Suits, I noticed some of them had streaks of ash where their sleeves had been. A few had burns on their faces and arms. Had I done that? I didn't know.

Nick led us around the Stone Mill and back through the gardens. Walking, Tully tried not to jostle me. I winced when he failed. I eyed the shrubbery and the path ahead, wary but hopeful that combat for the night had ended.

I started shivering with shock halfway through the first garden. My tailbone burned and stung. I had so many questions. I figured we all did. There was only one question I needed the answer to right now. I turned my attention to Nick.

"It's called Hidden City," he said. "Your character is one of many kinds of supers. Only a few people play humans. I thought that was you."

"I've been playing longest," Luke said. Hence the Senior. "When people join the game, they join as humans who get turned into supers by a current player. Nick started two years ago, so he is next after me to get the advantages of children, or new players."

Finder shook her head. "So you had no idea you were playing with real monsters?"

Luke shook his head. "Nope. One of Matilda's guys came into the shop one night when we were playing around the table. He watched and the next time we played she showed up and asked to join the game. Not many women play so we did our best to make her feel welcome. She set up her character as my . . . um . . ."

"We get it," said Finder.

"We all liked her," Nick said. "She was sweet and smart and a great player. So we thought."

"And she was hot," Finder said. Luke blushed.

"We're sorry," the older man said. "We thought you knew."

"We thought you were all players," Nick said.

"Wait . . .you biting Angela in the alley and that whole thing?" I asked.

"Live action. Acting. We play out certain scenes live to see what happens and for the benefit of other players who might be watching. It's like improv theatre only not quite so planned."

"The blood . . ?"

"Stage blood. It looked really good on that white dress, don't you think?"

Arriving at the Nature Center access gate, Nick pulled something from his pocket and jiggled the padlock. It was a long walk, Nick hadn't lied. It was worth it though, making it so we didn't have to climb the fence for a second time. Tully reorganized me in his arms.

Even after a major fight, he still smelled of pine trees and pancakes. No wonder Finder loved him.

"You should've told me about her dad," I whispered close in his ear.

"Not my secret to tell," he said. "You wouldn't have believed me anyway."

Well. That was true.

Nick pushed open the gate and gestured with a sweep of his arm for Finder to go through.

"Did you just pick that lock?" Surprise and respect sounded in her voice.

"Grew up playing this other role playing game and our rules were, 'If you can do it, you can do it.' Learned some handy skills."

"Willing to teach?" Tully said passing through the gate. "Not like I need to know but . . ." his voice trailed off.

"Handy when you lose a key," Nick said.

"Right. Handy. When you lose a key."

"Is it okay if I carry Stacy the rest of the way?"

Nick was not as well muscled nor as tall as Tully, but he was strong for a wiry guy and didn't have trouble hefting me the rest of the way to Tully's truck. He slowed as we approached the park fountain, lagging behind the others.

Even under duress and more eyeliner than he needed, his eyes were beautiful, wide and long lashed like a girl's. Now, though, he looked like a New Yorker on 9/11. Pale, dirty, hollow, as if something he had never thought could be possible had actually happened. And not just happened, but happened to him.

I shook harder. I knew how it felt to be helpless in a disaster, to have your power taken from you in a way that made you hurt, frightened and furious at the same time.

Matilda and her thugs had violated his rights as a human being, had taken him against his will and threatened his most precious possession, his life.

She could have taken it completely, too, but the truth was, she didn't care enough to bother. He meant nothing to her, his life no more valuable to her than a glass of orange juice. She was a true bully, selfish, narcissistic and greedy. Not a list of qualities I envied.

I looked up into those green-gold eyes, now returned to normal. The light in them still sparkled, but was more subdued.

"Thank you," he said. "For what you did for me and Luke tonight. Words don't cover it."

I had so much to say, but nothing came out of my mouth.

"I do still owe you a coffee," he said. His lip had that sweet little curve. "Chapter & Mercy must be a poor substitute for big city coffee, but if you wouldn't mind, I could call you. And we could go. Out. Like not in the game." He was nervous. He was rambling! He was an adorable goth boy.

"Chapter & Mercy coffee *is* very good," I said.

"It is?"

"Yes," I said.

"Yes?"

"Yes."

"Do you mean yes, yes? Or just the coffee is good yes?"

"I mean yes," I said.

"Oh. Wow. Okay. Good. Really?" His flustered-ness made me smile. Meredith was going to love this.

Back at the truck, Nick gently set me on my feet. I leaned on the door while Finder and he moved wood so I could lie down on a less lumpy pile in the back. We all squeezed in.

On the short ride back to the museum, we learned Luke lived in Midlothian with his wife and two basset hounds, but came to Carytown every week to role-play at his brother's game shop. Nick had started college early, finished his bachelors at VCU in Bio-Chemistry in three years, did a summer program to start becoming a veterinarian, but instead chose human medical school because he couldn't stand seeing animals get hurt. He was in his second year of pre-med.

Two cars were in the museum lot. Luke's was the hatchback.

Nick claimed the other car, a long olive green sedan. Not so much a junker as an antique, it had low tail fins and the widest cab I'd ever seen. He addressed Tully.

"I can take Stacy home."

"I'm spending the night at Finder's," I said. Nick's smile thinned in disappointment. Disappointment I shared.

"Let me see your hand," Nick said to Luke as he turned toward his car. The older man raised his palm into the parking lot light. Nick made a face.

"Do you guys have flashlights?" Nick asked. My disappointment turned to amazement as Finder and Tully held the flashlights from Finder's toolbox while Nick cleaned and stitched up Luke's hand using supplies from a field kit he kept in the massive sedan's trunk. Finder offered for him to give her instructions. She would do his.

"My roommate'll do it when I get home. Surgery is his favorite subject so a nice, jagged flesh wound will make him happy."

He eyed me when he said "flesh wound." I smiled, then grimaced, rolling over to give Nick his coat.

"I'd say go to the ER," he said, pulling the long coat on. His eyes glinted like soft pine in the streetlight, "Except you can't splint a," he paused. A tiny smile twitched the corner of his mouth.

"You can't splint your butt bone," I said. A bizarre half laugh came out of me. I might have laughed for real if the pain would've stopped shooting down my legs.

"The plus is that they can give you pain meds at the ER," Nick said. "And tell you for sure it's broken. That's about it."

"We have meds," Finder. "My mom's a pharmacist."

"What about you?" I asked her. "Are you really ok? Do you need a hospital?" I remembered Nick saying that Finder might have internal bleeding.

"I'm sore, but not much worse than a tournament. I'm telling you, that angel you summoned healed me. I'm filthy ugly for sure, but I'm not injured." Nick did a quick rib check just to make sure none were broken and Finder passed his test.

We agreed that an ER trip would not prove useful. If my tailbone was chipped or fractured (Nick said definitely yes), it hurt and there was nothing to do for it. If it wasn't broken, it hurt and there was still nothing to do for it. The fix is to wait for it to heal and hope no chips got stuck in the muscle.

I poked my neck under the bandage. All of the bite wounds, including mine, were healed. Much speculation would come later as to Finder's suggestion and the rest of our ideas about what or who had healed us and why. Meredith was going to have a major opinion.

I wasn't going back to New York though, not anytime soon. I wasn't exactly sure what had happened tonight, but I knew things had changed. I had changed. My dad was doing the best he could under trying circumstances. It wasn't in my best interest or his for me to keep hating my situation. I needed to make peace with Richmond, with my new life as whatever I was, and with the idea that if bad supernatural things can be real, then good supernatural things could be real, too. I talked to a vampire, why not a - what had Finder said? An angel?

Steve was going to need support as he made friends with his odd little monster and who better than his big sister to trust and help? And then there was Jill. I kept her out because letting her in would mean my mother was really gone, really mentally ill, really incurable, really not a mom at all. Maybe the time had come to face that reality, let Jill in, and let her shrink me. She should shrink Finder, too. At least now that I knew the deal with her dad, I understood better why she was the way she was. A cold wind blew my hair around my face in a puff. An image of the hat shadowing whatever was above that morphing neck stuck in my mind. The Man with No

Face, Steve's name for, I assume, the thing that we had banished tonight. I shivered and shoved it out of my mind.

"I'll call you?" Nick said helping me into the back seat of the pick up.

"I'll email you the number," I said.

"Tell me. I'll remember it."

I raised an eyebrow.

"Math team." His eyes twinkled. "Number one in the state."

Math Team?

He repeated my number back to me with perfect accuracy. Twice. Could he get any more adorable? I'd email it later, though, just in case.

"Night," Nick said. "Thanks again for. . .you know. Saving our lives." He inclined his head in a gesture exclusively southern.

"You're welcome," Tully said, shaking hands. Finder just shook her head. True to form, she rolled her eyes and said nothing.

"I don't know what we would've done without y'all, tonight," Luke said holding his injured hand at an angle.

"Died," Finder said.

"Probably," Nick said. "You'll have to tell us how you found us, why you came after us even. There's definitely more to this story than we know."

He looked back and forth among the three of us and Luke. His eyes lingered a moment longer on me.

Tully idled the truck until Nick and Luke got in their cars and pulled onto Boulevard. I would have waved, but I needed to lie down. On the way to Finder's my tailbone killed, my stomach rumbled, and I wondered how we'd all get through school in two hours.

I am alive. I am safe. Nothing bad is happening.

In this moment, all true.

Jostling down the Richmond side streets with my tailbone on fire, my heart secure and happy, I suspected this was only the beginning of the roller coaster that was going to be life in Richmond. Who knew?

New York had been so quiet.

To be continued . . .

in

TATTOOED ANGEL

The Unimaginables
Book II

Acknowledgements

I've always been fascinated by how many people get thanked by authors, and kind of unbelieving that so many people, in fact, helped. Now that it's my turn, I totally get it

Not only must I thank the unbelievable patience and plot problem solving abilities of my family, Shaun, Wyatt, Emmet, Clark & Roane, but the surprising number of other people without whose help, support, encouragement and endless texting this book would not be in your hands, or in your ears.

Since I'm unable to go about this in terms of importance, I'll just start with the obvious: This book would not exist without beta readers, people who read a book sometimes multiple times for no reward other than to have their two cents welcomed and incorporated: Eve Moennig (who knew me when I was Stacy's age and got me through those years with grace, sisterhood and a lot of ice cream), Jay Bushman, Christopher Kubasik, Coffee Polk, Ernie & Pamela Burnett, Bryan Coffee and Carolyn Faye Kramer, all writers, all brilliant, all willing to answer questions and help on a moments notice, all dear friends. Beyond the scope of beta readers is my soul-sister Charlotte Fandey (thank you, Jay) who caught one of my human babies at birth and has been nothing less than midwife to this book. She labored with me for an entire day as I read Stacy out loud to her. She read it more than once again on paper and e-reader, answered countless "emergency" texts, emails, and phone calls, unearthed the bands Stacy loves, and listened when I needed a sounding board. I thank you in unimaginable quantities from the very core of my heart.

No small thanks go to Emma Fandey & my son, Clark Furlong who also endured the full day read aloud, and who served with my daughter Roane as my go-to "ideal readers". They tolerated me with patience and very few eye rolls as I asked questions, worked the dialogue and cut the really bad nun jokes.

Thank you to Simbi Kali who made sure Finder and her family felt real, Jessica Mooney who taught me about Catholic School life, and to Abbie Zamcheck who generously shared his experience of being a student at Styvesant High School, the model for Stacy's JDS, on 9/11.

I am shamelessly indebted to the previously mentioned Carolyn and Bryan who not only inspired deeper character development for Stacy's parents, but who kept my energy, standards and awareness up during the writing of this book in more ways than I can name.

A major shout out goes to Moses Cardona at John Hawkins & Associates, an agent so excellent that after my decade plus long writing hiatus, he agreed to read this book. He gave me a fantastic round of comments that dramatically shaped the story as you experienced it. Moses, you are generous and kind and smart, qualities most needed in the world today. Thank you. Speaking of generous, kind and smart, a thank you also goes to a truly remarkable story artist whose career I can never hope to emulate, but who demonstrated faith in my storytelling, or in the fact that we share a birthday, by agreeing to write a circus with me back at the turn of this century. Mr. Neil Gaiman, you are an inspiration always. I hope that because of the proximity of our last names, my books will be able to fangirl all over yours in the bookstore.

Thanks to Rytis Valiunas, the first intrepid human to invite me to talk about this book and read a bit of it on his online interview show. I also thank Cory at Bad Robot, Caroline at A-Line Pictures and Corey Miller from The Rookie all for helping me learn how and what to do to turn this book series into a tv show (stay tuned!). Thanks to Valorie Hubbard at Actor's Fast Track who reminded me that marketing can be a joy and that actors create jobs for themselves all the time with pleasure and audacity. Last minute thanks go to Nicholas Santasier who showed me how to engineer and master my audiobooks, Don Baarns who saved my bacon with tech tips to fix my newbie mastering problems and Deborah Hawkins whose sharp eye and handful of last minute edits surely saved me plenty of embarrassment and post production groans. Thank you!

I want to acknowledge Jessica Porter at Crossroad Reviews for getting my PR train rolling, Allison Rosaci who makes whatever I ask for happen, Cami (CL) Walters, Jay Bushman and Amber Duell for the cover quotes, and YOU for the reading, listening, likes, emoji hearts, library requests & online reviews which build the steam for this engine! You are awesome.

I would be in very poor form to not acknowledge the magical work of two women who have held the space for me and this project in very unique and unimaginable ways, Tish Hicks of the V.O. Dojo and Music Goddess Melanie Bartenstein. Thank you, ladies. Mastermind trio for the win!

I'm going to wrap this gratitude party by thanking all the people I knew in high school and college who are in this book and the ones to come. Maybe you will recognize yourselves and maybe you won't.

Still, I love you so much. You're in here.

About the Author

J.S. (Jen Selby) Furlong has done a lot of things. Her professions have included writing and producing circuses, acting, stage managing, booking talent for events, teaching yoga, coaching actors, life coaching people who are not actors, house sitting, walking dogs, and throwing newspapers at apartment doors when she was nine. There are more.

Occupations she has not been previously paid to do are raising four fellow humans, keeping chickens & milking goats (oh the cheese!), chaperoning and managing her kids' sibling band, traveling as mom crew for her actor kids and writing a stack of novels, one of which you see here. Jen is a lover of food, art, large bodies of water, and things which make her amazed. She believes in untapped potential, the impossible, the power of the tribe and *you*. Even if she doesn't know you. Her guilty pleasures are ashtanga yoga, chai tea, cake, sushi & German beer. And pesto. One of her goals is to speak as many languages as she needs to run circuses and buy goats around the world. She lives in Virginia with her animals, her adorable husband and whomever else happens to be home. Follow Jen on IG at @iamjenfurlong.

P.S. Jen is also the author of Antagonists, a LARP manual for Vampire: The Masquerade by White Wolf Publishing under her maiden name, Jennifer Albright. Find all things Jen at jsfurlong.com.

Photo credit: Guido Venitucci Photography

Go MOBILE!

To access bonus content for The Unimaginables series, use your smartphone to scan the QR code below. Get more info about Stacy, Finder, Tully, AGB and other characters in the series as well as more information about the books and the author, J.S. Furlong.

1. Take a picture of the code above with your phone.

2. Explore the world of Stacy & The Unimaginables!